PRAISE FOR THE PUMPKIN LANTERN

"Seth Adam Smith is the American C. S. Lewis."

— CHARLOTTE ASHLOCK, CRAZYIDEALIST.COM

"Be warned, Smith has crafted something you won't want to put down."

— JASON F. WRIGHT, NEW YORK TIMES BESTSELLING AUTHOR

"Smith's writing style and storytelling is on par with popular storytellers such as Tim Burton and Neil Gaiman."

— ALICIA SMOCK, ROLLOUTREVIEWS.COM

"From page one, the author pulled me into an 18th-century New England full of interesting characters and magical intrigue."

— KIMBERLY CHRISTENSEN, TALK WORDY TO ME

"An origin story unlike any other! Rip Van Winkle and the Pumpkin Lantern is the perfect blend of humorous middle grade antics and at times, downright creepy fun! Highly recommended!"

— FRANK L. COLE, AUTHOR OF THE AFTERLIFE ACADEMY

"Seth Adam Smith breathes new life into this classic tale with his creative blend of history and fiction. Rip Van Winkle and The Pumpkin Lantern delivers imaginative characters, roller coaster adventures, magic and mystery, a spine-tingling ghost story, and an inspiring message of self worth. This book has something for everyone."

— KELLY NELSON, AUTHOR OF THE KEEPER'S SAGA

RIP VAN WINKLE AND THE PUMPKIN LANTERN

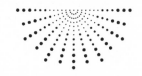

SETH ADAM SMITH

Illustrated by
HOWARD LYON

FIRE FISH MEDIA

For the Gonzo family:
Dan, Kerry, Logan, Aly, Ben, and Kalee.
You are the inspiration for the Van Winkle family.

And for baby Chance.

"That's the Van Winkle boy—the one they pulled from the grave —Rip. I'd recognize him anywhere."

Rip's hands began to tremble. "How do you know my name?"

Goodman chuckled. "I take it Jonathan hasn't told you much about me. I have a vested interest in things that are dead . . . as well as things that should be dead but aren't."

At this point, Goodman Brown leaned forward, revealing his face for the first time. Rip drew back in horror. Goodman was a living corpse! The man was missing a cheek, while the remaining flesh on his face was as white as cotton, curtained behind long, greasy clumps of gray hair. His eyes were pale and listless, like those of a dead fish. His black lips curled into a lopsided smile, exposing long, yellow teeth.

"So you see," continued Goodman calmly, "I was very interested when I learned about a baby who had been snatched from the hands of death and given the name of a grave."

CONTENTS

PREFACE

In 1819, Washington Irving, an American author, published a fictional story titled Rip Van Winkle, which takes place in colonial America sometime before the start of the Revolutionary War. In that story, Rip Van Winkle is a lazy, unambitious man who avoids work and responsibility.

One day, Rip goes into the mountains and meets a group of strange men who give him an enchanted drink. Feeling sleepy, Rip closes his eyes to take a short nap. When he wakes up, he learns that he has slept for twenty years—wasting his life and missing the American Revolution.

The story became an instant classic—a moralized fable on how we can sometimes "sleep through" the most exciting and wonderful times in history and in our own lives.

But that is not the full story of Rip Van Winkle, nor is it the true *meaning* of Rip Van Winkle . . .

America has fallen asleep. *We* have fallen asleep. We have forgotten the magic of All Hallows' Day, and we have forgotten the magic within ourselves.

This book was written so that you might awaken and remember . . .

- Seth Adam Smith

RIPPED FROM THE GRAVE

IN WHICH WE MEET A PAIR OF LIFE-GIVING GRAVE ROBBERS...

*O*n All Hallows' Eve, 1717, a dark figure slipped through the night and ran toward the South Burying Ground in Boston. There, in an open grave, the specter hastily abandoned the object it had been carrying —a tiny newborn babe. Then, without a word, the figure scrambled out of the grave and into the deserted streets of Boston, disappearing forever into the misty midnight.

The infant, left without food or clothing, cried into the darkness, flailing his arms and legs at the night sky. After about an hour, his cries dropped into a shuddering sob. In the gathering darkness, the boy's large green eyes dimmed, and as the cold settled in, he grew still.

ABIGAIL VAN WINKLE awoke with a start. Breathing heavily, she sat up and pressed her hands against her face. Her forehead was drenched in sweat. Abigail reached out and shook her husband. "Josiah!" she hissed. "Josiah, wake up!"

Her husband, a young, newly appointed judge, merely smiled in his sleep and mumbled something about a recent court case.

"Josiah!" repeated Abigail, this time much louder.

Josiah sat bolt upright. "Where's the pie?" he shouted. "Hmmm? What is this? Where am I?" It took him a few seconds to get his bearings. "Yes! Abigail! What's wrong, my dear? Did you have the nightmare again?"

Abigail nodded. "It was different this time," she said, still trembling.

"How's that?"

"I was walking in the graveyard, through the fog, and I saw the pile of gold . . . like before. Only this time I felt it was *ours*—all the money we have made, all the things that we own, *our* treasure. But as I moved toward it, the pile began to sink into the ground. I cried out and ran toward it, but the faster I moved, the faster it sank. And by the time I reached it, the pile had completely disappeared—replaced by a gravestone marked 'R.I.P.'"

"Rest in peace? That's odd."

"But that's not the strangest part," continued Abigail. "In front of the stone was an open grave, and when I leaned forward and looked down into the grave, I saw . . ." She shuddered. "I saw a baby."

Josiah's eyes widened in surprise. "A baby? Do you mean . . . a dead baby?"

"No, not a dead baby!" snapped Abigail. "Don't be morbid! The child was alive. He looked right at me."

"A baby in an open grave looked right at you?" repeated Josiah. "And you think *I'm* being morbid?"

Abigail gave her husband a scornful look.

"Well, why do you think you keep having this dream?" asked Josiah more sincerely.

Abigail shook her head. "I don't know. Maybe . . . we've been so blessed. I know we're supposed to feel thankful and satisfied . . . but I've just felt so *restless*. It's as if . . . it's as if something's missing." She bit her lip and twisted the edge of the blanket anxiously.

"If you're that concerned about it, perhaps we can give some of our money to the orphans," Josiah suggested with a yawn, turning over to go back to sleep. "Maybe if we share our treasure, then we can '*rest in peace.*' I know that's what I'd like to do," he muttered.

Abigail considered going back to bed, but then her lip began to tremble. "But I *can't* rest, Josiah! What about the baby? Oh, Josiah, he looked up at me with such pleading eyes, as if . . ."

A strange thought crossed Abigail's mind. Without another moment's hesitation, she tossed her blanket aside, fairly leaped from the bed, and hastily began to dress.

"Abigail, what is it?" said Josiah. "What are you doing? Where are you going?"

"I'm going down the street."

"To the church? It's almost certainly closed at this hour."

"I'm not going to King's Chapel," she snapped as she threw a shawl around her neck. "I'm going to the South Burying Ground."

"The *graveyard*?" said Josiah, sitting up again. "Are you mad? Abigail, it's All Hallows' Eve!"

"What's that got to do with anything?"

"The night of the dead?" said Josiah, waving his arms. "This is the night when the boundary separating the living from the dead is supposedly at its thinnest, and you want to go for a midnight stroll in a graveyard?"

Abigail put her hands on her hips. "I am not going for a stroll, Josiah. I am going to find that baby! Besides, I did not think you believed in all of that—what do you call it—'hocus pocus.'"

Josiah rubbed his forehead wearily. "I most certainly do not! But nearly everyone in Boston *does* believe in it. If anyone sees you going into a graveyard on All Hallows' Eve—"

"It is probably past midnight, anyway," interrupted Abigail, "which technically means that it's not All Hallows' Eve—it's All Hallows' Day."

"You're missing the point!" exclaimed Josiah. "A graveyard at night is still a graveyard at night, and people will talk. Besides, how can you believe there is actually a baby there?"

"Look, I understand this sounds a bit absurd, Josiah . . ."

"A bit?"

Abigail ignored his comment and placed a hand on her chest. "I didn't just *see* a child in my dreams—I *felt* it in my heart."

Josiah rolled his eyes before clambering out of the bed. "Well, then, give me a minute to put on my coat and trousers."

Abigail's eyes brightened. "You're coming with me?"

"Of course I am," he grumbled. "Darling, I would follow you through the blackest midnight—just not without my trousers!"

A FEW MINUTES LATER, Josiah and Abigail left the comfort of their home and made their way down the street. Each carried a brass lantern that pierced the darkness with bobbing yellow light. After a brisk walk, the couple approached the iron fence perimeter of the South Burying Ground. They skirted around the fence and cautiously approached the entrance to the graveyard. A cold, white fog swirled around the headstones before drifting toward the pair, as though it were a ghostly apparition reaching for the living.

With one hand on the fence, Josiah looked out over the gravestones and shrugged his shoulders. "Well, dear, I don't see or hear any baby. Let's go back."

"Josiah . . ."

The judge let out a long sigh, and the light from his lantern illuminated his breath in the cold night air. "Fine," he said. "I'll go in and walk down each row. Just stay right here and wait for me, all right? It's dark in there. I wouldn't want you to trip and fall."

Abigail nodded.

Satisfied, Josiah squeezed her arm gently. Taking a deep breath, he turned on his heel and walked into the graveyard, where he immediately faded into the fog.

Abigail waited anxiously at the iron fence.

A full minute passed by.

Then another.

And another.

The graveyard isn't that big! she thought. *What's taking him so long?*

"Josiah?" she called.

Silence.

She bit her lip. Suddenly, she heard a noise that came from deep within the graveyard. She raised her lantern and peered into the darkness, listening intently. She heard the noise again. Was it her husband? It sounded like a bundle of sticks being shuffled around.

Lantern poised ahead of her, Abigail left the fence, her curiosity drawing her toward the noise. The sound grew louder as she neared a large old maple tree. She raised her lantern.

"Who's there?" she called in a voice much softer than she had intended.

The mist parted, and suddenly she saw a huge, glowing face grinning at her! Abigail brought a hand to her mouth and stifled a cry of alarm. The glowing face was the carved pumpkin head of a scarecrow!

It stood next to the maple tree, wearing trousers, a vest, and a tattered frock coat. Tall and terrifying, the scarecrow lifted one of its long wooden arms and pointed directly at her.

Abigail felt fear as she had never known before. She wanted to scream. She wanted to run. But she couldn't do either. She was frozen to the spot.

This was definitely not part of my dream! she thought. Nor was she in a dream now; whatever this was, it was real.

Abigail stared wide-eyed at the scarecrow's pumpkin face. To her relief, its expression was not terrifying or cruel, but rather reflected a look of deep concern. Its facial features moved with as much fluidity as those of any human. The triangular eyes blinking at her were gentle and loving. What's more, the light emanating from its face was quite unlike the pale yellow light of a candle. It was like the light of the stars on a clear summer evening.

Her fear quickly melted away, replaced by a feeling of stillness. There was something comforting and oddly familiar about this scarecrow— something she couldn't quite place. It was as though she were being visited by an old friend. Abigail blinked heavily, almost sleepily. The world around her seemed to slow—as if time were standing still. And yet, in a strange way, she felt more awake and alive than ever before.

The slender scarecrow—who was still tall but no longer terrifying—beckoned to Abigail, motioning for her to come closer. She did so, stopping just a few feet shy of the figure, where she made an awkward curtsy. She wasn't sure why she had done that; she just sensed that it was the right thing to do. Abigail had lived her whole life in Boston and had never seen King George, but she imagined that being in the presence of royalty felt something like being in the presence of this scarecrow.

The scarecrow touched his forehead and bowed back at her.

"Welcome, Abigail," he said in a voice as sweet and warm as apple cider. "I knew you would come."

Abigail blinked. She didn't know who this scarecrow was or where he had come from, but she felt that she could trust him.

"There," said the scarecrow, pointing to an open grave next to him. "There is the seedling you seek; this child was planted on this earth to grow into greatness. But you must hurry. Bring him to the light before the darkness consumes him."

Raising her lantern, Abigail rushed to the edge of the grave and looked down. What she saw made her cry out. There, at the bottom of the gloomy pit—as pale and as still as death—was the newborn baby she had seen in her dream. Her first instinct was to jump down into the grave, but she knew she wouldn't be able to hoist herself back out with the child in her arms. She turned her head, looking for the scarecrow, but he had vanished.

Scrambling to her feet, Abigail yelled into the mist. "Josiah! Josiah, come quickly!"

A few seconds later the judge sprinted out of the darkness, clutching his side.

"Abigail?" he cried, gasping for air. "Abigail, are you all right? For heaven's sake, this is a graveyard. Keep your voice down!" But upon seeing the distress in her face, Josiah's tone changed. "What is it? What is wrong?"

"The baby!" Abigail exclaimed, pointing to the open grave. "The baby is down there!"

Josiah leaned over and peered into the grave. He let out a gasp and sprang into action. Dropping his lantern, he removed his coat and tossed it on the ground. Quickly, yet carefully, he lowered himself into the hole and reached for the child.

"Is he all right?" asked Abigail, her voice shaking with apprehension.

Josiah pressed his lips together. The child was as still as stone. The young judge squatted down and gingerly placed one hand on the infant's chest.

"Abigail! Throw my coat down!"

There was a flurry of movement as Abigail tossed her husband's coat into the grave. Josiah snatched the coat and hastily laid it out, then carefully bundled the infant inside.

"Josiah," called Abigail, "is he . . . is he *alive*?"

"I don't know," replied Josiah. "I've put him in the center of my coat and tied the sleeves over him. I'm going to hand it up to you so you can lift him out. Can you do that?"

"Yes!" She knelt down and braced her knees on the edge of the open grave.

"Here!"

Abigail reached into the darkness.

"Are you holding it?"

"Yes!" she answered, her heart quickening.

"Lift!"

Abigail hoisted the small bundle over the edge and laid it softly next to her. It was much lighter than she had anticipated. Gently, she unfolded the coat, and then bit her lip hard to prevent a sob from escaping. The pale baby boy lay still.

Instinctively, she threw off her shawl, opened her coat and shift, and held the baby to her neck. With his bare skin pressed against hers, she felt her warmth begin to flow into his tiny body. She struggled to close the coat over both of them, to wrap it in a way that would warm him. Josiah, who had managed to pull himself out of the grave, knelt beside his wife.

"Is he breathing?" he asked.

"He's cold," answered Abigail. "He needs more warmth. Help me!"

"What?" said Josiah, confused by his wife's request.

"Huddle close to the baby and wrap your arms around me."

Josiah wiped as much mud from his body as he could and then carefully wrapped his arms around his wife; thus bound together, they sheltered the child from the cold, dark night, enveloping him in warmth.

"Abigail," Josiah said, his voice trembling, "I think—I think this boy was alive when he was left here."

"Hush!" said Abigail. Her body was filled with raw emotion, but she would not permit herself to cry. "He will yet live; he belongs with us." She looked down at the baby in her arms. "Do you hear that, child? You have us. We are here for you. Come back."

In the quiet of the graveyard, the couple knelt together in soul-stretching silence—wishing, waiting, hoping, praying. Abigail lifted her head up and looked out across the graveyard with watery eyes. Suddenly, her gaze fixed upon something in the distance.

"Please . . ." she whispered.

Interrupting the quiet of the night, a warm breeze rattled the remaining leaves off the large maple tree. Then, after what seemed like hours, the baby began to stir. At first his movements were so slight that Abigail almost mistook them for the trembling of her own body. But soon the child's arms and legs began to twitch, and a muffled cry escaped his tiny mouth.

That cry was the most wonderful sound Abigail had ever heard.

"Josiah," she breathed, her voice overcome with joy. The baby's eyelids fluttered open, revealing a pair of large green eyes. Abigail had never seen a newborn baby with green eyes, and the mere sight of them caused tears of joy to flow down her cheeks.

"Oh!" she exclaimed, rocking the child back and forth. "There you are! Yes, there you are. You're safe now." Inwardly, she knew that they should head home, but she felt frozen in the moment, completely mesmerized by the miracle.

"Thank the Lord," whispered Josiah, breathing a sigh of relief. "I'll go to the leaders in Boston first thing in the morning."

"Why?" asked Abigail, still enamored by the baby's eyes.

"To begin the search for the child's mother."

Abigail gave Josiah a fierce and disapproving look. "His mother?" she said harshly.

"Yes," replied Josiah. "Abandoning a child is a serious crime. Obviously, this boy was born out of wedlock—"

"How do you know that?" snapped Abigail.

Josiah looked dumbfounded. "Well, because he was concealed. Why else would she leave—"

"And what makes you so sure that his *mother* abandoned him?" interrupted Abigail. "Every child has *two* parents, you know."

"Well, we need to find his *parents*, then."

"Why would we want to find them?"

"Because that's the *law*, Abigail!" said Josiah, fuming. "They are responsible for what they've done. They are his parents."

"Not anymore," said Abigail, clutching the baby tighter.

"What do you mean?"

"What do you think I mean?"

"Abigail, we're not taking this child in."

"And why not?"

"Because you don't just pick up babies in a graveyard and take them home!" he exclaimed. "We have an obligation to obey the laws of our community and find this child's parents. They nearly killed the boy, and they must be punished."

Abigail looked down at the baby and his beautiful green eyes.

"Who would leave a baby to die in an open grave?" she wondered aloud. As she marveled at the boy's tiny features, Abigail was filled with love and overwhelming wonder at what the child could become. "One human life is worth more than all the treasures of the earth," she whispered.

The words slipped out of her mouth before she even knew she was saying them, echoing in her ears and reminding her of the dream. She looked to her husband, her eyes shining in the lantern light. *"He's our treasure,"* she said.

"Come again?"

"The meaning of my dream," said Abigail tearfully. "All of our earthly treasure sank into an open grave, and in its place was this child."

Josiah raised an eyebrow. "Are you saying this child is going to *take* all of our money?"

Despite the gravity of the situation, Abigail couldn't help but laugh. "No," she said. "No, Josiah, that's not what I'm saying. I'm saying that I think I know what my dream means now. It means that no matter how much money we make, the value of our earthly treasure will never come close to that of our children."

"Our *children*?" repeated Josiah. "'You mean child, Abigail. This is one child, and he's not even ours!"

Abigail blinked at her husband, a look of reverence in her large, almond-shaped eyes. "There are so many children out there, Josiah—so many without homes. And we have so much to give."

"Yes, but *children*! Heavens, woman! We're not about to have some massive family. Who do you think we are? The Franklins? That Benjamin of theirs is a cheeky little upstart! Besides, we don't have *that* much to give!"

"We have more than most, Josiah," chided Abigail as she rocked the baby. "There's nothing more important in this world than caring for a child. If we have the power and the means, then we must help."

Josiah opened his mouth as if to say something, but nothing came out. Inside, his mind was wrestling with his heart. He knew that this baby belonged to his biological parents, that it was the parents' responsibility to raise the child; but truth be told, Josiah felt a love for the little boy that he couldn't quite explain—as if the child were somehow meant to be part of their family.

"Very well," he said, after a pause. "I'll still need to report all of this to the General Court, but I'll let them know that we're willing to take the boy in. And would you at least give me some time to think about taking in additional children?"

Abigail nodded, returning her gaze to the boy.

"So, this is now our son," said Josiah, hesitantly touching the top of the baby's head. "What will we call him?"

Abigail cradled the child thoughtfully. The baby yawned and nuzzled closer to her.

"Rip," she said at last.

Josiah raised an eyebrow. "Rip? As in 'Rest In Peace'?"

"Yes," said Abigail, rocking the infant softly as he drifted off to sleep. "Rip Van Winkle."

"Why 'Rip'?" asked Josiah.

Abigail's whispered response was carried away on the wind.

AND SO IT was that Mr. and Mrs. Van Winkle of Boston entered South Burying Ground near midnight on All Hallows' Eve and left on All Hallows' Day with their first child—a boy who had been ripped from the grave.

A boy named Rip.

2

A GROWING BOY

IN WHICH THE CHILD GROWS IN MORE
WAYS THAN ONE...

*T*rue to his word, Josiah Van Winkle approached the General Court the following day and related everything that had happened concerning baby Rip—everything, that is, except the fact that he and his wife had found the child in an open grave.

"They thought it was troubling enough that you and I were outside of our home on All Hallows' Eve," he later told his wife. "No need to add that we pulled a baby out of the grave and miraculously brought him back to life. We don't need all of Boston thinking we are *witches*. I mean, if they knew you had dreams about it . . . well, they might be tempted to drag you to the Common like they did Mary Dyer."

Abigail forced a laugh, trying to conceal an inner fear. Mary Dyer had been one of the original settlers of Boston—a Quaker woman whom many believed to be a witch. In 1637, Mary had given birth to a severely deformed, stillborn baby. Attempting to prevent the spread of rumors, Mary's physician had secretly buried the baby in a shallow grave.

But the secret of his burial wasn't kept.

As news of Mary's baby spread throughout the colony, Governor Winthrop ordered the body of the baby to be exhumed and examined. The Governor described the baby as "a monstrous baby, from a monstrous woman." Not long after that, Mary Dyer was executed—hanged from the branches of Boston's Great Elm Tree.

Truth be told, Abigail herself was disturbed by the implications of her dream. It *had* come true, hadn't it? What did that mean? As if the dream's reality hadn't been enough, Abigail had gone into a graveyard on All Hallows' Eve and met a living scarecrow with a pumpkin for a head. At the time, Abigail had wanted to tell Josiah all about the scarecrow, but hearing his comment about Mary Dyer made her decide not to say anything at all.

Fortunately for the Van Winkles, everyone in Boston respected Josiah. Judge Van Winkle was an honorable, no-nonsense sort of man, and the General Court trusted his judgment completely. After Josiah reported the incident, the leaders of Boston put up a public notice about a newborn baby found "under mysterious circumstances," and urged anyone with information concerning the child to speak with the Van Winkles.

But in the weeks that followed, no one came forward. There wasn't even a whispered rumor of who the child's parents might be. As far as the community knew, Rip had simply appeared out of thin air—or sprouted out of the ground like a tiny pumpkin plant. And so, after a sufficient amount of time passed, the General Court officially declared "Rip" a Van Winkle and closed the case.

Abigail, who had always wanted children of her own, was delighted by the newest addition to the family, and she took every opportunity to shower the baby with love and affection. Anxious for her still-hesitant husband to be more involved, she often dragged her rocking chair into Josiah's study. Once there, she rocked the baby to sleep while giving a detailed account of everything he had done that day. But Josiah, busy studying court documents, only muttered half-hearted responses.

"Oh, Josiah, do you see how tiny his hands are?" said Abigail.

"Minuscule," said Josiah, looking through several footnotes.

"And those bright red cheeks!"

"He's got them," agreed Josiah, dipping his quill into a bottle of ink.

"And would you look at the size of those eyes! Have you ever seen green eyes on a baby?"

"I'm sure I haven't."

"Oh, he's looking right at me!" Abigail laughed. "I wonder what he's thinking."

"He probably wants you to feed him," mumbled Josiah.

"I'll bet he's thinking about what he's going to be when he grows up," said Abigail, ignoring her husband. "You're going to do some great things, aren't you, Rip? That's why you're here, isn't it?"

Josiah snorted. "He's an infant! How would he know?"

Abigail cooed at the baby. "Every child is born with a purpose—isn't that right, Rip?"

Irritated by Abigail's constant interruptions, Josiah found himself unable to resist a moment of sarcasm. "Yes, Rip! Someday, many years from now, you will grow up and learn that your purpose in life is to work unbelievably hard, so that you can pay the king's taxes, then die."

"Josiah!" exclaimed Abigail, causing the baby to jump.

Josiah chuckled and returned to his papers. Abigail pursed her lips and sat back in her chair, and with eyes fixed firmly on the opposite side of the room, she rocked angrily back and forth. Josiah, though partly grateful for the silence, could never concentrate when his wife was quiet; it always unnerved him. Allowing the silence to continue was like allowing a cooked pot of stew to simmer over the fire indefinitely—if Josiah didn't do something, the whole house might burn down.

"What is it, Abigail?"

Abigail shook her head tersely.

"My dear, please tell me what's on your mind."

"What's the point?" said Abigail. "I know you won't believe me. You'll say it's all 'fairy-tale nonsense.'"

Like a sinner in Sunday school, Josiah felt uneasy. He could sense that Abigail was on the verge of another sermon. She was always on the lookout for some hidden spiritual meaning to everyday occurrences. And once she found that meaning, Abigail would always tell her husband *exactly* what it was—much to his chagrin.

Thinking it would be better just to get it over with, Josiah put down his quill. "All right, if you tell me what's on your mind, I promise I won't argue."

Abigail blinked her lovely eyes. "It's just . . . when I was a little girl, my grandmother would tell me stories about a pumpkin-headed scarecrow . . ."

Josiah raised an eyebrow. "Your grandmother? Didn't she claim to get her recipes from three women who lived in a gingerbread house?"

"I've never heard you complain about her cooking," said Abigail, tartly.

Josiah held up his hands. "I just want to be clear about who we're talking about—"

"We're not talking about my grandmother; we're talking about the scarecrow!" snapped Abigail. "She said he had a great big pumpkin for a head, and that he came to the early settlers when they were sick and dying. He healed them and brought them over to Boston. The 'Good Gardener,' they called him. My grandmother always said each of us is like seed, planted by the Good Gardener so we might grow into something majestic.

"There is something special about this child," continued Abigail. "I think . . . I think the Good Gardener led us to him."

Josiah leaned back in his chair and steepled his fingers. "Didn't your grandmother also claim to see an imp-like creature on the Governor's back?"

Abigail scowled at her husband. Josiah merely chuckled. "My dear, I think it is wonderful that this boy's life was saved. But *we* did that—not this pumpkin fellow. Men and women are what they make of themselves. Frankly, I think it is harmful to our progress as humans to believe that help may come from some magical force. I mean, the idea that there is anything beyond what we can see is—"

"Is what?" snapped Abigail. "Foolish?"

"I didn't say that."

"But you were thinking it."

"No, I was going to say that it would be *impractical*."

"*Impractical*," repeated Abigail. "A fancy word for 'foolish.'"

Josiah let out a long sigh. "Look, all I am saying is that life is very simple and straightforward; what you see is what you get. If you work hard, till the ground, and plant the seeds, then you will reap a harvest. Now, if there truly is a 'gardener' who 'planted' us here, then he must be an absentee landlord—a gardener who has abandoned his garden to let it grow on its own. We, therefore, must labor to improve our own condition. To believe otherwise is to believe in a dream."

"But that's just it," interrupted Abigail. "We found Rip in a graveyard at midnight, all because of a dream—*my* dream. It was a dream you did not see. And yet we saved his life because you *believed* in that dream. Why can't you believe there is something special about this boy, and that maybe —just maybe—there is something larger than us at work here?"

Josiah opened his mouth, but he couldn't think of anything to say.

Abigail appeared satisfied by this. "I refuse to believe that the only reason we are here is to pay taxes and die." She returned her gaze to the tiny child in her arms. "The Good Gardener planted each of us here for a reason, and that same Gardener is *still* in the garden."

Judge Van Winkle chose to remain silent, though he still didn't believe in Abigail's magical nonsense; he only believed in things he could see, things he could explain. And he believed that he would always feel that way.

But over the next few years, the Van Winkles would experience a number of things that Josiah could hardly imagine possible—let alone explain.

When Rip was less than a year old, Abigail gathered a handful of wild-flowers and put them in a jar on the windowsill next to her son's crib. The following morning, when Josiah was preparing to leave for court, his wife hurried into the kitchen with a bewildered look on her face.

"Josiah, how did you do that?"

"Excuse me?"

"The flowers," said Abigail. "You put more in Rip's room. How did you do it?"

"What do you mean?" asked Josiah, puzzled. "I didn't do anything. I didn't even know there were flowers in there."

"Oh, come now. You must be joking." Abigail said this with a laugh, but Josiah sensed a hint of concern in her voice. "I really don't mind. I just want to know how you did it."

"Abigail, I haven't the foggiest idea what you're talking about!"

"Well, here, come and see for yourself." She took Josiah by the hand and led him up the stairs. He started to protest, stating that he should really be on his way, but as soon as he crossed the threshold into his son's room, he stopped short and let out a gasp.

It was as if he had walked into a field of wildflowers. Bathed in the morning sunlight, tall, green grass covered the floor, interspersed with dozens of little white and blue flowers on long, delicate stems.

Josiah staggered forward, his shoes leaving the hardwood floor to tread on soft turf. The tops of the grasses billowed gently in the breeze that flowed in from the open window.

Abigail touched her husband's arm. "You really had nothing to do with this?" she whispered.

Pale-faced, Josiah turned to her and slowly shook his head.

From somewhere in the grass, they heard the familiar cooing of their child. Slowly, they made their way through the field to Rip's little crib. He was sitting up, his chubby fingers clasped around the jar that Abigail had used for the flowers she had picked. The child looked up at them delightedly, as if to say, "Mama! Papa! Look what I found!"

The Van Winkles simply stared at their child in wonder.

It took them several days to fully clear their child's bedroom—an activity they never thought they'd have to do. If anyone else in Boston had seen the grasses and flowers, they probably would have denounced the boy, deeming him some sort of witch-baby. But Judge Van Winkle was a thinking man, not some superstitious zealot. Besides, Rip was a just a baby! He was undeniably innocent of any mischief.

Nevertheless, Josiah was concerned. After all, how had an entire field grown—overnight—in Rip's room? The judge considered multiple possibilities. Maybe, over time, he had inadvertently brought in a large collection of seeds on the soles of his shoes. Well, no, that didn't make sense. Where would he have gotten the seeds? Perhaps the wooden floorboards already had seeds inside them, and the roots had been silently growing all along, waiting for a specific moment to sprout. But if that was the case, then why hadn't he ever heard of such a thing happening before? It just didn't make any sense!

Judge Van Winkle couldn't explain it and reluctantly accepted the event as a "mystery," in spite of his discomfort with such a concept.

Roughly three years later, another one of those inexplicable events took place. Rip was following his parents around the house as they searched desperately for the keys to Josiah's office in the State House. The toddler actually held the keys in his hand, but Josiah and Abigail—absorbed in their search—ignored Rip's calls for attention.

"Perhaps you left them in the garden?" suggested Abigail.

"I wasn't in the garden yesterday," replied Josiah, looking under a pillow.

"Papa?"

"Not now, Rip," said Josiah distractedly. "Papa can play later."

Nevertheless, Rip continued to tug on his father's coat. In an effort to move the child out of his way, Josiah lifted him up and plopped him down on a wooden bench, right next to a potted sunflower. After another frustrating minute of fruitless searching, Josiah and Abigail heard a dull thud, followed by a squeal of laughter. The couple turned to see Rip jumping on the bench, pointing excitedly up at the ceiling. They looked up.

There, lightly pressing against the ceiling, was the largest sunflower that Josiah and Abigail had ever seen. Its golden petals were the size of pumpkin leaves, and its roots (which had quietly broken through the clay pot) were as thick as ropes.

Not knowing what to say or do, they looked at Rip, then back at the plant.

They couldn't explain this one.

"Abigail, I'm starting to think there's something special about this child, after all."

She smiled as Rip held out his father's keys.

As the years passed, Rip continued to surprise his parents with an inexplicable power over things that grew in and around their home. The more Rip demonstrated this ability, the more nervous the judge became. Worried about the fearful superstitions of the townsfolk, Josiah warned Rip to never, *ever* demonstrate or even speak of his abilities to anyone outside of their family. Rip, being the obedient boy that he was, agreed.

The next extraordinary incident happened a few days shy of Rip's eighth birthday, while he was helping his mother tend her garden. Abigail was expressing her enthusiasm about the upcoming Harvest Festival when she let out a mournful sigh. "Oh, no."

"What is it, Mother?" said Rip, springing forward.

"It's the pumpkin," Abigail replied. Gingerly, she turned over the orange gourd, exposing a pale underside that was beginning to show signs of rot.

"I was going to take this to the Harvest Festival tomorrow," she said, shaking her head. "I was hoping to win that pumpkin contest." She sighed again. "I guess not this year."

Rip saw the sadness in his mother's eyes and instinctively wanted to help. He approached the pumpkin and placed a hand on its smooth skin. He furrowed his brow. "He's sad."

"What's that?" asked Abigail, looking at her son curiously.

"He's sad," repeated Rip, now with both hands on the pumpkin's side.

Abigail's eyes twinkled. "Well, what do you think we should do for him?"

"I'll ask him," said Rip. He placed his ear flat against the pumpkin. After several moments of listening, he wrapped both of his arms as far around the big, orange gourd as he could reach.

Abigail smiled, charmed by her son's naturally sweet disposition. But her smile quickly faded when she saw the pumpkin—already quite large —begin to expand rapidly, as though it were being filled with water. Abigail leapt up, grabbed Rip by the arm, and pulled him away from the swelling plant.

Rip cried out in alarm. "What's wrong?"

"It's growing!" she exclaimed. The two watched as the pumpkin continued to balloon outward, faster and faster. Soon, Rip and his mother were no longer looking down at a fair-sized plant, but standing in the shadow of an oversized monstrosity. The gourd had finally ceased growing—just short of causing a row of squash to live up to their name— but it was now taking up a quarter of the entire garden. Rip laughed and threw his hands in the air.

"Well done!" he shouted.

Abigail looked down at her son, trying to catch her breath. "What do you mean?" she asked.

"He told me he didn't think he could grow," said Rip, staring up at the pumpkin in awe.

"*He told you?*" repeated Abigail. "The pumpkin spoke to you?"

Rip nodded and reverentially placed his hands back on the pumpkin.

"He said he's different from the other plants, and that makes him feel lonely. He said he didn't feel like he belonged here."

"Did he?" asked Abigail, still trying to make sense of what had just happened. "And what did you tell him?"

"I told him that I feel the same way."

"You do?"

Rip shrugged. "Sometimes. I mean, I don't have any brothers or sisters. Besides," he added with a smile, "I don't know anyone else who can talk to plants."

Abigail's expression softened. "Rip, you know you belong here, right?"

Rip nodded vigorously. "Oh yes! Of course I do! And that's what I said to the pumpkin. I told him he belongs here, even if he's different. And I told him I would be his friend, because I know what it's like to feel alone. I think he took it to heart," he added, glancing at the gigantic pumpkin. Then, seeing the look of concern on his mother's face, Rip bit his lip. "Did I do something wrong?"

"Oh, no, of course not!" said Abigail, putting her hands on her son's shoulders. "Rip, listen to me: Helping someone feel they belong is a magic all its own."

As she hugged her son, Abigail recalled the night she had first held Rip. She remembered the pumpkin-headed scarecrow who had stood over her son's would-be grave. The scarecrow had said that Rip was destined to grow into greatness. Throughout his childhood, Rip had demonstrated an unusual gift when it came to plants. It seemed as though life literally sprang into whatever Rip touched. Could this be what the scarecrow had meant?

Abigail glanced back at the pumpkin, which was easily the weight and size of a cow. "I'm not worried about how the pumpkin grew," she said reassuringly. "It's just . . . your father is going to have a very difficult time taking it to the Harvest Festival now." She smiled at her son.

Rip grinned back at her.

THE NEXT DAY, Josiah—who had yet to see the pumpkin—offered to help his wife load the fruit into the wheelbarrow and haul it to the Boston Common.

"Oh, I think we will need something a bit bigger than the wheelbarrow," said Abigail, blushing slightly.

"Fantastic!" said Josiah enthusiastically. "Do you think this year's pumpkin will beat Mrs. Gookin's? I would love to wipe the smirk off that old crone's face!"

"Oh, I think so," said Abigail, winking at Rip.

"Wonderful!" said Josiah, recalling how small Abigail's previous pumpkins had been. "I'll gather my things."

After Josiah had done so, Abigail took Rip by the hand, and the pair led the excited judge into the garden. He had just finished putting on his gloves when he looked up and saw the gigantic pumpkin. It was so large and bright, he nearly mistook it for the setting sun!

Abigail grinned at her husband. "Do you think I'll win?"

Mouth agape, Josiah stared at the pumpkin for a full minute before he managed to speak. "I think I'll need to borrow Mr. Miller's wagon," he whispered.

"See if he'll give us some extra pumpkins," said Abigail with a smile.

Josiah furrowed his brow. "Extra pumpkins? What for?"

"I think this pumpkin could use a few friends," said Abigail, giving her son's hand a squeeze.

Josiah nodded dully, eyeing the monstrous gourd suspiciously. Was it just his imagination, or had the pumpkin swelled at the mention of the word "friends"?

3

FINDING CHARITY

IN WHICH RIP FINDS CHARITY TO BE
TWO DIFFERENT THINGS...

*E*arly the next morning, Josiah—with the help of ropes, ramps, two reluctant neighbors, and a team of horses—managed to lift the gargantuan pumpkin onto a borrowed wagon.

Eager to get going, Rip climbed onto the wagon and took a seat. Josiah, drenched in sweat, looked to his wife. "I'm just . . . going to go inside for a bit," he said, breathing heavily. "Get some . . . water."

Around midday, the Van Winkles hopped onto the wagon (which creaked precariously under the weight of the pumpkin), and made their way to the Boston Common for the Harvest Festival.

The Boston Common was a large swath of land originally owned by William Blaxton, a reclusive Englishman and the very first settler of Boston. Nearly one hundred years earlier, Blaxton had come to the New World with the intent to live and die alone. But in 1629 his plans were thrown off course with the arrival of the Puritans. After landing on the opposite side of the harbor, in a place they named "Charlestown," the Puritans fell victim to a mysterious illness that left many dead. Blaxton, whose farm and orchard were well established, invited the survivors to come live on his side of the harbor—Boston. For the Puritans, Blaxton's invitation was nothing short of a miracle. When they moved to Boston in 1630, Blaxton welcomed them with a harvest feast from his garden—a feast that the Puritans continued to commemorate every fall with a Harvest Festival.

Upon entering the Common, the Van Winkles (and their pumpkin) were greeted by looks of wonder and astonishment. In fact, most of the townsfolk, who had never before seen a cow-sized pumpkin, were prepared to award Abigail first place as soon as they saw the gigantic gourd; and they would have done so, had it not been for the Widow Gookin.

Mrs. Gookin was—to be perfectly honest—a bitter and cantankerous old crone. Her favorite pastimes included going to church, gossiping about those who didn't go to church, and listing all the ways she was better than her neighbors. Over the course of that summer, Mrs. Gookin had greedily watered her pumpkin plant several times a day, no doubt imagining the overwhelming praise and envy she would receive from her neighbors.

But on the day of the Harvest Festival, when the Van Winkles rolled into town with their pumpkin, Mrs. Gookin turned as green as a pickle. The old crone immediately set to work gossiping about Mr. and Mrs. Van Winkle, who, she said, "undoubtedly made the pumpkin grow using some form of witchcraft."

Abigail and Josiah ignored the old woman's gossip. Since finding a child "under mysterious circumstances," they had developed a thick skin when it came to rumors. Instead of reacting to the Widow Gookin, they turned their attention to the Harvest Festival and did their best to enjoy the day.

Be that as it may, the term "festival" was probably not the best word to describe this town event. As with most things in Puritan Boston, the Harvest Festival was somber, gray, and reverent. Apart from the sharing of food and the peddling of new clothes—which, Rip noted, looked exactly the same as the old clothes—there wasn't much in the way of celebration or activity. Here and there, he spotted other children desperately trying to have a bit of fun, but he also saw that their efforts were immediately squelched by stern parents.

Despite their solemn nature, the citizens of Boston insisted on cele-brating the festival year after year. The pumpkin contest was a crucial part of every Harvest Festival, for it was rumored that Blaxton himself had held a deep affinity for pumpkins.

And so, about an hour before sunset, Mrs. Van Winkle was officially awarded the first-place prize for her garden Goliath, receiving a respectful round of applause—much to the dismay of a certain someone. Truth be told, Mrs. Gookin had held a fair shot at winning second prize—that is, until an unfortunate mishap caused the Van Winkles' gargantuan pumpkin to roll off the wagon and land on hers, squishing it into oblivion.

This event was greeted by thunderous applause.

Soon after the contest, Josiah and Abigail were bombarded with praise, along with questions about gardening techniques—since apparently the Van Winkles were now gardening experts.

"How on earth did you manage to grow that fruit to such a size?" asked a young man named Jonathan Edwards.

"Will you make a pie out of it?" asked a small boy named Sam Adams.

"Oh, it will make a hundred pies," said Abigail with a big smile.

"What did it feel like to squash Mrs. Gookin's pumpkin?" asked Sam's father, also named Samuel. "I almost took a hammer to that wretched thing last month—the pumpkin, not the woman."

While Mr. and Mrs. Van Winkle did their best to answer everyone's questions, Rip, who had slipped away from his parents, saw something that immediately caught his attention—a tall, gangly person loping his way across the Common. At first Rip thought this person must be wearing some kind of elaborate costume—that of a scarecrow with farmer's clothes and a pumpkin for a head. But as he focused his eyes, he concluded that it couldn't possibly be a person wearing a costume. For one thing, there wasn't a single soul in Boston who would ever wear something so out of the ordinary and attention-seeking, and for another, no human could *possibly* be that tall and skinny! This figure—whoever or whatever it was— towered over the assembled Puritans like a man in a field of grass. Yet despite its height and features, it seemed as though it passed through the crowd like a gentle breeze—felt, but completely unseen. Rip couldn't believe it; it was as if the scarecrow were invisible to everyone but him!

The scarecrow reverentially approached the Van Winkle pumpkin and placed a long, spindly hand on its orange surface. Then it bowed its head as though in silent prayer. After a brief moment, the scarecrow looked up —directly at Rip—and winked!

Rip fell back a step. The scarecrow could see him! He looked to his parents for help, but they were surrounded by a throng of pumpkin-gawkers. Rip looked back toward the scarecrow but was surprised to discover that the being was no longer there! Casting his eyes around the Common, Rip glimpsed the long-legged scarecrow striding off toward the forest.

How did the scarecrow get there so quickly? wondered Rip. Without another thought, he sprang after the apparition. He didn't know why he was following it—he just knew he had to.

After a breathless minute, Rip came to the stone wall that separated the Common from a dark patch of forest. He stopped short and watched as the scarecrow headed into the trees. It paused and turned its large, glowing head to look at Rip once more; a question burned in its triangular eyes. Rip's heart was beating fast. Even though the scarecrow hadn't said a word, Rip somehow knew what it was asking: "Will you follow me?"

Rip hesitated. He wanted to follow the scarecrow, but he was afraid. Surprisingly, he was no longer afraid of the strange being—for in his heart he felt that it was somehow good—but he was afraid of what lay ahead.

He knew that beyond the forest, just out of sight, stood the large wooden gate at Boston Neck.

From his studies in school, Rip had learned that Boston was shaped like a pointed seed—a round peninsula connected to the rest of New England by a narrow strip of land known as Boston Neck. Shortly after their arrival in the New World, the Puritans had fortified the city of Boston by building walls and constructing an imposing gate at Boston Neck as well as a watchtower on Beacon Hill. Guards kept watch at both the gate and the tower, protecting the settlers by preventing wild animals, hostile Indians, and other dangerous, unknown things from entering the city.

Past the gate was the Gallows, an unholy place where murderers and other criminals were hanged for their crimes. Beyond that lay the wilderness of New England—a vast, unknown world, supposedly filled with darkness and evil. At least, all of this is what Rip had always been told. He didn't really know what was out there.

Of all the legends Rip had ever heard about the outside world, the most frightening was the one about the Dark Woodsman—an evil man who walked the wilderness at night, searching for souls to steal. Rumor had it that in the early days of Boston, the Dark Woodsman had stolen the souls of many and turned them into witches—witches who still haunted the forest. The mere thought of the Dark Woodsman and his witches was enough to keep most of the townsfolk, especially the children, safely behind the gated wall at Boston Neck.

"Hello?" said a timid voice.

Rip jumped. He had been so distracted that he hadn't noticed a girl in a red dress approach on the other side of the stone wall. She had olive skin and hazel eyes, and was perhaps a year or so older than Rip. A few curls of dark brown were visible from under her white bonnet. The girl looked at Rip with thoughtful interest.

"Sorry," said the girl. "I didn't mean to scare you."

"You didn't scare me. I was just . . ." He looked back at the forest. *The scarecrow was gone!*

"What's your name?" asked the girl.

Rip hesitated, still in awe of the sudden appearance and disappearance of the scarecrow. "Rip," he answered finally.

"Rip?" repeated the girl. "That's an odd name."

Well aware of the strangeness of his name, Rip let out a sigh. "Well, it's my name."

"My name is Charity," offered the girl.

"Charity's an odd name, too."

"It means love."

"I know what it means," replied Rip somewhat indignantly.

"It comes from the Bible," continued Charity. "To remind me to be a good person."

"Mine comes from a gravestone."

Charity's eyes widened with interest. "Your parents named you after a gravestone? Why?"

Rip shrugged. "I don't know. My mother gave me my name, but she never told me why. She said I would understand in time. That's her over there." He pointed at Abigail, who was far away, still busy talking to people.

"The woman next to the giant pumpkin?"

"Yes, that's her—and that's our pumpkin."

Charity's mouth dropped. "That's your pumpkin? Really? Gracious! How did it get so big?"

"Well . . ." Rip said hesitantly, "I talked to it."

Charity scrunched her nose doubtfully. "What do you mean you talked to it? People can't talk to pumpkins!"

"I talked to it!" he insisted. "He told me he was lonely. So I told him he belonged in our garden, and he was part of our family. After that, the pumpkin just grew bigger. My mother said that helping someone feel they belong is a magic of its own."

Rip suddenly wondered if he had said too much. The words had just tumbled out of him before he'd had a chance to think about what he was saying. He had never spoken with anyone about his gift with plants; his parents, particularly his father, had forbidden it. Yet, even though he didn't know Charity, Rip felt that he could trust her—the same way he had felt he could trust the scarecrow. Indeed, it was almost as though the scarecrow had led Rip to her.

Charity fidgeted with some loose stones on the wall. "Your mother sounds like a good person," she said, softly. "My mother disappeared . . . about a year ago."

Rip opened his mouth, but he didn't know what to say. He couldn't imagine how hard life would be without a mother. Just thinking about it made him sad.

"Did the pumpkin really talk to you?" asked Charity, clearly changing the subject.

Rip screwed up his face, trying to think of the right words. "It didn't exactly *talk*. I just sort of—felt what it needed. Does that make sense?"

Charity squinted her hazel eyes and shook her head.

Rip thought for a moment. "It's like going outside on a cold day," he said. "No one needs to tell you it's cold. You can just *feel* it."

Charity seemed to understand. "Can you feel anything in this?" She bent down, scooped up a small pile of dirt, and placed it on the rock wall. She smiled at Rip with curious anticipation.

Rip nodded. "Right here," he said, his hand hovering above the mound of dirt. "I can feel three dandelion seeds, some old, rotted maple leaves, and the root of a rosebush."

"Oh, I love roses!" said Charity.

Rip closed his eyes and his breathing slowed. At first, nothing happened. But after a few moments, a cluster of green leaves started to bubble and sprout from within the dirt. He removed his hand, and within a few moments, a very small rosebush sprang from the pile of dirt and began to bloom.

Charity laughed and clapped her hands. "Do it again!" she pleaded. "Please?"

But before Rip could do anything else, he heard his father call his name. "Rip! Is that you?" Josiah jogged over to his son. "Your mother and I have been looking all over for you. It's getting dark." He stopped abruptly, taking notice of Charity for the first time. "Hello! And who is this young lady?"

"This is Charity," said Rip. "She's my new friend."

The girl looked down.

"It's a pleasure to meet you, Charity," said Josiah.

When the judge extended his hand, Charity flinched and drew backward. Confused, he cocked his head to one side.

"It's all right," he said, smiling warmly. Slowly, Charity took the judge's hand, and Josiah shook it briefly before pausing to examine her wrist; it was marked with a large green and purple splotch. For a moment Rip wondered what that mark was. Then it dawned on him. It was a bruise—a dark, ugly bruise.

"Charity," said Josiah slowly, "where did you get that bruise?"

She looked at her wrist in surprise, and then quickly withdrew her hand. Rip couldn't understand why, but Charity seemed ashamed, as though she had just revealed a terrible secret.

Josiah furrowed his brow and spoke softly, as if trying to remember something. "Charity," he repeated. "As in, Charity . . . *Walker*?"

The little girl looked up at the judge with worried eyes. A harsh shout came from the edge of the woods. "Charity! Where are you?"

Josiah, Rip, and Charity looked toward the voice. All at once, a large man came striding through the trees. His clothes were some of the finest Rip had ever seen, yet there was something about this man's appearance that Rip did not like; it was cold and cruel. Rip turned to Charity and saw that her face had become very pale.

"It's my father," she whispered.

"Charity!" he barked. "What have I told you about talking to people! How dare you disobey me!" He moved menacingly toward his daughter. In a single move, Josiah swung his legs over the wall and placed himself between the children and Charity's father.

"Tom Walker," said Josiah with a forced friendliness. "I haven't seen you in a while—not since your wife disappeared."

"*Van Winkle*," acknowledged Mr. Walker, spitting out the name as though it were sour milk. Then, looking over Josiah's shoulder, he glared at his daughter. "You been talking to the judge?" he barked.

"She's been talking to my son," said Josiah. "They're friends."

"Friends?" spat Mr. Walker, turning his attention back to Josiah. "Why would she be friends with your little brat?"

Josiah tightened his jaw, all traces of amiability now gone. "You're looking rather extravagant today, Walker. I've noticed that you've been enjoying quite a few luxuries ever since your wife disappeared."

"Just what are you implying, Van Winkle?"

"I think you know *exactly* what I'm implying," said Josiah coolly. "When you're ready to tell me what *really* happened to your wife, Walker, you let me know."

Mr. Walker smiled slyly and smoothed his hair. "I already told you. She was kidnapped by Indians—"

"Outside the city walls," interrupted Josiah. "No evidence left behind. Then, almost overnight, you became unbelievably wealthy. That's a little convenient, don't you think?"

Mr. Walker laughed. Rip didn't like the sound of that laugh; it was harsh and unnatural.

"Van Winkle," said Mr. Walker, shaking his head, "what is this? Are you putting me on trial? I already gave my testimony to the General Court, and they found no fault with it. And yet, you're still not convinced."

"Perhaps it's because I don't care how many coins are in your purse," said Josiah. "You can dress as fancy as you like, Walker, but I know a liar when I see one."

Mr. Walker's eyes flashed. "You had better watch your mouth, Van Winkle! Or you might lose your reputation *and* your position!"

"*My position?*" repeated Josiah, his voice thick with indignation. "My responsibility is to forget about personal interest and focus on what is *just*. What about you, Walker? What kind of husband abandons his wife in the woods? If there's one thing I've learned from raising a child, it is this: you reap what you sow. So, whatever you think you've buried in your past—or out there in the woods—I can promise you that one day it will come back to haunt you."

For a brief moment, a genuine look of alarm swept across the brash man's face as he considered Josiah's words. But the expression faded as quickly as it had appeared, replaced by red-hot anger. He shoved Josiah aside and reached for his daughter.

"Come here, you!" he said, grabbing Charity by the arm. She stifled a sob as her father began dragging her away.

Anxious to help his new friend, Rip leapt over the wall to try to stop Mr. Walker, but Josiah was one step ahead of his son. The judge jumped in front of the brute, firmly blocking his path.

"Walker, I will not stand by while you—"

But Mr. Walker didn't let Josiah finish. With considerable force, he punched Josiah in the stomach, sending the judge to his knees. Rip cried out and ran to his father.

"Don't tell me what to do!" Mr. Walker bellowed, flecks of spit flying from his mouth.

Josiah, unable to catch his breath, looked up at Charity's father with eyes that burned like two hot coals.

Mr. Walker sneered down at him. "You know, I've got some friends in powerful places who really *do* care about the coins in my purse. I think I'll go to them tomorrow and tell them I don't like Josiah Van Winkle. Let's see how long you last after that!" Laughing, Mr. Walker yanked his daughter's arm once more and headed into the forest.

Rip stood next to his father, feeling helpless as he watched the Walkers depart. He had to do something! "Wait!" he shouted, surprising himself as much as he did the others.

Mr. Walker turned to face the boy, a dark expression covering his face. "What do you want?"

Rip felt a sudden pang of fear. He had a plan in mind, but he wasn't at all sure it would work, and Mr. Walker's cold, dark glare wasn't helping Rip's confidence. "The ground!" he blurted.

Mr. Walker stared at Rip in confusion, and then quickly dismissed him. "More Van Winkle nonsense!" he muttered as he turned to leave. Rip moved forward, yelling so that Mr. Walker would hear him.

"The ground," he repeated. "It knows! It knows your secrets!" He paused for a moment to think, then added, "And they're coming for you, Mr. Walker!"

The wealthy man whirled around, swinging his hand high as if to strike Rip, but stopped short. Something else had caught his attention— something between him and the boy. There, from a hole in the ground, a thorny bush was bubbling up and out—like water from a spring.

"What is that?" he exclaimed.

Rip, who had asked the rosebush to grow there, forced himself to make a fearful expression and started backing away from the plant. "It's your secrets, Mr. Walker. They're . . . they're coming out of the ground to get you!"

Mr. Walker's face turned as white as the moon. "No," he murmured. "It's not possible."

Calling upon the rosebush in his mind, willing the plant to grow deeper and stronger, Rip felt a sudden surge of strength. He realized, to his great surprise, that this rosebush trusted him completely; Rip could control it at will. The boy looked at the muttering, fearful Tom Walker and did his best to conceal a smile. Turning again to leave, the angry man dug his fingers into Charity's arm and pulled hard. The girl whimpered.

Rip angrily balled his hands into fists, and a huge, thorn-covered vine shot out of the rosebush and wrapped itself around the rich man's left boot, its sharp thorns visibly piercing through the leather. Mr. Walker cried out in pain and relinquished his daughter's arm.

"No!" he shouted. "It wasn't my fault; it was the pirates, I swear!"

"Oh dear, Mr. Walker," said Rip. "I don't think the plant believes you." Rip concentrated harder on the rosebush, and the vine tightened around the man's leg.

"All right!" Mr. Walker confessed. "I might've helped them . . . a little."

"Why?" pressed Rip. "Helped them with what?"

The end of the vine continued its growth, wrapping up to Mr. Walker's knee. He yelped in fright. Rip shrugged his shoulders, acting as though he didn't know how he could help the man.

"Maybe if you tell us what you did, the plant will let you go."

"I—I went outside the city walls and made a deal with the Dark Woodsman," said Mr. Walker through gritted teeth. "A deal for a lost treasure. My wife—she found out . . . confronted me in the woods. I had to stop her!"

Rip couldn't believe what he was hearing! He furrowed his brow, and two more vines shot out of the ground and reached for Mr. Walker's free foot. Terrified, the guilty man stumbled and fell backward, losing his boot to the rosebush completely. Without wasting another moment, he scrambled to his feet and shot off in the direction of his home in the woods.

Rip smiled. Suddenly, Mr. Walker didn't look so scary, hobbling away on one fancy boot. Satisfied, Rip turned to look at his father and Charity, both of whom were staring at him in amazement.

"Son," said Josiah slowly, "did you do all of that?"

Rip hesitated, worried that he may have upset his father. The boy nodded.

To his surprise, a proud smile crept slowly across his father's face. "Well done."

. . .

KNOWING that Mr. Walker was not likely to return, Josiah led the two children to Abigail. In hushed tones, he explained all that had happened, and before he even finished telling the story, Abigail was wrapping Charity in her arms, reassuring the frightened girl that everything would be all right. Abigail insisted that Charity stay at the Van Winkle home until things could be sorted out. Rip heard his father mumble something about the "legality of the situation" before leaving to find the city constable.

As Abigail made preparations to leave the Common, Rip approached Charity, who sat on a small bench, looking apprehensive and paler than ever. Rip sat down next to her. "Are you all right?" he asked.

Charity twisted the hem of her dress. "I'm scared."

"Why?"

"Wherever I go, I cause problems," said Charity.

Rip furrowed his brow. "I don't believe that."

"That's what my father always says," replied Charity, twisting the hem even tighter. "What if I just don't belong anywhere? Will I have to go back home and live with him?"

Rip was thoughtful for a moment, remembering what his mother had said to him in the garden about helping others feel accepted. "You can stay with us and be safe. My parents aren't like your father. Besides," Rip added, placing his hand on one of Charity's, "our home is a belonging place."

Charity's hands relaxed. She looked up at Rip with bright eyes.

EARLY THE NEXT MORNING, Josiah and Rip, accompanied by the city constable, went looking for Tom Walker to question him further about the disappearance of his wife. First, they went to the house in the woods, but finding it deserted, they went to Mr. Walker's business and found it in a similar state. Some of the locals claimed that they had seen him early in the morning, gathering his things in a hurry, and hauling out of town on a horse "as fast as lightning."

And so, with no way to question the man, Josiah took Rip to the General Court and provided testimony against the blackguard, reporting Walker's confession about smuggling goods to pirates and conspiring to murder his wife. Within the hour, a warrant was issued for Mr. Walker's arrest, and the Van Winkles were named Charity's temporary guardians until the issue could be resolved.

Inwardly, Rip suspected that the issue would never be "resolved." After their brief encounter in the Common, it was clear to Rip that the cowardly Mr. Walker loved his possessions more than his daughter and would never return to Boston. So, for all intents and purposes, the Van Winkle family tree had inadvertently grown another branch.

For his part, Rip was thrilled to have a sister. Charity was like the wondrous rose that somehow grows among thorns. Once the dark cloud of Tom Walker had fled from Boston, the sweet girl stepped into the light, and she revealed herself as the living embodiment of her name. Quiet, shy, and gentle, Charity was filled with a reverential love for all living things. And above all, Charity loved her brother, Rip. As time passed, the two became almost inseparable. They no longer felt alone. They had a belonging place. They were a family.

4

BELONGING PLACE

IN WHICH THE FAMILY TREE GROWS
PRODIGIOUSLY...

*A*bout a month after Charity's adoption, Rip overheard his father grudgingly admit something to Abigail about her "being right" (a phrase that always seemed to please Rip's mother very much). Shortly thereafter, Mr. and Mrs. Van Winkle informed Rip and Charity that their family would be opening their home to children who needed a family and a safe place to live.

Excited by the prospect of having a larger family, Charity and Rip agreed to help in any way they could, and they soon discovered that the world was filled with wandering souls, each searching for somewhere to belong. As it was, Boston was overburdened with needy children, and the Van Winkles wasted no time in giving them a safe haven.

In December of 1725, Josiah and Abigail took in Duncan, a thirteen-year-old mute boy whose parents had been killed by Indians on the outskirts of Massachusetts Colony. A pair of rangers had discovered the boy in an abandoned home, hiding under a bed. The rangers brought the boy to Boston's General Court, which, in turn, delivered Duncan to the Van Winkles. Haunted by frequent nightmares, the silent boy spent the first few weeks sleeping under his bed, trembling with fear.

Rip, who had never experienced something as traumatic as poor Duncan had gone through, didn't know how to make his new brother feel safe. With Duncan unable to speak, Rip eventually decided that all he could do was sit down on the floor next to Duncan's bed and tell him stories until he fell asleep.

Rip knew a lot of stories. His favorites were those he had heard from

Mrs. Elizabeth Goose—the wife of Isaac Goose and proud mother of *sixteen* children. Lizzy Goose told the most wonderful stories. There was the one about Jack and Jill who ran up Beacon Hill, one about a lion and a unicorn, and stories about Peter Pumpkin Eater, the legendary ranger of New England.

During the weeks following Duncan's arrival, Rip told the boy all of these stories and more, hoping they would ease his fears. Often, Rip was joined in his efforts by Charity, who sang soothing lullabies she had learned from her own mother.

One night after his storytelling, Rip began to feel discouraged. He didn't know if his efforts were helping Duncan at all. Thinking he should just forget it and go to bed, Rip yawned and rushed through a story. But as he turned to leave, Duncan's hand came out from under the bed and gently grasped his wrist. Rip peered under the bed and was surprised to see Duncan blinking back at him. Even though Duncan couldn't speak, there was something in the boy's expression that said more than words ever could. The look spoke of pain, loneliness, and deep sadness—and yet, deep inside shone a glimmer of hope. It was a hope that urged Rip to stay.

Slowly, Rip leaned back against the bed and started telling another story. As he did so, he noticed that, for the first time since Duncan had come to the Van Winkle home, he was smiling. From that day on, Duncan slept better and in his bed, and although he remained mute, he smiled often and learned to communicate with the Van Winkles through expressive gestures.

As the three siblings attended school, Charity and Rip often helped Duncan with his homework. In return, Duncan warded off potential bullies; the boy was so tall, he merely had to be present to intimidate most children. As time went on, Duncan's personality began to shine through. Even though he couldn't speak, the Van Winkles felt that he was a wise, old soul. He was quiet, but strong and reliable. He was as steadfast as an oak, and the Van Winkles loved him dearly.

THE MORNING OF OCTOBER 31, 1726, was cold but glorious. A gale-force wind from the night before had torn all of the remaining leaves from the trees, leaving the grounds of the Boston Common blanketed in a patchwork of autumn red and gold. Such beauty would have added to the celebration of All Hallows' Eve—that is, if the Puritan community actually celebrated All Hallows' Eve.

The citizens of Boston made a sharp distinction between All Hallows' Eve and All Hallows' Day. In the eyes of a Puritan, All Hallows' Day (November 1) was a church-sanctioned celebration of truth and life,

whereas All Hallows' Eve (October 31) was a pagan celebration that glori-
fied deception and death. Souling—one of the traditions of All Hallows'
Eve, where the poor would visit the homes of the wealthy, begging for a
treat—was seen as particularly distasteful. If the host refused to give
anything to the poor, the visitors sometimes threatened the host or uttered
a pagan curse upon the house. The Puritans viewed such behavior as irre-
ligious trickery and thus refused to participate. Nonetheless, Abigail Van
Winkle—a charitable soul by nature—always prepared cakes and treats for
any visitors who might come souling.

The children hurriedly bundled up and ran out to play in the Common.
They dashed through fresh piles of leaves, laughing as their movements
scattered red and gold leaves across the musty green grass. Caught up in
the joyfulness of the moment, Rip almost didn't see the young woman in
the yellow shawl walking down the street toward the Common. She was
carrying a small bundle in her arms and had two small daughters, one at
either side, clinging to their mother's skirt for warmth.

The woman stopped, brought a handkerchief to her mouth, and
coughed. Rip felt his stomach drop when the woman pulled the cloth
away; it was soaked in bright red blood! Amid the woman's coughing, Rip
could hear another sound. He strained his ears and realized that it was the
sound of crying; the bundle in the woman's arms was a baby.

Rip motioned to his brother and sister, who immediately ceased their
playing. He pointed at the young woman and asked, "You think she's all
right?"

Charity squinted down the street until she saw who Rip was pointing
at. Then, all at once, she leapt forward. "Those are the Delaney girls!" she
gasped as she ran toward them.

Rip and Duncan exchanged confused glances, and then followed their
sister up the road.

"Mrs. Delaney?" called Charity. "Are you feeling well?"

Startled, the young woman looked up. When Rip arrived, he was taken
aback by how pale she was. Her brown hair was matted against her face,
and there were dark circles under her tired eyes.

"My girls and I would like to leave a blessing on your house and family," murmured Mrs. Delaney. She paused, looking quite unsteady, before
adding, "I'm cold."

"Here," said Charity, touching Mrs. Delaney's elbow. "Let us take you
inside where you can get warm." She gently turned the poor woman
toward the Van Winkle home. The woman nodded half-heartedly, as
though barely aware of her surroundings. Her daughters stared at the Van
Winkle children warily.

Rip smiled warmly in response. "What are your names?"

The tallest of the two girls hesitated before speaking. "I'm Mary. She's Martha. And the baby is Molly."

Rip glanced up at the child in Mrs. Delaney's arms before responding to Mary. "It's nice to meet you, Mary and Martha," he said. He did his best to put on a brave face, though inwardly he was very worried about both the girls and their mother. Dressed in clothes that were no better than rags, they were all bone-thin and almost blue from the cold.

Rip offered Martha his hand. "Would you like to come inside?" he asked. "We can get you and your sisters something to eat."

Martha looked to her older sister before nodding. Mary and Martha took Rip's hands and followed Duncan, Charity, and Mrs. Delaney to the Van Winkle home.

Upon entering the house, they nearly collided with their father, who looked down at them in surprise. Mrs. Delaney let out a weak gasp and nearly fell to the floor.

"Judge Van Winkle!" she exclaimed as she made an awkward attempt at a curtsey. She immediately broke into a fit of coughing.

Rip glanced nervously at his father, who still appeared confused about what was happening.

"Mrs. Delaney? What's going on?"

She continued to cough, unable to speak.

"We found her on the street," explained Rip, gesturing to the bloodied handkerchief in her hand. "She's sick."

Josiah nodded and took command of the situation. "Duncan, take Mrs. Delaney's baby," he ordered. "Rip, escort our guests into the parlor to warm up by the fire. Charity, fetch your mother, and then ask the cook to bring tea and something warm for them to eat."

Everyone set to work. In no time at all, Mrs. Delaney was sitting in the armchair next to the fire, with her girls huddled on the floor beside her. Rip had found a few extra blankets for them, and Duncan stood close by, nervously cradling baby Molly in his stout arms.

It wasn't long before Abigail entered the room, followed by Betsy, the family cook, carrying a tray of tea. As Josiah brought Abigail up to speed, Betsy set down the tray on the oak side table and poured out tea for the destitute Delaney family. She then hurried out of the room to fetch bread and cheese.

After checking on the baby, Abigail went to the kitchen and brought back a wet cloth. She moved to Mrs. Delaney, who was coughing violently. Charity took some bread and cheese from Betsy and gave it to Mary and Martha, who immediately started eating. Josiah gave each of them a cup of milky tea.

When Mrs. Delaney finished coughing, she took a deep breath and leaned back into the armchair. Abigail did her best to soothe the poor woman, wiping her forehead with the cloth.

"Shhh," said Abigail. "You poor dear. Everything will be all right."

Mrs. Delaney opened her eyes, looking directly at the judge. "Forgive me, sir," she whispered. "I shouldn't have been out souling. I didn't mean to disturb you."

Josiah waved a hand dismissively. "No, no. I'm glad my children found you. But why were you out souling?"

Rip saw Mrs. Delaney's face fill with shame. "We were run out of our home last night, sir, and my bairns have had nothing to eat today."

Abigail gasped. "You've been on the streets since last night? But it's freezing out there!"

"Why were you run out?" asked Josiah.

Tears sprang to Mrs. Delaney's eyes. "Because my husband . . . my husband was lost at sea." The poor woman sobbed, putting her face in her hands. "And without my husband, I have nothing. I don't have any money to pay the landlord . . . or to buy food."

Mrs. Delaney let out a strangled sob that quickly turned into another fit of coughing. Abigail placed a gentle hand on the woman's shoulder. It seemed an eternity until the coughing subsided. Mrs. Delaney leaned back into the armchair again, looking paler than ever.

Mopping the woman's brow with the cloth, Abigail shot a concerned glance at Josiah.

"I think she has consumption," she whispered.

The judge nodded grimly. "Right, then. Charity, will you prepare a bed for Mrs. Delaney? Rip and I will head into town to see if we can find a doctor. Duncan?"

Duncan looked up in surprise. He had overcome his awkwardness about holding baby Molly and was completely engrossed with her, fawning over her as if she were the greatest thing in all of creation.

Josiah smiled. "You keep watch over the children."

Duncan made a serious face and nodded stiffly, like a soldier.

Everyone in the Van Winkle family set about their tasks, while the Delaney girls ate their fill and continued warming themselves by the fire.

Within the hour, Josiah and Rip returned with a doctor and some extra provisions, including milk for the baby. Abigail prepared the milk by warming it in a kettle over the fire. She gave it to Duncan (who, by this time, was even more taken with the child). Duncan dipped small chunks of bread into the milk and fed them to the tiny girl.

While the doctor attended to Mrs. Delaney, Rip joined Charity and the Delaney girls by the fire. Charity had taken them to her room and helped them into some of her clothes. The clothes, although somewhat large on the girls' skinny bodies, were a significant improvement over the tattered rags they had been wearing.

"Will our mother be all right?" asked Mary suddenly.

"I hope so," said Charity. "The doctor is tending to her."

"But what if she doesn't get better?" asked Martha, her eyes brimming with tears. "What if . . . what if . . . she dies?"

Rip sat down next to Martha. "Then you'll stay with us," he said. "We'll take care of you."

Martha sniffed and leaned into Charity, tears flowing freely down her sweet little face.

As THE DAYS PASSED, the little girls thrived, but Mrs. Delaney only grew weaker. She was visited by several doctors, who tried a number of treatments, but it was no use. Near the end of November, the dying woman, burning with fever, spoke with Mr. and Mrs. Van Winkle and asked them to watch over her girls. Josiah and Abigail agreed. Satisfied that her daughters were safe with the Van Winkles, the young woman saw her daughters one last time, kissing each of them on the forehead and giving them her blessing. Shortly thereafter, she passed away. Mary and Martha huddled around Abigail and sobbed. No amount of careful and caring discussion could have prepared them for the loss of their mother, but they had come to love and trust all of the Van Winkles, especially sweet Abigail.

With nothing to their name, the Delaney girls settled into the Van Winkle family with relative ease, and Charity was more than happy to share her room with them. The Delaney girls were pleasant, sweet, and quick to befriend the other three children. Duncan, who continued to be captivated by baby Molly, watched over her as a mother bear cares for her cub.

As winter turned to spring, Abigail mentioned to Rip that it was hard for her to imagine a time when Mary, Martha, and Molly were not part of the Van Winkle family.

While rocking Molly to sleep one night, Abigail turned to Rip with shining eyes. "Your father and I have been blessed with a wonderful family."

FOUR MONTHS before the adoption of the Delaney girls, Captain William Fly—a pirate with a terrifying reputation—was captured, tried, and hanged in Boston Harbor. Minutes before the pirate's execution, a local minister had tried to get the man to repent publicly, but Captain Fly merely laughed. With a smile on his face, the pirate leapt onto the platform, examined his own noose, and reprimanded his executioner for tying such a poor knot. Captain Fly then retied the noose with the skill of a sailor before placing it over his own neck. (Legend has it that the pirate also winked at the shocked minister seconds before he was hanged.)

After Fly's body was taken to a small island in Boston Harbor, all that remained of the Captain were his five-year-old twins—Silence, a girl, and Dogood, a boy. Because the children had been born and raised on a pirate ship, they were immediate outcasts within the stern and somber Puritan community. In fact, there was hardly a person in Boston who wanted anything to do with them. People were afraid that the children's souls were forever stained by the sins of their father.

Rip, however, had different ideas. Because of his father's position, Rip had been following the case of Captain Fly for months. After the pirate was executed, Rip immediately thought of the twins and asked if the children could be brought into the Van Winkle home. Josiah, who had seen Dogood bite one of the city guards, was not too keen on the idea of bringing a pirate's children into his family. But as soon as Rip suggested the idea, Charity and Duncan hopped on the bandwagon, and Abigail positively insisted on it. With such a ringing endorsement, Josiah reluctantly changed his mind and went to the General Court and offered to adopt Silence and Dogood. After several months of legal entanglements (there was some debate as to whether or not the children should go to a distant relative in Philadelphia) and about two months after the Van Winkles had taken in the Delaney girls, it was formally decided that Josiah and Abigail would become the legal guardians of the orphaned twins.

As it turned out, there was an inkling of truth to the rumors surrounding the children. They certainly weren't villainous pirates, but Silence and Dogood were almost always up to something mischievous— constantly on the lookout for their own brand of swashbuckling adventures.

Dogood was headstrong and reckless, while Silence was exceptionally talkative and clever. In this, it seemed that the children had been named by their father very ironically; Silence was rarely ever quiet, and Dogood seldom did good.

To further complicate things, the twins had a fascination with animals —particularly small woodland creatures they found and captured in the forest. It was not uncommon for Josiah to come home and discover some recently acquired creature that the twins hoped to make into a house pet (Josiah always considered the day the twins brought home and released an entire family of squirrels to be one of the worst days of his life). Nevertheless, Josiah and Abigail continued to allow the twins to explore the

Common. It gave them something to do, and it prevented Abigail from losing her mind.

IN THE SPRING OF 1727, there was a loud knock on the Van Winkles' door. Upon answering it, Rip was surprised to see the city constable standing on the stoop. The portly man had his hand on the shoulder of a boy near Rip's age. The boy, Rip noticed, was looking down and holding something close to his chest.

"Rip," said the constable, gruffly, "is your mother home?"

"I'm here," answered Abigail, approaching the door as she wiped her hands on her apron.

"Morning, Mrs. Van Winkle," said the constable. "We got a boy here— name's Joseph—arrived by ship not two days ago. His mother and father died at sea, and he's got no place to go. I took the lad to your husband, and he told me to bring him here."

Looking at Joseph, Abigail put a hand to her heart. "Oh, you poor thing!" she exclaimed. "You must be so frightened and lonely. Would you like something to eat?"

The boy glanced up, but didn't respond. Rip tried to catch his eye, but to no avail.

"It's no use," said the constable. "He ain't said a word since he arrived."

Abigail frowned. "Is he mute? Because Duncan—"

The constable shook his head. "The Captain says the boy talked a lot on the ship—excited to come to Boston. But ever since his parents died, he hasn't spoken. Grief, you know—"

"What're you holding?" asked Rip suddenly, posing the question to Joseph.

When the boy didn't answer, all eyes turned to the object in Joseph's hands. It was a small, wood-framed box, with a kind of spoon attached to it. The constable scratched his head. "Never really figured that out. Been holdin' on to it ever since I met him. Won't let me see it."

"Looks like something you made," said Rip, continuing to speak directly to Joseph.

The boy looked up and slowly gave a little nod.

"What is it?" asked Rip with genuine interest.

Joseph hesitated. "It's a catapult," he whispered after a moment. "My father helped me build it."

Abigail and the constable glanced at each other, then back at Rip, clearly astounded by what had just happened.

Rip smiled. "Can you show me how it works?"

Joseph timidly pulled the box away from his chest and pushed down on the spoon with his thumb. When he released the spoon, it sprang back to its original position.

Rip was impressed. "I wonder . . ." he said, screwing up his face thoughtfully. "I wonder if we can make a bigger one."

Joseph brightened. "You think?"

"Well, we have some spare wood," said Rip. "If you help us, then perhaps we can make a really big one."

"How big do you think it could be?"

Rip shrugged. "I suppose that's up to you. Do you want to help me build it?"

After casting a nervous glance at the constable, Joseph followed Rip to the garden. And just like that, Rip had managed to welcome another soul into the Van Winkle fold.

AS IT TURNED OUT, Joseph was an exceptionally intelligent boy who was constantly inventing things—little contraptions that usually involved weights, pulleys, wheels, ropes, and just a *touch* of gunpowder. To test these inventions, Joseph almost always enlisted the help of Duncan and Rip.

A few months after his adoption, Joseph, who had just finished constructing a large catapult at the edge of the Boston Common, shouted to his older brothers, "All right! I want you two to run far. I only have one cannonball, and I don't want to lose it! You have to try to catch it!"

Duncan and Rip nodded, as though this were a perfectly safe thing to do, though of course it most certainly was not. The two boys leapt over the stone wall and ran to the edge of the forest. As Rip waited, he heard a sound behind him. He looked back and noticed a small, barefooted, dirty boy, peeking out nervously from behind a tree. Without drawing too much attention, Rip nudged Duncan and motioned toward the ragamuffin.

"Hello?" said Rip, cautiously.

The boy ducked behind his tree.

"Hello?" repeated Rip, stepping closer. "What's your name?"

The barefooted boy didn't answer, but quickly scampered into the woods and vanished up a large tree.

Duncan and Rip exchanged perplexed looks, but before Rip could say anything else, a huge cannonball came crashing through the branches, landing violently on the ground at the boys' feet.

"Did it work?" shouted Joseph enthusiastically from the other side of the wall.

Duncan grinned and gave Joseph a thumbs-up.

Later, when the Van Winkle boys told their parents about the mysterious, barefooted visitor, Josiah and Abigail dismissed the whole thing as an imaginative story. After all, who ever heard of a young boy living all by himself in the woods of Boston?

"The only wild children we have are Silence and Dogood," said Josiah, eying the twins suspiciously. Silence stared up at the judge innocently while Dogood hurriedly stuffed a mouse in his pocket.

Later that night, Rip was confronted by the twins.

"Was there really a boy in the woods?" asked Dogood.

"And did he really climb up the tree like a squirrel?" asked Silence. "And disappear like a ghost?"

The twins were alive with excitement; the mere thought of such a child existing in the woods appeared to overwhelm their imaginations. Rip tried not to smile. The pirate twins were like two little wildflowers, uprooted from a turbulent, chaotic life on the sea and planted in the gray and somber soil of Boston. Rip loved the life and color they brought into the world.

Rip affirmed that he really had seen a frightened, barefooted boy in the woods, and that the boy really did indeed climb the tree like a squirrel.

"Does he have a squirrel family?" asked Dogood.

Rip shook his head. "I didn't see anyone else. I wonder if he's all alone."

"What if *we* see him?" asked Silence. "What should we do?"

Rip shrugged. "Try to be his friend," he said, echoing the advice his mother had given him long ago. "Make him feel like he belongs."

Silence and Dogood looked at each other and nodded, sly smiles spreading across their faces.

OVER THE NEXT two or three weeks, the Van Winkle household was unusually quiet—*suspiciously* quiet. On more than one occasion, Abigail noted (with great relief) that the twins were behaving very well; they hardly made a noise, ate their meals without complaint, and went to bed early. Around the same time, the Van Winkles also began to notice that several things were missing: a wheelbarrow, a small pile of scrap wood, a hammer and nails, and a considerable amount of rope and twine.

A few days later, while working with his siblings in the garden, Rip heard the distant sound of Silence and Dogood hooting and hollering like little Indian warriors. Straightening his back, Rip looked beyond the garden and saw that Dogood was pushing a wheelbarrow toward the Van Winkle home, while Silence, brandishing a long stick, danced about triumphantly. Rip's eyes widened in shock. On top of the wheelbarrow was a makeshift cage, and inside the cage was the small, barefooted boy!

Dogood grunted as the wheelbarrow came to a full stop in the garden.

Silence ran up to Rip. "Look what I did!" she proclaimed. "I caught the boy in the woods!"

"Hey, wait! I built the box!" said Dogood, wiping sweat from his brow.

Silence ignored her brother. "Rip, can we keep him?"

"Keep him?" repeated Rip, astounded by their request. "You want to keep him?"

"Of course we do!" said Silence. "You said we should be his friends and make him belong." At this, the little girl banged the stick against the cage. "Be our friend!" she ordered.

Pulling the stick from Silence's hands, Rip looked into the cage. He was followed by the rest of his brothers and sisters, who wanted to get a closer look. The boy had backed into a corner of the cage, trembling with fear. Rip noticed that the little fellow's hands and mouth were stained a dark shade of purple. At first Rip thought the purple stuff might be blood, but upon further inspection, he discovered a partially eaten blueberry pie at the bottom of the cage.

"You baited him with pie?" said Rip.

Silence shrugged. "Seemed like a good idea."

Dogood scratched his head. "Do you think Betsy will be mad at us for stealing the pie?"

"This isn't about the pie!"

Silence put her hands on her hips. "Well, then, I really don't know why you're so upset, Rip."

"You kidnapped a boy!" exclaimed Rip. "Don't you know that kidnapping is bad?"

Silence and Dogood suddenly looked uncomfortable, as though they had never before considered such a thing.

"It was Silence's idea," said Dogood, suddenly.

"Me?" said Silence. "You're the one who built the box!"

Silence and Dogood turned and ran in opposite directions. With a flick of his hand, Rip caused two large tree roots to spring out of the ground, grab the twins by their ankles, and hold them still.

"Rip!" shouted Silence, scrunching up her nose in frustration.

"Let us go!" said Dogood, tugging at the gnarled root.

"Boy eat pie!" exclaimed two-year-old Molly.

Rip and the twins turned their heads to see the boy shoveling large handfuls of blueberry pie into his tiny mouth.

"Let's call him Blueberry," said Martha.

"No!" proclaimed Rip. "We don't capture children and name them after pies!"

Rip opened the door to the box and peered inside. "Hello, boy."

The boy stopped eating and looked back at Rip, fearfully. Little chunks of pie dropped from his chin.

"I saw you the other day, remember?" said Rip. "What's your name?"

"Gabriel," said the boy apprehensively, his mouth still full of food.

The twins gasped, apparently unaware that their captive could talk.

"Well, Gabriel," said Rip, "have you been living in the woods?"

The boy nodded.

"Where are your parents?"

Gabriel fidgeted and his eyes welled up with tears.

Rip's expression immediately softened. "Where are your parents?" he repeated, only more softly this time.

"They died, sir. Late last winter."

Rip's heart sank. "And you've been living in these woods ever since?"

Gabriel nodded.

"Do you not have anywhere to go—no home or family?"

The boy shook his head. "No, sir."

Rip bit his lip, lost in thought. "Well, this is a belonging place. So . . . are you still hungry?"

Gabriel glanced around nervously before nodding.

"All right, then. Silence, take Gabriel inside and introduce him to Mother—since this was *your* idea. And Dogood, find Gabriel some of your clothes to wear—since *you're* the one who made the cage."

The scrawny boy looked at his captors in awe, no doubt wondering if this was all some kind of dream. Quietly, he stepped out of the cage and followed the twins into the house. Thus, the Van Winkle family tree had very unexpectedly grown yet another branch.

WITH THE VAN Winkle household now numbering twelve, Josiah and Abigail began to believe that their family was complete. But on a cold evening in February of 1728, there came a loud knock on their door. When Abigail answered, she was surprised to find her son Rip standing with a pair of young boys in tattered clothing. The two boys looked up at her with optimistic eyes.

"I caught these boys trying to pick my pocket," explained Rip. He then gave the elder of the two—a lad of six or seven—a small nudge.

The child cleared his throat, tipped his tricorne hat, and introduced himself as Matthias. He said the younger boy, a raggedy five-year-old, was his brother, Zachariah. Matthias apologized for their behavior and informed Abigail that the pair of them had been "livin' on the streets for quite some time" and were now ready to "live a clean and honest life and make the move into a fancy home."

At this point, young Zacharias peered around Abigail to get a look at the roaring fire.

Matthias continued his speech, saying that Rip had told them "tales o' the greatness of the Van Winkles," and how the family had "somethin' of an open-door policy" when it came to children. He concluded his speech, asking "ifn't the Van Winkles might not be willin' to take in such humble children as meself and me brudder—young, poor, *cold* Zachariah."

Rip then elbowed Zachariah, who responded by looking up at Abigail with pleading, bright blue eyes. She seemed charmed by this little production and invited the boys in for supper.

"But first," she said with a coy smile, "you must wash your hands and faces. I will not tolerate untidiness in this house."

Matthias grinned. "Well, if'n you's insist, marm, I don't see why not," he said, stomping the snow from his tattered shoes. He turned and helped his brother up the front step. Rip followed close behind.

Within a few minutes, the little fellows were scrubbed clean, their faces pink from the lye soap and rough rag. Josiah, who had been busy reading an old copy of *The New England Courant* at the kitchen table, was startled when he looked up and found two small, unfamiliar boys devouring a plateful of potatoes and pot roast. Rip watched his father raise an eyebrow and look to his wife for an explanation. Abigail merely smiled back at her husband with a familiar, determined expression. The bewildered judge shrugged his shoulders, pushed a basket of rolls toward the boys, and then went back to reading his newspaper. The little vagrants, Matthias and Zachariah, never went back to a life of skulduggery on the streets of Boston.

WHEN ALL WAS SAID and done, Mr. and Mrs. Van Winkle had become the proud parents of twelve children—a ragtag collection of souls with wildly different backgrounds and personalities. Yet, despite their seeming differences, the family somehow managed to find harmony. Rip, for his part, seemed to thrive in his role as a big brother and protector.

On a quiet summer evening, after a day of working in the garden, Rip sat down next to his father, who appeared deep in thought. When Rip asked him what he was thinking, Josiah nodded toward the garden, where most of the children were playing.

"I'm thinking about our family," he said in a reverential tone. "You know, Rip, ever since your mother and I brought you home, I've come to think of our family as a garden, and every child placed in our care is like a different plant or flower, sprouting up and growing in the world in which we live. Taking care of each of you has been work—hard work—but it's a labor of love. To see each of you blossom and grow, to see you thriving, to see you have hope for life when there once was none . . ." Josiah paused as though struggling to find the words. *"It's like magic,"* he said at last.

Rip didn't say anything. His father was rarely the type of person to speak his heart, and Rip didn't want to spoil the moment.

Josiah chuckled. "There was a time when your mother and I had a lot of money. But now?" he said, glancing at his son. "Now we're wealthy."

Rip sat with his father in silence, happy to belong to the Van Winkle family—a band of orphans and outcasts, bound tightly together by some unseen force and welcomed to a home of love and safety.

LITTLE DID Rip know that the contentment he felt at that moment was about to be shattered by another unseen force.

5

THE MIDNIGHT MINISTER

IN WHICH A DREAM BECOMES A LIVING NIGHTMARE...

*R*ip watched as Lizzy shifted in her armchair and leaned toward the Van Winkle children. It was the last day of August 1730, and they were listening to another tale from Elizabeth Goose, the great story-teller of Boston.

Elizabeth, whom the children affectionately called Lizzy, was an elderly woman with straight silver hair. Most times, Lizzy was an absentminded sort of person ("dotty" was the word Josiah used to describe her), ever forgetful and easily distracted. But whenever Lizzy told a story, she would sit up straight and her eyes would glaze over, as though she were actually seeing whatever she was describing.

The children, enchanted by Lizzy's gift, would frequently gather in her home to hear her stories, the light from her fireplace dancing in their wide eyes.

"This year marks the one hundredth anniversary of Blaxton's heroic rescue of the Puritans," said Lizzy excitedly. "Legend has it that during the week preceding All Hallows' Eve, Blaxton's ghost will return to Boston and light the watchtower on Beacon Hill like a candle on a candlestick."

"Is that true, Lizzy?" asked Zachariah, his chin resting on her lap.

Lizzy glanced down at the boy. "Well, All Hallows' Eve is only a couple of months away. I suppose we will have to wait and see."

"No, not that," said Zachariah. He glanced around fearfully and lowered his voice. "I mean, are ghosts real?"

Lizzy's expression became very serious. "Indeed they are, Zachariah. Indeed they are."

Zachariah swallowed hard.

"Oh, don't be scared, little one," said Lizzy, stroking the boy's hair. "Blaxton is a good ghost and a great protector of Boston."

"Is there any bad ghosts?" asked Matthias. He was sitting on the floor, holding his knees close to his chest.

Lizzy stroked her chin thoughtfully. "Well, yes," she admitted, "But truthfully, I'd worry more about the Midnight Minister."

There was a murmur of confusion while the children exchanged glances and shook their heads.

"Who is the Midnight Minister?" asked Mary. "Is he a ghost?"

The old woman shrugged. "No one knows for certain. It is said that the Midnight Minister is a servant of the Dark Woodsman and walks the forest at night—searching for parishioners, gathering his flock."

"His flock?" asked Martha timidly.

"That's right," said Lizzy. "Every minister must gather his flock and build his church. Well, the Midnight Minister's church is the wilderness at night, and his flock are those who wander strange, dark roads. Only, the Midnight Minister doesn't help people, like most other ministers."

"What does he do?" asked Dogood, who was huddled next to his twin sister, Silence.

"He steals their souls," whispered Lizzy.

All of the children gasped, except for Silence, who said, "That's amazing."

Lizzy chuckled. "I think you like these kinds of stories a little too much, Silence."

The pirate twin gave Lizzy a toothy grin.

"What does the Midnight Minister look like?" asked Gabriel.

"Like a minister!" said Silence. "*Obviously!*"

"Not quite," said Lizzy.

"What do you mean?" said Rip.

"He wears the dark clothes of a minister, yes, but he also wears a wide-brimmed hat. Attached to his hat, and covering his entire face, is a thick black veil."

"A veil?" repeated Rip. "Why a veil?"

Once again, Lizzy shrugged. "No one knows for certain. But there is one thing we know for certain: evil thrives in the shadows."

"Have you ever seen the Midnight Minister?" asked Charity.

Lizzy raised an eyebrow. "Seen? No. Heard? Yes."

Gabriel started. "What do you mean, you've heard him?"

"Because of his chain," said Lizzy.

Silence gulped. "His chain?"

"Yes," Lizzy cast her eyes around the room, carefully examining all twelve frightened faces. Rip could tell she was savoring the suspense. "You see, the Midnight Minister has a great black chain wrapped around his leg. And every time he moves, you can hear it rattle. So, if you're ever walking in the woods late at night, just stop and listen—listen carefully. Because in the distance, you might just hear the rattle, rattle, rattle of the minister's long black chain. And if you do, that means he's coming . . . ," she paused and suddenly pointed at Silence, "FOR YOU!"

Silence yelped and fell backward. The Van Winkle children burst into laughter.

"Not funny, Lizzy!" said Silence, although she too was laughing.

THE FOLLOWING MORNING, Rip came home from school feeling tired and weak. Nevertheless, he went outside to help his brothers and sisters with their chores. Gently touching a tomato plant, Rip used what strength he had to encourage the fruits to grow a bit larger. It lifted his spirits to see things grow.

Suddenly, Rip stopped what he was doing and stared blankly at his mother for several seconds. When Abigail asked what was wrong, Rip shook his head, lost his focus, and fell to the ground. Abigail cried out, rushed to her son's side, and called for help.

The last thing Rip remembered clearly was being carried to his bed by his brother Duncan. Everything after that was a blur.

Of all the diseases in the eighteenth century, smallpox was perhaps the most dreaded. Also known as the Speckled Monster, smallpox was marked by high fevers and puss-filled blisters. Highly contagious, the sickness often spread rapidly through communities; and the walled-off city of Boston was no exception.

Days passed, and Rip slept right through them. Now and then, he would open his eyes and catch glimpses of his siblings helping their mother to take care of him. In one of his waking moments, Rip noticed that Duncan had red spots on his face.

Over the course of the next two weeks, Rip faded in and out of consciousness. Nearly every time he opened his eyes, Charity was there, watching over him and doing her best to take care of his needs.

At one point, Rip awoke just long enough to see his father kneeling beside his bed, tearfully pleading with someone whom Rip couldn't see. He realized that his father was praying—a thought that made Rip think of his mother. It dawned on Rip that he hadn't seen her in a long time. The thought worried him, and he wanted to leave his bed to find her. But his body couldn't fight the overwhelming fatigue, and he slowly drifted back to sleep.

A few days later, Rip awoke again, only to learn from Charity that nearly half of the family had contracted smallpox. A wave of guilt washed over him. He rolled his head to one side and whispered, "This is all my fault."

"Hush, Rip," said Charity, soothingly. "You mustn't say such things!"

"But I was the first one to get sick." Tears pricked his eyes. "I brought it home. I'm the reason everyone is suffering."

Charity stroked Rip's hair in silence. It was several minutes before she spoke again. "You know, Rip, when I was younger, I used to think I was the reason my mother disappeared. At least," she added, sadly, "that is what my father used to tell me. He said my mother ran away because I was a mistake, because I was a burden to her. And I believed it.

"I felt so guilty," she continued, her voice laden with emotion. "And I just wanted to make things right. So I went into the woods looking for my mother, hoping she would forgive me and come back. It wasn't long before I became hopelessly lost. It grew dark, and I was scared. But then, I saw a small light in the distance. Feeling hopeful, I ran to it and was surprised to find myself in a garden—the most beautiful garden I had ever seen. And standing in the garden was a tall scarecrow with a pumpkin for a head."

At the mention of a scarecrow, Rip turned to face Charity, but she wasn't looking at him. Her eyes were unfocused, lost in memory.

"The scarecrow was alive, and he had the most wonderful smile," said Charity. "He invited me into the garden, and he healed my cuts and bruises. He showed me scores of fruits, flowers, vegetables, and I'll never forget how wonderful it was. I told him about my mother and how it was all my fault that she ran away. But the scarecrow stopped me. He shook his head and told me that my father had done a terrible thing." Charity paused momentarily, her chin trembling. "The scarecrow told me that I brought my mother more life than she had ever before felt. He promised everything would be made right. And you know what? A few days later I met you, Rip. You gave me a home. And you gave our brothers and sisters a home. Do not blame yourself for this sickness. You've given all of us more hope and life than we had ever before felt."

Rip looked up at Charity. He wanted to ask her more about the scarecrow, but he could feel himself falling back to sleep. He blinked up at his sister and smiled, grateful that she was with him. She smiled back at him. Content, Rip closed his eyes and drifted off.

As he slept, Rip thought he saw Charity standing on the street outside their home. It was midnight in his dream, and Charity held a lantern in her hand, its light illuminating her kind, lovely face. Suddenly, Rip froze, realizing that Charity was scared; she turned her head and screamed. Behind her stood a dark figure with a veil covering his face. It was the Midnight Minister, the nightmarish person who wandered the woods searching for souls. He was after Charity! Rip tried to call out to her, but she couldn't hear him. She turned away and ran down the street, the Midnight Minister in pursuit. Rip wanted to follow her—to protect her—but he couldn't move.

The scene changed. Rip was now standing in South Burying Ground. Again he saw Charity running, still holding the lantern. She fled through the gates with the Minister close behind her.

Before Rip could do anything, a cloud of darkness filled the graveyard, enveloping his sister. Again, Rip wanted to help her, but he couldn't. For some unknown reason, he was frozen where he stood. The Midnight Minister threw back his head and laughed in devilish triumph.

RIP AWOKE WITH A START, his heart beating fast. The dream was so real that he had to place his hands on his face to make sure that he was really awake. He looked around the room for Charity, but she wasn't there. He sat up slowly. Swinging his legs over the side of his bed, he took several deep breaths. As he stood, his legs shook. He sat back down and breathed even deeper. When he stood again, his legs held steady, and he breathed a sigh of relief.

He made his way to his sisters' room and was surprised to see it filled with the entire family. Most were huddled in a single corner of the room. He heard two or three of his siblings sniffle and noticed that little Zachariah was crying.

Rip saw his mother and called out to her. Everyone turned to look at him, their eyes red with tears. Rip's heart sank when he saw the expressions on their faces.

"What's going on?" he asked, a sense of dread rising within him.

Bowing their heads, the Van Winkle children parted, allowing Rip to see into the circle. A wave of icy numbness swept through his entire body, and he felt as though the floor had opened up underneath him to swallow him whole. Before him sat his father, tears trickling down his cheeks. In the judge's arms lay Charity, her skin dotted with faint red marks, her body still and lifeless.

"My child, my child," sobbed Josiah, rocking back and forth.

Abigail and the children gathered closer around Josiah, each desperate to find strength and comfort in each other. All the children took turns squeezing her hand or stroking her hair, saying goodbye to her in their own way.

Everyone but Rip.

He backed away from his family, watching his parents and siblings as if the whole thing were a dream—the worst possible dream he could imagine. Pressing his back against the wall, he willed himself to wake up. But it was no use. It wasn't a dream—Charity was dead!

No, not Charity! he thought. *Not her. No, not like this. No, no, no!*

Numb with pain, Rip sank to the floor.

Abigail called out to her son, her voice cracking under the weight of her own emotion. "Rip? Rip, come and be with your family. Please?"

He clutched his knees to his chest and shook his head.

"Rip, we need you," pleaded Abigail.

But he continued to shake his head. He couldn't look at his mother. He couldn't look at his family. He couldn't stand up and be with them. *I did this!* he thought to himself. *I killed Charity. This is all my fault!*

A heavy darkness descended upon him, and he felt cold—as though he had been thrown into an icy pond. His breathing was shallow and staggered. He wanted to scream. He wanted to cry—but he couldn't do anything. His whole body was numb with shock and grief.

Huddled against the wall, Rip thought of the dream, the nightmare. All at once he realized that it had come true—the Midnight Minister had stolen his sister!

6

THE HALLOW

IN WHICH THE NIGHT IS FILLED WITH LIGHT...

*L*ate in September, the Van Winkle family laid Charity's body to rest in South Burying Ground. The ceremony, although overflowing with sympathetic friends and family, was a humble one. Rip, still unable to accept his sister's death, kept his eyes to the ground the entire time, silently refusing to be witness to the burial.

The preacher, a man by the name of Jonathan Edwards, gave a sermon based on Charity's name, but Rip wasn't listening. When they lowered Charity's coffin into the ground, Rip tried to think about something else —*anything* else. But even nature itself seemed to be reminding him that his sister was gone; on the grass, and falling all around him, were the dead leaves of autumn. Try as he might, Rip couldn't escape the emptiness—the devastating hollowness—that grew inside him.

As the weeks droned on, Rip withdrew from his family and spent most of his free time in the room he shared with his brothers. When he finished his daily chores, he lay on his bed, dozing fitfully or staring up at the ceiling. Occasionally, he wandered around and flipped through a book or fiddled with the potted plants by his window. But all that did was remind him of happier times and the feelings he could no longer feel.

Why did she have to die? he thought over and over. *Why does anyone have to die? Does anything I do even matter, or will it just fade away when I die, too?* Rip felt so hollow. It was as if all color, all light, and all joy had been scooped out of his heart and buried in the grave with his sister.

On one of the sleepless nights that followed, Rip lay in bed, blinking in the darkness. Next to him was his brother Dogood (who was often too scared to sleep by himself). The rest of his brothers were sprawled out on the straw mattresses on the floor or on smaller beds throughout the room. From somewhere in the darkness Rip heard Duncan snore loudly.

Just as Rip was beginning to feel that he might be able to drift off, Dogood turned fitfully in his sleep, throwing his arm down on Rip's face. Rip let out a groan and pushed it away; his little brother continued sleeping peacefully.

Rip slid out from under his blanket and made his way across the room, carefully stepping over each of the boys. Glancing out the window, he saw the pale moonlight casting an eerie glow on the buildings. A thick, milky fog flowed along the street. Thinking of Charity, Rip turned his eyes toward the South Burying Ground.

As he stood there in silence, Rip noticed something flicker through the fog. He turned his attention toward the movement and saw a mysterious-looking man walking toward the graveyard. Dressed in a brown frock coat and a buckled black hat, and holding a lantern whose light sliced through the darkness before him, the figure strode forward.

Rip squinted, trying to get a better look. The object that the man was holding was not a lantern at all—at least, not a regular lantern. It was a pumpkin—a hollowed-out pumpkin with a carved face. It had two triangular eyes, a pointed nose, and a wide, gentle grin. The man, whoever he was, held the pumpkin lantern aloft by its long, hooked stem.

Strange though it was, the pumpkin didn't interest Rip so much as the light. Indeed, the light from within the lantern was unlike anything he had ever seen. The closer the man came, the brighter the light burned. In fact, the light became so bright and intense that Rip began to wonder why it wasn't waking the neighbors. It poured out of the pumpkin's face with the intensity of a bonfire.

Just then, the mysterious man came to an abrupt stop and turned to face the window, as if he knew that Rip was watching him. The light from the pumpkin grew even brighter, until its golden rays shone through the window, completely illuminating Rip. Terrified, he stood transfixed, unable to see anything but yellow light.

Then, as swiftly as it had overtaken him, the wave of light disappeared, plunging the room into darkness. Struggling to readjust to the change, Rip rubbed his eyes and glanced around the room. All six of his brothers slumbered peacefully in their beds, with Duncan snoring just as loudly as before.

When Rip looked out the window again, his heart leapt into his throat. Still standing on the street and looking directly at Rip was the mysterious man; only now his eyes were bright yellow, as yellow and as bright as the light from the pumpkin lantern.

With his free hand, the yellow-eyed man pointed up at Rip, and then motioned for the boy to come down to him. Heart thumping in his chest, Rip shook his head and hid behind the curtain. He pressed his body against the wall and willed himself to wake up.

"This is all a dream," he whispered to himself. "And you're going to wake up any second now."

But Rip was awake *and he knew it.*

After a few breathless moments he gathered the courage to peek out onto the street once more. The man had disappeared! Rip leapt out from behind the curtain. For some reason, *not* being able to see the yellow-eyed man frightened him even more than being able to see him. Rip glanced up and down the street, but to no avail; the stranger had completely vanished.

Just as he was about to leave the window and return to his bed, he heard something—something that made his blood run cold. It was the rattle of a chain.

Rip turned back to the window and saw a tall man, dressed in black clothing and carrying a small sickle, walking toward his house, a length of chain rattling at his ankle. The man's hands, the only visible flesh on his body, were as white as the moon, and hanging from his round hat, completely concealing his face, was a thick black veil.

It's the Midnight Minister! thought Rip, his whole body trembling. *He's real!*

Unable to tear his eyes from the street, Rip watched as the man crept through the fog like a spindly spider. Silent as a shadow, he strode forward, passing the Van Winkle home without a glance and heading straight for the graveyard.

Rip swallowed hard. *First the stranger with the yellow eyes and now the Midnight Minister? Is the Midnight Minister following the man with the yellow eyes? Why are they both heading for the graveyard?*

In a flash, Rip remembered his dream about the Midnight Minister, and his heart filled with dread. The Minister had chased his sister into the graveyard! Was he somehow chasing her even now?

Rip couldn't bear the thought of the Midnight Minister capturing Charity's soul. He dressed as quietly as possible, buttoning his frock coat over his vest. Despite the fear that billowed up inside him, Rip was determined to go to the graveyard. He was terrified of the Midnight Minister, but he was Charity's brother. He had already failed to protect her once; he wouldn't fail her again!

In less than a minute, Rip was on the dark cobblestone street, walking quickly, yet cautiously, toward the graveyard. The Midnight Minister was nowhere to be seen, but an ominous feeling still lingered. It was as if something wicked hung in the air, poised like a mousetrap, silently waiting for the moment when it would spring on him.

As Rip passed King's Chapel and approached the graveyard, he saw a dim light and could hear muffled conversation. He crossed the threshold of the cemetery, slowed his pace, and ducked down behind a gravestone. Breathing heavily, he poked his head out and saw the Midnight Minister standing under a tree, talking to the yellow-eyed man.

"Your time is up, William," said the Midnight Minister. "Give me the lantern."

The Minister's voice had a strange echo, as though two people were speaking the same words at the same time.

"Indeed, my time is up," said the yellow-eyed man. "But this lantern does not belong to you. It belongs to Feathertop, the son of Mother Rigby and the Great Spirit."

"The son of the Great Spirit," the Minister spat, saying the phrase as though it were some kind of joke. "Do you really expect me to believe that you got that lantern from Feathertop?"

"I don't expect you to believe anything," replied William. "Faith was never your strength."

"There is no strength in faith!" spat the Minister. "What good is faith? Faith was not enough to protect the Puritans from the Terrible Slumber and faith cannot save Boston now!"

"Faith is the deepest and truest form of magic," said William calmly. "Faith can turn the night to light. Yet, those who cling to the shadows will always hate and despise the light. It saddens me that you cannot see beyond what your eyes tell you. Without faith, you are as a crow who has forgotten his ability to fly; you peck at the dark, muddy earth when the bright mountains lie before you."

"Enough of your sermons!" shouted the Minister, his black veil billowing ever so slightly. "Your term of service has ended, William! Now give me the lantern!"

"You are not worthy of such light," said William. "Besides, I have come here to give this lantern—and its calling—to another."

"Another?" hissed the Midnight Minister. "Who?"

"To the boy who has been listening to our conversation."

Rip gripped the edges of the gravestone that shielded him from view, realizing that the yellow-eyed man was talking about him.

"Rip Van Winkle," said the yellow-eyed man. "Come—step into the light."

Rip froze. How did the man know his name? For a split second, Rip considered making a run for it. Then he remembered how the yellow-eyed man had stood on the street in front of his house and pointed right at him.

Rip knew that if he tried to escape, the man would find him at his home—and perhaps even harm his family.

Knees shaking, Rip stood up slowly and faced William, half expecting another burst of intense, yellow light. To his surprise, William only smiled back at him and gave a silent nod of approval.

"A boy?" scoffed the Minister. "You would give the pumpkin lantern to a boy?"

"It is not I who have chosen him," said William calmly. "But yes, this boy already carries the light."

The Midnight Minister let out a roar of anger. Horrified by the animal-istic sound, Rip stepped back, stumbled, and fell to the ground. Without warning, a cloud of darkness, thicker than any fog he had ever seen, enveloped him. He choked and gagged as a rancid smell of sulfur filled his nostrils. It was the smell of death.

Covering his mouth and nose with his arm, Rip looked up to see the Midnight Minister approaching him. The Minister's body elongated, twisting itself into a willowy figure with long fingers and a hunched back. The Minister looked more like a monster than a man, and Rip was seized with fear.

When the Minister spoke, his voice was cold and harsh, and the chain at his ankle rattled with every word. "Now, you listen to me, boy! If you carry that lantern, I swear I will hunt you down and *destroy* everything you love!"

Crippled with fear, Rip sank lower to the ground. He tried to call out, but no sound came. He couldn't move. He couldn't speak. He couldn't even blink. It was as if the darkness were not just around him, but inside him as well. It weighed down every thought of escape, strangling every hopeful feeling.

Rip was suddenly overwhelmed with memories—painful memories, *dark* memories. It was as if the Midnight Minister were in his mind, reading aloud his very worst thoughts. He remembered seeing Charity's bruises, the fear on her face when Mr. Walker yelled at her; the day he had been stricken with smallpox; the day he discovered that Charity had died. He remembered when his family laid her body in the graveyard.

The scene changed. Rip was lying in an empty grave and looking up at the night sky. A baby without clothing, he was scared and alone. He didn't belong here. He didn't belong anywhere. He looked up at the cold night sky and screamed.

In that moment, the darkness was pierced by spears of light emanating from William's pumpkin lantern. The Midnight Minister howled in rage, shielding his eyes as the darkness was washed away in a brilliant flood of light.

The Minister placed one hand over his chest and pointed a long, pale finger at Rip with the other. "This isn't over! I will find you! I will find you in your nightmares! I will find you in the darkness!"

"Be gone!" commanded William.

The Midnight Minister cursed before disappearing in a cloud of smoke.

William turned his attention to Rip, and the yellow glow in his eyes faded away until they looked normal. "Rip Van Winkle," he said, "I have waited for you for a very long time."

Rip stood on his feet, still trembling after his encounter with the Midnight Minister. "How do you know my name?" he asked.

"I know everything about you," said William. "I know you carry the name of a grave, and I know your mind is filled with thoughts of death. I know you have a special gift with plants, and yet you feel restless and unhappy. You have suffered loss—tremendous loss—and you wonder if things will ever get better. You wonder if there is any purpose to life itself —even your own life."

Rip felt his heart skip several beats. "How do you know all that?"

William's eyes shimmered in the darkness. "Because my eyes are filled with light and see things as they really are. I see *you* as you really are."

"Who are you?" asked Rip before adding, "Are you a ghost?"

At this, the man did something quite unexpected. He lowered the pumpkin lantern and laughed. It was a merry laugh and, given the gloomy circumstances that surrounded them, seemed out of context.

"Am I a ghost?" he asked, a hint of laughter in his voice. "No, I am not a ghost. At least, not in the way you understand them. My name is William Blaxton. I am a Hallow."

"William Blaxton?" Rip repeated. "The first settler of Boston?"

"Indeed, lad," said William with a grin.

Rip couldn't believe what he was hearing. "But how?" he asked.

"It is a long story," said William with a gentle sigh. "It began when I left England, driven away by grief. I sailed to this land with the intention to live by myself and for myself. Uninterrupted. Undisturbed. Alone.

"I had been so hurt by loss that I began to believe that hiding myself from other people would relieve my pain and sadness. But I was wrong, Rip. My sadness, like my shadow, had followed me across the ocean. Finally, I understood—to my great and utter woe—that I could not rid myself of the darkness within me. At least, not on my own.

"Soon thereafter, the Puritans began to arrive in the New World. They settled on the other side of Boston Harbor and invited me to join them, but I refused. I feared that if I befriended them, they would see the darkness within me and reject me. So, I kept my distance.

"Not long after their arrival, the Puritans became very sick. The land was cursed against them, and their minds became clouded. Unprepared for life in the New World, many of them died. Some of their leaders came to me for help, but again I refused them. I blinded my eyes to their suffering.

"Then, one October evening, I was met by a woman in rags. She begged for my help, but I refused—and not only did I refuse, but I demanded that she leave my property. It was then that revealed herself to be a witch."

Rip felt his heart skip a beat. "A witch?" he repeated. "They're real?"

"Aye, lad. They're real," said William. "And the witch who stood before me was and is the most powerful of all witches—Mother Rigby is her name—and she will neither deny, nor be denied, hospitality. And because of my refusal to help her, she cursed me. Cursed me in the most wonderful way." William paused, eyes shining. "Throughout the course of that night, I was visited by several other extraordinary beings, who showed me things that softened my heart and invited me to help those who were suffering. But each time, I rejected the invitation, unable to see beyond myself.

"Toward the end of the night, I was visited by a personage named Feathertop, a being of indescribable light and warmth. In all my long years of life, I shall never forget the look on Feathertop's face; for as he was leaving my home, he turned to look at me. In his eyes I saw a great and terrible sadness. 'Oh, my child,' said he, 'can you not see? You must let go of yourself. For if a seed wishes to live, it must sacrifice itself and grow outward, not inward. William, you must reach beyond your walls.'

"And then he left, and in the silence that followed, I came to understand that Feathertop was not only inviting me to help others, but he was also offering me the means by which I could help myself.

"With a changed heart, I left my lonely home and went to the Puritan settlement. I offered them food and water, along with everything else I had. The people received my offerings with gratitude and thanksgiving. Eventually, they moved to my side of the harbor, where I shared with them the harvests of my orchard and garden.

"It was another year before I saw Feathertop again. He came to me in October, one hundred years ago this very night. He asked me what I wished, and I told him that I wanted to help those who had struggled as I had struggled. I told him that I wanted to be a light in the wilderness of the world—as he was a light in the darkness of my heart.

"Feathertop smiled and took this pumpkin from my garden," said William, holding the lantern aloft. "He hollowed it out, gave it a face, and placed a light within it—a magical light, a light with power over life and death. From that day forward I became a Hallow—a person called by Feathertop to be a light in the darkness.

"For the past one hundred years, this lantern has preserved my life. During this time, I have traveled throughout New England, helping wandering and tortured souls find their way home. And now, as my mission comes to an end, I give the lantern to you, Rip Van Winkle."

William extended the lantern to Rip.

Rip looked at him in astonishment. "Me? Why me?"

"Because you are lost and restless, Rip," said William, his gaze firm and resolute. "And because, if you do not carry this light—if you do not become a light in the wilderness—then the city of Boston will fall to a great evil. Take the lantern, and with it, this charge: you must find Feathertop by All Hallows' Day. Do this, and Boston will awaken from a great slumber; fail to do it, and Boston will fall, consumed by the darkness."

Rip's mind was spinning. "Wait, Boston will fall? How? Why? And what can I possibly do about it?"

"I already told you," said William. "You must find Feathertop."

"But where?" asked Rip.

"*That* I cannot tell you," said William, leaning forward and placing the pumpkin in Rip's hands. "But seek him you must, for it is only through seeking that we find what we're looking for."

Rip, numb with confusion, absently took the lantern from William. The man breathed a sigh of relief, as though relinquishing the lantern had lifted a heavy weight from his shoulders. And then, against the backdrop of the midnight sky, William began to flicker and fade, like the dying light of a candle.

"Once I was a restless soul," he said, a smile of contentment spreading across his face. "But now it is time for me to rest in peace. Before I go, I must give you a warning. The pumpkin lantern is magical—it will magnify the power of the one who holds it. Because of this, the forces of darkness will seek to control it at all cost. Yet the lantern cannot be taken from you. The only way another can have it is for you to freely give it. So beware—beware of wolves in sheep's clothing! The forces of darkness will try to trick you into giving up the light that you hold. From this point on, Rip, things will rarely be what they *seem*."

Clutching the lantern by its handle, Rip continued to watch William fade, becoming less and less visible against the night sky.

The apparition took a long, deep breath. "And so I tell you, restless one, that no matter what happens, when things get dark, look to the light, and keep moving forward in faith."

Upon uttering these final words, William Blaxton—the first settler of Boston—vanished into the night, leaving Rip alone in the graveyard.

7

WOLVES IN SHEEP'S CLOTHING

IN WHICH A GRAVEYARD IS MORE LIVELY THAN USUAL...

*I*n the moments that followed William Blaxton's departure, Rip felt the night return to normal. The crickets chirped, a raven cawed, and a soft breeze rustled the dead leaves of the overhanging tree branches. Rip lifted the pumpkin lantern and turned it over in his hands. Its orange skin was taut and fresh, as though it had been carved just the day before. Yet its brown, hook-like stem was worn and polished, like the handle of an old man's cane.

However, the part that continued to draw Rip's attention was the lantern's yellow light. He had seen countless candles and lanterns, but there was something about this light that was different from anything he had ever seen. It seemed almost tangible—as though he could put forth his hand and *feel* the flow of light as one feels the flow of water.

Mesmerized by the light, Rip passed one hand over the face of the pumpkin. A mixture of light and shadow flickered across his face. In the light of the lantern, Rip could see his breath coming out in puffs of steam. It suddenly dawned on him that it was a very cold night, yet he didn't feel bothered by the chill in the least; on the contrary, he felt exceptionally warm—as though he had just finished drinking a mug of hot apple cider. Could it be that the light from the pumpkin was keeping him warm? Even now, he somehow felt stronger, more energetic, and more alive than he had felt in weeks.

Before he could think about it further, Rip heard a noise behind him. Startled, he whirled around, holding the lantern high. There was someone —or something—there in the fog. At first, he thought he was looking at an animal of some kind, but as the figure drew closer, Rip realized that it was actually a tall, beautiful woman. She was wearing a gray dress and a dark, hooded cloak.

The woman stopped short and smiled at Rip. "Child," she said in a soothing voice, "what are you doing in the graveyard at this hour?"

Unable to think of an adequate response, Rip simply stared at her. She moved closer. Rip was struck by how quietly the woman moved; she seemed to glide more than walk.

"Children should not linger in a graveyard at night," said the woman. "Especially when All Hallows' Eve is merely a week away. You never know what evil things could be out and about . . ."

Rip swallowed hard, remembering his encounter with the Midnight Minister. The woman was right! Why was Rip still in the graveyard when the Minister could still be nearby?

The woman nodded toward the lantern. "What is that in your hands?"

Rip glanced down. "It's a pumpkin lantern."

"I've never seen anything like it. Did you make it yourself?"

Rip shook his head warily. "No, I didn't make it."

"Then where did you get it?" asked the woman, and for the first time, Rip noticed a strange look in her eyes. Her expression showed an eagerness, a hunger.

"It was . . ." Rip hesitated. "It was a gift." He was beginning to feel uncomfortable about the stranger's questions.

"A gift?" repeated the woman, taking a step forward. "A gift from whom?"

Rip took a few steps backward. "Who are you?" he demanded.

The woman stopped. "It's all right, child. I mean you no harm." She showed her empty hands to Rip. "My name is Katy. I'm just curious about the lantern you carry. May I see it?"

He regarded the woman cautiously. Blaxton had warned him that the forces of darkness would try to take the light from him, but Katy didn't look like an evil person. She seemed very kind and beautiful. Then again, Blaxton had also warned him that things wouldn't be as they seemed. Should Rip let her see the lantern, or should he run from the graveyard? If he ran, where would he go? Wasn't he supposed to find someone named Feathertop?

As these thoughts coursed through his mind, Rip stood there in silence, unable to make a decision.

"The light is so beautiful," said Katy with a coo. "It shines like starlight."

The woman reached for the lantern, but before she could touch it, a large, black raven let out a fierce caw and swooped down, raking her hand with its talons. Clutching her hand to her chest, Katy reeled back in surprise and cursed at the bird. Her eyes were cold with anger.

The bird floated upward for a second or two before dropping down and landing gracefully on the shoulder of a tall man, who had been concealed in the shadows.

When the man stepped forward, dried leaves swirled around him and a sharp breeze whipped through the graveyard. Rip gasped in surprise. The man wore a broad, round hat and black clothes, which gave him the initial appearance of the Midnight Minister. But he wore no veil to cover his face; he had a strong, square jaw, pointed nose, and wolf-gray eyes. For a moment, Rip thought the man looked oddly familiar.

Katy, still clutching her injured hand, staggered backward and looked up at the man angrily. "I hate that bird, Jonathan!" she barked. "I swear, one day I'm going to catch it and eat it!"

Rip was surprised by the level of anger in Katy's voice. He was even more surprised when the raven, after ruffling its feathers indignantly, clacked its beak and spoke in a dignified, aristocratic accent. "Eat me? Ha! You would find me very disagreeable. I'd put up a fight the whole way down, *Katy Cruel*."

She narrowed her eyes. "I don't like that name, Nathaniel. But I'm more than willing to show you how I earned it—"

Jonathan raised a hand. "Peace! We did not come here to argue."

The man's voice was deep, cool, and strong, as though accustomed to commanding others. Rip then noticed the unmistakable white, rectangular bands of a preacher fastened around his neck.

"Then why *did* you come, Jonathan?" retorted the woman, haughtily. "You've had your little bird following me ever since I arrived in Boston. Don't think I haven't noticed!"

"It's best to keep an eye on you," said Jonathan. "I worry about the things you do in the shadows."

"I'm not the only one who has something to hide in the shadows," said Katy, flashing the preacher a knowing smile.

"What are you doing here?" said Jonathan, apparently ignoring her remark.

The woman shrugged. "Oh, nothing. Just following William Blaxton, is all."

Jonathan furrowed his eyebrows before turning his head to look directly at the glowing pumpkin lantern in Rip's hands. The preacher's mouth opened in astonishment.

"William Blaxton?" he whispered, glancing up at Rip. "The boy?"

The woman threw back her head and laughed. "And they call you the Library Keeper?" she exclaimed. "Really, Jonathan! I worry about you sometimes. No, not the boy! William Blaxton, the Hallow! He was here, not fifteen minutes ago! I picked up his trail in Salem and followed him through Boston, hoping to get my hands on his lantern. But it seems the boy beat me to it—"

"So the legends are true," said Jonathan, his eyes fixed on the pumpkin in Rip's hands. "William Blaxton really did have a pumpkin lantern."

"He did, indeed," said Katy. "Now, if you don't mind, I have a client who is very interested in it—"

"A client?" interrupted Jonathan derisively. "Still hunting for money, I see. I had thought better of you."

Rip saw a strange expression flicker across Katy's face. At first Rip thought the emotion was anger, but then he realized it was . . . hurt.

"I don't have a choice, Jonathan," she said. "I didn't have as many options as you did."

"We always have a choice, Katy," said the preacher firmly. "Only you can decide what you become."

Katy's lips twisted into a sneer of disdain. "Ah, yes, another famous sermon from Jonathan Edwards—the 'resolute' man."

Jonathan Edwards? thought Rip. *The name sounded familiar to him. Isn't he the preacher who presided over Charity's burial? Impossible! What is he doing in the graveyard at midnight—and with a talking bird? And what did Katy mean by "client"? None of this makes any sense!*

"Enough!" shouted Jonathan. Rip jumped. For a moment, he thought the preacher was talking to him, but Jonathan was pointing accusingly at Katy. "Who are you working for this time, Katy?"

The woman offered a coy smile. "Let's just say he's someone with a profound attachment to the lantern."

"Why?" asked the preacher.

Katy put her hands on her hips and stuck out her chin. "You know I don't just give information away. How much is the name worth to you?"

Jonathan tightened his jaw. "You owe me, Katy. And you know it."

The woman paused for a moment. "I can't give you a name, but I imagine he wants the lantern because of its power over life and death. My client has some . . . unfinished business with death."

"Is he going to use the lantern to bring someone back from the dead?" asked Jonathan.

Rip's eyes grew wide. *The lantern can bring someone back from the dead? That's impossible!*

Then Rip remembered the seriousness with which William Blaxton had spoken about the lantern, and how he, himself, had felt when he handled it for the first time. There was definitely a power within it that made Rip feel more alive.

Rip's thoughts were interrupted by the woman's laugh. "Bring someone back from the dead? Quite the opposite, actually!"

"He wants to kill someone?" asked Jonathan.

"You ask a lot of questions, Jon," said the woman, casually stepping forward. "Now it's my turn. What do you—a pious preacher—want with this lantern?"

Jonathan narrowed his eyes. "That's none of your concern, Katy."

"Of course it isn't," she replied with a look of disgust. "The preacher gets to keep *his* secrets. You haven't changed much."

"This isn't about the past," said Jonathan. "This is about your client. I don't know who he is, but something isn't right here. I don't trust him. I will not let you take the lantern to him."

Katy's eyes flashed dangerously. "You think you can stop me?"

At this point the raven cleared his throat and raised a wing. "Ahem! I don't mean to break up this, ah, 'lovers' quarrel'—but I don't believe either of you will be *taking* the lantern anywhere."

Jonathan cocked his head to the side to get a better look at Nathaniel. "What do you mean?"

"Well, you see," began Nathaniel, "I arrived in the graveyard around the same time as Katy—"

"So now you admit you were following me!"

"That was never in question," continued Nathaniel. "But as soon as she arrived, she fell back—afraid of what was waiting inside—"

"I wasn't afraid!" Katy protested.

Nathaniel ignored her and pointed a wing at Rip. "But then, this boy —'Rip,' is it?" Rip nodded dumbly. "Rip walked right into the graveyard! This fearless boy plunged headfirst into darkness and came face to face with the Midnight Minister himself."

Jonathan addressed Rip with a look of genuine surprise. "You saw the Midnight Minister?"

"Indeed!" said Nathaniel, answering before Rip could say anything. "Rip and the Midnight Minister fought each other, and William Blaxton was forced to use the lantern against the Minister. Who became so frightened that he fled the graveyard in a puff of smoke!"

"I didn't fight against the Minister," said Rip. "He just attacked me."

"Rip, please don't interrupt," said Nathaniel. "I'm in the middle of a story!"

"Nathaniel," said Jonathan impatiently, "what does this have to do with our inability to take the lantern?"

"I was getting to that," said the raven, glaring at Jonathan. "When the Minister finally left, William gave the lantern to Rip, telling the boy that it could never be taken from him—it could only be *given*."

"Fantastic!" said Katy, throwing her arms up in the air. "So, it's a Protective Curse."

"What's a Protective Curse?" asked Rip.

"It's a spell that prevents others from stealing an item," explained Nathaniel.

"Right," muttered the woman. "A curse. Which makes my job really difficult."

"You know, I like to think of it as a blessing, not a curse," said Nathaniel philosophically. "After all, everything that is given to us in life is either a blessing or a curse; it is—"

"Enough!" shouted Katy, clapping her hands to her ears. "Do you ever stop talking? You're the most aggravating bird I've ever met!"

"Aggravating?" repeated Nathaniel indignantly. "*Aggravating?* Touching that lantern could kill you, and you call me aggravating? Well, I beg your pardon. If you make it out of this graveyard alive, perhaps you'll find in your heart to forgive me for paying attention!"

"You should worry more about whether or not *you'll* make it out of this graveyard alive," Katy threatened.

Jonathan raised his hands for silence. "Would the both of you please just stop? We need to think about this."

Rip stood in absolute confusion. Here he was in a graveyard, surrounded by strangers who were arguing about a lantern that had been given to him by a man who was supposed to be dead. Rip was beginning to wish he had never left his house and that William Blaxton had never given him the lantern.

The lantern. That was it! Why did he have to keep the lantern? He could just give it to one of these strangers and go home as if the whole thing had never happened.

Using both hands, Rip raised the pumpkin high above his head, a movement that drew everyone's attention. "Look," he said nervously, "I don't know who any of you are. But I don't want this . . . this pumpkin. I don't even know why William gave it to me."

"Of course not, dear," said Katy soothingly. "Give *me* the pumpkin. I'll take it away, and you'll never have to worry about it again."

"Rip, don't listen to her," warned Jonathan. "She's dangerous."

"And he should trust *you?*"

Jonathan shot Katy a warning look but said nothing. The two then turned toward Rip, every muscle in their bodies poised for action. Rip hesitated. He didn't know whom to trust. Slowly, he began to lower the lantern to the ground.

"Wait!" exclaimed the preacher, raising his hand. A small but powerful gust of wind rushed through the graveyard. "What are you doing?"

Rip froze. Was it his imagination, or did Jonathan just cause that wind? Rip licked his lips nervously. "I'm not going to give the lantern to either of you," he explained. "I'm just going to leave it on the ground."

"You can't just leave it on the ground," said Katy. She appeared tense, perhaps rattled by the sudden wind. "You have to give it to someone. Doesn't he?" she added, looking to Jonathan.

The preacher furrowed his brow and shrugged his shoulders, as though such an idea had never occurred to him.

Nathaniel broke the silence. "Maybe if he places it on the ground, any one of us can take it."

"Keep your beak shut, Nathaniel!" commanded Katy. Rip could tell from the expression on her face that the woman was thinking hard, weighing her options.

Carefully, Rip placed the lantern on the ground. The pumpkin's wide, yellow smile glimmered up at him. With his fingers still on the handle, Rip wondered if he was doing the right thing. After all, when he had been given the lantern, William Blaxton had warned that Boston was in danger and that somehow, only Rip could save the city. But after meeting the figures in the graveyard, Rip felt more lost, confused, and unqualified than ever before. He couldn't make sense of what was happening to him in this moment; how could he be expected to carry the lantern to a person he didn't know in order to save Boston?

Rip let go of the lantern and took two steps backward. Jonathan and Katy eyed each other suspiciously. The air was heavy with tension, the preacher and the woman each waiting for the other to act.

Katy was the first to puncture the silence. "It's mine!" she shouted, sprinting forward.

Jonathan lifted his arm and Rip heard the sound of creaking branches. In an instant, a huge gust of wind rumbled past the preacher and slammed into Katy. She sailed through the graveyard and fell against a tall gravestone.

Jonathan lowered his arm, gave Rip a quick sideways glance, and stepped forward. Rip was astounded. Had the preacher really just commanded the wind to blow? Before he had a chance to think about it, a massive gray creature bounded out of the darkness and intercepted the preacher. In a split second, the beast tackled Jonathan to the ground, picked him up by an arm and a leg, and flung him across the graveyard. Rip watched in horror as the preacher collided against a tree and crumpled to the ground.

Realizing that he was suddenly alone with a monster, Rip's heart leapt into his throat. The thing—a gigantic, wolf-like beast—was standing on its hind legs, directly in front of him.

Covered in gray fur, both the monster's long arms and legs ended in cruel, black claws. Saliva dripped from its open jaws. Rip staggered backward, looking to the preacher for help. But Jonathan, who had managed to rise to his hands and knees, was struggling to catch his breath. The creature bared its teeth and began moving slowly toward Rip.

Desperate for help, Rip scanned the graveyard for Katy, but she was nowhere to be seen. *Where is she?* he thought. *Has she run away?* Rip continued to move backward but stopped when the beast let out a low, menacing growl. Its yellow eyes darted from Rip to the lantern, seemingly torn between which it should grab first. Then, eyes fixed on Rip, the beast lowered itself onto all fours and curled its mouth into a vicious snarl. At first Rip didn't know what the creature wanted from him. It continued to growl as it pointed its head toward the lantern. Rip realized that the monster wanted him to hand over the lantern.

Knowing that he wouldn't be able to outrun the creature, Rip raised his hands in a show of surrender and cautiously moved toward the lantern. He placed a hand on the stem and opened his mouth to speak, but was immediately stopped when another gust of wind ripped through the graveyard.

"Don't give her the lantern!" cried the preacher in a hoarse voice.

Her? thought Rip. *The beast is a female?* Understanding struck Rip's mind like a bolt of lightning. *Katy!* Rip stared at the wolf-creature in astonishment, recalling what Jonathan had said about the woman having secrets. *Could it be? Could this monster really be her?*

Whoever or whatever it was, one thing was now certain: Rip was not going to give the lantern to something that had *clearly* been a wolf in sheep's clothing! Clutching the pumpkin tightly, he turned to run away, but the beast was too fast. It swiped at his legs, causing him to fall on his face. In the confusion, the pumpkin tumbled out of Rip's arms and rolled up against a gravestone. Digging its heels into the ground, the beast waited until the lantern came to a stop, and then made a dive for it.

The moment the creature's claws touched the lantern, a huge flash of yellow light erupted from it like a cannon. The light thundered against the creature with so much force that it tumbled across the graveyard like a pebble skipping over water. The beast crashed against the cemetery's iron fence and went limp.

The light from the pumpkin returned to normal, and Rip sat in the semidarkness, waiting for his heartbeat to slow down. For about a minute, everything was still.

Then the preacher, still clutching his chest, limped toward him. "Hurry!" he said, gasping for air. "We need to get you out of here! I don't know how long we'll have until Katy wakes up."

Rip stood up, wincing at the pain in his legs. "What . . . what *is* she?" he asked, glancing at the now-unconscious monster. It was breathing, but just barely.

"She's a werewolf," said Jonathan.

"A werewolf!" exclaimed Rip. "Werewolves are real?"

"Of course," said Jonathan. "But there are far worse things out there than werewolves. And they'll want the lantern, too, if they can get their hands on it. We need to get you to safety!"

"Can't I just go home?" asked Rip. "My family will keep me safe."

The preacher shook his head. "Katy has your scent. As soon as she wakes up, she'll start hunting you. And she will find you—and your family—in no time at all."

As if on command, Katy twitched, causing Rip to jump. "What if I just give you the lantern?" he asked, thrusting it toward Jonathan. "I don't want it. Here!"

The preacher drew back and shook his head more vigorously. "No," he said firmly. "Blaxton gave the lantern to you, and he gave it to you for a reason. You'll have to carry it until we figure out why. Can you do that?"

Rip felt sick to his stomach. Why had he ever left his house? He should've just stayed in bed, minding his own business. Suddenly, an image of his sister Charity flickered in his mind, and he remembered how he had gone into the graveyard thinking of her. He had felt so strongly that he needed to walk into the graveyard for her sake. And now, after everything that had happened, that same thought gave him a renewed sense of hope.

With hands pressed firmly against the pumpkin's sides, Rip looked up at the preacher and nodded.

"Good," said the preacher. "We'll make our escape through Boston Burrows. Follow me!"

8

THE TERRIBLE SLUMBER

IN WHICH RIP LEARNS OF A COLUMBIAN AMERICA...

*J*onathan Edwards and Rip rushed through the graveyard. They passed dozens of gravestones etched with the faces of cherubs or skulls—mute witnesses to the events of the evening. As they ran, Rip wondered what other strange things these silent sentinels had seen but would never tell.

Lost in this thought, he nearly crashed into Jonathan, who had come to a full stop. Standing before them was a rectangular brick tomb, overrun with grass and weeds. Nathaniel swooped down and perched on top of the tomb. The structure was about four feet high and featured a small iron door that displayed a strange symbol Rip had never seen. The symbol had rusted and weathered over time, but to Rip it looked like an open eye, framed with long, straight lashes.

"What's that?" he whispered.

"It is the symbol for Columbia," explained Nathaniel. "The rising sun with an eye fixed in the center. It symbolizes our mission."

Rip leaned in closer. On second glance, he could now see what the bird had described. The lines that Rip had mistaken for long lashes were actually rays of light. "Mission?" he repeated. "What mission?"

Jonathan, who was hastily searching through his coat pockets, did not bother to look up. "To awaken the people, of course." He pulled a large key from inside his coat.

Rip was confused. "Awaken the people? What kind of a mission is that?"

"Ah, little fledgling," said Nathaniel, "you are taking things far too literally. Everything you see is merely a symbol for things you do not see. Most of the people of this world are asleep in their minds."

"What does that mean?" asked Rip. "Who is asleep in their mind?"

Jonathan gave Nathaniel a troubled look.

"He doesn't know," explained the bird.

"How can he not know?" said Jonathan. "He has the lantern!"

Nathaniel shrugged. "Believe me, I am just as confused as you are."

"What are you talking about?" said Rip, hopelessly lost in the conversation.

Jonathan, eyes still on Nathaniel, pointed a finger at Rip. "You are telling me that this boy is still asleep and yet Blaxton gave him the lantern?"

"I am not asleep!" said Rip, who had already tested—many times—to make sure he was awake.

"Do not take it so personally," said Nathaniel. "Nearly everyone you know is asleep in their minds. It is quite common, actually."

"So common that Blaxton was forced to choose someone who's asleep in order to make his plan work," grumbled Jonathan, turning his attention back to the symbol of Columbia.

Rip glanced at Nathaniel, who shook his head reassuringly.

"Do not mind him," said the bird. "Jonathan is always a bit grumpy at night. He will be better at sunrise, I promise."

Still grumbling, Jonathan pushed aside the pupil of the stone eye, revealing a secret keyhole. He inserted his key and turned the lock. Rip heard a dull click, and the door to the tomb opened, showing a narrow set of stairs descending sharply into darkness. Jonathan and Nathaniel began to make their way inside.

"Wait!" exclaimed Rip, his heart thundering in his chest. Both the preacher and the bird turned to look at him. "What are you doing? We have to get out of here! Katy could wake up at any moment. We'll be trapped! Whose tomb is this, anyway?"

"It's no one's tomb," said Jonathan irritably.

"Well, that's not true," said Nathaniel, thoughtfully. "It belongs to Captain Armitage."

Jonathan rolled his eyes. "But Armitage is not here right now, is he?"

"No, but the question was—"

Jonathan brought a hand to his forehead. "Must you always contradict me?"

Rip glanced over his shoulder, checking for any sign that Katy might be approaching. "But . . ." he stammered, "why are we going into the tomb?"

"Because this isn't just a tomb," said Jonathan, removing his hat and wiping the sweat from his forehead. "It's an entrance to the Boston

Burrows—a series of tunnels that connect under the city. It is how I was able to get here without drawing Katy's attention."

"I didn't know that there were tunnels below the city," said Rip.

"Few people do," said Jonathan. "It is a fiercely guarded secret within Columbia."

"You keep mentioning Columbia," said Rip in frustration. "What is it?"

"Columbia is another name for the American continent," said Nathaniel. "Named after Christopher Columbus himself. After all, it was he who discovered the New World and secretly organized our refuge."

"Your refuge?" asked Rip.

"Yes, boy," said Nathaniel, his black eyes sparkling. "Don't you understand? *We're magic.* America is the last great refuge of magical people and creatures."

"Magic?" repeated Rip. "What do you mean?"

"It is really quite simple," began Nathaniel. "Everyone in the New World is magic, to one degree or another—"

"We don't have time for this!" interrupted the preacher. "The boy did not even know about Columbia. How can he be expected to understand the Great Awakening?"

"Speaking of awakenings," said Nathaniel, anxiously peering through the trees, "I think Katy has finished her nap!"

Rip whirled around. Although he couldn't see Katy, he could definitely hear the grunting and snorting of a large beast. He lifted his lantern and saw the flash of yellow eyes in the distance.

Jonathan pushed him toward the tomb. "Inside! Quick!"

Rip needed no further encouragement. With Nathaniel close behind, he plunged down the narrow stairs and into the underground tomb. From above ground, there came a deafening roar. He turned his head in time to see Jonathan leap into the tomb and close the door behind him. There was a fierce yelp followed by a loud crash, as Katy's body slammed against the solid iron door of the tomb.

With a flick of his fingers, Jonathan twisted the lock and chuckled. "Sorry, Katy," he said, loud enough for the werewolf to hear. "Better luck next time, I suppose."

Katy growled and pounded on the door, but it was no use. Squeezing past Rip, the preacher gestured down the darkened hallway. "Come along, then," he said. "We'd best get a move on. Katy doesn't have a key, but she's resourceful and determined."

Outside the door, Katy barked angrily. Rip lunged forward, following the preacher into the narrow hallway. Holding the lantern aloft, he glanced at the surrounding walls. The space may not have been occupied by skeletons, but it was nevertheless unsettling to walk through a place that felt like a tomb.

After a few seconds of walking, Rip got up the nerve to address the preacher. "So . . . where are we going?"

"King's Chapel," grumbled Jonathan, without looking back.

"Across the street?" said Rip.

"Technically, *under* the street," said Nathaniel, a hint of humor in his voice.

"Why King's Chapel?"

"It's a place to think and regroup," answered Jonathan.

After a few seconds of brisk walking, Jonathan came to a stop at the base of a circular stone staircase that led up to the ceiling. Rip furrowed his brow. *Why would someone build a staircase leading nowhere?*

With the raven on his shoulder, Jonathan placed his foot on the first step and motioned for Rip to follow. Confused, Rip watched as the preacher walked up the stairs and—Rip gasped.

The preacher had disappeared!

Rip stood there in astonishment, not knowing what to think or do. A man had just vanished before his very eyes! A few seconds later, a black object shot out of the ceiling and landed gracefully on the stairs. It was Nathaniel.

"Sorry about that," said the bird. "We should have explained earlier. This is a magical ceiling—a faux floor, if you will. Come up the stairs and you will pass right through. It is quite safe."

Rip swallowed hard and tentatively made his way up the narrow staircase. Nathaniel, using an awkward mixture of hopping and flapping, stayed ahead of Rip by about four or five steps.

Reaching the last stair, the bird turned to Rip. "Watch," he said, before effortlessly pushing his head through the stone ceiling. Rip's eyes widened. Nathaniel's body remained on the stair, but now his head was gone. The bird tipped his body and his head reappeared.

"You see? Quite safe. Now, come along." Nathaniel then flapped his wings and disappeared entirely.

Rip looked down at the lantern in his hand and gripped the handle even tighter. He took a deep breath, closed his eyes, and jogged upward. After five or six steps, his right foot came down awkwardly. He had anticipated another stair, but his leg had come right back down and was now level with his other leg. He opened his eyes and saw that was standing inside an exceptionally small room, perhaps a closet, with just enough space to fit a full-grown man. In front of him was a rectangular opening—a doorway facing a wall. Rip stepped across the threshold and found himself standing inside the main assembly hall of King's Chapel, the tall, wooden church across the street from the South Burying Ground.

Jonathan Edwards, tall and brooding, stood in the shadow of an archway, arms folded. There was a rustle of feathers as Nathaniel flew over Rip's head and perched on the edge of the chapel's white podium. Rip realized that he had just emerged from a sort of doorway built into the podium itself.

"All right, lad," began Jonathan, "we're safe for the time being. Let's talk. What do you know?"

Rip blinked at the preacher in surprise. He wanted to either laugh or yell. "What do I know?" he asked, his voice echoing throughout the chapel. "I don't know anything! Who are you people? What is Columbia? Why did William give me the lantern? Why does Katy want it? And why can that raven talk?"

There was a long, uneasy silence broken only by the sound Rip's heavy breathing.

Nathaniel was the first to speak. "Right, I'll go first, shall I?"

In the light of the lantern, Rip could see Jonathan give a slow, almost imperceptible nod.

The bird continued talking. "My name is Nathaniel Flamm and that grumpy fellow over there is Jonathan Edwards, and we are official representatives of the Confederation of Columbia. We came here to introduce ourselves to William Blaxton and offer our services, such as they are."

Rip furrowed his eyebrows. "Columbia," he repeated. "Is Columbia one of His Majesty's colonies?"

Nathaniel snorted. "Ah, yes, His Majesty the *king*," the bird's voice was dripping with contempt. "*The king* has his countries. *The king* has his schools. And yes, *the king* even has his churches." Nathaniel spread his wings wide, gesturing to the walls of the building in which they now stood. "Did you know that when the king ordered the construction of this building, the Puritans refused to offer any land for its construction? So what did the king do? He built his church on Boston's first graveyard, forcing the Puritans to move many of their families' graves to the South Burying Ground. The nerve! That is one of the reasons why we built the tunnels under Boston. In case the king and his men ever decided to show up . . ."

"Columbia does not recognize English authority," said Jonathan. "Frankly, it is because of the king that we are in this mess."

"What mess?" asked Rip.

"Why, the Terrible Slumber, of course!" said Nathaniel.

"The Terrible Slumber? What's that?"

"A great forgetting—a terrible curse," said Nathaniel ominously.

"Remember when I told you that nearly everyone you know is asleep in their minds? *That's* the curse. They have forgotten the magic within themselves. This is what we mean by 'The Terrible Slumber.' Those who are awake, however—that is, those who are magic—are citizens of the Confederation of Columbia."

Rip glanced from Nathaniel to Jonathan and then back to Nathaniel. "So you are . . . you are all magic?"

The bird made a strange squawking noise. Rip interpreted this as a laugh. "After everything you have seen tonight," said Nathaniel, "is it really that hard to believe in magic?"

"Persecution drove our people from the Old World," said Jonathan. "Puritans, Calvinists, and Quakers, they called us—'strangers and *pilgrims* on the earth.'"

Rip's mind was reeling. "But . . . I thought pilgrims came here to escape *religious* persecution."

At this, Nathaniel laughed once more. "And how do you suppose all those magical people were able to get on those ships? Do you think they just walked up and introduced themselves as Luminaries? No! Better to introduce themselves as Puritans and Pilgrims. 'We're simple folk. No magic here!'"

"Luminaries?" repeated Rip.

"My apologies," said Nathaniel. "You wouldn't know what that means. Essentially, there are two forces at work in the world: the power of light and the power of darkness. Those who use the power of light are called Luminaries. The name itself comes from the Latin word *luminaria*, meaning 'lamp' or 'light.' But it can also refer to 'a celestial body'—like the sun, moon, or stars. Students of Greek mythology have long believed that our ancestors were given this name by Prometheus, a Titan with godlike power. Prometheus had great love for the creatures of the earth and wanted to help those who were struggling. And so, one day, he took starlight from the heavens and brought it down to the Earth as a gift for all. There, he used the starlight to build a large bonfire and invited all to join him beside it. As the story goes, those who sat with Prometheus— men, women, children, and animals—were taught magic and how to make fire of their own. Prometheus called these people Luminaries.

"All good magical folk are, in one way or another, connected to these first Luminaries; they gave us a tradition of magic that deals with the light —they 'passed the torch' to us, as it were."

"But not everyone sat at the fire of Prometheus," said the preacher, rather ominously. Rip shifted uncomfortably. He had almost forgotten that the preacher was there.

"Yes, I was getting to that," said Nathaniel. "According to the myth, there are those who stayed away from the celestial fire, choosing the power of darkness over the power of light. We call these followers of darkness Glooms . . . or Gloominaries, if you will," he added with a chuckle.

Rip placed the pumpkin on one of the pews and began rubbing the sides of his head. "But what does all that have to do with the lantern?"

"Everything, actually," said Jonathan.

Nathaniel bobbed his head enthusiastically. "Indeed! The lantern is a powerful symbol of the story of Prometheus. It is a light in the darkness. Some even say that All Hallows' Eve and All Hallows' Day are echoes of that ancient story—a reminder that light will always triumph over darkness. And so, darkness hates the light and Gloominaries are always looking for opportunities to smother the light. In fact, that's why most Luminaries were persecuted in the Old World, during a period ironically known as 'the Dark Ages.'"

"And that's why we came here," said Jonathan. "To build a New World —a nation dedicated to serving the light."

"But where did they, er, where did *you* all settle?" asked Rip.

"Columbia is a confederation of thirteen magical colonies," explained Nathaniel. "As such, our people are scattered throughout the New World with magical settlements in New England, New France, and even one in Florida! Isn't that exciting? There are whole communities of centaurs, satyrs, goblins, skeletons, giants, vampires—"

The preacher cut him off. "Nathaniel, there aren't any vampires. How many times do I have to tell you that? Vampires went extinct during the sixteenth century."

Nathaniel shook his head. "I respectfully disagree. You really should read the journals of Henry Hudson's crew."

Jonathan let out a long sigh. "Nathaniel—it's a dead end, *literally*. There are no more vampires! Trust me, *I* would know—"

"Um, excuse me," interrupted Rip, "but where do you two fit into all of this?"

The preacher raised an eyebrow. "I beg your pardon?"

"How are you connected to all of this?" asked Rip. "I mean, you're a preacher and a . . . well, a talking bird. Why are you here?"

"Ah!" began Nathaniel. "Yes, well, Jonathan Edwards is the official Library Keeper of Columbia and I am his humble assistant." At this, Nathaniel flourished his wings and gave a little bow.

"Library Keeper?" said Rip, his eyes darting from Nathaniel to Jonathan. "You're . . . librarians?"

Nathaniel narrowed his eyes. "It's a little bit more than that, thank you very much. Jonathan handles the most important documents, books, and histories of Columbia. He inherited the position from his grandfather,

73

Solomon Stoddard, after Solomon was . . . oh, what's the word I'm looking for?"

"Killed?" said the preacher, simply.

"No, no, no," said Nathaniel, touching the tip of his wing to his forehead. "That's not the word. After his—"

"Head was cut off?"

"Oh, don't be so crass, Jonathan!"

"Well, that *is* what happened . . ."

"Yes, but that's not the word I'm looking for."

"Decapitated?"

"Yes, decapitated!" said Nathaniel excitedly. "Jonathan became the Library Keeper after Solomon was decapitated. Oh dear, Rip. You look very pale. Are you hungry?"

Rip, who was feeling overwhelmed and a little sick after everything that had happened, teetered slightly before deciding to sit in one of the box pews. The face of the pumpkin lantern glowed up at him, smiling brightly. "And what am I supposed to do with this?" he asked.

Nathaniel and Jonathan exchanged glances.

"Yes, well, that's a most excellent question, Rip," said Nathaniel. "We were kind of hoping you could tell us."

Rip gave them a look of utmost incredulity. "You are asking me?"

"Well, I was perched fairly high in that maple tree," said Nathaniel, sheepishly. "It was hard to hear everything. But I'm assuming Blaxton told you where to go. Did he not?"

Rip frowned. So many things had happened during the past couple of hours that it was hard for him to remember everything Blaxton had told him. Slowly, he shook his head. "No," he said, "Blaxton didn't exactly tell me where to go."

Jonathan leaned forward. "And he didn't say anything about Columbia?"

Again, Rip shook his head.

"But that doesn't make any sense!" exclaimed the preacher. "Why wouldn't Blaxton mention Columbia? Blaxton was one of the original founders. Surely he would have told you to go to one of Columbia's governors."

Rip shrugged his shoulders, not knowing what to say. "I'm sorry. He didn't."

"Rip, this is very important," said Nathaniel. "You have to tell us *exactly* what Blaxton told you. Otherwise, we really don't know how to help."

Rip screwed up his face, trying his best to remember his conversation with the yellow-eyed man.

"He told me that his one hundred years of service were over, and that it was time for him to rest. He gave me the lantern and told me to take it to Feathertop."

At the mention of the name Feathertop, a look of utter bewilderment swept across the preacher's face. "Feathertop?" he repeated. "Blaxton said the name Feathertop? You're absolutely sure of that?"

Rip nodded.

"But that's impossible," whispered Jonathan.

In sharp contrast to the preacher's astonishment, Nathaniel let out a loud squawk and flapped his wings jubilantly. Under different circumstances, Rip might've found this gesture rather comical. As it was, Rip merely smiled nervously at the preacher.

"I told you, Jonathan!" exclaimed Nathaniel, bobbing his head excitedly. "I told you! But did you believe me? No . . ."

"Stop that!" commanded Jonathan.

Obediently, the raven stopped making noise, but he couldn't hide his look of triumph.

"Who is Feathertop?" asked Rip, now very confused.

"Feathertop is a fairy tale—"

"Ah, ah, ah, Jonathan!" interrupted the raven. "Don't color the story with your own disbelief. Just tell the legend and let the boy make up his own mind."

"Well then, you tell him the story!" snapped Jonathan, adjusting his hat. "And speak quickly! We haven't got all night."

"Oh, I do love this story!" beamed Nathaniel. The raven cleared his throat and paused for dramatic effect. "Truthfully, no one knows exactly what Feathertop is. Some records describe him as a man, while other stories refer to him as a mighty beast. However, the most enduring legend —and the one we ravens believe—describes him as a tall, pumpkin-headed scarecrow—"

Rip, who had been fidgeting with his hands, stopped and looked up at the bird in astonishment. "A pumpkin-headed scarecrow?" he repeated. His mind went back to the scarecrow he had seen at the Harvest Festival as a child. "Do you mean a living scarecrow?"

"Of course I mean a living scarecrow!" crowed Nathaniel indignantly. "You don't honestly think we have legends about inanimate scarecrows, do you?"

Rip was hardly paying attention. He glanced down at the lantern next to him. "What is it about pumpkins?" he murmured.

Nathaniel exhaled impatiently. "For your information, the pumpkin is a uniquely American plant, widely regarded as one of the most magical plants in all the world. Now please, don't interrupt. It's rude! Now, where was I? Ah, yes!" He cleared his throat again. "Feathertop is often described as a pumpkin-headed scarecrow—a powerful being in commoners' clothing. Legend claims he was created by Mother Rigby, a powerful witch. Unfortunately, we know very little about Mother Rigby—but there is one thing we know for certain: she was good. Now, if you're asking for my personal opinion, I think she is the personification of Mother Nature herself. My second cousin thinks that Mother Rigby is just a powerful witch . . . but my cousin lives in a barn on the outskirts of Salem; what would he know?"

"Get on with it, Nathaniel," growled Jonathan.

The bird rolled his eyes. "Yes, well, as I was saying . . . Legend has it that when Mother Rigby saw the suffering of the Pilgrims, she was moved to compassion. She wept great tears and resolved to bring forth a being who would help them.

"From the Pilgrim settlers she took only what was broken and rejected —a damaged broomstick, a cracked pudding stick, the handle of a hoe, parts of a broken chair, and miscellaneous sticks from an abandoned woodpile. The great witch fastened these things together, creating something that resembled the body of a man—a scarecrow. Then, she took a large pumpkin from her magical garden, carved a face into it, and placed it on the shoulders of the scarecrow. She lit the inside of the pumpkin with an ember from her pipe and named the being Feathertop.

"As the story goes, Feathertop rose from the ground, kissed his mother, and left the garden to care for the Pilgrims. He labored among them like a gardener tending to his garden—with great love and tremendous care. In time, he called the thirteen Hallows—"

"No he didn't," interrupted Jonathan. "The Hallows came from among us, and resolved to serve us of their own free will. Feathertop certainly never called them."

"Oh, I'm sorry," snapped the raven. "I'd be more than happy to correct the legend if you'd be so kind as to present me with viable sources. Could you recommend a few books to me? Perhaps the autobiography of Feathertop himself? Hmmm?"

"Uh, Nathaniel?" asked Rip, tentatively. "Why would William Blaxton want me to take the lantern to Feathertop?"

"Well, according to legend," emphasized Nathaniel, "Feathertop made a number of pumpkin lanterns and gave them to the thirteen Hallows. This makes sense, because the lanterns look like him—carved, glowing faces and whatnot. But more important, the lanterns behave like Feathertop; they are lights in the darkness. And light gives people hope. The pumpkin lantern, therefore, is a reminder of a Hallow's mission to be a light in the darkness. As to why Blaxton wants you to take this particular lantern back to Feathertop, I honestly can't say. Truth is, we know far more about the Hallows than the lanterns they carry."

"Wait," said Jonathan, stroking his chin. "The Hallows . . . that's it!" The preacher looked at Rip and Nathaniel, as though he expected them to know what he was thinking. "The original Hallows. We don't know much about the lantern or why Katy and the Midnight Minister want it, but we do know a lot about the original Hallows."

"Jonathan, I'm a talking bird, not a mind reader," said Nathaniel. "What are you trying to say?"

"Do you think the Skeleton Closet is open?" asked Jonathan.

Nathaniel's eyes widened. "The Skeleton Closet? That's in the marshland beyond the Gallows!"

Rip felt a pit in his stomach. "The marshland? You mean we're going outside the city walls?"

"Exactly," said the preacher. "We can take a tunnel underneath Boston Neck to the other side of the gate. If the Skeleton Closet is open, I'm sure we'll be able to find Goodman Brown."

"Goodman Brown!" cawed Nathaniel. "You must be joking! A man so evil they nicknamed him the Impure Puritan?"

"Oh, come on, Nathaniel!" replied Jonathan. It was the first time Rip had seen the preacher grin. "Where's your sense of adventure? I thought you were a raven, not a chicken. Besides, Goodman's the only one who knows more about this matter than we do."

"You know, the last time I saw Goodman Brown, he ate a turkey leg in front of me. A turkey leg! It wasn't even cooked!" exclaimed Nathaniel.

Rip shuddered. What kind of person was this Goodman Brown? And why would anyone live near the Gallows?

"Well, lucky for you, Nathaniel," said Jonathan with a smile, "you will not be coming with us."

Nathaniel perked up. "Really? Why is that?"

"Because if we're going to talk to Goodman Brown, we're going to need rope—a lot of rope."

9

THE WITCHES' NOOSE

IN WHICH RIP SEES THE PAST IN THE PRESENT...

$\mathcal{A}$ s the group traveled through the remainder of the tunnel in silence, the smell of earth and moss filled Rip's nostrils. Once again, he felt his head spinning as he desperately tried to understand everything Jonathan and Nathaniel had just told him. Why had he never heard of these things in school or from his parents? Was everything he knew about life a lie? Perhaps. Or maybe this knowledge was like his ability to help plants grow. Maybe there were some things people just didn't talk about—not because they were bad, but because other people wouldn't be able to understand.

After another few minutes, the trio came to a set of stone stairs that led to a door in the ceiling. Wedging himself between the door and the stairs, Jonathan gave the door a few hard pushes until it shuddered open.

Cool air flooded down on them. Rip was relieved to see the starry night sky and hear the sound of crickets in the distance. Judging by the darkness, he guessed it would be another three or four hours before the sun rose. He followed the preacher up the stairs and found himself standing in a field at the base of Beacon Hill.

Rip stared up at the massive, grassy hill, which seemed to glow under the pale moonlight. Sandwiched between two other hills of similar height, Beacon Hill was so named for the tall watchtower at its summit. Throughout each night, a watchman stood guard, looking beyond the city, ready to warn the residents of any possible threat.

As soon as Rip, Nathaniel, and Jonathan were all safely outside the tunnel, the preacher turned and closed the door, the top of which was covered in tall grass. As the door sank back into the ground, its rectangular outline disappeared, making it indistinguishable from the rest of the field.

"It's an enchanted door," said Jonathan, seeing Rip's amazement. "It hides itself in plain sight. Come along. We need to transfer to another tunnel."

Rip followed the preacher through the Boston Common, the tall grasses swaying gently around their knees. Here and there, he saw long, brown tables decorated with cornucopias and black and gray decor—early preparations for the Harvest Festival.

A few paces in front of them stood the Great Elm—an ancient, solitary tree that had existed long before the arrival of either William Blaxton or any other European. At a height of sixty-five feet, the Great Elm was an enormous spectacle—well deserving of its title.

Rip held the pumpkin lantern high, shining light on the coal-black tree. As the light passed across the trunk, he saw a woman drop from the branches and come to a sudden stop, suspended in mid-air. Rip gasped.

She was hanging!

He cried out and ran forward to help the woman, and Nathaniel shot off into the tree, frightened by Rip's sudden outburst.

The preacher whirled around in alarm. "What's wrong?" he exclaimed.

Rip turned to the preacher. "The woman!" he cried, pointing the lantern at the tree. Rip paused and narrowed his eyes. The woman was gone!

"Th-there was a body . . ." he stammered, "a woman. In that tree!"

"What do you mean?" Jonathan asked, following Rip's gaze. "I don't see anything."

"I saw a woman hanging from a noose. I saw her."

Jonathan examined the tree, but it was clear that there was nothing hanging from the branches. The preacher looked at Rip suspiciously. "Are you certain you saw a body?"

Breathing hard, Rip scanned the tree once more. He was almost positive he had seen a woman hanging from a noose. Now, he didn't know what to think.

"*How* did you see it?" asked Nathaniel, poking his black beak out from behind a thick branch.

"What do you mean?" replied Rip, puzzled.

"Did you see it with just your eyes, or did you see it in the light of the lantern?"

"The lantern, I guess," said Rip, giving a half shrug. "Does that make a difference?"

"The lantern is magic," said Nathaniel. "Didn't Blaxton tell you he could see things others could not see?"

"And you say it was the body of a woman?" pressed Jonathan.

Rip nodded.

"I'm not surprised," said the preacher, nodding at the Great Elm. "Today is Mary Martyr's Day."

"Huh?" Rip had never heard of such a thing.

"He means Mary Dyer," said Nathaniel.

Rip recognized the name from school. "Wasn't she a witch?"

"She was nothing of the kind!" snapped Jonathan. "At least, not in the way you are thinking. Mary Dyer was a faithful woman—a Hallow—who willingly gave her own life to protect the city of Boston."

"It's called a Martyr's Blessing," explained Nathaniel. "If a person willingly sacrifices his or her own life for a friend, that friend is not only protected but also given an abundance of power."

"And Mary Dyer gave her life for all of Boston," said Jonathan solemnly. "Mary was one of the first to awaken from the Great Slumber, and as such, she was unable to hide her magical gifts from others. Not long after that, she gave birth to a deformed, stillborn baby. The combination of this and Mary's mysterious powers caused the people to condemn her as a heretic and force her out of the city. While in exile, Mary became a Hallow and soon learned of an evil plot to destroy Boston. She rushed back to save the city. However, she was soon captured by the Governor's men, put on trial, and sentenced to death by hanging.

"As she was being led to the noose, Mary called upon her magic and blessed the city with her death—blessed Boston that it might be protected from the evil that sought to destroy it. Mary's blessing worked, and every year Columbia celebrates Mary Martyr's Day—the day a Hallow willingly gave her life for the 'city upon a hill.'" So saying, Jonathan looked up to the watchtower on Beacon Hill and stared at it in silence, as though in reverence of Mary Dyer.

Rip was astonished; he had never heard that story before. "But what was the evil that Mary was trying to prevent?"

The preacher glanced up, the edge of his hat casting a dark shadow over his eyes. "Mistress Hibbins," he whispered.

Rip's eyes grew wide. *Everyone* knew the legend of Ann Hibbins—the Mistress of Death. She was the most infamous witch in the brief history of New England. A wealthy widow, Ann Hibbins had been one of the first Puritans to settle in Boston. Not long after her arrival—and in defiance of town law—she began taking midnight walks in the forest surrounding Boston. It was after one of these walks that she claimed to have met a man in the forest—*the Dark Woodsman.*

Shortly thereafter, strange things started happening to Ann's enemies. For instance, a woman who had gossiped about Ann was struck with a fever, a carpenter who had done shoddy work on Ann's house went bankrupt, and a man who had called Ann a witch was nearly trampled to death by a horse. A strange illness swept through the city, leaving every citizen bedridden for days.

Everyone, except Mistress Hibbins.

Not long after, the leaders of Boston had tried Mistress Hibbins, found her guilty of witchcraft, and sentenced her to death. They had hanged the woman from the Great Elm—the same tree that now stood before Rip and his companions.

"It is a curious thing," whispered Jonathan as he peered up into the shadowy branches. "The Pilgrims came to the New World for the freedom to become themselves—yet, once they got here, they forgot who they were and persecuted each other."

"But Mistress Hibbins was evil, right?" asked Rip.

"As evil as they come," said Jonathan darkly. "She might've succeeded in destroying Boston had it not been for Mary Dyer. To this day, Mary's magical sacrifice keeps Mistress Hibbins outside the city wall. Because of Mary's magic, Mistress Hibbins cannot set foot in Boston."

Rip furrowed his eyebrows. "You speak as though Mistress Hibbins is still alive."

"That's because she never died," said Jonathan. "The Mistress of Death can never be killed."

"What?" exclaimed Rip. "But that can't be true! They buried her body!"

"They *said* they buried her body," retorted Nathaniel. Rip jumped and looked up. He had almost forgotten about the raven, who peered down at them with black eyes. "After leaving Ann's body hanging overnight, the Governor and his men returned the next morning to bury her in a grave set aside for pagans. But when they arrived, both Ann's body and the noose had completely vanished! The Governor did not want to frighten the people, so he claimed that he and his men had buried the witch's remains in a secret place. Years later, the Governor mysteriously died in the middle of the night. When his servants found him the next morning, they said he looked as shriveled as a corpse—as though something had literally sucked the life out of him."

The branches from the tree creaked in the breeze, sending down a shower of dead leaves. Rip shivered and pulled his coat a little tighter around his body. Jonathan grunted as he opened another grass-covered trap door that was hidden near the base of the Great Elm. He looked up at Rip with a grim expression. "Are you coming?"

Rip nodded and moved toward the door, the pumpkin lantern swinging in his hand. Suddenly, he stopped and looked up. In the light from the lantern, he could see the shadowy outline of several people, surrounded by an orange haze. Rip blinked into the murky haze. At first, he thought that what he was seeing was another trick of the mind—as when he had seen the image of the woman hanging from the tree. But then he remembered what Nathaniel had said about the lantern's magic, and he wondered if the light from the pumpkin was showing him something that others could not see. Holding his breath, Rip lifted the lantern a bit higher. Instantly, the shadowy orange became clearer.

A crowd of people were gathered around the tree. A fair-haired woman, no older than thirty, stood upon a small wooden ladder with a noose around her neck. The crowd jeered at her, but she held her head high, staring peacefully at the sky above.

"Mary Dyer," said a stern-looking man standing next to her. "Thou hast been found guilty of witchcraft and rebellion. Thou hast been deluded and carried away by the deceit of the Dark Woodsman. I implore thee to repent."

Mary closed her eyes. "Nay, man, it is the Dark Woodsman who has deceived you. He has darkened your mind with a Terrible Slumber. I have seen the light in the wilderness and I must follow it. I shall not repent of my faith."

A man at the front of the crowd sneered at her. "Methinks the noose will cure you of your 'faith.'"

Mary did not bother to look at the man. Instead, she stared straight ahead, her eyes fixed on the starlight. "No, sir," she said firmly. "It will take more than the noose to 'cure' me of my faith."

With a derisive snort, the man leapt forward and kicked the ladder out from under her.

"RIP!"

Rip jumped and the ghostly images vanished instantly. Lowering the lantern, he looked in the direction of the voice and saw Jonathan peering up from the tunnel.

"Are you coming?" barked the preacher.

Rip nodded dumbly and hurried down into the tunnel. The branches of the Great Elm swayed gently in the breeze.

10

THE IMPURE PURITAN

IN WHICH GOODMAN IS A BAD MAN...

*R*ip, Nathaniel, and Jonathan traveled through the tunnel until they came to a turn, which forced them to make a sharp left. As he rounded the corner, Rip was surprised to see water trickling down the walls and collecting in small pools on the ground.

"This tunnel leads directly underneath the swamp near Boston Neck," said the preacher. "Don't worry about the water. It shouldn't get any deeper than your ankles."

Stepping cautiously around the puddles, Rip kept a steady pace with Jonathan, tightly gripping the handle of the lantern to prevent himself from shaking. *The swamp near Boston Neck!* He was leaving Boston! For years he had dreamed about seeing the outside world, and now it was finally happening. Yet despite his excitement, he couldn't prevent a pang of fear from pricking his heart. What lay beyond the wall? He had already met the Midnight Minister. Would he meet the Dark Woodsman as well?

"This is it," said the preacher, stopping at a small set of stairs. He reached into a shelf in the stone wall and removed a large leather satchel, which he tossed to Rip. "Here. Put the lantern in this satchel. I don't want you to draw any unnecessary attention, and I certainly don't want anyone to know you have the lantern—*especially* Goodman Brown."

"But if I put it in the satchel, won't the light go out?" asked Rip.

"It's magical, so I doubt it," said the preacher. "But try it and see."

Rip placed the lantern in the satchel and closed the flap. After a few moments, he opened the bag just wide enough to peer inside. Sure enough, the lantern gleamed up at him, burning as brightly as before.

"All right then," said Jonathan, "come along."

They climbed the stairs until they emerged on the ground above, quietly closing the door behind them. A stiff breeze whipped through the trees, pushing Rip back a step or two. Nathaniel flapped his wings uneasily. The ground, thick with mud, squished under Rip's boots. But the thing that really caught Rip's attention was the smell; the air was thick with a stench like rotten eggs.

After glancing around to be sure that they were alone, Jonathan turned to the raven perched on his shoulder. "You know what to do," he said grimly.

The bird took flight, leaving Rip alone with the stern preacher. Satchel at his side, Rip followed him to a cluster of black buildings at the edge of the swamp. The narrow sloping of the houses made them appear almost alive—as if they were giant monsters looming above him, watching him hungrily.

"I've never seen buildings like this," he whispered.

"You're about to see a lot of things you've never seen before," said Jonathan, ushering Rip along.

They stopped at a building with tall, dirty windows and a sign that read:

SKELETON CLOSET: UNDEAD ONLY!

RIP COULD HEAR a wild assortment of noises just beyond the door: muffled shouting, loud music, boisterous singing, and bursts of raucous laughter. With one foot on the front step, Jonathan paused and put a hand on Rip's shoulder.

"Rip, I need you to listen very carefully to what I'm about to say. A lot of . . . *interesting* folk frequent this tavern, and some of them are quite dangerous. Frankly, the man we are about to meet is probably the worst of them. But don't worry—I promise I will not let anyone harm you. Just keep the lantern in that satchel, and stay close to me. Most important, *don't say a word*. If anyone tries to talk to you, just let me handle it. Understand?"

Rip nodded, pressing the satchel firmly to his side.

Jonathan squeezed Rip's shoulder. "Very well. Follow me."

The preacher turned the brass knob and pushed against the door to the building. As the door swung open, Rip's eyes widened and his jaw dropped. Inside was a tavern, filled with . . . *skeletons*—not inanimate bones, but moving, talking, laughing skeletons! Some wore sailors' clothes, some wore farmers' clothes, and others wore no clothing at all. Among them were what appeared to be female skeletons, dressed in dusty pink and bright red dresses, flirting with a group of stout skeletons who sat at a large, round table. There was even the skeleton of a small dog running back and forth between tables, yapping at all the commotion. In one corner of the room sat a small, hunchbacked figure with short legs and muscular arms. He was playing the piano, making a tune that sounded simultaneously eerie and strangely upbeat.

As soon as the preacher crossed the threshold into the tavern, all activity came to a dead halt. One of the skeletons threw down his poker hand. "All right! Who invited the stiff?"

Jonathan offered a small smile. "No worries, gentlemen. I didn't come here for you—at least, not today. I'm looking for someone—"

The bartender, a sun-bleached skeleton with remnants of a black beard, let out a derisive snort, cutting Jonathan off. "Can't you read the sign?" he snarled. "Undead only! We don't want what you're selling, preacher!"

"I'm looking for someone," repeated Jonathan firmly.

"Yeah? And who would that be?"

"The Impure Puritan."

The bartender tightened his jaw and leaned forward. "And what makes you think he wants to see you?"

"Because Jonathan Edwards is a sinner like me," said a voice from the back of the room.

Rip shuddered. The voice sounded like the crunch of dead leaves. Rip turned his head to see where it had come from. There, in a dark corner nearest the sputtering, dying fire, sat a lean man, wearing a round, black hat and smoking a long clay pipe. The shadows obscuring him were so dark that Rip couldn't see his face.

Jonathan, apparently taking the man's comment as an invitation, moved through the crowded tavern toward the figure in the shadows. Rip followed, tiptoeing between tables where skeletons sat watching him suspiciously through empty sockets.

"Jonathan Edwards," sneered the man in the shadows. "What brings a fine young preacher, such as yourself, to the very bottom of the social barrel?" Rip swallowed hard, noticing that the man's lips were as black as coal.

"Goodman Brown," acknowledged Jonathan. "I came here to find out what you know about the pumpkin lantern of William Blaxton."

The man in the darkness took in a long draft from his pipe and paused, before slowly blowing out a cloud of gray smoke. "The pumpkin lantern . . ." he repeated, apparently savoring the suspense. "Strange that you should ask about it—and on Mary Martyr's Day, no less! Why, just last week, I was talking to someone else about Blaxton's lantern." He put a finger to his chin in an overdramatic fashion. "Let's see, who was it? Ah, yes! It was Mistress Hibbins!"

Rip felt a chill run up his spine. "Why does *she* want the lantern?" he asked. Jonathan shot him a warning look, but Rip ignored it; he wanted to know. The mere thought of Mistress Hibbins made his blood run cold. Was she out there looking for Rip right now? What would she do if she found him with the lantern?

"Hello, boy," said Goodman, turning his attention to Rip. The tone of the man's voice was almost as unsettling as his mention of Mistress Hibbins. "You're a little young to be in a place as dark as this, don't you think?"

"He's my apprentice," interrupted Jonathan.

"Don't lie to me, Jonathan!" snapped Goodman. "That's the Van Winkle boy—the one they pulled from the grave—*Rip*. I'd recognize him anywhere."

Rip's hands began to tremble. "How do you know my name?"

Goodman chuckled. "I take it Jonathan hasn't told you much about me. I have a vested interest in things that are dead . . . as well as things that should be dead but aren't."

At this point, Goodman Brown leaned forward, revealing his face for the first time. Rip drew back in horror. *Goodman was a living corpse!* The man was missing a cheek, while the remaining flesh on his face was as white as cotton, curtained behind long, greasy clumps of gray hair. His eyes were pale and listless, like those of a dead fish. His black lips curled into a lopsided smile, exposing long, yellow teeth.

"So you see," continued Goodman calmly, "I was *very* interested when I learned about a baby who had been snatched from the hands of death and given the name of a grave."

"We didn't come here to talk about Rip," interrupted the preacher.

"Are you sure about that?" Goodman's lifeless gaze flickered toward Rip's satchel.

"Why was Mistress Hibbins asking about the lantern?" pressed Jonathan.

"Oh, for the usual reasons," said Goodman. "Revenge and all that nonsense. That woman's been riding the same broomstick for almost a hundred years. Can't seem to get over past wounds."

"Reminds me of someone I know," said Jonathan coolly.

Rip realized that Jonathan's last comment must've been an insult to Goodman, because suddenly the air in the room became very tense, as though everyone were collectively holding their breath. Goodman clicked his tongue and chuckled. Rip could feel everyone relax when the dead man leaned back in his chair.

"You know, that's a bit ironic coming from you, Jonathan. Especially when you look so much like your Granddaddy Solomon."

"*I'm nothing like my grandfather,*" said Jonathan, an edge to his voice.

"Of course you're not," said Goodman. "You're a redeemed man now!"

Rip heard two or three skeletons snicker.

"Tell me, preacher man, how exactly do all of your little restrictions and resolutions make you any better? Isn't life meant to be lived—not restricted?"

"Says the dead man who's rotting away in a tavern," Jonathan quipped.

Goodman stood up and slammed his fist down hard. "SILENCE!" he shouted.

Rip clapped his hands to his ears. Goodman must've used some form of magic when he yelled, because his voice echoed throughout the tavern, shattering glasses and extinguishing the light from every candle. The remaining embers of the fire faded into smoke.

Rip trembled at the sight of the Impure Puritan. Tall, gaunt, and rotten, the dead man was a terrifying specter. Shaking with rage, he glowered down at Rip and the preacher, as though silently debating all the ways he could kill them. Rip cast a sideways glance at the skeletons and could see that they, too, were frozen with fear. One of them sat with his jaw open, cards slipping through his bony fingers.

After another moment or two, Goodman blinked and seemed to regain his composure. "My apologies," he said, his countenance shifting to one of cool restraint. "I get a little, ah, grumpy when I haven't had a proper drink. Where are my manners? Please have a seat."

The dead man waved his hand, and from across the room, two wooden chairs magically skittered out of the darkness and came to a stop at his table. Jonathan hesitated before sitting down. Rip cautiously followed the preacher's lead. Goodman glanced up at the skeletons in the tavern, who looked back at him in frightened silence.

"What are you staring at?" growled Goodman. "Get back to drinking! Hop-Frog, play another tune on that horrible thing you call a piano. And Fortunato, bring me another drink of Amontillado!"

Instantly, the tavern blared back to life—at least, as much as could be expected in a tavern full of the undead. The skeletons picked up their cards, the hunchbacked figure resumed his awful rendition of a sailor's tune, and the bartender (whom Rip assumed to be Fortunato) brought Goodman a short glass filled with a yellow liquid. Without waiting for the drink to stop sloshing around, Goodman grabbed it and swallowed half of its contents in a single gulp. Small streams of the yellow liquid oozed from his open cheek.

"Ahhh," said Goodman, leaning back in his chair. "That's much better. All right, preacher. Ask me your questions and I'll see what I can remember."

Jonathan cleared his throat. "How many lanterns are there?"

"There were thirteen originally, but now," said Goodman thoughtfully, "now there are only twelve. One for each Hallow. Every time a new Hallow is called, he or she is given both a lantern and a mission. The magic from the lantern gives added power to the Hallow until his or her mission is complete."

"What makes the pumpkins so magical?" asked Jonathan.

Goodman shook his head slowly. "No, no, no. It isn't the *pumpkins* that are magical. Pumpkins have a magic of their own, of course, but the *real* magic comes from what's *inside* the lanterns—the embers. It's immortal—can't be extinguished."

"I see. And where did these *embers* come from?"

Goodman rubbed his forehead. "So many questions, Jonathan. Tell me, why do *you* want to know?"

Rip shifted uncomfortably, wondering how the preacher was going to answer that question without revealing that they, themselves, had a lantern.

"Next week marks the one hundredth anniversary of Blaxton's rescue of the Boston Puritans," said Jonathan, calmly. "There is a lot of talk in Columbia as to whether or not Blaxton will make an appearance."

"*Columbia*," said Goodman, his expression sour. "I doubt Blaxton or any of the other Hallows are going to visit Columbia any time soon."

"Why is that?"

"Because Columbia has lost its way," said Goodman with a wicked smile.

"Impossible," retorted Jonathan. "The governors of Columbia were chosen by the Hallows and are charged with awakening the people; they would never lead us astray."

"Of course not," said Goodman, his voice dripping with sarcasm. "Which is why you've come to me and not someone like Governor Chillingworth . . . ?"

Rip saw Jonathan tighten his jaw. Goodman seemed pleased.

"Now, as for the origin of the embers . . . I've heard it said that they came from the first fire of Prometheus, the Titan of Greek mythology. But I've also heard it said that they came from Stingy Jack—a man so evil that when he died, Hell itself wouldn't let him in. According to legend, the Dark Woodsman gave Jack a small ember to put in his lantern, and with that lantern Jack wandered the earth for centuries, unable to die. Now, out of the two myths, I tend to believe the latter—"

"What about Feathertop?" interrupted Rip.

It was as though Rip had said the worst word imaginable. Goodman scraped his long nails across the table, snapping one of them in half. "Where did you hear that name?" he demanded.

He was clearly angry, but Rip couldn't understand why. Rip was merely trying to understand. Blaxton had said nothing about Hell or Greek mythology; he had told Rip to take the lantern to Feathertop. And Nathaniel had said that the pumpkins were carved to look like the scarecrow. So, why was the mention of Feathertop's name so upsetting to Goodman Brown?

"I—I heard it from Jonathan," Rip lied.

"Is that so?" sneered Goodman, a hint of amusement shimmering in his dead eyes. "Well, if you're looking for Feathertop, you'd be better served talking to the Ginger Witches; they know more of the stories than anyone else. And since when does Jonathan Edwards preach fairy tales? I thought the level-headed preacher doubted the reality of Feathertop as much as I do."

"I have my doubts," said Jonathan. "But I'm not as faithless as other people—I don't go for walks in the woods looking for the Darkness."

"Perhaps not," said Goodman with a smile, "but where does your soul walk? Does it walk in the sunlit woods or hide in the shadowy forest? Because whenever I look at you, I see a man on the run, constantly hiding from himself and the people he's betrayed. You're still hiding—behind that collar, behind that skin. But I see you for what you are. You're a wolf in sheep's clothing, Jonathan."

Rip stiffened as he recalled Blaxton's warning: *Beware of wolves in sheep's clothing.*

At first, Rip had thought Blaxton might have been referring to Katy when he said this, because Katy had turned out to be a werewolf. But now, with Goodman's words about Jonathan ringing in his ears, Rip began to wonder if Blaxton had meant for him to look deeper.

"So, tell me, Jonathan," said Goodman coolly, "what *do* you believe in?"

"I believe in the mission and promise of Columbia," said Jonathan, his eyes fixed on Goodman. "I believe that Columbia will bring about the Great Awakening so that every soul can be reclaimed from the Dark Woodsman. My soul burns bright with faith in that promise. What about you, Goodman? How's your faith?"

"My Faith is gone!" snapped Goodman. "You cannot relight a fire once the candle has burned out. There is no redemption from the darkness of death!"

At the mention of the word "candle," an image of Charity flickered into Rip's mind. He pictured his sister holding a lantern inside their home, illuminating the family. Then, all too quickly, the light flickered and died, plunging the house into complete darkness.

"She still lives," said Jonathan quietly.

Surprised, Rip wondered if the preacher had been reading his thoughts, but he quickly realized that Jonathan was talking to Goodman.

"DON'T YOU DARE TALK ABOUT HER!" bellowed the dead man.

A sudden, terrified silence blanketed the tavern, and all eye sockets turned to face the trio in the corner. Without warning, Goodman snatched Rip up by the wrist and, with unnatural speed, rose to his feet and wrapped his free arm around Rip's throat. The boy cried out in alarm and tried to pull away, but the Puritan's grasp was surprisingly strong.

Jonathan stood up slowly. "Goodman, put the boy down."

But Goodman ignored the preacher and hissed into Rip's ear, blowing foul breath all over his face: "You think I don't know why you're here, little boy? You think I don't know you have the lantern there in your satchel? I can feel its presence in my rotten flesh; I can feel it in my hollow bones! I felt the lantern the moment Blaxton returned to Boston, and I felt it as you ran through the tunnels, bringing it closer and closer to me!"

"Goodman, stop!" shouted Jonathan. "Let the boy go!"

But the Puritan shook his head. "No, no, no," he said, pulling Rip closer. "The lantern has power over life and death! Do you know how long I've been waiting to have it? I knew Blaxton's mission was almost over, so I came back to Boston. Who do you think hired Katy to fetch the lantern in the first place? Imagine my surprise when I discovered I didn't need to hire her at all—you've brought it right to me! Trade one dog for another, I suppose!"

Rip struggled against his captor, his stomach laden with fear and resentment.

"Stop your squirming, boy!" barked Goodman. "You have no idea who you're dealing with! Now give me the lantern!"

"Leave the boy alone!" shouted Jonathan. "Take the lantern for yourself, if you must. But leave the boy alone!"

"I may be dead, Jonathan," growled Goodman, "but I'm no fool. I know the lantern cannot be taken; it must be given."

"Then you might as well just let us go because Rip's not going to give it to you."

Goodman chuckled. "Is that so? Well, I also know that it doesn't have to be given *voluntarily*."

Rip sensed an ominous edge to Goodman's use of the word "voluntarily." Jonathan seemed to sense it, too, because just then, outside the window, there came the sound of rushing wind. The preacher stood resolute, his fists clenched.

"If you think I'm going to let you harm the boy, you're wrong!"

"The boy?" said Goodman innocently. "Who said anything about harming the boy?"

Before Jonathan or Rip could react, Goodman raised a hand, and the preacher went flying across the room. Jonathan landed against the wall but remained suspended, his feet dangling two or three feet in the air. With the preacher out of the way, Goodman flung Rip to the floor.

The villain then moved toward the preacher. As he did so, a hurricane-like wind shattered the window and smashed against the Puritan, throwing him across a table and into several skeletons. Free from Goodman's spell, Jonathan slid down the wall and ran toward Rip, but Goodman Brown wasn't finished. Struggling against the ferocious wind, the villain extended his arms in opposite directions—one toward Jonathan, and one toward the wind that poured through the open window. Rip looked up. Straining against both Jonathan and the wind, the dead man had a look of rage like something from a nightmare.

The men continued to fight against each other until the gale from the window came to a sudden halt, and the preacher was once again flung against the back wall. Goodman Brown let out a groan and lowered his arms. As he did so, every bone in his body seemed to crackle and creak. Pinned to the wall, Jonathan struggled piteously against the Impure Puritan's magic.

Goodman returned to his table, lifted his glass, gulped down the rest of its contents, and then clutched his shoulder and gritted his teeth.

"You know, Jonathan, I'm not as strong as I used to be. The use of magic always takes a toll, and it exhausts me faster than it would exhaust you. But I daresay you're still no match for me. So much for your *righteous resolutions.*" Goodman then turned his attention to Rip. "Boy, I don't want to make this messy—so please don't force my hand. If you give me the lantern, I'll let you and the preacher go home. If you don't, I'll make you wish you had never been pulled from that grave!"

"Rip! Don't do it!" shouted Jonathan.

In response to this, a wooden stool upended and flew toward Jonathan with great speed. It slammed against the wall above his head, shattering into a dozen pieces.

"Tut, tut, Jonathan," said Goodman disapprovingly. "Can't you see I'm in the middle of a conversation?" He turned his attention back to the boy and spoke calmly yet dangerously. *"Give me the lantern."*

Rip didn't know what to do. For a brief moment, he thought about using his ability with plants to fight against Goodman—the way he had once used it against Tom Walker—but there weren't any plants in the tavern. Besides, Rip hadn't been able to communicate with plants since Charity died. Why would he suddenly be able to now? Even if he could control the plants, Rip knew he was no match against the Impure Puritan. Just then, Rip had an idea. He didn't know if it would work, but he didn't have any other options.

He reached into his satchel and pulled out the lantern. Its bright yellow light cast an eerie glow in the darkened room full of the skeletons.

Goodman looked at it greedily. "Yes!" he whispered. "Now give it to me!"

Rip paused. He lifted the lantern high and took three steps toward the Impure Puritan, concentrating very hard. The light from the lantern began to intensify.

Goodman noticed the difference almost immediately. "What are you doing?" he said, backing up.

Rip focused harder, concentrating on his memory of William Blaxton and how the ghost had used the lantern against the Midnight Minister.

"Stop!" cried Goodman.

But Rip persisted, amazed that his plan was working. The light grew and grew, until it illuminated the entire tavern, consuming every shadow. The light became so intense that Rip had to close his eyes. He heard the skeletons shout and fling themselves to the ground. Goodman himself let out a terrifying, unearthly scream.

Then, in an instant, the light faded and the room returned to its original darkness. Rip blinked a few times and glanced around the room. The first thing he saw was Jonathan. The preacher had freed himself from the wall and was staring at something behind Rip, a look of shock on his pale face. Rip followed the preacher's gaze.

Standing behind him was . . . someone who was no longer *Goodman*! At least, not the same Goodman as before. The man's eyes, once sunken and dead, were now alive and vibrant. His skin, once pale and decaying, was now clean and whole. The Goodman who now stood before Rip was no longer an undead corpse, but a living man!

The Puritan stared at his hands in astonishment. "What have you done?" he whispered.

"I—I don't know," said Rip.

Goodman began to tremble, and he balled his hands into fists. "WHAT HAVE YOU DONE?" he bellowed, shaking the room with his monstrous voice.

Rip fell back a step, shocked by the Puritan's rage.

"This isn't what I wanted!" screamed Goodman. "THIS IS NOT WHAT I WANTED!"

"I didn't mean to!" said Rip.

Goodman lifted his hand, and Rip felt himself rise into the air. "You have no idea what you've done!" shouted Goodman, his eyes burning with rage. "The lantern wasn't for me!"

Rip kicked and struggled, but it was no use; Goodman had him in his clutches.

Just then, there came a loud clank on the roof above. Goodman, Jonathan, Rip, and all of the skeletons fell silent and looked up.

"Too far—try again," said a muffled voice. Rip thought it sounded oddly familiar.

There was a short pause, followed by another loud clank.

"A little to the right," said the voice.

There was a longer pause, followed by a much louder clank; this time the sound clearly emanated from within the chimney. Goodman lowered Rip to the ground and pointed at one of the skeletons, who quickly leapt forward, poked his head inside the fireplace, and peered up.

"I don't see nothing," the skeleton said.

At that precise moment, a monstrous iron anchor thundered down on the skeleton, scattering ash and bone in every direction. Following the anchor, a large black object shot down the chimney and rolled out from the fireplace. As the smoke dissipated, the "object" stood up.

"Sorry I'm late," said Nathaniel, shaking the ashes from his wings.

Goodman cursed and glared up at Jonathan. "You brought the bird?"

Nathaniel cleared his throat. "Pardon me, but I do have a name. My, my, Goodman Brown. Is that you? You look different. Have you—ah—gained weight?"

Goodman narrowed his eyes. "You have a death wish, raven."

"Most certainly not," said Nathaniel dismissively, wiping the last bit of ash from his breast. "Jonathan, how are you? Good, I hope. Rip? Wonderful. Look, I'm terribly sorry about being late. We had an 'issue' about the best material to use. Jonathan suggested rope, but we weren't sure if it would have enough weight. Naturally, someone suggested chains, but I knew chains would be a bit harder to retract. In the end, we settled on one of the smaller anchors, which we tied to the end of this rope. Fortunately, it was large enough, yet small enough, to fit through the chimney. Thank you for putting out the fire beforehand. We birds naturally have a fear of open fires—rotisserie and whatnot."

Goodman pointed at the bird. "GET HIM!"

But Jonathan moved faster than any of Goodman's cronies. The preacher flung his arm forward, and a strong wind sent Goodman flying into a crowd of angry skeletons.

"Rip!" shouted Jonathan. "Grab the anchor! Quick!"

Rip needed no second bidding. Lantern in hand, he ran to the fireplace, placed his feet on the anchor's arms, and grabbed the shank with his free hand.

Nathaniel hopped onto Rip's shoulder and tapped the rope with his beak.

"Hang on tight!" he shouted.

Nathaniel wasn't kidding about holding on; in less than a second—and with unbelievable speed—the anchor soared up out of the chimney and into the night sky.

CAPTAIN STORMALONG

IN WHICH RIP FINDS FAITH TO BE TWO DIFFERENT THINGS...

*R*ip held on for dear life as the cold air whipped past him. Although grateful to escape the Skeleton Closet, Rip now felt that his life was endangered in a much more terrifying way. In fact, as he looked down at the marshland—far, *far* below—he almost wished to be back in that tavern; if his life *had* to be in danger, at least there it would be in danger on firm, solid, ground!

As Rip and Nathaniel continued their rapid ascent, the raven dug his talons into Rip's coat and shouted over the wind, "Behold! *The Courser*— the flying ship of Captain Stormalong himself! Brace yourself!"

Rip held his lantern high and looked up. There, suspended in the sky, against a backdrop of stars, was a large, magnificent ship. He tightened his hold on the anchor as it came to a sudden, jerky halt.

"Looks like we caught something!" bellowed an exceptionally loud, jolly voice.

The anchor—with Rip clinging to its side—had been pulled up over the side of the ship but was still dangling in the air, spinning slightly. It took a moment for it to stop turning, and when it did, Rip nearly lost his footing on the cold metal anchor.

There, standing at the edge of the ship, holding the weight of the anchor in one mighty arm, was the tallest, mightiest man Rip had ever seen. In fact, the word "tall" didn't do him justice. The man was a literal giant! Rip guessed that he must be eleven—maybe twelve—feet tall. He had a thick, brown beard and was covered from head to toe in bearskins, making him look like some bizarre mix between a Viking, a French trapper, and a pirate.

"Such a little fish on such a big hook!" laughed the giant, eyes full of mirth. He gave the anchor a shake, and Rip toppled onboard *The Courser.*

Nathaniel glided down to the boy's shoulder. "Rip Van Winkle," said the bird with a regal air, "allow me to formally introduce you to Captain Alfred Bulltop Stormalong."

Captain Stormalong winked and offered a weather-beaten hand to Rip —one that was easily five times larger than Rip's own. Cautiously, Rip allowed his own hand to be engulfed and shaken heartily.

"'Rip,' is it?" repeated Stormalong. "As in, 'Riptide'? Excellent! Welcome aboard my ship, young master Riptide!" From their various stations onboard, several of Stormalong's crew echoed a spirited welcome.

"This—this ship," stammered Rip, shakily rising to his feet. "It's a *flying* ship!"

"Of course it's a flying ship!" bellowed Stormalong, hooking his thumbs into his broad leather belt. "Made from the finest pumpkin wood of Newfoundland!"

"And her captain is the finest pirate of the North Atlantic," boasted Nathaniel.

Stormalong beamed. "In the North Atlantic? In all of Columbia!"

"He's the only pirate who has taken on the Kraken with his bare hands," chimed the bird.

"The Kraken?" repeated Rip. He remembered hearing stories about the giant octopus from Silence and Dogood, but he hadn't believed them. "You really fought the Kraken?"

"I'd almost forgotten about that," said Stormalong, with a look so full of pride that Rip was sure the giant hadn't forgotten. Then, without missing a beat, the Captain began telling the story.

"So there I was, swimming in the ocean, fighting the Kraken for the possession of a young white whale, and just when I almost had it, a huge whirlpool opened up and nearly swallowed all three of us—the Kraken, the whale, and me! Had it not been for Master Ahab's daring rescue," he added, nodding toward a man at the helm, "I might never have made it out alive!"

Ahab gave the Captain a solemn nod.

Stormalong looked back at Nathaniel and Rip, scratching his head. "Say, what happened to that preacher of yours? Did we splatter him on the road somewheres?"

Nathaniel gasped. "We left Jonathan in the tavern! I plumb forgot!"

"Never fear, never fear," said Stormalong. "Jonathan has a few tricks up his sleeve. Besides, I think my crew is hoping to see me go fishing again!"

There was a unanimous roar of approval from the crew as Stormalong leapt onto the edge of the rail and looked down.

"Now, where are you, preacher?" he muttered.

Nathaniel, who was already airborne, pointed his beak wildly at the buildings below. "There! There! I see him! He's on the street!"

Hastily stowing the lantern in the satchel at his side, Rip ran to the rail and squinted down. The bird's eyes must have been better than his own, because Rip could only make out a few of the buildings. One of Stormalong's men elbowed the boy and handed him a small silver spyglass. Quickly, Rip extended it to full length and used it to scan the street below. It took him a few moments to find what he was looking for. Sure enough, Jonathan had escaped the building and was hobbling down the street. Rip shifted his focus away from the preacher and discovered that Jonathan was being pursued by Goodman Brown and a pack of skeletons. But the villains were struggling to move forward, and the Puritan hobbled along, holding on to his hat while his cloak billowed behind him.

The wind! thought Rip, excitedly. *They can't get to Jonathan because he's outside, using the wind to protect himself!* Despite this bit of good news, Rip could tell that the preacher's use of magic was taking a toll on him; Jonathan looked as though he was barely able to put one foot in front of the other.

"Right!" shouted Stormalong. "This is going to take some precision! Ahab! Bring the ship forward! I want to reel him in straight!"

"Aye, aye, Cap'n!" yelled Ahab.

Rip held on to the rail as *The Courser* lurched forward. Stormalong grabbed the anchor and a large portion of rope. Using incredible strength, he swung the anchor around and around before releasing it like a net, out and over the rail of the ship. Rip brought the spyglass to his eye and watched as the anchor sailed through the air, arced gracefully, and finally landed with a loud crack on the street below—a mere three or four feet in front of Jonathan Edwards.

Clearly surprised by the sudden appearance of the anchor, the preacher stumbled backward and landed on his backside. He looked up at *The Courser* and shook his head in astonishment. Stormalong merely hooked a thumb into his belt and beamed with pride.

The preacher gathered himself up and grabbed the anchor just as Goodman and his cronies closed in on him. Then, waving his free arm, Jonathan sent one last gust of wind that toppled all of the skeletons and left Goodman standing alone. As Jonathan was lifted to safety, he tipped his hat to Goodman in mock salute.

Stormalong laughed as he reeled in the rope. "We caught ourselves a preacher!"

Moments later, Jonathan stumbled aboard *The Courser*. He was pale, haggard, and sweaty, but otherwise appeared quite happy to be alive.

"Looks like things got a little tense down there," said the Captain, slapping Jonathan on the back.

Jonathan laughed. "*That* much is certain."

"Reminds me of that time in Salem . . ."

"*Which* time in Salem?"

"When you were fighting that fellow—what was his name—Burlap?"

"Billy Burlap?"

Stormalong grinned and slapped his thighs. "Yes! That's the one. You were grateful to see me then, too!"

"That's an understatement!" replied Jonathan.

Stormalong suddenly brought a finger to his lips. "Shhh! You hear that?"

Everyone grew silent. Goodman must have been using magic to project his voice, because Rip could clearly hear the man shouting words that Puritan children were taught never to say. Stormalong strode back to the rail and looked down.

"Is that *really* Goodman Brown?"

Jonathan nodded.

The Captain squinted, clearly able to see things farther away than Rip himself could. "He looks . . . different," remarked the giant. "Healthy, I daresay."

"That he is," said Jonathan, glancing up at Rip. Rip looked away uncomfortably and pushed the satchel behind him.

"You'd think he'd be happier about it," muttered Stormalong.

Using his spyglass, Rip looked down to see what Stormalong was talking about. Caught up in a furious rage, Goodman was magically hurling objects up at the ship, but to no avail. The objects either fell short or merely bounced off *The Courser*'s massive hull.

A sly smile spread across Stormalong's face. "Ahab!" he bellowed.

"Yes, Cap'n?"

"Let's make it rain!"

Ahab matched his Captain's smile. "Yes, sir!" The man then pulled a lever next to the helm.

The Captain winked at Rip. "Now you get to see why they call me 'Stormalong'!"

Rip could feel the ship rumble beneath his feet, and he grabbed the rail to steady himself. Beyond *The Courser* spread a flash of light, followed by the sound of thunder. Looking over the rail, Rip saw black clouds billowing out from beneath the hull. He glanced nervously at Nathaniel, who was lazily preening his feathers—not a care in the world.

Turning his gaze back to the gathering storm, Rip watched in wonder as the dark clouds grew twenty, thirty, forty feet in diameter! Three flashes of light shot out, and the deck rumbled again. A curious noise immediately followed. Straining his ears, Rip realized that he was hearing the sound of rain. He thought himself foolish for not recognizing it right away —but then again, he had never been on the opposite side of a rain cloud before.

Rip glanced up and saw Captain Stormalong leaning over the rail with his ear turned toward land. Noticing Rip's eyes on him, the Captain pulled back and grinned with satisfaction.

"It seems Goodman isn't very happy about being wet," he laughed. "I could listen to that old codger complain for hours!"

"Sadly, we cannot," interrupted Jonathan. The preacher had managed to pull himself to his feet and was now propping himself up against the rail. "Goodman is still very dangerous, and he has ways of getting to us. He still has the Lightning Horse, remember? That animal can travel anywhere in New England in the blink of an eye."

Stormalong furrowed his bushy eyebrows. "Who, Gunpowder? That beast can travel with the lightning, it's true—but *The Courser* has its own magic. Creatures like Gunpowder can't magically appear on my ship."

"Even so," continued Jonathan, "we're on a rather tight schedule. And Goodman will eventually figure out where we're headed and find a way to get to us. At this point, our only hope is to stay one step ahead of him."

"Fair enough," agreed Stormalong. "Where are we going?"

"To see the Ginger Witches," said Jonathan. Rip recalled the name from their conversation with Goodman Brown.

Stormalong's eyes brightened. "The Ginger Witches? You thinking about getting some pie?"

Rip heard some of the men murmur in excitement.

Jonathan shook his head. "No, not pie—*information*. Goodman hinted that the witches might be able to help us on our journey."

"Well, you're in luck, Johnny, because we've got a shipment of apples that we need to deliver to those ladies."

"Let's get a move on, then! Besides," Jonathan added with a smile, "I suppose it wouldn't hurt to pick up a little something for ourselves while we're there."

The crew eagerly set to work. In no time at all, the ship was on its way over Boston Neck, pulling along the storm it had created. Rip glanced around. Below them and to the east, the Atlantic Ocean looked calm and peaceful, but Rip couldn't help feeling a little unsettled.

"Um, Nathaniel?" he asked, getting the bird's attention. "Do you think it's wise to see the Ginger Witches? I mean, they are . . . *witches*, right?"

The bird paused for a moment before he seemed to understand the question. "Ah," he said at last, "you believe all witches to be bad, yes?"

"Well, aren't they?"

"Of course not!" Nathaniel snorted. "Technically, the term 'witch' refers to anyone who uses magic. Sadly, the word has, for the most part, become a derogatory term among those who are 'asleep.'"

"So the Ginger Witches—" began Rip. "I mean, they're good, right?"

"If by 'good' you mean their cooking is amazing, then yes!"

"They're cooks, too?"

"Indeed! They run a quaint cooking cottage at the far end of the harbor. Although I must admit, calling them cooks, witches, or Luminaries would not be entirely accurate. Truthfully, no one really knows *what* the Ginger Witches are. They're very powerful and very old. Then again, most magical people have a certain power over aging. *But* if you ask me," added Nathaniel under his breath, as if to keep the others from hearing, "I think their 'cooking business' is something of a smokescreen—a distraction."

"What makes you say that?"

Nathaniel shrugged his wings. "You'll understand when you meet them. Those women seem to dwell in two worlds at the same time. I get the sense that they know more than they're willing to reveal."

The sky paled in the east as the sun began to rise. Rip stared at the horizon in wonder. Had he really been up the entire night? Had all of the events happened in just one night? Rip marveled at how much his life had changed in such a short span of time.

But what surprised Rip even more was the fact that he didn't feel the least bit tired. Glancing down at the lantern in his hand, he wondered if his alertness might have something to do with the magical light within the pumpkin. He remembered the first time he had held it—the life and energy he had felt. He also remembered what Goodman Brown had said about the light being eternal and also having power over life and death. Maybe that light was what had healed Goodman.

The thought of Goodman's transformation sent a shiver up Rip's spine. Why had he been so angry about being healed? Could it be that he had wanted the lantern for some evil purpose? Was Goodman Brown a Gloom —a servant of the dark?

Remembering what Nathaniel had said about Luminaires and Glooms made Rip's heart sink. For the past month, he hadn't been able to make plants grow. Instead, he had been overwhelmed by a feeling of darkness growing within himself—a darkness he couldn't shake. This darkness filled him with terrible thoughts about life and about himself. If this darkness was inside of him, did that mean he was a Gloom? Was he going to become someone like Goodman Brown? If people knew about the darkness inside of him, would they even want anything to do with him? Rip decided never to tell either Nathaniel or Jonathan about how he felt inside; he didn't know how the others would react.

"Rip, may I speak with you for a moment?"

Rip jumped. It was Jonathan. The preacher had been quietly standing on the edge of the stairs with one hand on the rail. Rip swallowed hard and moved toward the preacher, certain that the conversation wasn't going to be good.

"Rip, I want to talk to you about what happened in the Skeleton Closet—"

"I'm sorry!" Rip blurted, without even waiting for Jonathan to finish.

"Sorry?" repeated Jonathan. "What are you sorry about?"

"About what happened," explained Rip. "I healed Goodman and made him stronger, didn't I? I wanted to stop him—the way Blaxton stopped the Midnight Minister—but I couldn't. I think I—I think I just made everything worse."

Jonathan cleared his throat. "Rip, you didn't do anything wrong. In fact, what happened in the Skeleton Closet probably did more good than you know."

Rip was startled by this. "It did?"

"Yes," said Jonathan encouragingly. "The lantern has power over life and death, and you used it to give life to a man who believed he was dead inside. That's a good thing."

"But Goodman is a bad person."

The preacher smiled wistfully. "You know, before tonight I would have agreed with you . . . but it is never as simple as that. There is good and bad in all of us, and as strange as it may sound, there seems to be more good in Goodman than even he knows. You used the lantern to encourage the life still lingering within him. Think about it; you gave light to a man who dwells in darkness. From what I understand, that's the work of the Hallows, isn't it? To be a light in the wilderness. The labor of a Hallow is to bring light to every life, because *every* life has immense value."

Rip stared out at the sea and narrowed his eyes. "If every life has immense value, then why do people die?" He tightened his jaw. "If every life has value, then why did my sister die, and why did my parents abandon me as a baby?"

Truthfully, Rip was a little stunned by his own words. He had never expressed his feelings about being abandoned to anyone—anyone, that is, except for Charity.

Jonathan paused. "Your parents abandoned you?"

"My *real* parents," said Rip, looking down at the deck. "They didn't want me, so they left me in a graveyard to die. My mother and father—the people who found me and raised me—took care of me because they couldn't find my real parents."

"I'm sure the people who raised you love you," said Jonathan.

Rip lowered his head. For a long time there were no words, just the sound of the wind snapping in the sails as the ship moved forward.

The preacher was the first to break the silence. "Rip, do you feel alone?"

"What?" Rip was confused by what seemed to be a random question.

"Do you feel alone?"

Rip paused. "Well . . . yes, actually."

"Do you feel burdened with secret grief?"

"Yes."

"Do you feel like you don't belong?"

"In general, or on this ship?"

Jonathan laughed. "Both."

Rip nodded.

"Do you feel that if people knew who you really are, they would reject you?"

Rip looked at the preacher in surprise. It was as if Jonathan had read Rip's very thoughts. "How did you know that?"

"Because it's often how I feel." Jonathan turned his gaze to the sea. "And I think it's how our pilgrim ancestors felt, even in the crowded streets of Europe. They were different. They were strange. They were outcasts. Rejected by their own families, they came to the New World in search of a safe haven. I do not think what you are feeling is wrong. I believe each of us is a pilgrim in our own way; we are all lost souls, trying to find our way home."

"But what if *I* wasn't meant to be found?" blurted Rip. "What if my parents weren't supposed to find me? What if I wasn't *supposed* to have the lantern?"

"Rip, Blaxton gave *you* the lantern. Not me. Not Nathaniel. Not Katy, or anyone else. He gave it to *you*. Blaxton wandered New England for a century. If you weren't the right person to give it to, I'm sure he would have waited and given it to someone else. But he didn't, did he? Have faith in the light you carry—not only the physical light in the lantern, but the light inside you. Trust in that light to help you find your way."

Rip examined the pumpkin in his hands, watching the light as it glowed softly and steadily. Jonathan's encouragement reminded him of the first time he saw William Blaxton on the street. Rip remembered how

Blaxton had stopped in front of the Van Winkle house and looked directly at him. It was as though Blaxton were calling upon Rip. Blaxton had found him, even when Rip thought he couldn't be seen.

For some reason, recalling that memory brought comfort to him. But there was something that bothered Rip. "Jonathan," he said hesitatingly, "when we were in the Skeleton Closet, you and Goodman were talking about faith. You said that your soul burns bright with faith, but Goodman said his faith was gone—that it was impossible to relight a fire once it is burned out. What did he mean by that?"

Jonathan furrowed his brow momentarily, but then his eyes filled with understanding. "Well," he began, "first of all, Goodman and I weren't exactly talking about the same thing."

Rip was confused. "How's that?"

"I was talking about faith in general. Faith is believing in something you cannot prove for certain. However, Goodman wasn't talking about that kind of faith. He was talking about his wife—Faith Brown."

Rip raised his eyebrows. "His wife's name was Faith?"

Jonathan nodded. "She died a long time ago, and Goodman never quite recovered."

Despite his intense dislike of the Impure Puritan, Rip felt a pang of sadness for the man. Losing Charity was the hardest thing Rip had ever had to go through. He didn't know if he would ever feel normal again—and he didn't know if he really wanted to. Suddenly, and quite unexpectedly, he began to understand Goodman's bitterness.

"But why did he look like a corpse?" asked Rip.

Jonathan hesitated, as though choosing his words very carefully. "Goodman's situation is . . . unique."

"How is it unique?" pressed Rip. He was thinking about his sister, wondering why someone like Goodman Brown could stay alive while Charity couldn't.

Jonathan lowered his voice. "Rip, how do you think Goodman knows so much about the lanterns and the Hallows?"

Rip shrugged. "He's been around a long time?"

"And why do you think Goodman's been around for such a long time? Why do you think he's alive when he should be dead?"

Rip was confused. He knew that Jonathan was trying to make a point, but he couldn't figure out what it was. He looked up at the preacher with a blank expression.

"Rip, the reason Goodman didn't fully die is because he retains some power over life and death. Goodman Brown is still alive because he was one of the original thirteen Hallows."

12

THE SIMMONS SISTERS

IN WHICH RIP GETS A TASTE OF A
DIFFERENT KIND OF MAGIC...

*A*fter some time, *The Courser* began a slow descent toward a cluster of trees. For a moment, Rip was worried that Ahab was on a collision course, but his fear was put to rest when Nathaniel pointed out a long wooden dock, suspended in the air between two trees.

"Stormalong built it himself," said the raven. "His whole system of delivery is really quite marvelous. Because New England is so, well, *new*, there are a number of magical communities in need of quality goods. In response to those needs, Captain Stormalong devised this rather ingenious system of shipping. Using a flying ship that generates a storm for cover, the Captain can secretly transport magical goods to nearly every city in Columbia! Stormalong is one clever giant."

"Are there other giants like him?" wondered Rip aloud.

"Ah, not *quite* like him," said Nathaniel. "Most giants live in the North. They like the cold more than most folks, which makes Stormalong a bit odd for his kind; while his family prefers the cold and the seclusion of snow-capped mountains, Stormalong prefers the warm, open air. Aside from that," added Nathaniel with a twinkle in his eyes, "Alfred fancies one of the Simmons Sisters."

"The Simmons Sisters?"

"The Ginger Witches," explained Nathaniel. "Their last name is Simmons, and they're sisters—Amelia, Amalia, and Amanda. Captain Stormalong is quite charmed by Amanda, which is ironic, because she happens to be the shortest of the three sisters."

Rip chuckled. "Really?"

"Oh yes," said the raven, speaking under his breath. "Alfred and Amanda have been writing to each other. Although, from what I gather, Amanda is somewhat dissatisfied with the Captain's letters."

"Why's that?"

Nathaniel shrugged. "Well, I suppose it has something to do with the content. Amanda is the kind of person who would pour her heart and soul into her letters, while Stormalong is the type who would write about fish guts and sea monsters. In any case, whenever we visit, Amanda is always pressing me for more information about Stormalong. 'How's my Alfred?' she asks. 'What's Alfred doing? Has he said anything about me?'" Nathaniel shook his head. "That woman talks far too much! It's terribly annoying."

Rip smiled, finding it ironic that Nathaniel could be annoyed by someone talking too much.

"At any rate, I do wish you luck," said the bird as he stretched his wings. "Visiting the Ginger Witches is always an eye-opening, *mouth-watering* experience."

Rip cocked his head to one side. "Wait, you're not coming with us?"

"Ah, not this time. With you, Jonathan, and Stormalong all going, having me there would be . . . what's the expression? 'Too many cooks in the kitchen.' Besides," added Nathaniel with an air of humor, "I'm a delicious bird! With feasts and festivals just around the corner, who knows what those cooks might do to me?"

Winking at Rip, Nathaniel flapped away.

The Courser leveled out from its descent and hovered over the harbor next to the trees. With practiced efficiency, two crewmen threw hooks and ropes into the foliage, and began pulling the ship closer to the wooden dock. Once *The Courser* was fastened securely, Captain Stormalong laid out a massive plank between the ship and the dock, creating a walkway.

"After you, Johnny," said the giant to the preacher.

Jonathan tipped his hat and motioned for Rip to follow him across the plank. The two of them walked carefully to the dock and stopped beneath the canopy of trees. Beyond this point was a long rope bridge made of thick wooden slats. The bridge zigzagged from one large tree to another.

They heard Stormalong grunt from behind them and turned to see him lift two large wooden barrels onto his shoulders. The barrels were easily as long as canoes.

"Well, what's the hold-up?" shouted Stormalong cheerfully. "Across the bridge, Johnny. You know the way!"

Following the preacher's lead, Rip stepped onto the bridge and began moving forward, albeit very slowly. As he walked, he noticed something odd about the planks—they weren't like regular slabs of wood, but softer and smoother.

Stormalong's voice boomed behind him. "Everything all right?"

Rip jumped, startled to hear the giant so close by. "The planks!" he said, unintentionally shouting his response. "They're different. And the air . . . it smells like—"

"Gingerbread," finished Stormalong with a smile.

"Gingerbread?" repeated Rip. Instantly his mouth began to water. Gingerbread was a delicacy in New England. Once, during the Harvest Festival, Rip had actually been lucky enough to eat several gingerbread cookies. Soft and warm, the cookies were the perfect mixture of maple syrup, rosewater, and gingerroot. Rip looked out across the gingerbread bridge and gripped the rope rails tightly.

"What's wrong, master Riptide?" asked Stormalong.

"Uh," said Rip, looking down fearfully. "Can this bridge hold our weight?"

Stormalong laughed. "Can it hold our weight? Of course it can! It may look soft, but it's stronger than steel! Why, I almost built my ship out of gingerbread!"

Rip did his best to calm his nerves, and the trio continued their journey, crossing the bridge before heading up a series of ginger steps that wrapped around the trunk of a large oak tree. Near the top, they crossed over onto another large bridge. Rip could see a cottage-like treehouse on the other side, nestled in the branches of a gargantuan maple tree. From the roof, tendrils of smoke curled out of two separate chimneys. Rip sniffed the air. Whatever was cooking inside smelled delicious!

As the group moved closer to the cottage, Rip couldn't help but notice several oddities. For one thing, the cottage didn't appear to be made of logs or wood, but out of the same material as the bridge—gingerbread! Rip's mouth dropped open, and he stared in disbelief.

It was a gingerbread treehouse!

The walls of the house—decorated with large, colorful sweets—were held together by thick, elegant trails of icing. The shingles of the roof were thin, curved sweets, each as bright and as colorful as the different shades of the rainbow.

Before the companions had a chance to knock, they were startled when the door swung open and a tiny creature emerged. The creature was no taller than Rip's knee and looked like an oversized hedgehog walking on its hind legs. It wore a burnt apron that was two sizes too big, and it grumbled in an incoherent language as it kicked the ground and tugged its spikes in apparent frustration.

"What on earth is that?" exclaimed Rip.

The creature looked up in frightened surprise before dashing inside and slamming the door.

"*That* was a pukwudgie," said Stormalong.

"What's a pukwudgie?" asked Rip.

"Small, magical woodlanders," explained Jonathan. "They like to work, but they do *not* like to be seen. In fact, we probably wouldn't have seen that one if All Hallows' Day weren't so close."

"Why's that?" asked Rip.

"Festivals, of course!" said Stormalong. "In a few days, everyone in Columbia will be celebrating All Hallows' Day. The Simmons Sisters are working overtime to fill orders. They hired the pukwudgies for some extra help."

As if on cue, the door to the cottage burst open, and out stepped a tall woman with brilliant red hair and sleeves rolled up past her elbows. In the crook of one arm she held a large bowl, and with her other arm she was whisking so furiously that Rip thought she might be trying to start a fire.

The woman turned and yelled back into the cottage. "Stop your belly-aching, Nibs! I don't care if Teak lit your apron on fire! You've still got half a day's work ahead of you, and if you don't finish it, I'll take your apron and toss it into the fire myself!"

From inside the cottage there came a gasp of surprise, followed by a few words that Rip couldn't understand.

"Yes!" the woman replied. "The *whole* apron! Now get back to work!"

Satisfied, she blew a curl of red hair out of her face and turned to face her visitors. Rip's eyes grew wide. On either side of the woman's head were two long, curved horns!

The woman stopped stirring and put a hand on her hip. "Alfred Bulltop Stormalong! I hope you're just bringing apples, and not additional orders."

"Just the apples, Amalia," said Stormalong merrily. "These two would like to ask some questions about Feathertop."

"Feathertop, eh?" said Amalia, still mixing the batter at a blinding speed. "Well, you've come to the right place! We don't have too much time to spare—none, in fact. But we can answer your questions if you don't mind watching us cook. Is that boy all right?"

Rip had been standing with his mouth and eyes wide open, too stunned by Amalia's horns to speak. After a nudge from Jonathan, Rip swallowed hard and tried to speak as casually as he could. "Yes—every-thing is fine."

Amalia stopped stirring and ran a hand through her curly hair. "It's my horns, isn't it?"

Thinking he might have done something terribly rude, Rip shook his head and stammered, "No, no! Of course not—it's just . . . it's your house!"

But Amalia didn't seem to believe him. "I'm not surprised. Most Puritans are terrified by the horns. They think it has something to do with the Devil. Nonsense! Don't they realize that horns are a symbol of the harvest? For heaven's sake, even the Puritans in Boston decorate their Harvest Festival with horns!"

"What?" said Rip, unable to stop himself. "No, they don't." He had never seen horns at the Harvest Festival. The General Court would *never* allow such a thing.

Amalia narrowed her eyes. "Is that so? Well then, tell me, little Puritan, what are cornucopias? Hmmm? Just a pointed basket full of food? No! They're horns—symbols for the horn of plenty. When the Greek god Zeus was a baby, his mother hid him in a cave. And you know what? He would have died if it had not been for our mother, Amalthea. She became his adoptive mother and nursed him back to health. In gratitude, Zeus blessed her horns that would always give life. Now, does that sound evil to you, little Puritan?"

Rip hurriedly shook his head while simultaneously marveling at the story. It reminded him of his own adoptive mother. "I never knew the cornucopia represented a horn," he said.

Amalia shook her head. "It's the Terrible Slumber—that rotten curse! It causes everyone to demonize what they don't understand."

Stormalong grunted, causing the barrels on his shoulders to rise up and then go down again. "I don't mean to interrupt story time, Amalia, but where do you want me to put these?"

The woman pointed around the corner. "Behind the cottage. And you'd better have more than that!"

"*Much* more," grunted Stormalong. "It'll take me a while to unload everything. Have some pie ready for me before we leave."

Amalia smirked. "Don't I always?"

The giant lumbered off, and Amalia ushered the visitors inside the cottage. For Rip, stepping across the threshold of the Gingerbread treehouse was like stepping into a life-sized beehive. The interior of the cottage—which was much larger than the outside belied—was one big kitchen, bursting with life and activity.

Pukwudgies of various colors and sizes scampered about the house, working with impressive eagerness and zeal. The little creatures were baking, basting, blanching, blending, boiling, caramelizing, dicing, drizzling, dusting, flaking, glazing, grilling, grinding, kneading, mincing, mixing, peeling, paring, roasting, searing, shredding, simmering, stewing, stirring, tossing, and whipping!

And oh, the things they were making! All around the room, in every available nook and cranny, was something set aside to cool. At one end of the room, there were plates piled with roasted beef, mutton, veal, and wild turkey. In another area, on a long table in front of the fire, was a collection of puddings—Indian pudding, bread pudding, almond pudding, and apple pudding. Up against the wall, stacked neatly on rows and rows of shelves, was an assortment of pastries, pies, and cakes. There were plumb cakes, johnnycakes, seed cakes, carrot cakes, and strawberry shortcakes. There were apple pies, blueberry pies, rhubarb pies, cranberry pies, and pumpkin pies.

On a round table, next to the window, was a collection of syllabubs—lemon and raspberry sodas—overflowing with vanilla cream.

Rip was tempted to reach out and grab one of the drinks but stopped himself when Amalia shouted across the kitchen, "Amelia, Amanda! We have guests!"

There was a clatter of pots and pans, and another red-headed woman—this one considerably shorter than Amalia—burst out from behind a stack of shelves.

"Is it Alfred?" she squeaked breathlessly.

"Just his friends, Amanda," replied Amalia.

Amanda's face fell. "Oh," she said.

The preacher rolled his eyes. "Stormalong's here. He's just unloading the apples. "

"Oh!" exclaimed Amanda, straightening her hair to make her short, black horns more visible.

"Is that Jonathan Edwards I hear?" said a cheerful voice from somewhere in the room.

Before the preacher could reply, a third horned, red-headed woman, this one tall and graceful, strode out from behind a narrow row of shelves. Rip assumed that this woman was Amelia. In her arm, she carried a large bowl and was stirring very slowly. A few steps behind her was a tiny pukwudgie. Rip noticed, to his amusement, that the little creature was copying Amelia's every move. In its own arm, it held a teacup like a bowl and was stirring with a small stick.

"John!" exclaimed Amelia, playfully smacking the preacher's elbow with the end of her long wooden spoon. Mimicking Amelia, the pukwudgie whacked Jonathan's ankle with his stick and accidentally spilled all the contents of its teacup. Rip winced, but the pukwudgie quickly scooped up as much batter as possible and resumed stirring as if nothing had happened.

Amelia grinned. "How are you, old friend?"

The preacher smiled and rubbed his elbow. "I was doing just fine until you hit me."

"What are you doing here?"

"They came here to ask us about Feathertop," explained Amalia, scooting three pukwudgies off a table as if they were pet cats. "Or was it pumpkins?"

Amelia raised an eyebrow. "Pumpkins? Are you looking for pumpkin recipes? I hope not! I'm saving them for my book, you know."

"You've been working on that book for ages!" shouted Amalia. She turned to Rip and lowered her voice. "Personally, I don't think she's *ever* going to finish it."

"When's Alfred coming in?" chirped Amanda anxiously. "I mean, not that I really care. It's just that he didn't reply to my last letter, and I just think that's quite rude. I mean, pirate or no pirate, a person should at least be able to write a letter saying he's alive—"

"Did you build this house yourselves?" said Rip, unintentionally interrupting Amanda.

"We did indeed," said Amelia with a hint of pride. "We had to build it in the trees because whenever children stumbled across our old home, they would start eating it."

"Terribly annoying," muttered Amalia.

Amelia nodded in agreement. "Whenever we told them off, they'd get mad at *us*, and accuse *us* of devilry. Children can be so nasty when you deny them sweeties."

Amanda nudged Rip and lowered her voice. "So, did Alfred say anything about coming here?"

Rip blinked at her.

"Captain Stormalong?" she prodded. "He's coming to see me, isn't he?"

"Oh, right," said Rip. "Yes, um, he said that he was looking forward to eating some of the food."

Amanda narrowed her eyes. Clearly, this was not the answer she had been hoping for.

"And what's the name of this little gumdrop?" said Amelia, turning her attention to Rip.

"His name is Rip Van Winkle," said Jonathan.

"A boy with three names," said Amelia with a smile. "I like him already."

"Alfred has three names," mumbled Amanda.

Amelia ignored her sister and pointed at Rip's satchel with the end of her spoon (the tiny pukwudgie did likewise). "What's in there?"

"That," said the preacher, "is the reason why we're here. Rip has the pumpkin lantern of William Blaxton."

Amelia raised an eyebrow. "You don't say."

The witch put the bowl down and wiped her hands on her apron (the pukwudgie dropped its teacup and smeared its paws on its fur belly).

Amelia held out her hand to Rip. "May I see the lantern?"

Rip hesitated. He looked to Jonathan, who gave him a reassuring nod. Then he looked back at the Ginger Witch. He sensed that he could trust her, but he had seen what the lantern had done to Katy and didn't want to risk something similar happening to Amelia.

"It's all right, young one," said Amelia, with a wink. "You can give me the lantern. It won't harm me. And I promise to give it back."

Swallowing hard, Rip nodded, removed the lantern from his satchel, and handed it to the Ginger Witch. To his relief, nothing happened. Amelia raised the lantern so that it was level with her face.

"Ah, yes," said Amelia, peering into the light. "The pumpkin lantern is a fascinating thing. The light within is eternal, and yet the pumpkin itself is a symbol for mortality."

Jonathan folded his arms. "How does the pumpkin symbolize mortality?"

"How does it not?" said Amelia. "Like mortals, the pumpkin seed is planted in the darkness of the earth, where it is left to search for the light. When the plant finally sprouts, it travels along the ground, as if in search of its place in the world. Then, once the pumpkin has found its place, it blossoms into a fruit that towers above all others. And when the pumpkin is ripe, it's a veritable life-giving force. Why, if it hadn't been for pumpkins, the settlers of New England would have been undone."

"Why's that?" asked Rip.

Amelia blinked at Rip in astonishment. "Because the pumpkin was essentially all they had to eat!"

"They ate the seeds, the pulp, the meat, and even the shell," said Amalia, without looking up from the table.

"They would bake it, roast it, stew it, dry it, even eat it raw," said Amanda cheerfully. "It could be the main dish, the side dish, the dessert, or simply feed for the livestock."

Amelia nodded. "You see, the pumpkin is, in many ways, a life-giving, life-saving plant. Personally, I think that's one of the reasons why Mother Rigby made Feathertop's head out of a pumpkin."

The Ginger Witch handed the lantern back to Rip, who held it with renewed awe. Amelia rolled up her sleeves and placed her hands on her hips. "Now, I have about ten minutes before I need to get back to work," she said, turning her head from Rip to Jonathan. "So, let's get to your questions."

Jonathan cleared his throat. "Yes, well—my question is actually about Feathertop." The preacher paused for a moment, as though silently debating with himself. Finally he asked, "Where can we find him?"

Amelia smiled shrewdly. "Are you sure that's your question, John?"

The preacher shifted uncomfortably. "What do you mean?"

"Well, it seems to me that what you *really* want to know is whether or not Feathertop is *real*."

Rip saw Jonathan tighten his jaw. Apparently, Amelia had struck a nerve.

"Forgive me," said the preacher, slowly. "I just have a hard time believing that a living pumpkin-headed scarecrow is anything other than a myth."

Amelia shook her head wistfully. "Ah, Jonathan. You'd like to think of yourself as a faithful man, but in actuality, you're quite faithless."

Rip's jaw dropped.

Jonathan furrowed his brow. "Excuse me?"

"You only believe in the things you can see," said Amelia simply. She picked up her bowl and resumed stirring the batter. (Her pukwudgie companion, apparently bored by the conversation, had curled up next to its teacup and was fast asleep.) "You trust in the power of Columbia," continued Amelia, "and you trust in your own strength—how many resolutions have you written down, John? Forty? Fifty?"

"Seventy," said Jonathan. Rip noticed that the preacher's face was as set as stone.

"Exactly," said Amelia, dipping her finger into the batter and sampling it. "Seventy written resolutions—all of them entirely dependent on your own strength. That is to say, all of them depend on what you can *see*. That isn't exactly the same thing as faith, is it? And unless my ears have deceived me, you were teaching the boy a little something about faith—believing in something you cannot see and cannot prove for certain? Hmmm?"

Rip was startled by Amelia's last comment. Jonathan had talked about faith while he and Rip were on Stormalong's ship. Had Amelia somehow overheard their conversation from that distance? What else did she know? What other powers did she have?

"My resolutions have given me strength," said Jonathan sternly. "I have an iron will."

"So far," admitted Amelia. "But willpower, though important in its own way, is never enough. In order for you to be truly powerful, you must open up and trust in something *beyond* yourself—something you cannot prove for certain."

Jonathan scoffed. "And you're suggesting that 'something' is Feathertop?"

"Suggesting?" repeated Amelia. "I'm not suggesting anything. I'm *warning* you, Jonathan. There is a darkness inside of you—a beast you think you've caged with your resolutions. You cannot defeat darkness by running from it, nor can you conquer your inner demons by hiding them from the world. In order to defeat the darkness, you must bring it into the light.

"Now," continued Amelia, smiling wryly, "as to whether or not Feathertop is a myth . . . he most certainly is."

Rip couldn't believe what he had just heard. Jonathan himself looked taken aback by Amelia's startling admission.

"He is?" asked the preacher.

"Oh, absolutely!" said Amelia. "But not in the way you might think. You see, myths are different than fairy tales or legends. Legends are stories based in history and are more or less true. Myths, on the other hand, are stories containing a deeper truth—stories that transcend time. If you were to travel the world, you would find myths that are remarkably similar to one another—stories of heroes fighting the darkness with the light. For example, one of the world's most popular myths is about a powerful being who left his home to rescue people who were on the brink of death. Now tell me," she said, turning her attention to Rip, "who is that story about?"

Rip started, immediately trying to think of the right answer. "Um, Feathertop?" he guessed.

"Really?" said Amelia, her eyes twinkling with amusement. "I thought the story was about William Blaxton."

Rip paused. Thinking back on Blaxton's story, Rip realized that it was indeed very similar to the story of Feathertop.

"Then again," added Amelia thoughtfully, "it also sounds like the story of Squanto, the Indian who helped the Pilgrims of Plymouth. Or it could be the story of Prometheus, the Greek Titan who gave the gift of fire to mankind."

Rip was amazed. He had never thought of these stories as being similar to one another. Jonathan, on the other hand, seemed unimpressed.

"But that doesn't answer the question of whether or not Feathertop is real," said Jonathan.

Amelia grinned back at him. "Are you sure?"

Jonathan furrowed his brow, clearly confused by Amelia's roundabout method of answering his question.

The Ginger Witch chuckled. "Let me put it to you this way: Throughout time and across cultures, there are recurrences of the same type of stories, because these stories teach immortal truths. Feathertop is the living embodiment of the greatest truth in existence—namely, the power of light. So," she added, looking at Jonathan with penetrating eyes, "I have answered the question you *should have* asked. And that is a resounding yes; Feathertop is *very* real—for there is nothing more real than light."

"But where is he?" asked Rip. "Where can we find him?"

Amelia leaned forward. "Where do you find light?"

"Huh?" said Rip.

"Where do you find light?" repeated Amelia.

Rip was confused. He sensed that this was some sort of trick question and felt sure that he didn't know the right answer. He shrugged apprehensively. "Wherever it shines?"

"Exactly!" said the witch, her eyes on the lantern.

"*Amelia*," said Jonathan, clearly losing patience with the Ginger Witch. "There must be an actual place we can find the scarecrow."

Amelia let out a long sigh. "A *place*," she muttered, rolling her eyes. "Mortal minds are always unsettled by eternal things; they want to catch the infinite and nail it down to something finite. Impossible!"

Rip felt lost. "Are you saying we can't find Feathertop?"

"You *can*," admitted Amelia, "but not in the way you're expecting."

"Then how?"

"Ah," said Amelia with a sad smile. "Goodman Brown wondered the exact same thing. He too searched for Feathertop, desperate for answers to his own questions . . . but sadly, Goodman never found what he was looking for."

Suddenly, Amelia snapped her fingers. "Which reminds me— Goodman Brown is on his way! He should be here any moment!"

13

BRUISED APPLES

IN WHICH EVERYTHING IS A SYMBOL FOR THINGS UNSEEN...

*J*onathan sprang to his feet. "What?" he barked. "*You invited Goodman?*"

Amelia waved her hand dismissively. "Calm down, John. No, we didn't invite him. Goodman has apparently invited himself." She closed her eyes and brought a hand to her head, as though concentrating on a distant memory. She paused a few seconds before speaking again. "Yes, he believes you're here. He's readying his Lightning Horse as we speak."

Rip stood up next to Jonathan and braced himself to fight. "Right! Do you have any weapons?"

In response to this, Amelia and her two sisters laughed so hard that they were soon wiping tears from their eyes.

"Weapons?" repeated Amelia. "No, no, little gumdrop. We're *the Simmons Sisters*. We don't need weapons! Besides, we have the pukwudgies."

Out of the corner of his eye, Rip saw one of the creatures trip and fall into a large bowl of cake batter. While the surrounding pukwudgies snickered, Rip seriously doubted the mercenary power of these woodland creatures.

Amalia, who appeared not to notice the pukwudgie's fall, clapped her hands together and spoke. "Now, about those pies of yours! Amanda? Would you be a dear, and fetch the cauldron?"

Cauldron? thought Rip. *Why would they want a cauldron? Don't bad witches use cauldrons?*

"Apple, cranberry, or pumpkin?" asked Amanda.

"Pumpkin, I should think."

Amanda opened the door to a deep closet, and about a dozen pukwudgies followed her inside. After a tremendous clatter, the pukwudgies emerged, pushing an enormous cauldron the shape and color of a hollowed-out pumpkin. The pukwudgies rolled the cauldron on its side to the center of the room, where they hung it over a fire pit. Meanwhile, a separate group of pukwudgies took turns standing on tiptoes, dumping large jugs of water into the massive orange cauldron. Amanda emerged from the closet, grabbed a long spoon from the wall, and approached the giant pot.

At that precise moment, Captain Stormalong opened the door to the cottage and ducked his head inside. "Afternoon, ladies!" he bellowed.

Amanda's spoon clattered to the floor.

"Alfred!" she cried, her face as red as her hair. "What a surprise! How have you been?"

"Hello, Amanda," said Stormalong, the tip of his nose turning pink. "I'm doing very well. How are you?"

"Oh, you know," said Amanda, twirling her hair in her fingers. "Just cooking a lot of things. Getting ready for the big feasts. Also, I was planning on making a delicious dinner. So, if that's something you're interested in . . ."

Amalia rolled her eyes. "Oh, fine! I'll do the stirring." She snatched the spoon from the floor and immediately set to work.

Stormalong turned his attention to Jonathan. "Sorry I'm late! One of the barrels had a few bad apples—switched them out for some fresh ones. What did I miss?"

Jonathan adjusted his hat. "Amelia was just telling us that Goodman Brown is on his way."

The giant looked puzzled. "How do you know that?"

Amelia tapped her forehead with a knowing smile.

"Wonderful," muttered Stormalong. "Goodman Brown again. Now *there's* a bad apple!"

Amelia shook her head. "I wouldn't say he's a bad apple—more of a bruised one."

"What's the difference?" asked Rip.

"A bruised apple is not all bad," said Amelia sternly. "It still has tremendous potential." She paused and shook her head. "Oh, dear Goodman! After the death of his wife, he was simply too wounded to go on. He surrendered his lantern to someone who used its power against the early settlers."

"Who?" asked Rip.

Amelia cocked her head to one side. "Mistress Hibbins, of course."

Rip was astonished. He cast Jonathan a disbelieving glance, but the preacher didn't appear the least bit surprised. It seemed Goodman's treachery was common knowledge.

"But wait," said Rip, turning back to Amelia. "If Goodman already gave his lantern to Mistress Hibbins, then why does she want the one I have?"

"Because Mary destroyed the other one, dearie," said Amelia.

"Mary Dyer?" said Rip.

"It was the Martyr's Blessing," said Amalia, sampling a bit of the batter from the pumpkin cauldron. "Mary sacrificed her own life to destroy the pumpkin lantern and protect Boston against Mistress Hibbins."

"The lantern shattered the moment Mary was hanged," said Amelia with a sad sigh. "She had such great love for the people of Boston."

"Love *is* a powerful magic," chirped Amanda, looking at Stormalong and preparing pie crust in the most flirtatious way possible.

"But I thought you said the lantern is eternal," said Rip. "How could it be destroyed?"

"I said the *light* within the lantern is eternal—much like the light within each of us. Darkness gains power over each of us when we stop believing in the light." Amelia tossed a few spices into the pumpkin cauldron.

"And therein lies the folly of Goodman Brown!" shouted Amalia over the din. "When Goodman stopped believing in the power of light, he brought a darkness not only upon himself, but upon New England as well. Ironically, Goodman continually rejects the very thing that could lift him out of his despair."

"Poor Goodman Brown," said Amanda. "He's like a lonely pumpkin plant that refuses the light—rotting away in his swampy patch of land."

Rip suddenly remembered the pumpkin that once stood rotting in his mother's garden. The pumpkin had told him it was lonely and felt like it didn't belong. Was that how it was with Goodman Brown; did he feel lonely and out of place? Did Goodman feel as lost as Rip himself did?

"There was a time when Goodman was the brightest of the Hallows," said Amelia. "But after years of searching for Feathertop, he simply gave up. Heartbreak can break the best of us."

Hearing these words, Rip felt his heart sink even lower. "*Years?*" he repeated. "But if Goodman searched for Feathertop for years—and never found him—then how am I supposed to find Feathertop by All Hallows' Day?"

Amelia lifted her spoon and pointed it in Rip's direction, spattering flecks of batter onto the boy's coat. "You keep missing the point! It's not *where* Goodman was searching, but *how* he was searching! He had abandoned the light and could no longer find his way. Child, don't you understand? Everything you see is a symbol for what you don't see!"

"That's something you'll have to remember as the new Hallow," grunted Amalia, who was now scooping gobs of pumpkin pulp into the bubbling cauldron.

"New Hallow?" repeated Rip. "Who's the new Hallow?"

Amelia looked back at the boy. "You," she said, matter-of-factly. "That's why William Blaxton gave you the lantern."

Rip shook his head. "No, no, no," he said with a forced laugh. "I'm not the new Hallow. William just told me to take the lantern to Feathertop."

Amelia cocked her eyebrow. "Did he, *really?*"

Rip was startled by her question. Under different circumstances he would have answered in the affirmative, but something about Amelia's all-knowing gaze made him question himself.

"Yes?" answered Rip, although it came out more like a question.

Amelia stepped closer. "Are you sure that William wanted you to take the *lantern* to Feathertop?" she asked, with particular emphasis on the word "lantern."

Rip was confused, but the three sisters exchanged curious, knowing glances.

Jonathan, who was rubbing his temples, appeared to have lost all patience. "Amelia, Rip's just a boy. Of course he's supposed to take the lantern to Feathertop. Now, can you give us any idea as to where we can find that blasted scarecrow?"

Amelia let out a low sigh. "I can give you a *clue*, but you must understand that life is less about finding and more about seeking. I cannot tell you where to find Feathertop . . . I can only tell you where to seek him. Now, whether or not you find him there is another matter altogether."

Rip's heart was beating fast. "Where? Where can I seek him?"

"The best place to look is at the old home of his mother," said Amelia.

Jonathan stirred. "Mother Rigby? Where is she?"

"Everywhere," said Amelia with a smile. "But I didn't say to seek his mother; I said to seek the old home of his mother—two very different things."

Captain Stormalong scratched his head. "Well, where's that?"

"Cape Tragabigzanda!" burst Amanda.

Jonathan looked puzzled. "I'm sorry, what did you say?"

"Sounds familiar," muttered Stormalong.

"Cape Tragabigzanda is another name for Cape Ann," grunted Amalia, who was now helping the pukwudgies scoop the contents of the pumpkin cauldron into large round pans.

"It's north of here," continued Amalia. "Not far. It was first named

Cape Tragabigzanda by Captain John Smith. We told him he should use a simpler name—one that would be easier to spell—but he refused. He insisted on naming it after the love of his life—a Turkish princess who rescued him from captivity. Love makes us do strange things."

At the mention of love, Amanda batted her eyes at Captain Stormalong. Rip saw the giant's face turn a distinct shade of pink.

"Wait a minute," said Rip. "You knew Captain John Smith?"

"Of course we did!" snapped Amalia. "Who do you think brought us here? I mean, originally we wanted to settle somewhere closer to the city of Salem—"

"Which was also named by John Smith," interrupted Amanda.

"But that place was noisy even before it was the capital of Columbia," finished Amelia. "It seems Mother Rigby found it noisy as well; she lived on Cape Ann *long* before John Smith explored the area."

"How long did Mother Rigby live there?" asked Rip.

Amelia shrugged. "Who knows? Mother Rigby is the most powerful Luminary in history—time means little to her. Those who have met her and walked in her garden have often described the experience as something beyond the confines of time."

Amelia interrupted her sister. "Speaking of time, we really do need to get back to work! We only have a few days left until All Hallows' Day."

Just then, Rip heard the distant rumble of thunder.

"Hmmm," said Amelia thoughtfully. "That'll be Goodman Brown. He's mounted the Lightning Horse. You really must get going. His horse can't magically appear on Stormalong's flying ship, but it can most certainly appear on the bridge just outside this cottage—which is what I think Goodman intends to do. So, it might be best if you left through the back."

A fat pukwudgie, standing on the shoulders of an even fatter pukwudgie, opened the back door, and Amelia ushered her visitors outside. Dark clouds were rolling in.

"Wait!" cried Amalia. "Don't forget your pies!"

Amanda wobbled over to her sister while balancing three exceptionally large pies on each arm, and another on top of her head. Amelia took the pies from Amanda's arms and handed them off to Jonathan, Rip, and Stormalong.

Amanda removed the last pie from the top of her head and delivered it to Stormalong personally. "I made this one special for you," she said with a wink.

Stormalong glanced down at Amanda with fondness and spoke in an uncharacteristically high voice. "Oh. Well, that's . . . nice. Really . . . you're nice, Amanda."

Even the pukwudgies cringed at this awkward exchange.

Amelia waved her arm. "Now, back to the safety of your ship, little gumdrops!"

"Wait!" exclaimed Rip. "Where *exactly* is Mother Rigby's home?"

Amelia let out an exasperated sigh. "There you go again, wanting an exact location! Would you like a map? Would that make you happy, little Hallow?"

Rip was confused. "I—I guess?"

"Amalia, do we still have Captain Smith's map?"

"Didn't we give it to Goodman Brown?"

"No, no, no. We gave Goodman the sword."

"You gave John Smith's sword to Goodman?" asked Rip.

Amelia waved her arm distractedly. "A story for another time."

A shadow passed over them as heavy black clouds blotted out the afternoon sunlight. Rip heard another clap of thunder—only this time, it felt much closer.

"Here's the map!" cried Amanda. Brandishing a rolled-up parchment, the young witch rushed forward. After giving the document to her sister, the breathless Amanda leaned against the door frame and batted her eyes at Captain Stormalong. The giant tugged on the collar of his shirt.

Amelia unrolled the parchment and looked it over. "Yes, this is it," she said, nodding. "Oh, and would you look at that—he even included Norumbega!" Amelia rolled the sheet back up and handed it to Rip. "Here you are, little Hallow. Here is a map that will help you feel better about your journey. However, I must give you this warning: your journeys will rarely ever go as you plan. You will make mistakes, and you will feel lost. Whenever that happens, *look to the light and keep moving forward in faith.*"

Rip looked up at Amelia in surprise. He had heard something like that before, but from William Blaxton. Had Amelia somehow overheard that conversation too? Suddenly, her face became quite stern. She turned to face the front of the cottage. "Here he comes," she said.

Rip felt a wave of energy course through his veins as a bolt of lightning struck the bridge on the other side of the cottage. Rip peeked out from behind Amelia and felt the air drain from his lungs; there on the bridge, sitting astride a large, fearsome black horse, was Goodman Brown!

Amelia closed the back door, and Stormalong quietly led Rip and the preacher down a set of stairs that wound down the trunk of the gargantuan maple tree. In no time at all, they were standing on a smaller bridge directly beneath the one Goodman now occupied. Through the cracks in the bridge, Rip could see the Impure Puritan on his pitch black horse. Amelia stepped across the entrance to the Gingerbread House, toward Goodman Brown.

Goodman wasted no time with pleasantries. "Where's the boy?" he barked.

Amelia stepped forward. "Good afternoon, Goodman. Would you like something to eat?"

The man raised his arm and pointed a long finger at Amelia. "Tell me where he is, witch! I have to stop him before he ruins everything!"

Amelia folded her arms and tapped her foot, apparently unfazed by Goodman's outburst. "Before he ruins everything?" she echoed. "My dear Goodman, you have a very warped perception of how things really are. Have you spent so much time in the darkness that you cannot understand the light? Feathertop believes in him."

"Feathertop is a lie!" shouted Goodman.

"Feathertop is the truth," stated Amelia firmly. "*And he still believes in you, Goodman.* As do I. Once again, I invite you to come in for food and friendship—such as you once knew them. But if you will not accept my hospitality, then I must ask you to leave."

From his place on the lower bridge, Rip couldn't see Amelia's face, but her voice was like a chocolate-covered razor blade—the outward sweetness belying a deadly core.

"I'm not scared of you, witch," growled Goodman, shifting in his saddle.

"No?" said Amelia with a chuckle. "Then what about the pukwudgies?"

All at once, dozens of pukwudgies rushed from the cottage and across the bridge, where they scurried up Goodman's horse with unnatural speed. Using tooth and claw, the little creatures attacked Goodman Brown like a swarm of bees. Gunpowder whinnied and kicked, while Goodman howled in pain and fought against the creatures—but to no avail. The pukwudgies were both small and exceptionally agile. Barking like small dogs, they ducked in and out, biting, kicking, clawing.

Spitting out a curse, Goodman pulled on the reins, and his horse reared up onto its hind legs. A bolt of lightning suddenly split the sky, striking both Goodman and Gunpowder. Rip had to blink several times before he could see clearly enough to realize that the Puritan had vanished.

Goodman's attackers, the pukwudgies, lay on the bridge—a little stunned but otherwise unharmed. After a few brief moments, the creatures stood up and began congratulating each other in their own language.

Captain Stormalong laughed merrily as he and Jonathan headed down the bridge toward *The Courser*. Rip followed after them. Over his shoulder, Rip heard Amanda calling after them. "Don't forget to write, Alfred!"

14

MISTRESS HIBBINS

IN WHICH THE DAY IS DARK AS NIGHT...

*T*he trio boarded *The Courser* and quickly divided the pies among the crew. As the ship set sail for Cape Ann, Rip tried to get some sleep. He tossed and turned restlessly for about an hour before deciding to rise and busy himself with the chores of the ship. While he worked, Rip was struck by the fact that he hadn't slept for nearly two days. Even so, he didn't feel the least bit tired. Undoubtedly, his energy was because of the pumpkin lantern. If Rip stood still and concentrated long enough, he could almost feel the lantern's flicker—like his own heartbeat.

While he worked aboard the ship, Rip pondered all that Amelia had said about pumpkins and what they symbolized. Rip thought about the Hallows, and wondered why Amelia and her sisters had thought he was a Hallow himself. True, he carried the pumpkin, but that certainly didn't mean he was meant to be a Hallow like William Blaxton or Mary Dyer.

Besides, weren't the Hallows supposed to help people, to rescue them from harm? In his own situation, it seemed Rip was the one who needed to be helped or rescued at every turn. Rip wondered if someone like Jonathan, Stormalong, or Amelia ought to be made a Hallow instead of himself.

And weren't the Hallows supposed to be a light in the wilderness? After Charity died, Rip felt so dark and empty inside. It was as if all the light inside him had been sucked out completely, and he didn't know how to make it come back.

As he thought about this, Rip recalled something Goodman Brown had said: "You cannot relight a fire once the candle is dead. There is no redemption from the darkness of death!" Rip realized that the Puritan wasn't talking only about his own personal belief, but also about the loss of his wife.

Again he felt an unexpected twinge of sympathy for the former Hallow. Goodman, like Rip, was struggling with the painful loss of light. Perhaps Jonathan was right; perhaps there really was more good in Goodman than the Puritan himself knew. Rip wondered if there was a way to rekindle Goodman's faith. It was an odd thing, but thinking about this actually gave Rip a glimmer of hope for rekindling the light within himself.

As evening drew near, Rip glanced out to sea and noticed a patch of dark clouds in the south, which seemed to roll in at an unnatural speed. He turned to Stormalong, who was at the wheel. "Do clouds normally move that quickly over water?"

"No," said Stormalong grimly. "And I've never seen green clouds."

The clouds that billowed toward them were indeed a dark, sickly green —like the color of swamp slime.

"Do you think it's Goodman?" asked Rip.

Stormalong shook his head. "He wouldn't even try. His horse can't board this ship, remember?" The giant leaned over the wheel. "Johnny!" he called. "Any idea what that is?"

The preacher ascended the stairs and looked southward. "No idea," he said. "But I don't want to get caught in it."

"Agreed!" said Stormalong, turning the ship's wheel to the left.

"How far until we reach Cape Ann?" asked Jonathan.

Stormalong stretched out his arm. "That's it right there," he said, pointing to a distant strip of land. "At this rate, it shouldn't take us more than an hour."

Rip cast a nervous glance over his shoulder. Was it just his imagination, or had the green clouds changed direction to follow the ship? Whatever the case may have been, the clouds were picking up speed and growing closer.

"I don't like it," muttered Stormalong to Jonathan. "There's only one person who can make a storm as big as mine, and you know who that is."

"Mistress Hibbins," whispered Jonathan.

At the mention of the witch's name, Rip's blood ran cold.

"You mind giving the ship a little push?" asked Stormalong.

The preacher nodded and extended his arms. Almost immediately, a steady stream of wind rushed across the ocean, filling The Courser's sails and sending it forward with incredible force.

"I think we need to go faster," said Stormalong, still eyeing the mountainous clouds behind them.

SETH ADAM SMITH

"Easier said than done," grunted Jonathan. Nevertheless, he closed his eyes gritted his teeth, and the ship accelerated.

Rip looked back and gasped. Despite the preacher's efforts, the clouds were much closer now—a mere stone's throw away.

"Come on," Stormalong muttered to himself, gripping the helm and gritting his teeth.

The green clouds lurched forward, bubbling over the rail like green vomit.

"What is this stuff?" shouted Stormalong as the murky mist began swirling around his ankles.

Jonathan bent down to touch it. "I feel so . . . so tired," he said, dreamily. Before anyone could respond, Jonathan's eyes rolled into his head, and he fell backward in a heap.

Rip cried out and ran to Jonathan, but Stormalong stopped him.

"Wait!" he hissed. "Don't bend down! It's the clouds!"

"What?" said Rip.

"The clouds!" repeated Stormalong, pointing at the deck. "Look!"

Rip looked out across the ship and saw what Stormalong meant. The green smoke snaked its way across the deck, enveloping Stormalong's crew. One by one, each of his men yawned and fell to the deck.

"It's putting them to sleep!" exclaimed Rip.

Stormalong blinked heavily. "But why haven't you fallen asleep?"

Rip glanced at his satchel. "The lantern! It must be protecting me."

"I don't know whose magic this is," said Stormalong, his head nodding, "but it's strong! I don't think I'm going to last much longer. Can you climb to the crow's nest? Maybe . . . maybe you can find a way out. Right now, you're the only one who can help us." The giant yawned, struggling to keep his eyes open.

Rip nodded apprehensively. The thought of being alone, without anyone to help him, made his blood run cold. Finally succumbing to the clouds' power, Stormalong slumped against the rail and slowly slid down.

"Hurry, Riptide," he whispered. "Whoever is doing this to us is not a friend."

Heart beating fast, Rip ran down the stairs. He hopped gingerly over each of Stormalong's slumbering crew members and nearly tripped over a fat sailor who was peacefully sucking his thumb.

Rip clambered up the ladder of the main mast and threw open the hatch door of the crow's nest. Once inside, he placed his hands on the rail and squinted through the cold, wet fog. The clouds around him were as thick—and as green—as the mist down below. Whatever this evil was, it had made the day as dark as night.

Rip could hardly see a thing! He needed light. He fumbled with his satchel, removed the pumpkin lantern, and hoisted it into the air. What he saw made him cry out and stumble backward.

There, standing in the crow's nest before him, was a pale-faced woman —staring back at him, watching him with a wicked smile.

"Wh-who are you?" asked Rip tremulously.

"Oh, come now," said the woman with a wink. Her voice sounded sweet, yet there was something about it that Rip did not like. It made his stomach twist up into knots. "I'd think a Boston boy like yourself would know who I am." Her face was haughty and proud, and dark brown hair cascaded down her back.

Rip swallowed hard. "Mistress Hibbins?"

The sinister look on the woman's face confirmed it, and Rip's stomach filled with a sickening dread. It was Mistress Hibbins—the Boston witch who was hanged from the Great Elm and who swore to destroy Boston— standing in the crow's nest not two feet away from Rip! What was she going to do to him?

"Well done," said Mistress Hibbins. "It's nice to know Boston still remembers me—despite their foolish attempts to get rid of me."

Rip didn't know what to say. He merely stared at the witch in stupefied horror. Mistress Hibbins seemed pleased by the effect she was having on the boy.

The witch's eyes flickered to the pumpkin in Rip's hand. "Is that the lantern?"

"You can't have it," said Rip, more out of reflex than anything. He briefly considered fighting the witch, but after everything he had heard about her power, he wasn't sure he'd be able to stop her.

"Child, I'm not going to take the lantern from you," said Mistress Hibbins, shaking her head. "I want you to give it to me. Give it to me so I can put it in the hands of the Midnight Minister."

Rip swallowed hard. "Do you work for the Minister?"

"Oh, no, no, no," said Mistress Hibbins, shaking her head girlishly. She lifted her arm, and on her wrist there suddenly appeared a short length of black chain. "He works for me . . . *Rip*."

Rip froze. "How do you know my name?" he asked.

The chain vanished and the witch's eyes shimmered in the darkness. She paused for a moment, then whispered wickedly, "*I asked your family.*"

Rip was shaking now. "How—how did you find my family?"

Mistress Hibbins ignored Rip's question and leaned back against the rail. "Tell me," she said, "what's a little Puritan boy like you doing in the wilderness of the world? Shouldn't you be at home, safe inside the walls of Boston, protecting your brothers and sisters? I'm sure they're scared without you."

"What do you mean?" said Rip. "Did you do something to them?"

"Oh, Rip, why worry about them now? You weren't worrying about them when you left Boston. You certainly didn't worry about them after Charity died."

Rip felt sick to his stomach. How did this witch know so much about him? How did she know about Charity? What had Mistress Hibbins done to his family?

"Don't worry," she continued, now advancing toward the boy. "I haven't done anything to your family—*but I could*. Besides," she added with a sneer, "I don't need to do anything to them. You've already hurt them enough on your own. Do you realize how much of a burden you have been to them? You were an unwanted baby, thrown away like garbage, and raised by people who never even wanted you. Before you came into their lives, your parents were rich, happy, and free. Now they're poor, sad, and overburdened. Is that why you exist—to be a burden to others?"

Tears sprang to Rip's eyes. *She's right*, he thought. *I've only been a burden. And not just to my family, but to Jonathan Edwards, Captain Stormalong, and so many others.*

Mistress Hibbins shook her head sadly. "Rip, there's something evil inside you. You brought smallpox to your family. Because of you, they suffered. Because of you, Charity died."

Rip sank to the bottom of the crow's nest, his body numb with shock. He was breathing heavily now, desperately trying to hold himself together. "I didn't mean to do it!" he cried.

"How can that matter?" hissed the witch. "You brought the disease home! You killed your sister!"

Tears trickled down Rip's face. *She's right!* he thought to himself. *I brought the smallpox home. I almost killed my whole family; I killed Charity!* "How can I ever make it right?" he cried.

"Well," began Mistress Hibbins, "there might be something you can do . . ."

Eyes red from his tears, Rip looked up at the witch. "What is it?"

"Let go," whispered the witch. "Surrender your mind to the Slumber. You can't be expected to do this. You were never meant to have the lantern. Give it to me, and surrender to the Darkness. Once you fall asleep, you'll understand that your entire existence has all been one—bad—dream."

Rip paused, his body trembling with self-loathing. Maybe Mistress Hibbins was right. Maybe he should just give up. After all, what was the point of going on? He just kept hurting people.

The more Rip considered the witch's words, the heavier his eyelids felt.

She's right, he thought. *I can't do this.* His head began to droop. *I'm an unwanted burden.*

"If I give up," he whispered, lifting the pumpkin, "will my family be happy?"

A wicked smile curled across the witch's face. "Of course."

Rip stood up slowly. He was so tired. His body felt tingly and strange, as if his life were draining right out through his toes. He looked up at Mistress Hibbins and extended the lantern to her.

Eyes wild with excitement, the witch sprang toward the lantern. But before she could lay her hands on it, a large black bird swooped out of the sky and raked her hand with its talons.

Nathaniel!

Mistress Hibbins let out a terrifying screech and clutched her hand to her chest. Rip awakened to his senses and immediately withdrew the pumpkin lantern.

"Don't listen to her, Rip!" shouted Nathaniel, now circling high above the crow's nest. Talons outstretched, the raven made a second dive, this time aiming for the witch's unprotected face. Mistress Hibbins screeched once more and struggled against the bird. After a moment of furious fighting, she hit the rail of the crow's nest and tumbled over it, falling backward into the fog.

The raven landed on the rail, breathing hard.

"Nathaniel!" exclaimed Rip. "How are you still awake?"

"The witch's spell wasn't intended for me!" gasped the bird. "Rip, don't listen to her. She's a liar. She wants you to give up the lantern—and with it, your life. But you mustn't! Fill your life with light!"

"But I don't have any light inside of me!" cried Rip.

"Yes you do!" said Nathaniel. "Remember the graveyard. Your life—your very existence—is a light!"

At that precise moment, a green bolt of fire smashed against Nathaniel, knocking him unconscious. The bird pitched forward and crumpled to the bottom of the crow's nest.

"Nathaniel!" Rip shouted.

But before he could do anything for his friend, he heard a cruel cackle come from somewhere behind him. He turned around quickly, looked up, and saw Mistress Hibbins. She was sitting astride a broomstick, hovering in midair. Her entire arm was alive with a magical green fire. Slowly, the witch began circling the crow's nest. Her encounter with Nathaniel had left her face and arms covered in scratches, but as she circled Rip, the red lines faded away.

"Goodman Brown isn't the only one with power over death," sneered the witch. "I had to sell my soul in the woods, but I got my power."

"Who did you sell your soul to?" said Rip, the lantern wobbling with the movement of his trembling hand.

The witch cackled. "Oh, dear child, how little you know of the world! I sold my soul to the Dark Woodsman, and he taught me how to live forever. All I had to do was give my death to a baby. It's an old curse—the opposite of a Martyr's Blessing. It keeps me young and makes me impervious to death. But now I want something more."

Rip stared at Mistress Hibbins in horror. He didn't know how someone could be so evil, so cruel, or so malevolent as to sacrifice a baby.

"What more could you possibly want?" asked Rip, breathing heavily.

The witch sneered and glanced out across the ocean. "When we first came to Boston, Governor Winthrop told us that the eyes of all people were upon us. He told us our hearts should be 'knit together' in love—and if they were, Boston would be 'a city upon a hill,' a light to the world. He said that if we ever dealt falsely with each other, then Boston would be destroyed."

Mistress Hibbins turned her attention back to Rip. The expression on her face made his blood run cold. "*Boston dealt falsely with me!*" she hissed. "Boston rejected me! I had no place in their New World." As she spoke, a thin green snake slithered out of her sleeve and wrapped itself around her arm. "You ask me what I want? I want *darkness*—darkness and death for every citizen in Boston! I want to extinguish the light upon the hill!"

"Is that why you want to give the lantern to the Midnight Minister?" asked Rip. "So he can use it against Boston?"

"Very good, little Puritan. You see, the lantern can magically give life, but it can also magically take life. Now," she extended a fiery green hand, "give me the lantern."

Rip's eyes drifted to the fire in the witch's hand, and he felt his breathing begin to slow. He was mesmerized by the fire's movements, unable to look away. As he stared into the open flame, thoughts of Charity and his own life bubbled to the surface of his mind. Rip was again overcome by feelings of sadness and despair; he felt as though his life was meaningless and his situation was hopeless. He just knew that he was a burden to his family and that he was no match for Mistress Hibbins.

Once again, Rip felt that the only thing he could do was give up. Slowly, he lifted the lantern to give it to Mistress Hibbins. As he did so, the warm light from within the pumpkin flickered on his face, drawing his gaze away from the witch. All at once, Rip remembered something.

"Feathertop," he whispered.

"What?" hissed Mistress Hibbins, sounding very much like an angry cat.

But Rip wasn't listening to the witch; he was looking into the light of the pumpkin, recalling a distant memory. In it, Rip was a baby, lying in an open grave. Naked and alone, he looked up at the stars above and shivered. It was cold and dark, and he was scared. He started to cry. Suddenly, a figure appeared—a scarecrow with a glowing pumpkin for a head. The scarecrow reached out and touched Rip on the chest.

"Hush, child," it said. "The sun will rise."

Back on the ship, Rip raised his head and looked directly at Mistress Hibbins. "Feathertop!" he repeated, only louder this time.

"Feathertop is a lie!" screeched Mistress Hibbins.

"No he isn't!" proclaimed Rip, raising the lantern high above his head. "He is the light in the wilderness!"

It was as if Rip had touched an open flame to a barrel of gunpowder. Like an explosion, bright, fiery light erupted from the lantern. The surrounding mists of darkness were immediately dispelled, and the brilliant sunset on the horizon shone forth.

"No!" cried the witch.

Down below, Rip could hear the shouts and groans of Stormalong's waking crew. The witch's sleeping spell had been broken!

Mistress Hibbins made a desperate lunge toward Rip, but she was knocked off course by a sudden gust of wind. Rip looked down to see Jonathan Edwards pulling himself to his feet while simultaneously directing the wind. The witch crashed between the mast and sail but managed to latch onto one of the ropes. She clung to the rope and pointed her broomstick toward the crow's nest. The green snake slithered from the witch's arm, down the broomstick, and onto the upper part of the mast, where it wrapped its body around the wooden structure and moved toward Rip.

As it moved, the snake doubled, then tripled, and quadrupled in size! In no time at all, its body had grown to the size of a tree trunk. Without waiting to see how much bigger the snake would get, Rip stashed the lantern into his satchel, opened the door to the crow's nest, and fled down the ladder. The snake followed after him at a blinding speed, nearly close enough to nip his shoulder.

In his haste, Rip missed one of the ladder rungs, lost his footing, and fell the last few feet to the deck below, landing on his back. He looked up and saw the giant snake open its jaws wide. Rip held out his hands in a weak attempt to defend himself, but he didn't have to. Captain Stormalong, free from the witch's curse, leapt forward and punched the snake in the jaw with the force of a cannonball.

The snake hit the mast and began swinging around the thick pole like a tethered ball. The creature quickly unraveled itself, and then fell to the deck with a smack. Stormalong thundered toward his opponent. The snake looked back at him, flicked its tongue in the air, and vaulted toward the giant. With remarkable agility, Stormalong caught the snake in mid-air, swung it around his giant head, and threw it across the deck. Without waiting for the snake to recover, Stormalong dove into the creature's mass of coils and began pummeling the snake's head with his bare hands.

Rip stood in awe. Watching the giant wrestle the monstrous snake was like watching a hurricane grapple with a tornado. The struggle was a furious tangle of coils and limbs, fists and fangs.

High above him, Rip heard Mistress Hibbins cackle. He looked and saw the witch tossing green bolts of fire onto the deck below. All around him, sailors were dashing about. Some were helping their Captain by slashing at the giant snake with swords, while others were simply trying to avoid the wrath of Mistress Hibbins and her fire bolts. No doubt sensing Rip's eyes upon her, she looked down and smiled malevolently.

Rip didn't linger. He took off across the deck toward Jonathan Edwards. The pale-faced preacher was leaning heavily against the rail of the ship, obviously weakened by the effects of the green mist. Rip dashed up the steps, careful to avoid several planks of wood that were lying about.

"What do we do?" asked Rip.

Jonathan shook his head. "I can't do anything!" he shouted. "She's too strong."

The witch, who seemed to have heard this, turned on her broomstick and made a rapid dive toward Jonathan, a bolt of green fire in her hand. But before the witch could strike the preacher, Jonathan suddenly stood up straight and raised his arm. A sharp breeze surged across the deck, scooping up a plank of wood in the process. The wood flew on the wind with great speed and smashed against the oncoming witch. For a brief moment, Mistress Hibbins hovered in midair as her eyes rolled up into her skull. Then she slumped over and fell onto the deck, her broomstick clattering out in front of her.

The preacher smiled and readjusted his hat.

Rip, astonished by what had just happened, looked from the preacher to the plank, then back again. Jonathan had lured Mistress Hibbins down so that he could pummel her with that plank.

"You tricked her?" said Rip. "But you're a preacher. Preachers don't lie."

Jonathan shrugged. "I never said I was perfect. Now, come on! We have to help Stormalong!"

The Captain was on his side, his entire torso wrapped in the snake's coils. The beast tightened its grip, and the giant's face turned an unnatural shade of purple. One of Stormalong's men dashed forward and sliced the snake's exposed skin. The monster roared, relaxing its grip just long enough for Stormalong to breathe and wrench out his left arm. In one quick movement the Captain grabbed the snake's head and squashed it like an overripe peach. Rip had to look away.

Still gasping for air, Stormalong wriggled free of the snake's body—which, although headless, was still writhing violently. "Well, that was fun," breathed Stormalong.

Several crewmen chuckled, albeit halfheartedly; most of them were still recovering from the sleeping spell.

The relative peace of the moment, however, was quickly shattered by an animalistic scream. Mistress Hibbins was on her feet, a trickle of blood streaming down her forehead. Raising her hands, the witch blasted green fire in all directions, scattering both men and debris.

Captain Stormalong lowered his head and dashed toward the witch like a stampeding bull, but she was too quick for him. With a flick of her hand, Mistress Hibbins blasted Stormalong back against the mast of his own ship. Rip didn't know whether it was the mast's wood or Stormalong's head that made the cracking noise. Either way, the giant fell to the ground, unconscious.

The witch's green eyes landed on Rip. Had those eyes been able to shoot poison, Rip was sure he would have died on the spot; everything about the woman's presence screamed venom.

Ahab, Stormalong's first mate, drew his sword and dashed toward the witch, slashing her arm. Taken by surprise, Mistress Hibbins turned to fight with Ahab. With the witch distracted, Jonathan yanked on Rip's arm. Rip turned to see that the preacher was standing on the edge of the ship, holding the witch's broom.

"Do you have the lantern?" Jonathan shouted.

Rip's hand went to the satchel at his side. He nodded.

"Then jump!" he said.

Before he even had time to think about what was happening, Rip followed the preacher's lead and dove off the ship into the open air. For a brief moment the two tumbled toward the ocean below, before Jonathan managed to get the broom steadied under himself and scoop up Rip next to him. Once the two were astride it, the broomstick pulled out of its dive almost immediately and started bouncing through the air like a stone skipping across water. Jonathan clung tightly to the broom with both hands, while his legs dangled helplessly.

Heart thumping madly, Rip looked ahead and saw something that made his stomach churn.

"Trees!" he shouted.

Jonathan looked up. Straight ahead of them, and approaching fast, was the shoreline of Cape Ann—filled with numerous tall trees. Jonathan made a quick attempt to change the broomstick's course, but it was too late. They sailed into the trees at a blinding speed.

After a breathless moment, Rip felt his chest slam against a large branch, and everything went dark.

15

THE LOST PEARL

IN WHICH EVERYONE LOSES THEIR WAY...

*R*ip could see Charity.

She was standing in a beautiful garden, the likes of which Rip had never seen, and she was aglow with a most wonderful light. Rip opened his mouth to speak, but all that came out was a muffled sound, as if he were underwater. He stepped toward his sister, but she raised her hands and shook her head vigorously. Rip was confused. Why didn't she want him to come to her? His heart sank. Was she angry with him?

With an expression of deep concern on her face, Charity pointed to something behind Rip. He glanced over his shoulder and saw a bent and shriveled man reaching out to him. Alarmed, Rip stepped out of the way, and the man fell to his knees. Rip drew back in horror at what he saw next: on the man's back was a hideous creature. Small and thin, the creature looked like a freakish child with long limbs, floppy ears, and a pointy nose. It clung to the man with a lengthy black chain and glared up at Rip with devilish black eyes.

The old man held out a rotten apple and spoke in a hollow, husky voice. "Little boy, would you like this delicious apple? I promise it will make all of your pain go away."

Disgusted, Rip looked from the man to Charity, who shook her head and mouthed the words, "He's lying." Rip was perplexed. Of course the man was lying; that was obvious enough. Why did Charity feel the need to explain that?

A shadow descended on Rip. He looked over his shoulder and saw the Midnight Minister looming over him. The Minister reached out with a long, spidery hand and grabbed Rip by the throat. Overcome by a bitter coldness, Rip closed his eyes.

RIP AWOKE with a start and sat bolt upright, bringing his hands to his neck. He glanced around, shivering in the cold night air, and discovered that he was sitting on the ground in a forest, faintly illuminated by the red glow of a dying fire. Rip's eyes lingered momentarily on the fire. Who made that fire? Did Jonathan make it? Where was he?

Rip straightened his back and groaned. There was a sharp pain in his chest. He was covered in scrapes and bruises. He glanced around and saw the satchel lying next to his leg. He was relieved to see the slight glow of the pumpkin lantern from within. Slowly, he forced himself to his feet.

"I wouldn't move if I were you," said a girl's voice.

Rip attempted to whirl around, but not having the strength, he merely cried out, stumbled, and fell backward. The girl emerged from the trees. She wore a hooded cloak. It was too dark for Rip to see much of her face, but he could tell that she was carrying a bundle of sticks and logs.

Seeing Rip on the ground, the girl shook her head. "What did I just tell you about trying to move?"

"Who are you?" said Rip, a little more forcefully than intended.

"You might try saying 'Thank you.'" She dropped the wood next to fire.

"'Thank you' for what?"

"For saving your life," replied the girl. Without another word, she knelt down and coaxed the fire into a pleasant blaze.

"How did you save my life?" said Rip.

"I was walking through the woods and saw you fall through the trees and land on a branch," said the girl. "Boys don't normally fall from the sky, so I knew something must be wrong. I thought about leaving you there, but then I decided to pull you down."

Rip glanced up at the tall trees and wondered how the girl had been able to reach him, let alone carry him down. "Who are you?" asked Rip, not knowing what else to say.

The girl narrowed her dark eyes. "My name is Pearl. Pearl Prynne."

Rip screwed up his face in confusion. "Pearl? Your name is Pearl?"

"You catch on quick," she said sarcastically. "Are you planning on standing there for the rest of the night?"

Rip shook his head dumbly.

"Well, sit down, then," she ordered. "I've got some bread and cheese, and I might share it with you if you wipe that stupid look off your face."

At the mention of food, Rip's stomach growled. He couldn't recall the last time he had eaten anything. He sat down next to the fire. Pearl handed him a large chunk of cheese.

"Thank you," said Rip.

"About time you said that," replied Pearl tartly. "Now, what's your name?"

"Rip Van Winkle." He took a cautious bite of cheese while watching Pearl out of the corner of his eye.

Pearl poked the fire with a stick. "Why are you staring at me?"

Startled, Rip turned away. "Sorry!" he said, taking another bite of cheese.

"It's all right," said the girl. "I guess I'm used to it. Where are you from?"

"Boston."

"*Boston*," repeated the girl, contemptuously. "Figures."

"You've been there?" asked Rip.

"I was born there."

"Really? And your last name is Prynne? I don't think I know any Prynnes."

"You might have heard of my mother," muttered Pearl, "but she disappeared a long time ago."

There was a long silence. Finally, Rip spoke: "I'm sorry to hear about your mother. My sister Charity died a little while ago. It hurts to lose someone you love."

Pearl's expression softened. "I'm sorry to hear that."

"What about your father?" asked Rip, changing the subject.

Pearl snorted. "Which one?"

"Huh?"

"My father or my *step*father? If you're asking about my *real* father, I never really knew him. I don't think *anyone* really knew him."

Sensing the anger in Pearl's voice, Rip decided that it might be best to change the subject. "Where do you live? Where's your home?"

"I don't have a home," said Pearl, staring into the fire. "I used to live with my stepfather, but then I ran away."

"You ran away?" repeated Rip. "Why would you do a thing like that?"

Growing up in such a large, loving family, Rip couldn't understand why any child would want to run away from home. He felt a pang of guilt mixed with fear remembering the terrible things Mistress Hibbins had said about his family. Was his family really better off without him? Nathaniel had told Rip that the witch was lying, but Rip had his doubts.

Nathaniel! Rip had almost forgotten about Nathaniel! The last time Rip had seen the bird was in the crow's nest. Was the raven all right?

"I ran away from home because I had to," continued Pearl, interrupting

SETH ADAM SMITH

Rip's thoughts. "My stepfather is an evil, evil man. Besides," she added with a glare, "if I hadn't run away from home, I wouldn't have found you. Why did you fall from the flying ship? I mean, I'm *assuming* you fell from the flying ship—"

"You saw the ship?" asked Rip. Instantly, his mind was flooded with concern for his friends. Had Mistress Hibbins hurt Nathaniel? What about Captain Stormalong and his crew? Were they still alive? He wanted to ask Pearl all of these questions, but he didn't know what she had seen or how much she knew about magic. He didn't yet know if he could trust her.

"Of course I saw the ship!" exclaimed Pearl. "It was an enormous *flying* ship—kind of hard to miss."

"Then you know about magic?"

Pearl looked at Rip incredulously. "Of course I know about magic! How do you think I kept her from finding you?"

"Who did you keep from finding me?"

"Mistress Hibbins! My goodness, boy! Did you hit your head, or are you always this thick?"

Rip was taken aback by the girl's brazenness. "I'm only trying to understand," he said defensively.

The girl rolled her eyes. "Yes, she was flying overhead looking for you." Pearl threw another log on the fire. "She called upon her broom to return to her and flew over the trees, looking for you. She probably would have killed you if I hadn't found you first. That Mistress Hibbins is a real piece of work. I've had a few run-ins with her, myself."

"But how did you prevent her from finding me?" wondered Rip out loud, remembering the incredible power of Mistress Hibbins.

Pearl grinned mischievously. "Do you think this patch of forest is real?" she asked.

Rip was confused. *What does she mean by that?* "Yes?"

Pearl snapped her fingers, and the surrounding trees evaporated. Rip jumped in surprise. He glanced around and saw that they were actually sitting in a small, grassy field. The real line of forest began about thirty or forty feet away.

Rip was astounded. "How did you do that?"

Pearl smiled and shrugged her shoulders. "It's a trick I learned from my stepfather. Deceptions are his specialty. He's a professional liar, that one."

"Is that why you ran away?"

Pearl took a deep breath and looked up at the night sky. "I ran away because nobody wanted me. No one has ever wanted me. Not my father, not my mother, and certainly not my stepfather. I don't belong anywhere."

Rip's heart sank. He felt sad for Pearl. Her words reminded him of the day he first met Charity.

"You could always stay with me and my family," he offered.

Pearl smirked. "What?"

"Yes," said Rip. "I'm sure you would be welcome."

Her look of disbelief only deepened. "Why would your family want someone like me?"

"My parents adopted all of my brothers and sisters. There are twelve of us. Well," he added, remembering his sister Charity, "eleven . . . now."

Hugging her knees close to her chest, Pearl gazed at Rip curiously. "You really think your family would let me stay?"

Rip smiled. "You're a good person. Why wouldn't they?"

Pearl blinked back at Rip with a puzzled expression, as though such a thought had never occurred to her.

In the distance, they heard a rustling in the trees, and suddenly a figure emerged from the forest.

"Jonathan!"

Rip, despite the pain in his chest, stood up and stared at the preacher in astonishment. Jonathan was pale and haggard, and looked like he was about ready to collapse.

"Rip," he breathed, "where have you been? I've been searching for you all day!"

Rip cocked his head to one side. "All day? How long have we been separated?"

"It's October 30, Rip!" barked Jonathan. "We have less than two days to get the lantern to Mother Rigby's house!"

October 30! thought Rip, his stomach sinking into his boots. Had he really been unconscious for a full day?

"Mother Rigby?" repeated Pearl. "You're trying to find Mother Rigby?"

"Who is this girl?" demanded Jonathan. "What have you told her?"

Rip was surprised by the level of anger in the preacher's voice. "I haven't told her anything! She saved my life and kept me hidden from Mistress Hibbins."

Jonathan turned a furious gaze on Pearl. "How did you keep him hidden? I must have walked through this area a dozen times! What are you, some kind of *demon*?"

Pearl got to her feet, fire blazing in her eyes. *"DON'T CALL ME THAT!"*

A sudden wind blew through the campsite, fanning the small fire into a large flame. Rip rushed forward and stood between his two friends.

"Will everyone please calm down!" he shouted.

Jonathan ignored Rip. "You haven't answered my question!" said the preacher, pointing a finger at the girl. "Who are you?"

She narrowed her eyes. "Pearl."

Jonathan's lips parted slightly. "Pearl?" he repeated. "Pearl *Prynne*? The daughter of Hester Prynne?"

Pearl made no reply. She simply glared up at the preacher.

Rip watched Jonathan's expression change—the anger was still there, but now it was mixed with something else. It was as if the preacher were looking at some relic from the past—an artifact that disgusted him.

After an uneasy pause, Jonathan broke the silence and spoke very slowly. "Rip, get your satchel. We're leaving right now."

"But where are we going?" asked Rip.

"There's a path that leads northward. It's not far from here."

"I wouldn't take the path if I were you," said Pearl ominously.

"And why not?" said Jonathan, clearly nettled by the girl's suggestion.

"Because that path leads straight to Dogtown."

"Anything's better than here."

"Then let me come with you," said Pearl. "I was just there. I know my way around—"

Jonathan pointed a long finger at the girl. "You'll stay away from us!" he ordered. "I don't ever want to see your face again—do you understand?"

Pearl narrowed her eyes and backed away. Rip was dumbfounded. He had never seen the preacher act this way before. What was wrong with him? What was it about Pearl that made him so angry?

"Come on, Rip!" said Jonathan. "If we hurry, we can be there in a few hours." Without waiting for Rip to comply, the preacher readjusted his hat and stormed off.

Biting his lip, Rip picked up his satchel and started following Jonathan, but stopped after a few paces. He turned around and jogged back to Pearl, who had been silently staring down at the ground. She looked up in surprise.

"What are you doing?" she said.

Rip hesitated momentarily before giving Pearl a tight hug. "Thank you," he whispered.

Pearl blinked up at him in astonishment. "Y-you're welcome," she stammered awkwardly.

Rip squeezed Pearl's wrist reassuringly. "I meant what I said. If you're ever in Boston, you can stay with us. The Van Winkle home is a belonging place, and you will always be welcome."

Pearl nodded, disbelief etched into her face. With that, Rip turned to leave, but the girl suddenly reached out and caught him by the hand.

"Be careful, Rip," she whispered. "Dogtown isn't what it appears to be." With that, Pearl let go of his hand, grabbed a small bag from the ground, and took off into the woods.

For a brief moment, Rip wondered what Pearl meant about Dogtown. But before he could give that much thought, he heard the preacher call his name angrily. Rip turned and sprinted in the direction of Jonathan's voice.

The preacher was waiting for Rip on a narrow, winding dirt road. "What were you two talking about?" he demanded.

"I just went back to thank her," said Rip defensively. "And I told her that she could stay with our family in Boston."

Jonathan appeared mortified. "Why would you tell her that?"

"Because she's all alone," explained Rip. "She said no one wants to be her friend."

"There's a reason for that, Rip," growled the preacher. He turned sharply on his heel and moved down the path.

Rip followed, but he couldn't help feeling a little resentful. Why was Jonathan so angry?

Besides, it's not as if I chose to be unconscious! Rip thought. *I didn't do anything wrong, and neither did Pearl.*

As Rip and Jonathan pressed on through the forest, the path became less and less visible. Even with the light of a full moon, Rip was having trouble seeing his way ahead. Finally, they came to a stop at the foot of a giant boulder. The preacher removed his hat, exposing his head to the moonlight. Rip couldn't help but see that the preacher's forehead was drenched in sweat.

Noticing Rip's gaze, the preacher replaced his hat and rubbed his eyes. Rip thought the man looked dazed and confused. "Jonathan, are you all right?"

"I'm fine!" snapped Jonathan.

"Do you know where we're going?"

"Of course I do!" barked Jonathan. "I'm just a little . . . turned around, that's all."

Rip glanced around and scratched his head. There seemed to be faint paths branching off in nearly every direction.

"It's this way!" said Jonathan, pointing to a path that curved around another large boulder.

Obediently, Rip followed the preacher around the bend, only to discover another cluster of diverging paths. With a grunt of frustration, Jonathan quickly chose a path that led up a small hill. Before long, the preacher turned around and headed back down.

"Dead end," he muttered before storming off down a different path.

Rip was worried. With no signs or markers, there was no way of knowing which path was the correct one; he wasn't even sure if he knew how to get back to Pearl's campsite from here. Rip's breathing quickened. With so many choices and no clear direction, it was beginning to feel as though he and the preacher were stuck in a spider web. It was then that Rip heard something that made his blood run cold.

Rattle. Rattle. Rattle.

Jonathan stopped and looked back at Rip. "What was that?"

Rattle. Rattle. Rattle.

Rip swallowed hard. "It's the Midnight Minister," he whispered. "He's in the forest."

Fear swept across the preacher's face.

Rip pulled the pumpkin lantern from his satchel and held it out in front of him, casting its light across the trees.

Rattle. Rattle. Rattle.

Out of the corner of his eye, Rip saw something. He turned and peered into the trees. Was it just his imagination, or had one of the trees moved? He took a step closer, breathing slowly. In the darkness, he saw a huge figure. Rip felt his heart skip a beat. At first, he thought it might be the Midnight Minister, but it wasn't. It was something else. It had a large round head and glowing triangular eyes—eyes that gazed directly at Rip.

It was Feathertop!

The scarecrow paused and motioned for Rip to follow before plunging deeper into the woods. Rip called out to Jonathan. "It's Feathertop!"

Jonathan was startled. "Are you sure?"

"Yes!" Rip pointed his lantern into the woods. "He went that way."

Without waiting for Jonathan's response, Rip ran after the scarecrow. Soon he was standing on the exact spot where Feathertop had stood. He stopped, and heard the preacher jogging to catch up to him. Rip glanced around, scanning the forest for any sign of the scarecrow. He heard a crack to his right and turned just in time to see Feathertop disappear behind a boulder.

"Wait!"

"Rip!" called Jonathan. "Slow down!"

But Rip ignored the preacher. He had to get to Feathertop! As he rounded the corner of the boulder, Rip let out a cry of dismay; Feathertop was not there. Once again Rip raised the lantern and looked in every direction, desperate for any sign of the scarecrow.

Far ahead, in the midst of a dense thicket of trees, Rip thought he saw a faint glow. He ran forward, heedless of the brush and brambles that tore at his clothes and cut his skin. As he ran, the light in the distance disappeared. Not knowing where to go, Rip was forced to come to a complete stop. Breathing heavily, he wiped the sweat from his forehead as he continued to scan the area.

Just then, a small figure ran into the clearing and came to an abrupt stop in front of Rip. Alarmed, Rip took two steps back before realizing that the person, a boy roughly his age, was covered in an orange glow. The same glow he had seen surrounding his vision of Mary Dyer.

The boy was clutching his left arm and glancing around the forest. He was obviously terrified. Rip's eyes darted from the boy to the pumpkin lantern.

It's not real, thought Rip. *It's just another vision—like the one with Mary Dyer. But who is he?*

Rip narrowed his eyes, carefully examining the boy. There was something about him—something oddly familiar about his pointed nose.

"Grandpa?" said the boy, his chin trembling. "Grandpa, where are you?"

Rip noticed blood dripping from the boy's arm.

"Grandpa?" called the boy again, his eyes brimming with tears. "Please help me! There's something in the forest!"

There came a loud rustling in the trees, and both Rip and the boy looked to see what it was.

Jonathan Edwards burst into the clearing. "Rip!" he cried, angrily. "What on earth are you doing?"

Rip glanced back to the spot where the boy had been standing. He was gone!

"I-I thought I saw Feathertop," stammered Rip.

"Of course you did," muttered Jonathan. "Whatever happened to that map of yours?"

The map! thought Rip, slapping his forehead. *Of course!* Amelia had given him a map that included Cape Ann. Surely the map would help them find their way out of this mess!

"Umm," mumbled Rip, stuffing his hands into his pockets. "I don't . . . I don't . . ." he could feel his face turning red. "I don't think I have it."

Jonathan's face was livid. *"What?"*

"I must have left it on Stormalong's ship."

"That means it's in the hands of Mistress Hibbins!" said Jonathan, his fists clenched. "You know, Rip, when someone gives you a map and tells you it will help you find your way, you don't just toss it aside!"

Rip's mouth fell open as his mind made a startling connection. "Jonathan . . . what happened to you?"

The preacher narrowed his eyes. "What do you mean?"

"In the forest," whispered Rip, "when you were a boy . . . "

Jonathan's pale face went slack. "What do you—what do you mean?"

"I saw you, as a boy, in the light of the lantern. You were running—running through the woods. You were looking for your grandfather . . ."

Jonathan's breathing quickened, and Rip saw a childlike, fearful expression sweep across the preacher's otherwise stern face. "My grandfather," he began, his voice barely above a whisper, "my grandfather was . . . a very bad man."

"It looked like you were running from a monster," said Rip.

"No," said Jonathan, the blood draining from his face. "My grandfather . . . *my grandfather* was the monster. He took me into the woods and . . ."

Jonathan blinked, and all at once he seemed to regain himself, his expression once again cold and harsh. He let out a string of foul words.

Rip was shocked. "Jonathan, what's wrong with you?"

"What's wrong with *me*?" Jonathan advanced toward Rip. "*I'm* not the one who forgot the map and led us on a wild goose chase through the woods! It's all that girl's fault!"

"Pearl?"

"She put some kind of evil spell on this forest—or on you!"

"She's just a girl!" exclaimed Rip.

"Just a girl!" snorted Jonathan. "She's much older than she looks. Do you know who her mother is?"

Rip shook his head, his anger rising. Why was Jonathan treating him this way? And why should it matter who the girl's mother was?

"Let's just say that Pearl's mother did a very bad thing," said Jonathan, "and Pearl is the living embodiment of that mistake."

Rip felt a wave of white-hot anger surge inside of him. "You're saying that Pearl is a mistake?" He was thinking about Charity, and how her father had said something similar to her.

"What her mother *did* was a mistake," corrected Jonathan, "and it hurt a lot of people—"

"But you're calling her a mistake!" interrupted Rip, his anger bubbling over. "Is that what you really believe? That people should be punished for the mistakes of others?"

Jonathan sneered. "We're *all* sinners in the hands of an angry God, Rip!"

"But she helped me!"

Jonathan grabbed Rip roughly by the shoulders. "Rip, did you ever stop to think about *how* she helped you? Hmmm? Pearl hid you in plain sight for a full day. Think about it, boy," Jonathan added, shaking Rip. "She hid in the shadows and covered up the truth. If that's not dark magic, then I don't know what is. Darkness always tries to hide the truth!"

"Like you do?" said Rip, glaring up at the preacher.

Jonathan froze. "What did you say?"

Rip's eyes were burning with resentment. He hadn't intended to say that, but the preacher's words about Pearl had cut Rip to the core. Without a family or home, Pearl was, in many ways, a lost and wandering soul—Rip knew what that felt like. But instead of being sympathetic toward Pearl, the preacher's words were thoughtless and cruel. Rip couldn't let Jonathan talk about Pearl like that.

"What did you say?" repeated the preacher, shaking Rip again.

Rip wrenched himself free of Jonathan's grasp and fixed his eyes on him. "Everyone says you're hiding something. Katy said you have secrets, and Goodman said you're a wolf in sheep's clothing. What does that mean?"

Jonathan paused. "You wouldn't understand," he said.

"So, you *are* hiding something!"

"I said you wouldn't understand!" repeated Jonathan furiously. "No one could!"

"You judge Pearl—a girl you don't even know—while you knowingly hide the darkness in yourself?"

"It's different," said Jonathan. "That girl's mother couldn't control her passions. She brought evil into the world. I obey the law; I keep my darkness caged!"

"Is that why you have all those resolutions?" said Rip. "Because you're trying to 'cage' the darkness? How can that work? Amelia was right. You can't defeat the darkness by keeping it caged inside you."

Jonathan snorted and wiped his brow. "So you think you can teach me morals? All right, Rip. Let's see if you can find the moral in this story: Years ago, Ann Hibbins and Mary Dyer were the best of friends. At the time, Ann was in love with a man, a minister by the name of Arthur Dimmesdale. But Arthur didn't love Mistress Hibbins. Arthur was in love with Hester Prynne, Pearl's mother.

"Against Boston's laws, Arthur and Hester met together in secret. Mary Dyer learned about the affair but kept the truth hidden from Ann. Nonetheless, Ann found out, and the betrayal drove her mad with jealousy and rage. That rage was what inspired Ann to wander into the forest and make a deal with the Dark Woodsman. She sold her soul for the power to ruin everyone who had wronged her. Mary was the first to be cursed, followed by Hester. Mary gave birth to a monstrous child, and Hester gave birth to a child named Pearl—a child who would never grow old.

"Now, tell me," said Jonathan, advancing on Rip, "what is the moral of that little story?"

The preacher paused, giving Rip time to answer. Slowly, Rip shook his head.

"*Never disobey*," hissed Jonathan. "Never give in to your passions. Cage whatever evil is inside of you, and never let the monster out. Some things are too dangerous to be brought to light."

Jonathan's eyes flashed yellow, and Rip took two steps back. The preacher, apparently satisfied that he had made his point, turned and began walking down a different path. As Rip watched the preacher move away, a thought suddenly sprang to his mind. He called out to Jonathan.

"I don't think that's the moral of the story!"

Jonathan turned on his heel, his eyebrow raised. "Is that so?" he sneered.

Rip swallowed hard. "I think the moral is that we should be true. I mean, Hester, Arthur, Mary, and Mistress Hibbins—they all had secrets. Their secrets caused all the problems, not their passions. Maybe that's the *real* cause of the Terrible Slumber."

Jonathan tilted his head. "What do you mean?"

Rip swallowed hard. "Well, Nathaniel said that the Luminaries came to the New World pretending to be Puritans—pretending to be simple folk. They hid their light from the world. Maybe, after a while, they just started to believe they *were* simple—that they were merely 'sinners in the hands of an angry God,' as you said. Maybe they forgot their true magic because their real identities were buried under layers of darkness. My father once told me that the only way to fight the darkness around us is to light a fire within us. I never really understood what he meant . . . until now."

Jonathan's hardened face suddenly relaxed. He stared at Rip with an almost reverential expression, as though the boy had somehow provided the answer to a long-held question. Rip wanted to ask what the preacher was thinking, but before he could speak, they heard growling in the bushes.

Rip jerked his head around. "What's that?"

Jonathan raised a hand to Rip, gesturing for him to be still. "Dogs," he said. "Quick! Put the lantern back in the satchel."

Rip did as he was told and just in time, for they were soon encircled by a pack of wild dogs. Rip's heart leapt into his throat. Normally he liked dogs, but these animals were big, vicious, and obviously hungry. Teeth bared, the animals moved in slowly, forcing Jonathan and Rip to stand back to back.

"Any ideas?" said Jonathan to Rip.

"Me?" hissed Rip. "I was hoping you had an idea."

"I can't move the wind, if that's what you're suggesting," said Jonathan. "I don't know if you've noticed, but I'm not *exactly* feeling myself at the moment."

"Oh, really?" said Rip sarcastically.

Several dogs snapped their jaws and moved in closer.

"Who goes there?" said a commanding man's voice.

Three stout soldiers emerged from the trees, each carrying a long musket directed at Rip and Jonathan. As the men entered the clearing, the dogs relaxed and backed off slightly.

Rip was surprised by the men's uniforms—they were made of some of the finest linens Rip had ever seen. It was clear that these weren't back-woods farmers or rangers, but well-trained, professional soldiers of the highest order.

"Identify yourselves!'" commanded a tall, bald soldier, his musket still raised.

"Jonathan Edwards," said the preacher.

The bald man lowered his musket. "The Library Keeper?"

Jonathan nodded, and the officer gestured for the other soldiers to lower their weapons. "Unbelievable," he muttered, extending a hand. "I'm Captain Armitage of the Columbia Militia."

The preacher took the man's hand. "Captain Armitage," he acknowl-edged, "how wonderful to finally meet you. We made use of your 'tomb' in the South Burying Ground of Boston a few days ago."

Captain Armitage nodded toward Rip. "And who is this?"

"This is my apprentice, Rip Van Winkle."

"How do you do?" said the Captain, with a slight nod.

Not knowing what to say, Rip just stood there awkwardly.

"Since when does the Columbia Militia use such aggressive dogs?" asked Jonathan, an unmistakable note of suspicion in his voice.

"What, these pups?" laughed Captain Armitage. He turned to the dogs, all of which stared back at him with cold hostility. "We use them for extra security, is all."

"Now I know where Dogtown gets its name," muttered Rip.

"What brings the two of you here, anyway?" asked the Captain.

Jonathan hesitated. "It's a long story."

"Well, save it for later," said the Captain. "I imagine Governor Chilling-worth will want to hear the whole story."

"Roger's here?" asked Jonathan.

"That's right," confirmed the Captain. "He arrived just yesterday morning."

"Well, lead on, Captain," said Jonathan. "I must admit, it would be nice to get some real food and a good night's rest."

"You look like you could use it," said the Captain. "If you don't mind my saying so."

Jonathan smiled grimly. "Not at all."

Rip watched the entire exchange without saying a word. Despite the casual conversation between the captain and the preacher, Rip couldn't quite shake the feeling that something was wrong. They were headed for Dogtown, yet Pearl had warned Rip that Dogtown wasn't what it appeared to be. What could she have meant by that? Were the people there hiding something?

As the soldiers accompanied them toward town, Rip glanced back at the dogs. Following at a distance, the animals glared back at Rip with cold, hungry eyes.

16

DOGTOWN

IN WHICH RIP HEARS A CHILLING
ACCOUNT...

*A*fter walking on the path for some time, the group came to a place where the woods parted, exposing a large clearing, dotted with numerous homes. This, they were told, was Dogtown.

Nearing the town's center, Rip was awestruck by the size and construction of each of the buildings. Every shop, home, and structure was obviously made out of the finest material that money could buy. In fact, if it were not for the presence of an extraordinary number of stray dogs, Rip might have thought he had stepped into a magnificent painting. There were grand, stately homes; impressive gardens; elegant statues; and beautiful, crystal-clear fountains.

"This is incredible," Rip whispered to Jonathan.

The preacher nodded in agreement. "It looks a lot different from the village it was a few years ago when I visited. Governor Chillingworth has obviously made some improvements."

"Who is Governor Chillingworth?" asked Rip. "Why have I never heard of him?"

"He's not a governor of New England. He's a governor of Columbia."

"How many governors does Columbia have?"

"Thirteen," replied Jonathan. "In reflection of the thirteen Hallows."

"And you know Governor Chillingworth?"

Jonathan shrugged. "Not very well. We've actually only talked a few times, but he's a brilliant man. Has a keen interest in books. I've seen him once or twice in the library at Yale College. Although he used to live in Boston."

"What's he doing in Dogtown?" asked Rip.

"Like most governors, Chillingworth is quite wealthy and can afford more than one home. I heard that he had built one here."

"I can see why," said Rip as they passed a tall marble statue.

The group came to a halt, and Captain Armitage signaled for his men and the dogs to stay behind. He then led Jonathan and Rip to a building that resembled a church with tall columns. Barrel-chested men with long muskets stood guard in front of the large double doors.

"Welcome to the Governor's mansion," said Captain Armitage. He nodded to the guards who opened the heavy oak doors and ushered the travelers inside.

Once inside, the first thing Rip noticed was the noise. The walls echoed with loud, raucous laughter—so much laughter that, for a moment, Rip thought they had entered a tavern full of drunks instead of the mansion of a sober-minded governor.

After passing through a narrow hallway, they came to a stop at the threshold of a large, spacious room. At the center of the room, underneath a great chandelier, stood a long, ornate table. Surrounding the table, sitting on high chairs, were the most dazzling people Rip had ever seen. Had they not been laughing and moving about, Rip might have mistaken them for august sculptures, so perfect were their appearances.

But the people, beautiful as they were, didn't hold Rip's attention for long; heaped upon the table, in a resplendent display, was the most lavish, mountainous feast imaginable. It looked even more delicious than the food at the home of the Simmons Sisters, if that was possible.

There were plump turkeys, golden-brown geese, steamy piles of lamb, sizzling strips of bacon, wreaths of sausages, joints of beef, and roasted pigs stuffed with cherry-cheeked apples. There were fresh salads, golden cobs of corn, and baked potatoes drizzled in butter. There were puddings, pastries, and cakes of every shape and size, each coated in icing and smothered in strawberries, blueberries, or nuts.

As Rip stared at the food longingly, his mouth began to water. He hadn't realized how hungry he was until now.

"Do I spy Jonathan Edwards? The Library Keeper?"

The room grew silent, and everyone turned their attention to the man who had spoken—the figure at the head of the table. He was a tall, regal-looking man, with long black hair and striking gray eyes. He had been sitting with his feet propped on the tabletop, one ankle crossed over the other, looking out at the feast casually—almost indifferently. But once he spotted Jonathan and Rip, the man stood up and made his way through the crowd to the visitors. Rip stared at him quizzically; he looked strangely familiar.

When the man reached the beleaguered pair, he extended a hand and pumped Jonathan's arm enthusiastically. "Jonathan Edwards! What a most wonderful surprise!"

The preacher nodded wearily. "Governor Chillingworth. I must admit, it is good to see a familiar face." Jonathan paused and squinted at the Governor. "You look . . . very . . . young."

Chillingworth laughed. "I assure you, I feel a great deal older than I look."

In response to this remark, several of the men and women sitting at the table laughed. The once-boisterous crowd was listening intently to the exchange between their governor and the visitors.

"And who is this strapping young man?" said the Governor, looking at Rip.

"This is Rip Van Winkle."

"Van Winkle?" repeated the Governor. "You wouldn't by any chance happen to be related to Josiah Van Winkle, would you?"

Feeling the eyes of everyone in the room settle directly on him, Rip blushed. "Yes, sir. He's my father, sir."

"Excellent!" said the Governor warmly. "I knew him when he was little, no higher than my knee."

When he was little? thought Rip. *How is that possible?* Governor Chillingworth looked younger than Rip's father.

"I'm sorry, Governor," said Jonathan. "We didn't mean to interrupt your festivities."

The Governor waved his hand. "Nonsense! You've actually caught us at a good time. We have some distinguished guests coming tomorrow night, so we decided to celebrate All Hallows' Eve a day early. You're welcome to join us if you'd like."

Jonathan looked at the food and licked his lips. "Honestly, Roger, that would be wonderful."

"Then it's settled!" The Governor clapped his hands together once, and motioned to a servant who stood at the edge of the room. "Two chairs at the head of the table!"

After a flurry of movement and noise, Jonathan and Rip were soon seated on either side of the Governor while the rest of the participants resumed eating and laughing. As Rip waited for plates and utensils, he couldn't help but admire the Governor's mansion. Behind Chillingworth was an opulent purple banner embroidered with the golden emblem of Columbia. On the walls hung gorgeous paintings of proud and alluring men and women. The wood floors and banisters were of the finest craftsmanship, and the glass chandelier—which was almost the shape and size of an upside-down oak tree—sparkled like a thousand diamonds.

"Do you like my home?" asked the Governor, a hint of pride in his voice.

"Very much," admitted Rip. "Did it used to be a church?"

Governor Chillingworth narrowed his eyes, and his mouth twitched slightly, as though he were fighting the urge to say something unpleasant. After a moment's hesitation, he laughed it off. "Long ago," he answered. "But not anymore. This is a *government* building. In Dogtown, we don't mix religion and government; doing so never leads to anything good, you see."

Jonathan cleared his throat. "It led to the construction of this building —and, if I'm not much mistaken, the colonization of New England."

"Ah, Jonathan," began the Governor, "my apologies. I had forgotten that you are a *preacher*."

The Governor spoke the word "preacher" disdainfully, as though merely forming it was enough to make anyone ill. Some of the men and women at the table scoffed.

Jonathan raised an eyebrow. "Is there something wrong with that?"

Chillingworth held out his hands apologetically. "I'm sorry, my friend. I meant no offense. It's just that I lived in Boston for a while and saw a lot of religious hypocrisy. I was there the day they hanged Mary Dyer—it soured my opinion of religion in general."

Rip's jaw dropped. "You saw them hang Mary Dyer? But that was back in 1660! You must be really, really old!"

"Rip!" hissed Jonathan.

Chillingworth laughed. "It's quite all right, Jonathan," he said, turning his attention to Rip. "Yes, I saw them hang Mary Dyer, and yes—I'm *really* old."

Rip blinked at the Governor in astonishment. "But you don't look old at all."

"Why, thank you," said Chillingworth with a grin. "Before I was Governor, I was a physician and I lived among the Indians. They taught me some of their magic. It has preserved my life and kept me young. Unfortunately," added the Governor, "my magic couldn't save the life of Mary Dyer . . . or her child."

"You saw Mary's stillborn child?" asked Jonathan.

"Saw it?" repeated the Governor. "I *delivered* it."

Rip sat forward. "'Mary's 'monster'?"

"Indeed," said the Governor in a low voice. "Although, 'monster' doesn't even *begin* to describe it."

"What did it look like?" asked Rip, his mouth going dry. He had heard rumors about Mary's monster in school. Some said it had horns, while others said that it had been born with two mouths and clawed feet. Rip wasn't sure what to believe.

The Governor hesitated, silently tipping his wine glass from side to side. "This is hardly the kind of conversation one should have at dinner." But after a few moments he spoke, uttering three words that Rip would never forget: *"He was headless."*

Rip felt that he might be sick. "Headless?"

Jonathan cocked his head to one side. "Anencephaly?"

The Governor pointed his glass toward the preacher. "Very good, yes. Anencephaly."

"What's that?" asked Rip.

"It is an extremely rare medical condition," explained the Governor. "So rare, in fact, that up until that night, I had only ever read about it in books. It happens when a child is born without part—or in this case, all—of its head. In the case of Mary's baby, the features of the child's head—the eyes, the nose, the ears, and mouth—" The governor paused uncomfortably and brought a hand to his mouth before speaking again. "They were located in the child's chest. It was the most . . . gruesome thing I've ever seen. And it certainly didn't help Mary that the leadership in Boston—under the influence of the Terrible Slumber—already suspected her of witchcraft. When that baby was born, I knew the rest of the city must never find out; they would surely interpret the child's deformities as 'a sign from God' that Mary was a witch, and hang her for it. So, in an attempt to save Mary's life, I buried the baby in secret—"

"But someone found it," interrupted Jonathan.

The Governor gave the preacher a meaningful look. "No doubt it was Ann Hibbins who found the grave—after all, she was the one who had cursed Mary's baby in the first place."

Jonathan was about to reply when a door on the other side of the room opened, and two servants appeared with clean plates and utensils.

While his guests were being served, the Governor changed the subject. "So what brings you to Dogtown?"

Jonathan gave a full report, detailing everything that had happened to them from the time Rip encountered Blaxton in the graveyard until their fight with Mistress Hibbins on board *The Courser*.

Unable to concentrate on the conversation, Rip stared at his food with wonder and thanksgiving. Not only did the meal look delicious, but it smelled intoxicating! Picking up his knife and fork, Rip was about to start eating when he noticed something out of the corner of his eye. He turned to get a better look.

There, skulking in the shadows at the back of the room, were a pair of dogs. They were skinny, hungry-looking things with bleary eyes and long faces. Alarmed, Rip cast his eyes around the room and was surprised to see several more dogs, each as emaciated as the first two. Why hadn't Rip noticed these dogs before? Why did they look so hungry when there was so much food here?

"Rip?" asked Jonathan.

Rip jumped. He had been so focused on the dogs that he hadn't realized Jonathan was trying to get his attention.

"The Governor would like to see Blaxton's lantern," said the preacher.

Rip lifted the satchel onto his lap, but then hesitated and looked around the room. All eyes in the room were fixed on him. Even the stray dogs, with their vacant expressions, stared at him in silence. Something about the situation made Rip feel extremely uncomfortable.

"It's all right, Rip," said Jonathan with a reassuring smile. "Governor Chillingworth is a friend—like Amelia. He wants to help us."

"What about the dogs?" said Rip.

Governor Chillingworth cocked his head to one side. "Dogs? What dogs?"

"The dogs at the back of the room." Rip pointed behind Jonathan. Everyone turned their heads to see what he was pointing at, but to Rip's astonishment, the dogs had vanished.

"Do you mean the dogs outside?" asked Chillingworth. "I will admit, we do have a lot of stray dogs."

"I—I, no," stammered Rip. "There were dogs in here. In this room. I saw them!"

"Oh, my dear boy," said the Governor, "we would never allow dogs in here. You must be very tired from your journey. Here," he added, procuring a bright red apple from the pocket of his frock coat. "Perhaps you would like a delicious apple?"

Rip froze. Those words . . . he had heard them before! He suddenly recalled his disturbing dream and the shriveled old man with the monster on his back. Rip's mouth fell open in shock as he looked up at the Governor. Then it dawned on him why Governor Chillingworth had looked so familiar when they'd first arrived; he *was* the old man from the dream! Here in Dogtown the Governor was younger, of course—much younger—but the resemblance was uncanny. It had to be him; Rip was sure of it!

Heart beating fast, Rip crossed his arms over his satchel. "No, thank you," he murmured.

The Governor seemed taken aback by Rip's sudden shift in temperament. "I'm sorry?" he said, placing the apple on the table. "Did I say something wrong?"

"No," whispered Rip, pushing his plate of food away. "I'm just—I'm actually not that hungry."

"Rip," hissed Jonathan. "The Governor is being very generous."

Governor Chillingworth raised a hand. "It's quite all right, Jonathan. I'm sure the boy is just tired. Now, about that lantern," he added with a charming smile. "May I have it?"

Arms still crossed over the satchel, Rip's eyes darted from the Governor to the preacher. He couldn't shake the ominous feeling that something wasn't right. He recalled Pearl's words about Dogtown not being what it seemed, and although he wasn't sure why, Rip knew he shouldn't—under any circumstances—let Governor Chillingworth have the lantern.

Slowly, Rip shook his head. "I can't give you the lantern," he whispered.

"What did you say?" said the Governor, a note of incredulity in his voice.

Jonathan cleared his throat. "Roger, it's not you. You see, Blaxton told Rip to give the lantern to . . . well . . . um . . . Feathertop."

For a brief moment, Rip thought the Governor looked slightly unnerved by Jonathan's comment.

"*Feathertop?*" said the Governor with a forced laugh. "Please don't tell me you believe in that hocus pocus, Jonathan."

Several men and women laughed along with Chillingworth.

"I never said I believed in it," retorted Jonathan. "But Blaxton told the boy to take the lantern to Feathertop. So that's what Rip is trying to do."

"Well, Jonathan, I hate to be the one to tell you, but Feathertop is a complete lie. You can search all you want, but you'll never find something that isn't there. Surely, Blaxton meant for you to give the lantern to someone real and tangible—to a leader in the government of Columbia —didn't he?"

"That's what I wondered at first," said Jonathan, looking questioningly at Rip.

Once again, all eyes turned toward Rip, and he felt his face flush with embarrassment. He could sense that the room was filled with people who disbelieved in the existence of Feathertop, yet Rip knew that what Blaxton had told him was true!

Slowly, and almost defiantly, Rip shook his head. "Blaxton didn't say anything about giving the lantern to someone in Columbia. He told me to give it to Feathertop."

Forcing another laugh, Chillingworth leaned forward and lifted a large, clear bottle of brownish liquid. He uncorked the bottle and poured the drink into Jonathan's glass.

The minister looked down. "What's this?"

"The best apple cider you'll ever taste," said Chillingworth. "From my own orchard." Then he offered the bottle to Rip.

Rip, still unsettled by the similarity between the Governor and the man from his nightmare, politely declined. The Governor gave Rip a curious expression before putting the bottle back down. "I'm sorry, Rip. Did my comments about Feathertop upset you?"

Rip didn't say anything.

The Governor bit his lip thoughtfully before gesturing to the banner behind him. "Do you see that flag, Rip? It is the flag of Columbia—the image of a rising sun with an eye in its center. When the Hallows formed Columbia, they charged its governors with two tasks. The first task, to awaken the people, is symbolized by the open eye. The second task, to bring the people to Feathertop, is symbolized by the rising sun.

"And for many years, this is what the governors tried to do; they labored to help people remember who they really were and bring them to Feathertop. But after years and years of hard work, do you know what the governors discovered? People prefer to remain asleep; they don't want to work, they don't want to change. The people just want to be left alone—hidden behind the walls of their communities, tucked inside their warm beds, unaware of the truth about themselves.

"And you know what else, Rip? After all these years of being a governor, do you know how many times *I've* seen Feathertop?"

Rip shook his head, nervously fingering his satchel.

"*None*," said Chillingworth with a sad shake of his head. "So either this Feathertop person doesn't want anything to do with us, or . . . he doesn't exist. Either way, we're on our own."

"But Blaxton *told* me to take the lantern to Feathertop!" said Rip.

"Child, I have no doubt of that," said Chillingworth sympathetically. "But did Blaxton ever tell you *where* to find Feathertop?"

Rip lowered his eyes. "No, not really."

Chillingworth nodded. "If Blaxton *truly* wanted you to find Feathertop, don't you think he would have made it easy for you? Why should it be so hard for you to do something that is supposed to be right?"

Rip's shoulders slumped. Chillingworth had made a good point. Why was it so hard to find Feathertop? After all his searching, why had Rip never caught more than a momentary glimpse of the scarecrow? Didn't Feathertop want to see Rip? Was Feathertop really a lie?

The Governor nodded sadly. "Now you know something of the weight that has been upon *my* shoulders. We tried to bring the people to Feathertop—but he's nowhere to be found. So instead of placating the people with fairy tales and lies about some mythical scarecrow, I now encourage them to eat, drink, and enjoy what has been given to them. Speaking of enjoyment," added the Governor, snapping his fingers, "we actually have some entertainment planned for this evening."

Rip looked up at the Governor, feeling sick and confused. "Entertainment?"

The Governor grinned. "Yes, a group of traveling performers. They arrived, not two days ago, with a new production—one that I hear has been quite popular in Salem. It's called *Featherbottom.*"

Upon hearing the title, several of the attendees clapped their hands and shouted enthusiastically.

"*Featherbottom!*"

"Give us entertainment!"

"Yes, *Featherbottom!* Let us see *Featherbottom!*"

"Wonderful! Stupendous!"

Rip noticed that one of the guests, a beautiful young woman, appeared puzzled. "What's *Featherbottom?*" she asked.

"You haven't heard of *Featherbottom?*" said an older gentleman seated next to the woman. His mouth was agape, as though the young woman had committed a capital offense.

She glanced around and shook her head nervously.

The man rolled his eyes before explaining. "It's a musical, my dear—far better than those dry and dreary Puritan hymns and Psalms. It tells the story of a group of Puritans sent to the New World in search of a mythical being. Along the way, they meet the natives and have a bloody conflict with the Indian King, Philip. It's really quite a brilliant production; everyone in Salem loves it. Such a marvelous satire on the hypocrisy and foolishness of the Puritans."

The woman, seeing everyone's eyes on her, bit her lip and nodded, somewhat enthusiastically. Rip furrowed his eyebrows. *The hypocrisy and foolishness of the Puritans?* he thought to himself. *Everyone in Salem loves it?* How was that possible? Wasn't Salem the capital of Columbia? Weren't the people of Salem Puritans as well? Didn't they believe in Feathertop?

At a word from Chillingworth, the performers entered the main hall and gathered behind the Governor's chair. Using the purple tapestry as a kind of curtain, they assembled their stage on the raised floor of the former church. After the performers finished their preparations, Chillingworth had his servants turn his chair around, which gave him a front row seat to the performance.

From somewhere behind the tapestry, there came a cheerful, lively tune. The candlelight dimmed, and the tapestry rose. Almost immediately, the crowd burst into laughter. Standing onstage were a group of actors dressed in outlandish, oversized clothing that made them look like ridiculous caricatures of the early settlers. With their faces covered in excessive makeup, they wandered around the stage and made lewd expressions that elicited laughter from the audience.

Rip couldn't understand what was so hilarious. The people onstage looked silly, but that was it—nothing they were doing seemed funny to him. The audience, however, could hardly contain themselves. After a few musical numbers, the "Puritans" met the "Indians" and tried to speak with them. There was some confusion, and the Indians made several vulgar comments. Rip was shocked by their words, but the audience merely laughed.

At length, the Puritans began fighting with the Indians. Another catchy tune flared up when the Puritans declared they were living "in Featherbottom's honor" by going to war with the Indians.

Then they hoisted up an absurd, life-sized puppet of a clownish pumpkin-headed scarecrow. The puppet—which had actual feathers glued to its trousers—was greeted with a roar of approval from the audience. Everyone pounded the table with their fists and howled with laughter, tears streaming down their cheeks. Rip cast a sideways glance at Jonathan, wondering what his reaction might be. But the preacher wasn't paying attention; he was nodding off in his seat.

Rip, for his part, felt disturbed and offended. The puppet being paraded onstage hardly resembled the scarecrow he had seen as a boy. The Feathertop that Rip had seen and heard about was humble, noble, and majestic. The onstage spectacle felt like a crude mockery of something quite beautiful.

Nevertheless, the people surrounding Rip continued to laugh and clap, and Rip couldn't help but wonder about Feathertop. Could the scarecrow really just be an invention of the Puritans? After all, every time Rip had seen Feathertop—or thought he had seen him—Rip had been unable to reach him. Was the scarecrow just a figment of Rip's imagination? Had he traveled all this way only to discover that Feathertop was just a lie?

Having lost his appetite completely, Rip pushed his food farther away and slumped miserably into his chair.

AT THE CONCLUSION of the show, Rip discovered that Jonathan had fallen into a deep sleep. Rip gently prodded his friend, but the preacher refused to budge.

The Governor chuckled. "Leave him be. I'll have my servants escort him to his room." The Governor then stood and motioned for Rip to follow. "Come with me. I'll show you to your own room."

Chillingworth led Rip up a long set of stairs into an elegant hallway filled with portraits of dignified men. Rip and the Governor stopped at an oak door at the end of the hallway, and there came the sound of jangling as the Governor pulled out a large iron loop filled with keys.

Rip's eyes grew wide with surprise. "That's a lot of keys."

The Governor smiled without looking up. "I have a lot of responsibilities," he said, singling out a heavy black key. He unlocked the door and pushed it open. But before Rip could go inside, Chillingworth turned and placed a hand on the boy's shoulder.

"Rip, about what I said earlier—I didn't mean to upset you. Long ago, I traveled the road you now wander. It took me years to accept the fact that my journey was a foolish delusion. I don't want you to struggle as much as I did. If I were in your position, I'd prefer the truth—however painful—over some fantasy. Besides that," added Chillingworth, a note of sympathy in his voice, "I sense you are burdened with a great sadness."

Rip looked up. "How do you know that?"

The Governor gave a half smile. "I told you I used to be a physician. I have a gift for these things. What troubles you, Rip?"

Rip lowered his head. "My sister died . . . about a month ago."

Chillingworth let out a heavy sigh and squeezed Rip's shoulder. "I know how hard that must be. Years ago, I lost someone who was very dear to me. I searched for hope anywhere I could find it. For a time, I thought maybe Feathertop would be able to help me . . . but I never found him. I look at you now, and I have to wonder if you are doing the same thing. I wonder if you are holding on to this idea of Feathertop as a way of escaping or denying the pain you are feeling."

Rip glanced up at the Governor anxiously. "Did you ever find any hope?"

The Governor shrugged. "In a manner of speaking, yes. Truthfully, the pain never quite goes away. The best you can do is numb it, and learn to cope."

"How do you do that?"

"With this," said the Governor, reaching into the pocket of his coat and producing the apple he had previously offered Rip. Red, plump, and juicy, it looked more delicious to Rip than ever—especially after he had skipped dinner.

"This apple comes from my orchard, here in Dogtown," said the Governor. "As I said, I once lived among the Indians. They taught me much in the way of medicine and showed me an herb that was very sweet —an herb that numbed not only the pains of the body, but also the pains of the heart. I put it on all the foods here. It not only makes things taste better, but it also makes those who eat it *feel* better." The Governor held out the apple to Rip. "I promise it will help."

Rip hesitated as confusion filled his mind. He couldn't shake the feeling that his dream from the night before had warned against this very thing. Then again, the person in his dream had been a sad, shriveled old man, whereas the person standing before him was young and happy.

Aside from that, Governor Chillingworth had promised that the apple would make Rip feel better. Rip was tired of running from place to place, tired of feeling so lost, and tired of feeling so empty inside. Physical and emotional fatigue overwhelmed him. He wanted relief, and he wanted it now. Besides, it was just an apple. *Apples come from the earth, and are good for you,* he reasoned to himself. *No harm ever came from eating an apple.*

With some trepidation, Rip held out his hand.

The Governor smiled and gave him the apple. "There you are. You'll feel right as rain in a moment."

Rip licked his lips nervously before taking a small, cautious bite. As soon as the apple touched his tongue, he realized that Governor Chillingworth had been right; the apple was the sweetest thing Rip had ever tasted! It was better than his mother's apple crumble, better than pumpkin pie from the Simmons Sisters, better than anything that could *ever* be cooked or baked! Before Rip realized what was happening, he had devoured the entire apple—everything except the stem! Then, without warning, he was swept up in a wave of euphoria. He felt almost disconnected from his body, completely detached from all his pain and sorrows.

Rip thought he heard Governor Chillingworth mention something about stopping by the following night, but Rip didn't care. He was happy —floating and free! He drifted over to the bed, and without even bothering to undress or climb into the sheets, he landed on the bed and curled up on his side. His eyes were swimming in his head.

Free! he thought to himself. *I'm finally free!*

But as he drifted into a dizzying sleep, Rip felt a strange pain in his stomach . . .

17

THE DARK WOODSMAN

IN WHICH TOM WALKER IS STUMPED...

*W*hile yet asleep, Rip dreamed he was wandering through a swampy forest—the likes of which he had never before seen. It was dense and thickly grown with monstrous, gloomy white pines and nettlesome weeds. Pungent odors of sulfur and rot assaulted his nose and throat. Yet, despite a feeling of intense foreboding, Rip, for reasons unknown to him, felt compelled to go deeper into the forest. Cautiously, he picked his way across the swampy terrain, lightly stepping from one tuft of overgrown roots to another, careful not to fall into any of the muddy quagmires.

At length, Rip made it to a firm strip of land, which led, like a peninsula, into the very heart of the swamp. As he proceeded, he heard the caw of a crow and felt the gaseous rumble of the swamp, churning like an upset stomach. Rip put his hands on his own stomach. He could feel himself getting sicker as he moved deeper into the bog. He had taken a dreary road, darkened by all the gloomiest trees of the forest. His heart careened against his chest, beating as loudly as an Indian drum.

Thump. Thump. Thump.

Rip paused when he realized that it wasn't the sound of his heartbeat, but something else entirely. He strained his ears. It was the sound of someone cutting wood.

Thump. Thump. Thump.

And it was coming from somewhere up ahead, from somewhere within the darkness.

Rip felt his pulse quicken, but he did his best to gather his wits. He had to go into the forest—he had to get through! He swallowed hard and moved forward, stepping as quietly as a cat. As he did so, the woodcutting grew louder.

THUMP. THUMP. THUMP.

Rip tried not to think about the stories he had heard as a child, tried not to think about the Dark Woodsman. Instead, he tried to make himself as small as possible, tried to stifle the sound of his breathing. But all that did was cause his breath to come out in short bursts, matching the woodcutter's beat.

THUMP! THUMP! THUMP!

Then, all at once, the noise ceased.

"You're late," said a deep, growling voice.

Rip came to a dead stop and felt himself go numb with fear. The voice was unlike anything he had ever heard. It wriggled through his ears and traveled down his spine like an icy snake.

"Master!" said a second voice, this one filled with fear. "Please, forgive me!"

Rip stood still and listened, not daring to move.

"You tried to take a shortcut," growled the first voice. "Have you learned nothing? There are no shortcuts through the wilderness of life. There is only the way forward."

"M-master," trembled the second voice, "I need more time. More time to pay my debt—"

"MORE TIME?" roared the first voice. "Your time is up, *Tom Walker!*"

Rip started. It had been years since he had heard that name! *Tom Walker? Charity's father? What was he doing here, in this swamp? And who was he talking to?* Instinctively, Rip crouched down and silently moved to a cluster of bushes. Parting the branches, he peered through and did his best to stifle a gasp.

Before him stood a massive man dressed in heavy, dark clothes and a large, red belt. His face, swarthy and begrimed with dirt, was curtained with long black hair and bespeckled with two great red eyes. Over his shoulder he bore a mighty axe.

The Dark Woodsman! thought Rip, his breath quickening.

There could be no doubt about it. The man who towered before him was truly the Dark Woodsman of New England legend; his presence radiated terror and dread.

"But please!" said a voice to Rip's right. He jumped, but quickly recovered himself and peeked around a corner of the bush. Rip could just make out the form of Tom Walker, his clothes tattered, his face sunken and white.

"I just need more time!" begged Tom. "More time to settle my debts, that's all. *Please!*"

At this, the Dark Woodsman let out a peal of terrifying, unnatural laughter, the sound of which caused Rip to feel sick. The Dark Woodsman was enjoying Tom's torment. He threw his axe down into an old stump.

"More time to settle your debts?" repeated the Dark Woodsman. He pointed to a large white pine tree, the trunk of which was nearly hewn through; chunks of its wood were scattered across the forest floor. "Look upon yonder tree and tell me how much *TIME* you have left!"

Trembling with fright, Tom Walker did as he was told. He clapped his hands to his head and let out a cry of horror. Rip followed the man's gaze and saw the name "TOM WALKER" scored on the bark of the tree.

"This tree is you, Tom Walker—and it is time for me to reap what you have sown. One more blow from my axe and you will fall!"

Tom fell to his knees. "Please! Please, there must be something you can do! Mercy, please!"

"You are asking the wrong person. I am the Dark Woodsman. I know nothing of mercy!"

Laughing, the Woodsman bent down and lifted one end of a heavy black chain. In a move that defied his stature, he swiftly threw the chain around Tom, enveloping his torso in black links. Tom squealed with fright.

"There must be something I can do," he jibbered. "There must be some hope!"

The Woodsman paused and glared at Tom, his dark, heavy brow casting even darker shadows over his red eyes. "Hope is not found here," he said. "Hope is found somewhere else."

Still bound, Tom hobbled forward and fell to his knees. "Tell me!" he begged. "Tell me where I can find it!"

The Woodsman's gaze went slowly from the ground up the white pine tree and to a small patch of starry sky. "An appeal to Heaven," he murmured.

Tom looked up suddenly. "What do you mean?"

The Dark Woodsman let out a growl and struck Tom in the face. The man spun around and landed on his back, chains rattling and blood spurting from his nose. The Woodsman threw the other end of the chain around the trunk of the tree.

"Your time is up, Tom Walker!" he barked. "It's All Hallows' Eve, and the Terrible and Everlasting Slumber is upon you!"

With that, the Dark Woodsman lifted his axe and gave it one last mighty swing. It struck the tree with a deafening *thud*. The force of the impact shook the ground beneath Rip's feet. The tree groaned and lurched forward, crunching and snapping under its own weight.

Tom shrieked as the tree fell into the swampy water, pulling his chain along with it. Unable to use his arms, he was dragged, screaming, into the muck and mire and soon vanished from sight. Two bubbles in the bog were all that remained of the nefarious Tom Walker.

Rip, unable to fathom the horror he had just witnessed, felt his mouth run dry. The Dark Woodsman, however, seemed unfazed by what had just happened. With his back to Rip, the Woodsman slammed his axe into the stump of Tom's tree and moved his head from side to side, cracking the bones in his neck.

Then, quite unexpectedly, he turned to face Rip, his red eyes burning like two hot coals. "I know you're there, Rip." His voice rumbled through Rip's bones.

Terrified, Rip fell back a step.

The Woodsman unwedged his axe and held it high above his head. "I'm coming for you, boy!"

Rip stumbled backward as he scrambled to his feet. He turned and ran, racing through the forest as fast as his legs could carry him.

"Run while you can," growled the Woodsman. The forest shook under his deep voice. "My black chains will be wrapped around you soon enough!"

Rip staggered along, clutching his stomach. He felt sick. He wanted to stop, but he had to keep going! Hearing a noise to his left, he cast a sideways glance and ran into a tree. Stepping back, he realized to his horror that it wasn't a tree at all—it was the Midnight Minister!

"What did I tell you, child?" exclaimed the Minister, the chain on his ankle rattling. "I told you I would find you in the darkness!"

Shaking with fear, Rip clutched his stomach, staggered backward and collapsed on the ground.

SECRETS BROUGHT TO LIGHT

IN WHICH RIP LEARNS THE UGLY TRUTH...

*R*ip awoke with a start. He had fallen out of his bed and landed on the hard floor. He groaned softly and held his aching stomach. It took him a while before he realized he was in the Governor's mansion in Dogtown.

It was just a nightmare, he reassured himself. *It wasn't real.*

His head, drenched in sweat, felt like it had been hit with a hammer. He looked up, wondering what time it was. Daylight streamed in through cracks in the boarded-up windows, stinging his eyes.

He sat up.

Boards on the windows? he thought to himself. *Why are the windows boarded up?*

He looked up at the window above his bed and confirmed that thick slabs of wood had been nailed over it. He glanced across the room and saw that the two other windows had also been nailed shut. Why hadn't he noticed this before?

It was then, after taking in his surroundings, that Rip became aware of just how disgusting the room was. Dust and grime coated the floor. The paint on the walls was cracked and peeling, and his bed was a dilapidated, moth-eaten shamble. Having grown up in a large family, Rip was used to living in a chaotic and messy home, but this was different. This room appeared condemned. Why would the Governor put Rip in a room like this?

He heard a small click, followed by the sound of the door creaking open. He turned and was startled to see a girl poke her head into the room —a girl who looked almost exactly like his sister Charity.

"Pearl!" exclaimed Rip.

She brought a finger to her lips. "Not so loud!" she hissed. "You don't want them to hear you!"

"Them?" said Rip, lowering his voice.

"The imps," whispered Pearl.

Rip blinked back at her in surprise. "Imps?"

Pearl nodded.

"Where?"

She stepped into the room and quietly closed the door behind her. "You've already met them."

Rip was confused. "I haven't seen any imps."

"Of course not," snapped Pearl. "Imps are magic and can only be seen in the daylight."

"But then how have I met them?" asked Rip.

"You met Governor Chillingworth, didn't you?"

"He's an imp?"

Pearl gave a half-shrug. "More or less. Actually, he *has* an imp—they're like leeches. They latch onto people and animals—and control them while slowly draining the life out of them."

"But I didn't see any imps last night," began Rip.

"That's because imps are extremely magical and secretive," explained Pearl. "They make things appear to be what they are not—especially at night, when things are dark and easily concealed! If, at night, you see a man possessed by an imp, he could make himself look, to you, like he's the king of England. They can even make buildings look more beautiful than they really are."

Rip felt his stomach twist as he remembered his arrival into Dogtown the night before. He had been so amazed by the Governor's mansion—the feast, the artwork, the people, the chandelier—was it all an illusion created by the imps?

"And they can attach themselves to . . . anybody?" Rip looked over his shoulder to check for an imp.

"Anyone who eats their *food*," emphasized Pearl. "It's bewitched; if you eat it—and they find out about it—they can wrap their magical black chains around you."

Still recovering from his nightmare, Rip shivered at the mention of black chains. Then he remembered something that made him feel worse: he had eaten the Governor's apple! Chillingworth had said it was different from other apples—that he had added something special that made it taste better. Did that mean it was imp food? How could something that tasted so good, and brought so much relief, be so bad?

As if in response to these thoughts, his stomach writhed in pain.

Pearl seemed to notice the look of anguish on his face. "Rip?" she asked tentatively. "Are you all right?"

He nodded, beads of sweat dripping down his forehead.

"I need you to be honest with me. Did you eat any of their food? Did you have dinner with the people in this building?"

Rip felt shame burning his cheeks. He didn't want to admit his mistake. He didn't want Pearl to think him a fool. "No, I didn't have dinner with them," he said, carefully dodging Pearl's first question. "I just didn't sleep well, that's all. Maybe later today I'll be able to get some rest."

Pearl looked concerned. "Rip," she said slowly, "do you know what time it is?"

He shrugged. "Well, we arrived here late last night, so it must be eight or nine in the morning?"

Pearl pointed at the window. "That's not morning light, it's evening light. It's All Hallows' Eve!"

Rip's stomach churned violently. "All Hallows' Eve? No, no, no! I've failed! Blaxton told me to deliver the lantern to Feathertop, and it's already too late!"

Pearl put her hands on Rip's shoulders. "What on earth are you talking about? Blaxton who?"

"William Blaxton." Then, before he had time to think about what he was saying, the words tumbled out. "He gave me the lantern and told me to take it to Feathertop before All Hallows' Day. Only, we didn't know where to find Feathertop, so the Simmons Sisters told us to go to his mother's home. They said we might be able to find him there. But," he added, tears burning his eyes, "I don't know where Mother Rigby's home is, and it's already All Hallows' Eve!"

"Mother Rigby?" repeated Pearl. "What does her home look like?"

"How should I know?" retorted Rip angrily. "I've never been there. It probably doesn't even exist!"

Pearl ignored Rip's outburst and looked at him steadily. "Is it a home with a garden?"

Rip blinked. "I think so. Why?"

"Because I think I've been there."

Rip tilted his head to one side. "You have?"

Pearl rolled her eyes. "I'm not just saying so to make you feel better."

"And you've seen Mother Rigby?"

"I haven't seen her," admitted Pearl, "but I'm almost positive it's her home. My mother took me there when I was a little girl."

Rip felt a wave of relief, the thrill in his heart outweighing the pain in his stomach. "Let's go, then! We haven't a moment to lose!" he declared.

He dashed to the edge of the bed and retrieved his satchel. Out of habit, he opened the flap and glanced inside. The light from the lantern beamed up at him. Rip paused. Was it just his imagination, or was the light within the pumpkin slightly dimmer? Rip frowned and closed the satchel, not wanting to look at the pumpkin anymore. He was grateful that he would soon be rid of it. Then he, Pearl, and Jonathan Edwards could go home and get on with their lives.

Rip stopped. He had forgotten about the preacher! "We have to get Jonathan!"

"Jonathan?" repeated Pearl.

"The preacher. He'll want to come with us."

"Oh, him," said Pearl, her voice dripping with obvious contempt. "Where is he?"

Rip shouldered his satchel. "I assume he's in one of the other rooms down the hallway."

"Down the hallway?" asked Pearl, cocking her head to one side. "There aren't any other rooms. There isn't even a hallway! This is the attic of the church."

"What?" Without waiting for her to reply, he leapt across the room and opened the door. He let out a gasp when he realized that Pearl was right. There was no hallway—no elegant carpet leading to the room and no portraits of proud, noble figures. There was just a small, dusty landing with a narrow set of rickety wooden stairs leading down.

"But how is this possible?" whispered Rip. "I saw a hallway. Chillingworth led me down a hallway!"

"You saw what Chillingworth wanted you to see. He's a master of deceit. Evil will always make things appear to be what they are not."

A strange thought entered Rip's mind, and he whirled around, examining Pearl with suspicion. "How do you know so much about imps, anyway? How did you get into Dogtown without being discovered?"

Pearl folded her arms. "I used to live here," she said matter-of-factly.

He jerked his head back in surprise. "You did?"

"Yes. I was running away from Dogtown when I met you in the forest."

"You said you were running away from your stepfather."

"That's right," said Pearl. "My stepfather is Governor Chillingworth."

Rip's mouth dropped open. "So are you . . . are you an imp, too?"

Pearl rolled her eyes. "Are you always this dense? I said he was my stepfather—stepfather! Not my actual father! Chillingworth tricked my mother into marrying him."

"But how did you avoid eating the imp food?"

Pearl let out a long sigh. "I'm not stupid! I saw straight through the Governor's façade, and he's always hated me for it. Now, come on! If we're going to find that preacher, we'd better do it now, before the sun sets."

"But where is he?" asked Rip.

"Where was he the last time you saw him?"

Rip pressed his lips together. "Last night . . . in the dining room."

"My guess is he's still there."

"Do you think he's all right?"

Pearl shrugged. "I don't know. We'll have to see for ourselves. It'll be tricky, because that's where most of the imps sleep."

She moved out onto the landing. Rip swallowed hard, fearing what they might see in the dining room. Nevertheless, he put on a brave face and followed Pearl down the wooden staircase. About halfway down, Pearl turned to him, pressed a finger to her lips, and pointed ahead. Lying at the base of the stairs, breathing raggedly, was a large, emaciated dog. Legs twitching, the poor creature was covered in heavy black chains, and it shivered and whimpered in its sleep.

Rip gasped.

Curled up on the dog's ribcage, clutching the ends of the chain like the reins of a horse, was a small green creature with long arms, pointy ears, and a sharp nose. The monster's eyes, which were tightly closed, were encrusted with dried pus. Just looking at the scene made Rip's already sick stomach feel worse, and he fought back the urge to vomit.

And yet, as the monster tugged on the chain unconsciously, Rip thought there was something vaguely familiar about what he was seeing. Once again, he recalled the dream he had had the night he met Pearl—the dream about the man with the hideous creature on his back. The monster from his dream had looked very similar to the one lying on top of the dog —although the one in his dream had been much taller. When Rip remembered what Pearl had said about Governor Chillingworth, he suddenly wondered about the veracity of his dream. Had it been some kind of warning? Were his dreams showing him things that were about to happen? He shivered as he thought about his most recent nightmare—the one with the Dark Woodsman.

"That's an imp," whispered Pearl, bringing Rip back to reality. "They go into a deep sleep during the day, but if you're not careful, you can wake them up."

They descended the rest of the stairs, carefully stepped around the dog, and made their way to the main hall. After moving under the archway, Rip had to squint in order to see anything clearly in the dimly lit room. But once his eyes adjusted, what he saw made him wish he couldn't see.

Gone were the music and the laughter. Gone were the feasting and revelry. Gone were the happiness and mirth. What lay before them now was something Rip could only describe as *agony*.

Strewn across the floor were dozens of humans and dogs, each sleeping fitfully, tossing and turning and groaning in anguish. The emaciated dogs kicked in their sleep, yelping with fear while the withered humans rolled from side to side, clutching at their heads or struggling against some unseen enemy. Rip vaguely recognized some of the men and women from the feast the night before, but now they were thin, frail, hollow shadows of their former selves.

Wrapped around every man, woman, and dog were thick black chains that rattled with every movement. As he looked upon the feverish crowd, Rip noticed that each member was possessed by a sleeping imp. The imps varied in shape and size. Some were short and fat, while others were tall and gaunt. Some had flat noses, while others had snout-like faces with tusks. But no matter their features, each of the imps was equally hideous.

Casting his eyes to the front of the room, Rip noticed that the great symbol of Columbia, once an elegant tapestry with gold embroidery, was nothing more than a tattered old flag, riddled with holes. The light from the setting sun, which came through small cracks between the boards on the windows, shone upon the large dining table. In the dim light, Rip saw that the table, once filled with a scrumptious feast, was now laden with rotten food, alive with maggots and cockroaches.

Gagging, Rip looked away from the food and noticed a tall cage standing in a corner of the room. Sitting inside the cage was a man wearing black clothes and a broad slouch hat. When Rip stepped forward to get a better look, he realized that the man was Jonathan Edwards!

Rip dashed forward, careful to step around the imp-bound bodies of humans and dogs. When he reached the cage, he saw that Jonathan was slumped forward, his head nodding. Rip reached through the bars and shook the preacher gently, yet urgently.

Jonathan jerked awake and stared at Rip with wild, bloodshot eyes. Rip pressed his finger to his lips.

"Rip?" whispered the preacher. "What are you still doing here?"

"Rescuing you," replied Rip, testing the strength of the bars.

"You—you came here to rescue me?" Jonathan's voice was heavy with weariness. "After the way I treated you?"

"Of course!" said Rip. "You're my friend. What did you expect?"

"The Governor must have drugged my drink . . . how did you find me?"

"Pearl helped me."

The preacher shifted his gaze to look at Pearl, and his eyes filled with deep regret. "Pearl Prynne," he whispered, "forgive me for what I said earlier. I was angry and struggling with my own demons—"

Pearl shook her head. "We don't have time for that! The sun is setting! The imps will wake up any minute."

"Pearl says she knows where to find Mother Rigby's home," explained Rip.

Jonathan's eyes lit up, and he grasped the bars of the cage. "She does?"

"Yes," whispered Pearl, grabbing the lock. "But we need to get you out of here! Even these bars are enchanted. They make you weaker than you really are. If we can just release you, you'll feel much stronger. Do you know where the key is?"

Jonathan nodded in the direction of the rotten feast, where Rip saw a figure sitting at the head of the table. Wrapped in chains, a withered man sat doubled over, dozing fitfully.

"It's Chillingworth," whispered Pearl.

Rip shuddered. The figure slumped over the table looked like the hollow husk of the man who had entertained them the night before. "Where's his imp?" asked Rip.

Pearl pointed under the table. Rip gasped and drew back. It was the same monster from his nightmare! Tall, thin, and grotesque, it sat with its back against the man's legs, snoring peacefully. Occasionally it unconsciously tugged on the chains in its ugly hands, causing the man above to groan in his sleep. Rip glanced at the tortured man's bony hands and saw that he was holding a set of keys. Rip bit his lip. They had to get those keys!

"The sun's almost gone," said Pearl. "We must hurry."

Rip swallowed hard and nodded, following Pearl over to the dining table, again careful to avoid stepping on any fingers, toes, or tails. As he neared the table, he was suddenly struck by the overwhelming smell of rotten food and had to cover his nose in order to proceed. How had he not noticed that odor the night before? Chillingworth had to be very powerful to conceal such sights and smells!

Rip glanced down at the withered man. Chillingworth's brow was furrowed, as though he were fighting through a fevered nightmare. Pearl nudged Rip, urging him to hurry. Fortunately for Rip, the withered man didn't appear to be holding the keys very tightly.

Licking his lips nervously, Rip reached out and gently tugged on the iron loop, easily pulling it from the Governor's grasp. With a sigh of relief he passed the keys to Pearl, who instantly darted back to the preacher's cage. Before Rip could follow her, he heard the rattle of chains.

"Please," said a dry, hollow voice.

Heart beating fast, Rip turned to face Governor Chillingworth.

The man blinked up at him with gray, tormented eyes. "Please," he croaked again, "help me."

Rip's breathing quickened. Nervously, he cast his eyes around the room, hoping that nobody had heard the man's plea.

"How?" Rip whispered.

Chillingworth twisted his neck to look at a bowl of rotten apples. "Give me one of those apples," he pleaded. "I feel so empty."

Rip was disgusted. He shook his head. "Those apples are rotten! They'll make you sick!"

Chillingworth looked back at Rip in surprise. "No, no," he moaned. "Those apples are delicious. They're the only things that can help me. They're the only things that make the emptiness go away."

At these words, the pit in Rip's stomach grew deeper. He had eaten one of those apples. Inwardly, he knew that he had done something very wrong. He had known it at the time—though he didn't want to admit it to himself—but he felt it even more now. All he could do was hope that no one found out what he had done.

Rip shook his head. "I-I can't help you," he stammered.

In response, the Governor's eyes grew dark with anger. He slammed his fist on the table, knocking over a goblet. "Give me an apple!" he barked.

Rip turned to run but felt something tug on the tail of his coat, holding him back. He whirled around and saw, to his horror, that Chillingworth's imp was fully awake and clutching the end of Rip's coat. The monster looked up at Rip and grinned, revealing two rows of jagged yellow teeth.

Just then, Chillingworth sat up and began to twist violently. Rip could hear the man's bones popping as he rocked from side to side. All of a sudden, the Governor stopped and slammed both of his fists on the table. He looked up at Rip, his eyes cold and black. The expression in the governor's eyes told Rip everything he needed to know.

The imp was back in control.

Chillingworth let out a low, disgusting laugh. "You've been a naughty boy, Rip."

Then, quick as thought—quicker than Rip could ever dream possible—Chillingworth stood and hurled a huge black chain at Rip's ankle. The chain wrapped itself around his leg and magically linked itself together. Chillingworth gave the chain a violent tug, sending Rip sprawling to the ground. He fumbled on the floor, desperately searching for something to hold on to, but the Governor was too strong for him. He dragged Rip across the floor toward the decrepit table.

A loud clatter from the corner of the room caused Chillingworth to pause. Rip craned his neck and saw that Pearl had successfully freed Jonathan Edwards.

Chillingworth pointed a long, ugly finger at Pearl. "You!" he shouted angrily. "I'll deal with you later!"

"You will not!" bellowed Jonathan, his eyes burning with anger. He raised his hand in the direction of Chillingworth, and a violent burst of wind slammed into both the man and his disgusting imp. Chillingworth released Rip's chain and moved to protect his imp.

"WAKE UP, YOU BLOCKHEADS!" roared Chillingworth against the wind. "THE PRISONERS ARE TRYING TO ESCAPE!"

Without wasting another second, Rip gathered up his end of the chain and ran toward Jonathan and Pearl, dodging the humans and dogs who were beginning to rouse from their slumber. He cast a terrified glance back and saw a cavalry of imps riding dogs charging into the room, blocking the only exit!

Jonathan pointed to the tattered flag of Columbia. "Behind there!" he said. "Quickly!"

Rip needed no second bidding; he and Pearl ran up a short set of stairs and dove behind the flag. Hidden behind it was a tall, dusty podium—the kind that a preacher would use—and Rip was reminded that the building used to be a church. Governor Chillingworth had probably hung the flag in front of the podium in order to hide the stand from view. In the wall was a massive bay window, and, like all the other windows in the building, this one had been boarded up. One look at the cracks between the boards told Rip that the sun had set completely.

Only a few hours until midnight! he realized.

Then he heard the voice of Captain Armitage. "Shall I send the dogs in, my lord?"

"No," croaked Governor Chillingworth. Rip did not like the sound of the man's voice; it was thin, raspy, and hateful. "This is much more entertaining than last night's performance. Besides, we're in no hurry. Mistress Hibbins will be here any minute. After tonight, Boston will finally fall!"

The chamber echoed with the ragged, hollow laughter and howls of both men and beasts.

Jonathan furrowed his brow. "That's impossible!" he shouted from behind the flag.

"You think so, preacher?" laughed Chillingworth, his voice thick with delight. "Mistress Hibbins is only a few steps away from taking the city and cleansing the New World of all that hypocritical, puritanical rot!"

"Funny to hear you talk about hypocrites!" Jonathan shot back. "You gave a fine speech about hypocrisy last night, and yet here you are—the ugliest hypocrite of them all!"

"I give the people what they want," growled the Governor. "No one wants to be awake, Jonathan! No one wants to experience the harsh realities of life. The truth is too hard for people to bear. I offer them an escape. I offer them hope!"

Jonathan shook his head angrily. "You make yourself out to be some kind of savior, when in reality you're the exact opposite! Your way doesn't make men free—it makes them slaves!"

"And has your way made you free, John?" The Governor's voice dripped with amusement. "Can your resolutions save you now? And what about the boy? He ate an apple, John. That magic cannot be undone."

A devilish choir of laughter rose from the crowd of imps.

Fear gripped Rip's heart as he recalled the image of Tom Walker being pulled into the swamp. He turned to the preacher. "Is that true? Isn't there anything you can do about the chain?"

Jonathan examined the chain around Rip's ankle. He shook his head slowly. "I'm sorry, Rip," he said at last. "But undoing dark magic is beyond my abilities."

There was another peal of laughter from beyond the flag.

"That's right! There's nothing you can do," taunted the Governor. "Once someone eats our food, they're forever trapped. There's no hope for the boy!"

Rip's lip trembled. The feelings of guilt, shame, and fear were so overwhelming that he wanted to cry, but he held back his tears and looked to the preacher for help.

"Pearl," whispered Jonathan, "how far is it to Mother Rigby's house from here?"

"About a half mile through the woods," she whispered.

"Come out, little rabbits," taunted Chillingworth.

Rip saw Pearl narrow her eyes. Instantly, a bolt of red fire ignited and hovered above her palm. Before anyone could stop her, Pearl stood up and hurled the fire angrily past the flag and into the room beyond. Rip heard an explosion, and several imps yelped in a language he couldn't understand. Pearl ducked down, narrowly avoiding a javelin, which embedded itself into the wall next to them.

"You little witch!" squealed Chillingworth.

Rip assumed that Pearl's bolt must have started a fire, because he could hear the crackling of flames amid the angry shouts of imps. He got down on his knees and peeked through a small hole in the tapestry. Sure enough, in the far corner of the church, a large fire began to lick its way up the wall.

"Leave it!" shouted Chillingworth, his tall imp sitting astride his neck. "After tonight we won't need this chapel anyway! All of Boston will be ours!"

Jonathan grimaced and closed his eyes. "Everything I ever believed about Columbia is a lie." He pressed his lips together and bowed his head as though offering a silent prayer for help.

Rip could sense the restlessness of the imps in the room as the crackling of the flames grew louder.

Jonathan opened his eyes and fixed them on a discarded prop from the performance the night before. It was the puppet made to look like Feathertop, lying in a heap next to them, the pumpkin head grinning up at them. The preacher set his brow. "Rip, I want you to follow Pearl. Follow her to Mother Rigby's house. Find Feathertop. He's the only one who can help us now."

Rip felt his chin tremble. "Are you not coming with us?"

"I can't," replied Jonathan. "Someone has to hold the imps back in order for you to have time to escape."

"But you said you didn't believe in Feathertop," whispered Rip.

"He's the only hope we have left." Jonathan looked up at Rip, and his eyes grew wide with regret. "You were right, Rip."

Confused, Rip returned the preacher's gaze. "What do you mean?"

"You were right about the story—the story about Mary Dyer and Mistress Hibbins. It's not about being strong and resolute; it's about being true. Truth is the greatest strength we have against darkness. Honesty is the only way to fight the inner demons."

The imps were advancing now. Once again, Pearl stood up and hurled a bolt of fire beyond the flag. This time Rip heard several dogs yelp in pain. With a look of triumph, she threw another bolt, and then another.

"I should have told you earlier, Rip," continued Jonathan.

"Told me what?" Beyond the podium, Rip could hear the dogs snarl and move in closer.

The preacher set his brow. "I should have told you what I really am."

With that, Jonathan pushed Rip aside with one hand and flung his opposite fist in the direction of the window. Like a battering ram, a thunderous force of wind smashed through both the wooden planks and glass, fanning the flames and creating a shower of broken glass and splintered wood.

The preacher then spun around, placed a hand on Rip's shoulder, and yelled, "Run!"

A look of fierce pain swept across Jonathan's face before he doubled—then tripled—in size. His black clothes ripped open, torn to shreds by thick muscle and gray fur. A long snout, filled with sharp, white fangs, grew from his face. He stood up on his hind legs, swiped the flag from the wall, and let out a terrifying, ear-splitting howl.

Jonathan Edwards was a werewolf!

Rip watched as the beast bent down and, with very little effort, tore the podium from its stand and lifted it high above his head. At the mere sight of this display, several of the imp-possessed humans and dogs scattered in fright. Chillingworth's imp looked particularly terrified.

Rip felt Pearl yank on his arm.

"Come on!" she urged, leaping out the now-open window and landing on the ground a few feet below.

With the satchel at his side and the slack of his chain in his arms, Rip leapt after Pearl. He landed next to her and cast one last glance back at Jonathan. The werewolf hurled the podium into the mass of imps. Then, with a savage bark, it charged the crowd of humans and dogs, scooping several of them up in his massive hands and flinging them across the room. Within seconds, Jonathan was surrounded by men and beasts, all fighting tooth and nail to chain his massive body down.

Once again Pearl yanked on Rip's arm. "Hurry!" she shouted. "They'll catch us if we wait here any longer."

Rip hesitated. He didn't want to leave Jonathan to the imps, but he knew he didn't have a choice. He had to get to Mother Rigby's house before midnight. He had to find Feathertop!

With Pearl in the lead, they ran through a grassy field to the edge of a black forest. As they entered the woods, the shouts and roars emanating from the ruined chapel faded into the distance.

ALL HALLOWS' EVE

IN WHICH THE DEAD RISE WHILE THE LIVING FALL...

*R*ip ran through the forest, following after Pearl at breakneck speed. In his arms, he carried the slack of the chain that was wrapped around his leg, and with every step, the combined weight of the chain and the satchel grew heavier and heavier. The pain in his stomach, which he had tried to ignore while in the chapel, was now much worse. He felt nauseated and dizzy. His heart pounded furiously.

At length, he stopped and shouted ahead to Pearl, "I need to rest!"

Pearl jogged back to where Rip was doubled over. He had dropped the chain and was gasping for air.

"You lied to me," said Pearl. "You told me you didn't eat their food, but you did!"

"I'm sorry," groaned Rip, fighting back tears of frustration. "I was hungry—*so hungry*. I didn't know it would cause pain like this!"

Pearl's expression softened, and she touched his shoulder.

Rip frowned. "My stomach—I feel awful!"

"That's what imp food does. At first, it makes you feel good; then it makes you feel pain, worse than ever."

"Is that why Governor Chillingworth wanted another apple?"

Pearl nodded.

Rip's legs gave out, and he fell to his knees. "Will the pain ever stop?"

Pearl bit her lip. "I don't know, but Mother Rigby's house isn't far away. She might be able to help you."

Rip glanced ahead and saw a patch of grass in the distance, illuminated by the moon. The clearing really wasn't far away, but as Rip knelt there with sweat dripping off his forehead, he was unable to bear the thought of running again. He felt a sudden pain in his leg and winced. It felt like the chain was getting tighter.

"Did you know that Jonathan was a werewolf?" asked Pearl.

Rip shook his head.

"That might have been the reason why he was so angry the other night," said Pearl. "Werewolves can only transform at night. He was probably fighting against the change. Although, the only werewolf I've ever met who could control the transformation is Katy Cruel."

Rip heard what Pearl was saying, but only barely. *A werewolf*, he thought. The words of William Blaxton, Katy Cruel, and Goodman Brown thundered down on him like water from a broken dam. Each of them had warned Rip about wolves in sheep's clothing, and now Jonathan had revealed himself to be werewolf—a wolf disguised as a preacher.

Rip thought about all the oddities he had noticed in Jonathan Edwards —the man's strange history with Katy Cruel, his secretive nature, and his fierce determination to keep his resolutions. Jonathan himself had said that he made those resolutions to "cage the beast within." Was that how he fought the transformations—by clinging to his resolutions? Was that why he had been helping Rip? Was he hoping to be cured of being a werewolf?

Rip's thoughts were interrupted by the sound of barking. He rose to his feet, causing the chain around his leg to rattle.

"The dogs!" said Pearl. "They've picked up our trail! They'll be here at any moment. We have to keep moving!"

Rip tried to move forward, but a sharp pain in his stomach forced him back to his knees. He cried out in anguish.

"Come on!" said Pearl, pulling Rip into a standing position. "It's almost midnight!" She lifted his chain and stuffed as much of it as she could into the satchel. Then she threw Rip's arm over her shoulder, and they hobbled down the path together. The pain in Rip's stomach had become so intense that he didn't know how he was even moving his legs.

As they stepped into the clearing, he saw an old stone house flanked by two overgrown trees. He wondered if it could really be Mother Rigby's house. It looked dark and desolate, as though it had been abandoned ages ago.

Just then, Rip heard a familiar cackle from overhead. He looked up. There, hovering in the air above them, was Mistress Hibbins, her hand aglow with green fire. Rip felt himself enveloped by a fresh wave of fear.

The witch, eyes wild with sadistic malice, flung the fire downward. Pearl, acting quickly, threw her weight against Rip, causing the pair of them to fall just out of the reach of the witch's fire. The green bolt hit the ground and exploded like cannon fire, scattering debris over the field.

Before the dust settled, Pearl was on her feet and throwing magic of her own back at Mistress Hibbins. A bolt of red fire landed on the witch's broom, and the hag reeled back in surprise. The flames spread remarkably fast, causing Mistress Hibbins to spin out of control. She landed on the ground with a sickening thud and lay still as the flames consumed her broomstick. Out of the corner of his eye, Rip thought he saw a flash of green light come from the run-down cottage.

Once again, Pearl reached down and pulled Rip to his feet. Growing delirious with pain, he shook his head, but Pearl dragged him toward the house. He could take only two or three steps before stumbling and falling to his knees again.

"I can't," he murmured. The barking of the dogs grew louder. "I can't. . ."

"Then give me the lantern!" shouted Pearl. "I'll take it to Mother Rigby's house!"

Rip nodded and opened his satchel. Slowly and painfully, he removed the excess chain; then he withdrew the lantern. The light within the pumpkin was dim, as though it were on the brink of flickering out. Rip looked up at Pearl, but he couldn't bring her face into focus.

"Take the lantern," he murmured. "It's yours."

As the sound of barking grew even louder, Pearl snatched the lantern, ran to the house, and disappeared inside. Rip looked over his shoulder just as a pack of dogs emerged from the forest. They were soon followed by two or three dozen people. Because of their magic, Rip couldn't see the imps, but he knew that they were there, controlling the movements of both the humans and the dogs. The group stopped at the edge of the forest and glared at Rip, their expressions dripping with hatred.

It was a few seconds before Governor Chillingworth stepped to the front of the crowd. The magic of his imp made him appear as handsome and charming as ever, but Rip wasn't fooled. He knew that the monstrous imp was underneath Chillingworth's façade. The Governor pointed a finger at Rip.

"Rip Van Winkle," he said, his voice disapproving—almost fatherly. "You've done some very terrible things lately. Come back to my mansion and we'll take those nasty memories away."

Finally catching his breath, Rip felt a surge of new strength. "What have you done to Jonathan?" he shouted.

The Governor snickered. "Have no fear. We put your guard dog in a kennel. He's safe . . . for now. If you come back without a fight, I promise I shall let him go."

Rip knew the Governor was lying. All he could do now was hope that Pearl would deliver the lantern to Feathertop in time. It was then that he realized Chillingworth was no longer looking at him, but over his shoulder, toward the cottage. The Governor's look of triumph had disappeared, replaced with a disgruntled frown. Following the man's gaze, Rip saw something that shocked him to the core.

Standing at the threshold of the dilapidated stone house was the tall, dark form of the Midnight Minister! And next to him stood Pearl, her eyes cast downward. Rip's stomach dropped when he realized what the Minister had in his hand—Pearl had given him the pumpkin lantern!

The Minister held the pumpkin as though it were a precious jewel, carefully examining the light within. Rip noticed that the flame within the lantern was no longer warm and bright, but cold and dark, tinged with a sickly green hue.

Mistress Hibbins, who had risen to her feet, ran forward and clapped her hands. "At last!" she squealed, her voice shaking with feverish excitement. "After all these years I have the lantern!"

Despite his fatigue, Rip forced himself to stand. "Pearl!" he cried. "What have you done?"

Pearl ran out to meet him. "Rip, I'm sorry! I didn't have a choice! Mistress Hibbins found me last night and made me tell her everything I knew about you. She made me go back to Dogtown and rescue you."

As understanding dawned on Rip, he felt overcome with anger. "You saved me to gain my trust! You wanted me to give you the lantern!"

Pearl clasped his hands. "Rip, you don't understand! Mistress Hibbins said she would kill you if I didn't bring it to her!"

Rip wrenched his hands free and shoved Pearl away. "You tricked me! I trusted you, and you tricked me! You're just as bad as Jonathan said you were!"

"But . . . I did it to save you!" Tears sprang to her eyes. "I did it so we could go home to Boston!"

Rip couldn't believe what he was hearing. "*Home?*" he repeated. "You think you can just go home with me as if nothing happened? You're not welcome in Boston. *You don't belong!*"

Pearl staggered backward, as though Rip's words had knocked the wind out of her. Their mutual sorrow was interrupted by the laughter of Mistress Hibbins.

"Boston!" she said derisively. "Yes! Go back to the safety of your home and dream that all is well. It really doesn't matter what you do now, because everyone in Boston will die!"

At this point, Governor Chillingworth, who had been watching the whole scene in stupefied silence, stepped forward. He looked incredulous. "Die?" he repeated. "What do you mean, die? You promised the goblins the chance to enslave the city!"

Mistress Hibbins swiveled her head to look at him. "That was before the boy taught me a new trick," she said, smiling coyly at Rip.

Rip was startled. "Me?"

"Oh, don't be so modest," she smirked. "Yes, you! Remember our encounter on the giant's ship, when you made all that light? It was then that I realized the lantern has the ability to magnify the light and power of the person who wields it. If I'm right, then just imagine what it could do in the hands of the Midnight Minister—my instrument of death. Why, if he stood on the watchtower at Beacon Hill, he could snuff out each and every Luminary in Boston once and for all!"

Rip felt sick. Governor Chillingworth, on the other hand, appeared angry. "This is not what we agreed on, *witch*!" he spat. "You promised the imps could enslave Boston!"

Mistress Hibbins pouted her lips in mock sincerity. "Oh dear. I guess I'll have to break that little promise. Whatever will you do, Roger?"

The Governor tightened his jaw and signaled to his dogs. The animals tensed their muscles and growled.

The witch tapped her chin. "I take it you want to test my new powers?"

Chillingworth lowered his arm and the dogs ran toward her, jaws snapping wildly. In response, the Midnight Minister strode forward and raised the lantern. Instantly, a cloud of darkness poured out of the pumpkin and engulfed the animals. When the cloud dissipated, all the dogs were lying on the ground—as still as stone.

The Governor's face grew very pale. He motioned to his men, who quickly raised their muskets to their shoulders. "Shoot the witch!" he screamed.

Mistress Hibbins was inspecting her fingernails when the booming sound of musket fire echoed through the clearing. At the same time, two flashes of green light erupted from the Minister's black veil.

When the smoke from the guns dissipated, Rip saw the witch clutching her chest and stomach. She was twisting her body in a strange, almost melodramatic way.

"Oh no!" she gasped, a hint of laughter in her voice. "You shot me, Roger! I'm done for!" Then she stopped moving and pulled her hands away. Rip let out a gasp. There were two holes in her bodice, but not a trace of blood.

"Shoot me again, Roger," said the witch. She moved forward and stopped just a few feet short of the trembling Governor. "Shoot me again," she repeated, eyes flashing defiantly. "I dare you."

Chillingworth didn't hesitate. In one swift movement, he removed a pistol from his side and fired directly at the witch's heart.

Mistress Hibbins didn't even flinch. Then, from under the Midnight

Minister's veil, there came another flash of green light. The witch reached out and slowly—delicately—removed the pistol from the Governor's hand.

One by one, his supporters dropped their weapons, turned, and ran into the forest.

"Stand your ground!" cried Governor Chillingworth, his voice hoarse. But it was no use; all of the imps had fled.

"Poor Roger Chillingworth," said the witch, tossing aside the pistol. "He's all alone."

The look on the Governor's face was one of pure terror. "What is this devilry?"

"*Devilry?*" returned the witch, a bemused expression on her face. "Honestly, Roger, I'm surprised at your reaction. After all, I learned this trick from the imps."

"You did?" whispered Chillingworth.

The witch bit her lip coyly. "Yes, but I had to sell my soul to the Dark Woodsman to make it work for me. You see, when you were living in Boston, I saw how you latched on to someone else and slowly drained the life out of him. I wondered . . . was it possible for old Mistress Hibbins to do something like that? Could *I* preserve *my* life by draining the life out of someone else? And then I had an even better idea!" She snapped her fingers. "What if, instead of draining the life out of *one* person, I created something that could drain the life out of multiple people?"

Rip watched the Governor shake his head. "Impossible! For that kind of magic to work, you would have to first raise someone from the dead or else. . ." Chillingworth paused.

The witch's face split into a wicked grin. "Or else what, Roger?"

"Or use an unborn seed," whispered Chillingworth. All the color had drained from his face, and he stared at the Midnight Minister with a mixture of horror and amazement. "No, it couldn't be . . ."

Mistress Hibbins trembled with excitement. "Now you understand! The Midnight Minister is the son of Mary Dyer—the boy *you* delivered and the boy *you* buried."

Rip's mouth dropped open. *The child of Mary Dyer was the Midnight Minister!* The slender figure stood as still as a statue.

"He's my own little imp," continued Mistress Hibbins, dusting the Minister's shoulders with admiration in her eyes. "Except, instead of draining *my* life, he drains the life of everything and everyone around him. And then he gives it to me!" She held out her wrist, shaking the small length of chain that dangled from her wrist. "The day before they hanged me in Boston, I had the Minister visit a large family that lived on a farm just outside the city. They all died that night . . ." The witch closed her eyes as though savoring the memory. "And I have never felt such strength! They hanged me the next day—but I merely dangled there with my eyes closed. Bound to the Minister, I can never be killed. I would have destroyed Boston had it not been for Mary Dyer's 'blessing.' No matter, imagine what the Minister can do, now that he has the pumpkin lantern!"

"But that child . . ." said the Governor, shaking his head in disbelief. "That child was . . ."

"Was what?" demanded the witch. "WHAT WAS HE?"

Governor Chillingworth couldn't speak, but Mistress Hibbins didn't wait for his reply. At her signal, the Minister reached up and tore off his hat and veil. Rip gasped and Chillingworth screamed.

"HEADLESS!" shouted Mistress Hibbins.

Without warning, the Minister's headless body bolted forward and snatched at something in the air above Chillingworth's shoulder. When the he drew his hand back, Rip saw that the Minister held Chillingworth's imp by the throat. The Governor cried out in pain as the illusion surrounding him was suddenly shattered, revealing the withered man who had been hidden beneath the surface.

The headless Minister held the pumpkin close to the imp's face. The creature writhed in pain, shielding its eyes from the dark lantern.

"Long have I waited for this night," hissed the witch. "The night when I would obtain the lantern and take my revenge on Boston—the city that rejected me! But first," she added, her malevolent gaze boring into the Governor's imp, "I think I'll put an end to the wretched little creature who just tried to stop me."

"But I can serve you!" gasped Chillingworth. Rip thought it odd that the man was so desperate to save the imp. Indeed, the Governor, with his hands pressed tightly together, looked as though he was on the brink of a nervous breakdown.

"Please!" begged the Governor. "Let me serve you!"

Mistress Hibbins narrowed her eyes, and the Minister tightened his grip.

"You?" said the witch. "An imp? Imps don't serve anything but themselves—that much is clear."

The creature must still be speaking through Chillingworth, thought Rip.

The imp turned an ugly shade of purple, and Chillingworth clapped his hands to his head. "Please, let me serve you!" he squealed.

"You want to serve me?" whispered Mistress Hibbins.

Chillingworth nodded fearfully. The witch's smile broadened and she brought her hand down. The Minister yanked on the imp, snapping the chain that connected the creature to the man. The Governor yelled in agony as the Minister tossed the now-unattached imp to the ground.

"Here's how you can serve me," said the witch to the imp. The Midnight Minister raised the lantern. "You can be the next to die!"

The creature's scream was cut short by a flash of green light that illuminated the night sky. When the light disappeared, the imp lay on the ground, as still as stone. Chillingworth, the man, staggered to his feet. Rip noticed that he looked much different without the imp attached to him. He looked healthier. The man gave Mistress Hibbins a terrified look before sprinting into the forest.

Mistress Hibbins cackled. "And now! Now, on All Hallows' Eve—when the veil between the living and the dead is thinnest—summon the dead! Bring forth an army that will take us into Boston!"

The Minister tightened his grip on the lantern, and green fog spewed forth, spilling onto the ground like gaseous vomit. As the fog grew toward Rip, he felt the urge to run, but he couldn't move; he just knelt there in the grass. It swept across the grass and filled the entire clearing in a matter of seconds. The ground began to rumble and crack. Rip cried out as several pale, rotten hands burst through the earth.

Corpses!

He felt a cold hand on his shoulder and whipped around in fear. It was Pearl. She was pulling on him, trying to get him to safety. Despite his anger toward her, Rip allowed her to help him to his feet and pull him toward the cottage. His chain dragged heavily behind him. They clambered through the narrow door and peeked out from behind one of the broken windows.

Outside, the ground was wriggling with dozens of corpses rising from their graves. Wrenching themselves free, the dead moaned and groaned, filling the air with a haunting chorus, each face twisted into an expression of pure agony.

Mistress Hibbins raised her hands in a welcoming gesture. "Follow me, restless ones, down the path and onto *The Courser*. We leave for Boston!"

The witch turned and practically skipped away, leading the corpses to Dogtown. They staggered behind her, continuing their horrific wailing.

Watching the scene unfold, Rip thought about his family in Boston and was filled with a renewed sense of dread. He had to do something! If he didn't stop Mistress Hibbins and the Midnight Minister, they would destroy his family along with everyone else in the city. He gripped the stones in the wall and rose to his feet. He gathered his chains and stuffed them into his now-empty satchel.

"Rip!" Pearl hissed. "What are you doing? Don't go out there!"

He ignored her and hobbled outside. Squinting, he could just make out the form of the Midnight Minister at the end of the line of corpses. The headless man held the pumpkin lantern at his side. Rip focused on what little energy he had left. He had to get that lantern! He stumbled down the path as best he could. His stomach ached and sweat dripped from his forehead, but he couldn't allow himself to think about that now. His family was in danger! He couldn't fail, or they would die . . . like Charity.

Drawing closer to the Midnight Minister, Rip held his breath. The pumpkin lantern was almost within his grasp. All he had to do was reach out and take it; then he could make it light up as he had on Stormalong's ship. The light would scare the Minister, and everything would be made right.

The pumpkin bobbed up and down, matching the Minister's slow stride. Rip reached forward, his arm trembling with a mixture of fear and exhaustion. He was so close! He licked his dry lips and lunged.

The moment Rip's fingers grazed the lantern, there came a burst of green light that slammed against Rip's body like a tidal wave. He soared through the air and landed hard on the ground. As he regained his senses, he was immediately filled with a searing, biting, agonizing pain.

The Midnight Minister was on Rip in a flash and placed a heavy, booted foot on the boy's chest, pinning him to the ground. Rip felt his ribs creak and groan as the Minister bent down and reached into Rip's satchel, pulling out the black chain of the imps. Before Rip could defend himself, the Minister had looped the chain around his neck and hoisted him into the air. He kicked his legs and dug his fingers into the chain around his neck, struggling to breathe.

For several moments, the Minister simply stood there in silence and held Rip's chain like a tree holds a noose. When he spoke, it was with two voices: his own, and the voice of Mistress Hibbins.

"That's the problem with having a head. Someone can always hang you."

"The . . . lantern," Rip sputtered. "It . . . belongs . . . to Feathertop."

"*Feathertop?*" repeated the Minister. Rip could hear glee in the witch's voice. "Look around, orphan! Feathertop abandoned the New World the way your real parents abandoned you—and the way *you* abandoned your family to die in Boston!"

With that, the Minister flung Rip back to the ground. "I would kill you," he said, "but you've already sealed your fate by touching my lantern of death. You've killed yourself. The Terrible and Everlasting Slumber is coming upon you, Rip Van Winkle."

Lying on the ground, still tangled in his chains, Rip let out a strangled sob as his vision blurred. Somewhere in the distance he heard the Minister depart. He turned onto his stomach and crawled along the ground, picturing his family—his brothers and sisters, his mother and father. He couldn't help them now. He had failed them!

Rip's arms gave out and he fell into the mud. He felt as if his whole existence had been one failure after another. All he wanted now was for the pain to end. He thought of Charity and how he would soon be joining her. Thinking of her made him remember her father, Tom Walker, and his encounter with the Dark Woodsman.

"There must be something I can do," Tom had said. *"There must be some hope!"*

"An appeal to Heaven," had been the Dark Woodsman's reply.

As Rip rolled onto his back, he thought he heard a voice. Whether it was a voice in the distance or merely a distant memory he could not be sure.

"Rip," whispered the voice. It was Amelia—Amelia Simmons. She was in her kitchen, and yet she was talking directly to him. "Where do you find the light?"

He felt his heartbeat begin to slow. He opened his mouth. "Wherever it shines?"

He could sense Amelia's smile. "Exactly."

Rip's eyes flicked upward at the night sky, dimly lit by tiny pinpricks of starlight.

"Please . . . " he heard himself say, his voice hollow and ragged. "Please, Feathertop . . . if you're real, please . . . help me."

With that, his vision clouded over, and his heart stopped beating.

20

THE CATHEDRAL OF NATURE

IN WHICH RIP FINDS HIMSELF NEARLY
AWAKE...

*R*ip was in a world of darkness, consumed by unfathomable pain. He wanted to escape, but he trapped—mired in a frozen lake of agony. From somewhere in the darkness he could hear the voice of a woman calling his name. He wanted to respond—to scream for help—but he could hardly open his mouth. He couldn't do anything other than writhe in torment.

The woman spoke again: "My dear little sprout, what have you done?"

The voice reminded Rip of his mother. Thoughts of his family flooded his mind. He thought about how he had let them down again, how he was responsible for everything bad that had happened, and how he had given Mistress Hibbins the power to destroy Boston.

A fresh wave of guilt and shame washed over him. *I am a failure!* His stomach roiled, and his whole body trembled. Then he felt a hand gently stroke his hair. A cup was pressed against his lips.

"Here," said the woman. "Drink this."

Fumbling in the darkness, Rip placed his hand on the cup, took a sip, and gagged. The drink was exceptionally bitter. He tried to push the cup away, but the woman persisted.

"Drink," she repeated, this time a little more forcefully. "This bitter cup is the *only* thing that will help you."

Rip clutched his stomach with his free hand and let out a moan. His insides were burning! He no longer cared what had to be done; he just wanted the pain to end. He took the cup from the woman's hands and, with a muffled sob, pressed it to his lips and began to drink. The bitterness

185

of the drink was almost unbearable. He wanted to vomit—he wanted to stop drinking—but couldn't endure another minute of the pain. There was nothing else to be done, so he finished the bitter cup.

Several seconds later, the pain in his stomach began to subside. He breathed heavily and his muscles relaxed. Then he rolled to one side and fell into a deep, peaceful slumber.

ALL AT ONCE Rip became aware that he was awake. He rubbed his eyes. It was a bright, sunny morning, and high above him was a canopy of maple trees, whose branches swayed gently in a warm breeze.

Morning sunlight filtered through the leaves and fluttered across Rip's face, warming his body. He took a deep breath through his nose. The air was crisp and alive, fresh and sweet; he could smell honey. There was a newness in the air that was unlike anything he had ever before smelled— as though the air he had breathed up to this point in his life had been stale and rotten. Here, every breath he took now gave him renewed strength and vigor.

Rip furrowed his brow, realizing that the branches above his head were curiously shaped. Instead of reaching out horizontally, they pointed directly upward. He sat up. If he didn't know any better, he'd have thought that the branches formed a vaulted ceiling.

"Do you like my home?"

Rip jumped and whipped his head around. There, sitting on a wooden stool and smoking a long clay pipe, was the strangest, most magnificent woman Rip had ever seen. She was barefoot and wore a tattered dress that was patched together with various pieces of brown, green, and yellow fabric. Her hands and wrists were adorned with curious twine bracelets, and around her neck was a necklace of bones, shells, and the skull of a crow. Her tangled black hair hung to her shoulders and was laced with various flowers—daisies, sunflowers, forget-me-nots, and others Rip did not recognize. He noticed four—maybe five—honeybees flying from flower to flower in the woman's hair, gathering nectar and pollen.

The woman's olive skin was so smeared with dirt and grime that at first glance she looked something like a farm wife—a woman who worked all day in the fields. Even so, Rip couldn't help but sense an unmistakable light emanating from her. Though covered in dirt, she shone like the sun. Rip stared at her in awe.

"Mother Rigby!" he breathed.

"Is that what they're calling me now?" said the woman with a smile. "My, my! I have so many names it's hard to keep track. The Greeks knew me as Gaia and the Romans called me Terra. The Natives speak of me as

Nokomis, the Grand Mother. But the sprouts of the New World," she added, thoughtfully sucking on her clay pipe, "you seem to fancy the name Mother Rigby. So, Mother Rigby it is."

Rip shook his head in disbelief. "Am I dreaming?"

Her eyes twinkled as she let out a puff of smoke. "No, lad. In fact, you're very nearly awake."

"Where are we?"

"My home," she said, gesturing to the surrounding trees. She looked back at Rip and raised an eyebrow. "You didn't really think I lived in that sad little hut, did you?"

Rip glanced around him and saw that it looked more like a large room formed out of living trees, sunlight pouring through the spaces between the trunks, filling the chamber with light and illuminating the red and gold leaves that blanketed the floor. High above Rip's head, clusters of wisteria hung from the canopy ceiling like white and purple chandeliers. Rip saw two or three deer grazing in the background while numerous colorful birds flitted about.

"The trees," he murmured. "They make it look like a—"

"A what?"

Rip hesitated. "The inside of a church?"

Mother Rigby grinned. "Very good, lad. Except you've got it backward. All churches are an echo of this—the Cathedral of Nature. For to love the creations of the Earth is to worship the Being who created them."

"Why did you bring me here?" he whispered, breathless from the sheer beauty of it all.

Mother Rigby seemed pleased by Rip's amazement. "Why? Because I offer my hospitality to all, be they good or bad. And because you asked Feathertop for help, and I will always show my power to those who reverence my creations. Besides," she added with a grim expression, "you would have died had I not come."

Rip's face burned with shame, and he lowered his eyes. In doing so, he noticed for the first time that the heavy chain was gone from his leg. He looked up at Mother Rigby in surprise. Once again, she smiled back at him.

"The chain!" he exclaimed. "I thought it would never come off! How did you do it?"

Mother Rigby gazed at him proudly, almost haughtily. "I am Mother Nature." She lowered her pipe and pointed at the vaulted ceiling above. "All of creation bows before me. When people leave their cities and learn of me—walk in my woods, bathe in my rivers, eat of my harvest—they will find healing to their souls. But stray from me and return to the supposed wisdom of men, and they will find themselves in chains once more."

Rip felt a familiar pit forming in his stomach at the mention of cities and chains. Mother Rigby seemed to sense his anxiety. Leaning forward, she asked, "Child, what is it?"

Rip hesitated. He wanted to tell her that Boston was in trouble, but in doing so he would have to confess that he had given up the lantern—that it was all his fault. For a brief moment he considered telling her that it wasn't actually his fault, that he had been tricked—by Pearl, by the imps, and by the Midnight Minister. But something about Mother Rigby's demeanor told Rip that she wouldn't accept excuses.

"It's Boston," he admitted. "We have to do something before it's too late!"

"Oh, I wouldn't worry about that," she said dismissively. "Time has no authority here. You have found an intermediate space—where the passing moment lingers and becomes the present. Why, just the other day, Father Time himself was here, resting where you now sit."

Rip was bewildered by Mother Rigby's comment. "Father Time?" he repeated. "He's a real person?"

Mother Rigby laughed. "Of course he's real! And a real stick-in-the-mud, too! He's always going on and on about how hard and fast he has to work down in your world. Some days he'll just come here to take a nap or ask Feathertop for advice. Which reminds me . . ." she added, smiling wryly, "my son would like to see you."

Rip's mouth went dry. "Feathertop?"

"Yes." Mother Rigby dumped the ash out of her pipe. "He's in the garden just outside. And though time may not mean much here, obedience does. He said it was urgent, so I wouldn't keep him waiting."

Nervously, Rip rose to his feet and followed Mother Rigby across her cathedral-like home. He wondered what could be so urgent that Feathertop wanted to see him right away. His heart sank as he remembered the pumpkin lantern. Undoubtedly, the lantern was what this meeting would be about. The scarecrow was going to be furious when he discovered that Rip had lost it—or did he know already?

As they crossed the threshold of Mother Rigby's house—a natural arch formed by two converging trees—she stopped and pointed down a path that disappeared into a line of trees. "You will find Feathertop in the new garden at the end of that path. Of course, 'new' is a relative term—we've been working on that plot for ages. Oh, and before you go," she added, extending her pipe to Rip, "would you be a dear, and give this to my son?"

Rip took the pipe. "Um, sure."

"Thank you, lad."

Rip glanced toward the path, which wound down a well-lit field before it veered sharply into a dark forest. He glanced back at Mother Rigby. "The way looks dark."

The woman's eyes twinkled. "Always go as far as you can see, then let faith take you the rest of the way. Now, off you go."

Without warning, Mother Rigby gave Rip a strong (but not unkind) kick in the seat of his pants that sent him stumbling forward. Surprised, he quickly righted himself and glanced back at Mother Rigby. She smiled and then turned on her heel and disappeared into her bower. Rip took a deep breath and trundled down the path that led into the forest.

21

THE GREAT AWAKENING

IN WHICH RIP HOLDS A CORNUCOPIA OF LIFE...

*A*s he walked through the field, Rip was amazed by the vibrancy and life emanating from everything around him. Aromas of the earth filled his lungs. The wind itself seemed to breathe a story in this place. He turned a corner, passed under the bough of a sycamore tree, and let out a small gasp. There, standing on the path in front of him and leaning against a pruning hook, was Feathertop, the legendary scarecrow. He was taller, larger, and grander than Rip had remembered or could have ever possibly imagined.

The scarecrow looked down at Rip and smiled. The light from his pumpkin head filled Rip with an indescribable warmth. Even the surrounding plants seemed to sense Feathertop's power; they blossomed and bloomed with unnatural speed, responding to him as though he were the sun itself.

"My dear Rip," said Feathertop, "I am so very grateful that you have come."

Rip stared up at the scarecrow in reverential awe. It was the first time he had heard him speak. Feathertop had a pleasant, almost melodious voice; it reminded Rip of summer rain or the song of a bird.

At a loss for words, Rip held out Mother Rigby's pipe. The scarecrow approached him in two quick strides, and the flowers that surrounded Feathertop followed his movements, turning their petal-ringed heads toward him. Feathertop lifted the pipe from Rip's hand and placed it in the pocket of his own vest.

"Thank you," said he, patting his vest. "I will need that later."

The scarecrow hoisted his pruning hook and threw it onto his shoulder before offering a cornucopia-shaped wicker basket to Rip. "Now, would you be so kind as to carry this for me? All Hallows' Day is nearly upon you, and there is much work to be done."

Not seeing any reason to object, Rip reached out and took the basket in his hands.

"Thank you, lad," said Feathertop with a wink. "Come, follow me."

With that, he turned and strode off in the opposite direction. Rip started to follow but stopped suddenly. "Wait!" he called.

Feathertop looked over his shoulder.

"What about the lantern?" asked Rip. "Don't you want it?"

"Lantern?" echoed Feathertop. "What lantern?"

Rip couldn't believe his ears. "The pumpkin lantern!"

"A pumpkin lantern?" repeated Feathertop, his eyes brimming with humor. He let out a laugh so deep and rich that Rip couldn't help but smile; listening to that laughter was like listening to the sound of sunshine, if that were possible.

"Look at me, Rip. I *am* a pumpkin lantern! Why would I need one?"

"But . . . but William Blaxton told me to bring it to you!"

"Is that so?" Feathertop's face glowed brighter than ever. If Rip hadn't known any better, he'd have thought the scarecrow looked a bit mischievous.

"I don't understand," said Rip. "I thought I was supposed to bring the lantern to you."

Grinning broadly, Feathertop stuck his pruning hook into the ground and folded his arms. "Well, you seem set on it. So, come on, then! Let's see this pumpkin lantern of yours."

Rip's face fell. "I, uh . . . I lost it."

"What?" exclaimed Feathertop, the tone in his voice clearly jovial. "But weren't you supposed to bring the lantern to me?"

"I thought you were going to be upset," said Rip, by now quite confused.

Feathertop grinned. "But I'm not. And do you know why?"

Rip shook his head.

"Because I never wanted you to bring the pumpkin *lantern* to me—I wanted the lantern to bring *you* to me."

Rip was shocked. "What?"

"My dear boy," said Feathertop, "I can make hundreds of thousands of pumpkin lanterns—and I have—but there is only one you. And you are worth *infinitely* more than you could possibly imagine." The scarecrow winked before lifting his pruning hook once more. "Now, come along. There is work to be done, and you are the only one who can help me do it."

Obediently, Rip followed. Walking briskly to keep pace with Feathertop's strides, he marveled at the beauty of the surrounding garden. Every now and then the scarecrow stopped, and he and Rip pulled a few weeds, moved stones, or cleared out dead branches; other times they plucked ripe berries, plump fruits, and large vegetables. Anything they harvested went into Rip's basket.

As they worked in the garden, Rip felt enveloped in a feeling of immense joy—a feeling that almost surprised him. For so long, he had felt overwhelmed by darkness and confusion. But as he labored alongside Feathertop and pondered the scarecrow's words, Rip's heart swelled with immense gratitude for life. His cornucopia was soon overflowing with fruits, vegetables, nuts, and berries—so much so, that he soon realized he didn't have enough space for any more.

"You have a very big and beautiful garden," grunted Rip, straining under the weight of the harvest. "So much life!"

Feathertop tilted his orange head. "My garden? This is not my garden."

Rip stopped. "What do you mean it's not your garden?"

"Well, I own the land, and I care for the plants—but this is not my garden."

"Then whose is it?"

"Yours," answered the scarecrow, simply.

"Rip furrowed his brow. "What do you mean, mine?"

Feathertop smiled, bringing a hand to his triangular eyes. "Remember, Rip, everything you see is a symbol for what you do not see. This garden represents your life and all the things, and people, within it. Look yonder." He pointed to two trees. "There are your parents—two maple trees, mighty and strong. And before them is Duncan, a young oak tree—firm, loyal, and resolute. And to the right are three small aspen trees. Do you see them? Why, those are Mary, Martha, and Molly. And there is Joseph," he said, pointing to an apple tree. "And the raspberries and the blackberries are Silence and Dogood—prickly little things—but so wonderful. And the grapevine growing on the trellis is, without question, Gabriel. He's always been a good climber, that Gabriel. And those two pear trees, yes, the small ones there—those are Matthias and Zachariah; they will become mighty, fruitful trees, I have no doubt.

"Yes, Rip," said Feathertop, spreading his arms wide, "this garden is your life. Of course, there are the occasional weeds—but more than anything, this garden is filled with so much life!"

Rip glanced down at the cornucopia in his arms and felt a lump form in his throat. "But where's Charity?"

The scarecrow knelt down and put his branch-like hands on Rip's shoulders. "That's the best part. Look up."

Rip did as he was told and realized that he was standing under an arbor—a wooden archway. The arch was covered with a climbing rose-bush, overflowing with magnificent red roses.

"Charity is the entrance to the garden," said Feathertop. "And she's watching over you—all of you."

Rip set down the cornucopia and wiped his brow, choking back tears. After some time, Feathertop stood up and gestured to an obscure part of the garden.

"Come," said he. "I must show you something."

Rip followed him to a large, gnarled tree with dead branches. "What's that?"

"A hollow apple tree," said the scarecrow, placing a hand on the trunk.

Rip frowned. "It looks as though it's dead."

"It does look that way, doesn't it?" said Feathertop, a touch of melancholy in his voice. What happened next took Rip by complete surprise. The scarecrow brought his hands to his face and began to weep. "What more can I do for this tree?" he cried.

Filled with dismay, Rip left his basket and moved toward Feathertop. "Can I help?"

Feathertop spoke slowly. "You can, but will you?"

The scarecrow's words took Rip by surprise. "Yes?" he answered nervously.

Feathertop nodded and gently took Rip's hand, placing it on the trunk of the tree. "There was a time when you believed in yourself," said the scarecrow. Rip wasn't sure if Feathertop was talking to him or to the dying tree. "Have faith," he said earnestly. "Turn to the light."

Rip felt something stir beneath the palm of his hand—like the tremor of a beating heart.

"Ah!" said the scarecrow with a smile. "Look!"

Rip removed his hand. There, growing on the trunk of the tree, was a tiny shoot with green leaves. Rip held out his hands in astonishment and felt tears prick his eyes. It had been a long time since he had been able to help something grow.

Feathertop ran his hand along the tree and nodded, his face beaming with joy. "There is hope for the Sleepy Hallow."

He then crouched low and peered at a small patch of earth. He gestured for Rip to come closer. "You see this?" he asked, pointing down at the ground.

"What is it?"

"A wonder of wonders," said Feathertop, affectionately. "The most miraculous magic you will ever see."

Rip knelt down to see what Feathertop was talking about. It was a plant—a tiny sprout—pushing its way through the soil. Rip blinked in confusion. *This is the most miraculous magic I'll ever see?* "I don't understand," he said. "What is so special about this?"

"It is very special, indeed," said Feathertop, nodding warmly. "This little plant is having *a great awakening*."

Rip furrowed his brow. "I thought the Great Awakening was about overcoming the Terrible Slumber."

"Ah. And what do you think is happening here?"

Rip looked down in surprise. He had never considered the growth of a seedling comparable to the Great Awakening.

"You see, Rip, *this* is the miracle of all miracles—when life sacrifices itself to become something greater. When it awakens to its potential and rises in power. *That*," emphasized Feathertop, "is true magic. And it is happening here and now."

Rip crouched lower to get a closer look at the plant. "What is the seed going to become?"

Feathertop shrugged. "I suppose that all depends on you."

"Me?" echoed Rip. "Why me?"

The scarecrow's yellow eyes softened. "Rip, don't you understand? This plant is *you*."

Rip felt goose bumps prickle his neck. "What?"

"Another symbol," said Feathertop, "like the pumpkin lantern is a symbol of me. This plant represents what's happening inside of you." He motioned to the ground. "The world, like the soil, is cold and dark—layered with a history of destruction and death. You were planted in this world to rise above it. Do you not see? The very existence of this darkness gives you the opportunity to become a light to the world. For each of us, there comes a time when we must awaken and become what we were born to become."

As Rip glanced down at the tiny plant, he felt his chin tremble. "What am I supposed to become?"

"You already know," said Feathertop.

Despite being in the presence of Feathertop, Rip felt a wave of doubt wash over him. "But how? How can *I* be a Hallow? I'm nothing like a Hallow. I've made so many mistakes. I'm nothing like a Hallow!"

Feathertop blinked at Rip thoughtfully before turning to a large tree, laden with a beautiful white fruit. He reached up, plucked one, and held it out in front of Rip. "Do you see this fruit? It looks nothing like the tree, and yet deep inside, it has the potential to become like the tree. But before it can do that, the fruit must fall." Feathertop released the fruit and let it drop to the ground. "Battered, bruised, and broken, the fruit will open up and begin the journey to become what it was meant to become. It is the journey that all men and women must take—*through the wilderness of the world*. You have fallen, Rip, but if you awaken to your true self, you will become a Hallow—a light to the world."

Rip's breathing quickened. He could feel all the ugliness inside of him bubbling to the surface. "But I'm not a light!"

Feathertop gazed deeply into Rip's eyes. "And why is that?"

"Because there's something . . . inside of me," said Rip, his voice shaking with emotion. "A darkness I cannot see. I brought it home, and . . . and I hurt my family. Charity got sick. It's my fault . . . I was supposed to protect her, and I—I killed her!"

Overcome with grief, Rip buried his face in his hands and began to sob. It wasn't long before he felt the hand of the scarecrow rest on his shoulder. He looked up and saw something that surprised him more than anything he had seen thus far. Drops of water were trickling down Feathertop's orange face. Feathertop—the great and noble scarecrow—was crying for Rip.

"My dear boy," whispered the scarecrow, "you did not cause Charity's death. In fact, if you did anything at all, you gave her life."

Rip furrowed his brow and a tear fell down his cheek. "What?"

"There *is* something inside of you. But it is *not* darkness."

"What is it?"

The scarecrow was thoughtful for a few moments before speaking. "Rip, do you know why my mother named me Feathertop?"

Rip sniffled and shook his head.

"Because when my mother created this body, she placed upon it a dusty three-cornered hat with the longest tail feather of a rooster. She thought it was the finest hat in all the land." At this, Feathertop chuckled. "But in reality, it was really quite ugly."

Rip couldn't help but laugh.

"Ever since then," continued the scarecrow, "she's called me Feather-top. I've since lost the hat—I think it's somewhere in New Orleans or Jamestown—but the name remains. The point is," he added, lifting one of his branch fingers, "*that* is why my mother gave me my name. Do you know why your mother gave you your name? Do you know what it means?"

Slowly, Rip shook his head.

Gently, Feathertop took both of Rip's hands and placed them on either side of his own pumpkin head. "Then look to me, and see yourself as you really are."

Rip stared into the yellow light that streamed from Feathertop's face and fell into a trance. He found himself standing in the South Burying Ground at midnight. At first, he thought he must be dreaming, but the cold air on his face made him think otherwise. He heard a noise to his right, looked toward it, and saw Feathertop standing next to a tree. The scarecrow was beckoning to a woman who was carrying a lantern.

Rip squinted and realized that the woman was Abigail, his mother. Aside from looking younger, she also looked . . . different. Her whole body, from head to foot, was aglow with a strange light that outshone even the light from her lantern.

She approached Feathertop and made an awkward curtsy. The scarecrow spoke to her and pointed toward an open grave. As she rushed toward the grave, Feathertop looked up at Rip. He motioned for the boy to come closer. Rip obeyed.

He heard his mother cry out and then call to Josiah for help. Rip saw his father run out of the darkness. He was also aglow—though his light wasn't nearly as bright as Abigail's. Josiah removed his coat and climbed down into the grave. After a few moments of struggling and scrambling, Abigail was cradling the limp body of a baby boy. Rip's mouth went dry as he realized that the boy was him.

This was the night they found me!

He watched as his father wrapped his arms around Abigail and the baby. The two of them sat there in soul-stretching silence.

Rip was startled when his mother suddenly looked up. For a moment he thought she could see him; she seemed to be looking directly at him! But she was looking past him, at Feathertop . . . or . . . at the stars.

"Please . . . ," she whispered.

The scarecrow nodded and moved forward as gently as a breeze. Quietly, he removed Mother Rigby's pipe from the pocket of his vest. He then dipped his finger into the pipe and slowly twirled it around. The pipe's bowl expanded magically until the item looked more like a ladle. Feathertop stretched his arm high above his head and swept the ladle across the starry, milky sky, as if scooping something into it. He then reached toward the Van Winkles and slowly poured the contents of the ladle over the baby. A sparkling white light—as bright as starlight—flowed from the pipe's bowl, settling on the baby's chest. From there, it reached outward until it had spread to Abigail and Josiah. Rip stared at his parents in astonishment. Against the backdrop of midnight, the Van Winkles glowed as brightly as a bonfire.

The baby began to stir, and Feathertop stepped back. Abigail was crying and Josiah was choking back emotion. After a while, Abigail regained her composure and told her husband that she wanted to name the child Rip.

Josiah raised an eyebrow. "Rip? As in 'Rest In Peace'?"

"Yes," said Abigail, rocking the infant softly. "Rip Van Winkle."

"Why 'Rip'?"

"Because now I know why I've felt so restless," whispered Abigail, her eyes brimming with tears. "I was missing this boy. Josiah, *I've never felt this kind of peace.*"

Rip felt a lump form in his throat as the graveyard faded from his view. He was again standing in Feathertop's garden, his hands still on the scarecrow's face.

"Do you see it now, Rip?" asked Feathertop, quietly taking Rip's hands into his own. "Your life brings peace. It has always been so."

Feathertop stretched forth his finger and touched the boy on the forehead. Instantly, Rip's mind was flooded with memories. He saw himself as a young boy—a boy who radiated a light as bright as starlight. Wherever he went, plants responded to his light in marvelous ways. Yearning to be close to Rip, the plants reached out and grew toward him. In his mind's eye, Rip saw the day he had wrapped his arms around his mother's failing pumpkin. He noticed that the light from his body flowed into the gourd, causing it to expand rapidly.

Next, Rip recalled sitting next to Charity at the Harvest Festival the day they first met. He noticed that she had a light about her as well, but it was very dim—like the last glowing ember of a dying fire. Rip had placed his hand on Charity's as he explained that the Van Winkle home was a belonging place. Watching the memory, Rip noticed that, as their hands touched, light passed from himself to Charity. Eventually the girl looked up and her eyes brightened.

From outside the vision, Rip could hear Feathertop's voice: "Do you see the light within yourself, Rip? Do you see how you have given it to others?"

Feathertop recalled another memory for Rip. Duncan was hiding under his bed. Rip noticed that his mute brother also had a light about him, though his was very dim, and the surrounding darkness was threatening to snuff it out. Rip saw himself sit by Duncan's bed and tell the boy stories. Duncan looked up at him in gratitude and wonder.

Rip watched as Duncan reached out and held him by the wrist. In that instant, light traveled from himself to Duncan, leaving both of them glowing in equal measure.

"Do you see the light within yourself?" repeated Feathertop. "Do you see how you have given it to others?" Once again, the scarecrow pressed his finger against Rip's forehead, and Rip found himself standing on a street in Boston. Rip was surprised to find Feathertop standing next to him here.

"This is a vision of the past," explained the scarecrow. "It is shown from *my* perspective."

Rip looked out and saw Mrs. Delaney hobbling down the street, the cold autumn wind battering her frail body. She held baby Molly in her arms, as Mary and Martha clung to her skirt. The woman and the girls each had a light of their own, but their lights were weak, flickering in the wind as they staggered forward.

Rip saw Feathertop stride toward the woman and wrap a yellow shawl around her shoulders. The shawl flapped in the wind like a small banner. Rip remembered how he had taken notice of that bright shawl and how it had prompted him to call out to Charity and Duncan. Soon, the Van Winkle children were with the Delaneys and helping them inside the house.

"Look!" commanded Feathertop, pointing to Duncan. "See what your brother does with the light you shared with him."

Rip watched as Duncan (who was now positively glowing with a white light) took little Molly into his arms and held her close to his chest. The infant looked up at Duncan and beamed, her light quickly growing to match that of the boy who held her.

"Look!" commanded Feathertop again, now pointing at Charity. "See what your sister does with the light you shared with her."

Charity returned to the room and immediately attended to the two older Delaney girls. As she did so, Rip noticed rays of light pass from Charity to Mary and Martha.

"Do you see the light within yourself? Do you see how you have given it to others?"

The scene changed, and Rip found himself standing next to Feathertop on the deck of a ship. Not far away, Joseph stood by the deck's rail. The boy was leaning over, trying to get one last glimpse of his parents' still bodies as they were lowered into the sea. Somehow, Rip could tell that Joseph had once been filled with light and energy, just as Rip himself was. But the loss of his parents was almost more than the poor boy could bear, and his light had nearly gone out. Grief-stricken, the child stood there, numb and despondent, clutching the small wooden invention—his last physical connection to his father—close to his chest. Rip saw Feathertop approach Joseph and place his hands on the boy's shoulders. This seemed to sustain what little light remained within the boy.

The scene changed once more, and Rip saw the city constable come and guide Joseph to the Boston courthouse, where Judge Van Winkle was working. Feathertop did not leave the boy's side. After hearing about the death of Joseph's parents, Josiah looked down at the boy in bewilderment. At this point, Feathertop stepped forward and touched Josiah on the chest, directly over his heart. The light within Josiah grew until it filled the entire courthouse.

Feathertop stepped back and spoke to Rip again. It was clear that the others in the vision couldn't hear the scarecrow. "Your father's parents died when he was Joseph's age. As a result, he sees himself in that boy— and well he should. It created an empathy in him that has helped him love and care for Joseph in a very special way.

"You see, Rip, every man, woman, and child on this earth is a wandering pilgrim in his or her own way—each searching for a belonging place. That sense of belonging is found only as we care for one another."

Rip looked upon his father in amazement. He hadn't known about his grandparents' deaths.

"You can stay with us," the judge said to Joseph, his eyes watery. "Our home is your home." As Joseph looked up at Josiah, his own light brightened.

Feathertop tugged on Rip's elbow. "Come," he said. "There is more I wish to show you within these walls."

Rip followed the scarecrow out of the room and down the narrow hallway of the courthouse. At the end of the hall, Feathertop opened an oak door and stepped through. Rip felt his heart sink when he saw what was inside. The pirate twins, Silence and Dogood, were huddled in a corner of the room, holding one another.

"Nobody wants us," whispered Silence to her brother, weeping bitterly.

"Dear children," said Feathertop, kneeling down and wrapping his arms around the twins. "You are *always* wanted by me."

The twins were unable to see or hear the scarecrow, but they suddenly began to glow with a soft light. Dogood squeezed his sister's hand. "It will be all right," he said.

Feathertop turned his great head toward Rip. "In their first five years of life, these two children had never known a comfortable bed, never known a mother's hug, never celebrated a birthday, and never, ever felt wanted or loved. And they would have continued on without such things had it not been for you, Rip. You shared your light with these wild berries by urging your father to rescue them." The scarecrow let out a mournful sigh, and two shining tears fell from his eyes. "Rip, you gave them a belonging place —you gave them life. Can you not see that?"

Wiping tears from his own eyes, Rip lowered his head and saw that he was no longer standing on the wooden floor of the courthouse room, but on a faded dirt path. He looked up to see that the vision had changed. He now stood in a forest at twilight, and he could just make out a skinny, barefooted boy sitting next to a small fire. It was Gabriel. Feathertop sat across from Gabriel, watching over him.

"Gabriel's parents died of consumption," Feathertop told Rip, his eyes never leaving the small boy. "He never speaks of it, but to this day, Gabriel blames himself for their deaths."

Rip's mouth opened slightly. "He blames himself? But why?"

Feathertop shrugged. "He was the first to get sick. Because of that, he thinks it is his own fault. He blames himself for living while his parents are dead."

"But consumption is a disease!" exclaimed Rip. "It's not Gabriel's fault!"

"And what of smallpox?" asked Feathertop, turning his head to look at Rip. "Is that not also a disease? Is it your fault that your family contracted it after you did?"

Remembering Charity's death, Rip felt a familiar pang in his heart. "That's different," he objected.

"How?" pressed the scarecrow. "Gabriel ran into the woods because he believed that he had killed his parents. He actually believed that he was going to be arrested and charged for murder. Imagine how Gabriel must have felt when the son of a judge reached out to help him, freed him from a cage, and offered him a new home. Imagine the light that filled the heart of this poor boy when you did that."

As Rip glanced down at Gabriel, who was holding his knees close to his chest and quietly stoking the fire, he was overcome by a feeling of deep sympathy. He wanted to go to his brother; he wanted to put his arm around Gabriel and tell him that everything would be all right.

Feathertop lifted his hand and pointed directly at Rip. "Look!"

Rip looked down at his own arms and saw that he was now aglow with light. "What's happening?" he asked breathlessly.

"You are remembering who you really are."

The scarecrow snapped his fingers, and the vision changed once more. This time, Rip was standing on a wintry street in Boston as the sun set in the west. Rip looked around for Feathertop and finally caught sight of the scarecrow standing some distance away, watching over two small boys. As the boys peered out from behind the corner of a building, Rip recognized them at once. It was Matthias and Zachariah. Rip shivered from the cold and made his way over to them.

Feathertop glanced at Rip before reaching out and touching Matthias on the shoulder. "Poor child," he whispered. "Matthias is doing his best to care for his younger brother, but he is very weak and weary, and the night is bitterly cold. He may very well die tonight."

"No," said Rip. "Not Matthias."

"Do not worry," said Feathertop, looking out at the street, "for help is on its way. Remember?"

Following the scarecrow's gaze, Rip saw a younger version of himself walking down the street—glowing as brightly as William Blaxton had. As Rip's younger self walked by, Matthias and Zachariah nodded to each other and stole forward. The two brothers walked quietly behind the younger Rip, reaching out toward his coat.

"They are not trying to pick your pockets," said Feathertop. "Not really. They are following you because they can no more endure the cold and dark and you are warm and bright. You are a beacon, Rip."

Rip watched his younger self whirl around and snatch Matthias by the wrist. Almost immediately, the boy was filled with light. Young Zachariah looked up at his brother's captor with a reverential awe.

Feathertop breathed a sigh of relief, as though he, himself, had been deeply concerned for these two boys. "Matthias and Zachariah are among the few who can actually see light within other human beings," said the scarecrow. "And they saw it within you, Rip. You took them to your home and gave them a belonging place. Therein lies your *true* magic. You have a gift with plants, yes—but your greatest power is giving light and life to others.

"Come," he said, gently tugging on Rip's shoulder. "There is one more child I wish to show you."

Rip was confused. He had seen all of his brothers and sisters. What other child could there be?

As Feathertop strode across the street, the stones and buildings melted away, revealing a spacious field with a small, decrepit hut in the distance. The midnight sky was overcast and laden with heavy storm clouds. A girl ran from the house and knelt over the body of a boy lying in the field.

"Rip!" she sobbed. "Rip! Wake up! Please, wake up!"

Rip realized that the girl was Pearl.

"I'm sorry!" she sobbed, cradling Rip as rain began to fall. Thunder rumbled in the distance.

"Poor Pearl," said Feathertop. "Of all Boston's children, she is, perhaps, the most lost. She was cursed to live forever as a little girl and denied by her real father. Then her mother disappeared, and her stepfather has abused her in every imaginable way. All Pearl has ever wanted was to live somewhere safe—to have a home, a belonging place."

Rip cast his eyes downward, remembering the last thing he said to Pearl—that she didn't belong. Yet she had betrayed him because she wanted a home. As the scene faded, Rip felt Feathertop's hands on his shoulders once more. The scarecrow knelt down in front of him.

"Do you understand now, Rip? Your garden is in this 'New World,' and it is part of my labor. This land is a refuge for the homeless, the tired, and the poor, who yearn for a belonging place of their own. I *am* the Pumpkin Lantern—I am the light in the darkness. I bring light to the children of the Earth. I bring them home. I ask you now, Rip, *please* . . . awaken to who you really are and share the light within you. Pearl needs you. Your family needs you. Boston needs you. *I need you.* Help them wake up and find their way back to me."

Rip's chin began to tremble. "I just don't know if I can do it."

Gently, Feathertop reached out and placed a small object in Rip's hand. He looked down and was surprised to see a pumpkin seed. He looked up at Feathertop once more; the scarecrow's bright orange face was as warm as the sun. "Have faith, Rip. Believe in yourself, and believe in me—for in me there is always hope. No matter how dark things may seem, remember that the sun will always rise. Light will always triumph over darkness."

Rip closed his hand around the seed and nodded slowly. "I'll go."

"I knew you would," said Feathertop. The scarecrow laid his hand on Rip's chest, directly over his heart. "Where once you felt hollow, may you now feel hallow."

Rip felt a warmth course through his entire body.

"Your world," continued Feathertop, his hand still on Rip's chest, "your world is filled with pain. It will hurt for others to wake up, just as it has hurt for you. But I promise the pain will diminish as you move forward."

Rip stared into Feathertop's eyes and nodded once again. "I'm ready."

"Then wake up," said the scarecrow.

Rip cried out. He felt as though Feathertop had punched him in the chest, but the scarecrow hadn't moved. Feathertop simply looked back at Rip, his face as calm as a summer's morning.

"Wake up," he repeated.

Once again, Rip felt something slam against him. He staggered backward.

"Wake up."

Again, something struck Rip in the chest—this time with the force of a club. He fell on his back, clutching his chest.

"Wake up, Rip!" The voice he now heard sounded different—deeper and rougher than the scarecrow's gentle tone.

He felt the blow again, and this time the impact was so hard that he blacked out from the pain.

"RIP, WAKE UP!"

He opened his eyes and gasped. Cold air flooded into his lungs. Looking up, he found himself lying on his back in a dark field. His eyes immediately grew wide with fright. Kneeling over him, with a raised hand clenched into a tight fist, was Goodman Brown!

THE SLEEPY HALLOW

IN WHICH TWO PEOPLE ARE AWAKENED...

*G*oodman glared down at Rip before slowly unclenching his fist and letting it drop. "You're alive," he acknowledged. "Good. You had us worried."

Baffled, Rip turned his head and saw that Pearl was also there. She was kneeling alongside Goodman and looking at Rip with an expression of relief. Rip sat up slowly, wincing at the pain in his chest.

"Sorry about that," said Goodman. "I had to strike your chest several times in order to revive you."

Rip looked at Goodman in astonishment. "You . . . you revived me?"

The Puritan nodded grimly.

"But why?"

"Turns out he's not half as bad as people think he is," said a familiar voice.

Rip tilted his head to see Nathaniel perched on Goodman's horse.

"Nathaniel!" exclaimed Rip. "You're alive! Where have you been?"

The raven beamed, cleared his throat, and puffed out his chest; he had obviously been waiting for this triumphant moment. "Yes, the story of my daring escape from *The Courser*—an epic tale full of mystery, adventure, and bravery—"

"Oh, get on with it, Nathaniel!" growled Goodman.

The raven lowered his beak. "Ah, yes, well, in the interest in time . . . after our encounter with Mistress Hibbins, I apparently lay unconscious in the crow's nest for several hours. When I came to, it was morning and the ship was flying somewhere over Cape Ann. I could hear the witch from the deck below, muttering to herself and rattling that horrible chain on her arm. Given the fact that she was alone, it took me some time to realize that she wasn't speaking to herself but was actually speaking *through* the Midnight Minister, who was somewhere else entirely."

"She controls him like a puppet," said Rip.

"Yes, exactly!" said Nathaniel, flapping his wings excitedly. "Apparently, the Midnight Minister had met a girl in the woods, and from my covert position in the crow's nest, I was able to hear what the witch was having him say."

At this point, Pearl cast her eyes downward but Nathaniel carried on. "It was a one-sided conversation, of course, but I was able to gather the gist of it. The plot was to bring you here and trick you into giving the lantern to the Minister. I knew I had to warn you—and Jonathan—but I didn't know where to find either of you. I left the ship and made for Cape Ann, and that's when I ran into Goodman Brown."

"Literally," muttered the Puritan.

The raven let out a deep sigh of annoyance. "I said I was sorry! Besides, when you're being chased by a witch, you're hardly looking forward."

"Mistress Hibbins chased you?" asked Rip.

"Yes! And I made a rather daring escape, if I do say so myself. But that's the 'adventure and bravery' part, which I have been forced to omit." He glared at Goodman.

The Puritan rolled his eyes. "Suddenly, running away is considered a form of bravery."

"*At any rate,*" emphasized Nathaniel, "I flew into this deadbeat, and he drove the witch away."

"Now *that's* bravery," remarked Goodman.

The raven ignored him. "After Goodman explained a few things to me, we joined forces in search of you. Although," he added sadly, "it seems we weren't quite fast enough."

"It's all my fault," said Pearl, keeping her eyes to the ground. It was the first time Rip had heard her speak since he had awakened. "I brought Rip to this place. I wanted to protect him, but I nearly got him killed."

"Pearl," said Rip, "don't blame yourself. We were both tricked into making some pretty terrible choices, and . . . I said some things that I didn't mean."

He reached out and touched her arm. When she looked up at him, he saw starlight reflected in her eyes. Rip smiled and squeezed her wrist. "The best thing we can do now is look to the light and keep moving forward—"

"*In faith,*" finished Goodman.

Rip glanced up in astonishment. The Puritan's voice, though still quite rough, was marked with a note of sincerity that Rip hadn't expected to hear. Goodman glanced away and stared at something in the distance. "I know that phrase well," he said quietly. "It was repeated to me many times when I was a Hallow before . . . before my wife died."

Rip held his breath. There was a stillness in the air, a reverence in the moment—as if nature itself were leaning in, waiting for what Goodman would say next.

"I never thought I was worthy to be a Hallow," said Goodman, still gazing out across the field. "I used to believe that the only way I could make it through this life was to cling to my wife and follow her to heaven. *She* was my light. She . . . she was my life. And when she died . . . ," Goodman paused, ". . . it was as if I had died, too. I felt . . . *hollow*, not *hallow*. I became bitter and distrustful. I searched for Feathertop—not for the sake of others but for mine. I wanted him to bring my wife back. But I never found him. In my despair, I surrendered my lantern to Mistress Hibbins and shrank into the shadows." The Puritan let out a deep moan. "It was *my* faithlessness that nearly destroyed the city. It was Mary's faith that saved it. Had it not been for Mary Dyer's sacrifice, Mistress Hibbins would have destroyed Boston."

Goodman lowered his head. "Rip, the reason I wanted your lantern was because I thought I could stop you from making the same mistake I had. I didn't want the lantern to fall into the hands of Mistress Hibbins. I wanted the chance to stop her and . . . to be like Mary Dyer. I wanted a chance *at redemption*."

Rip peered curiously at Goodman. There was something about the Puritan's demeanor that reminded him of what he had seen in the garden with Feathertop. Or was that all a dream? Had he really seen Feathertop? Rip felt something small and pointed jab into his palm. Turning his hand over, he discovered a pumpkin seed—the one Feathertop had given him.

Rip peered up at Goodman. "You still believe in the light, don't you?"

Goodman said nothing.

Rip turned the seed over, concentrating hard. "While I slept, I had a dream—or maybe I was seeing things as they really are. I don't know. Either way, I saw Feathertop and . . . I saw you."

Goodman glanced up in surprise. "You saw me?"

"A symbol of you, yes," nodded Rip. "You were . . . a tree, a dying apple tree, and Feathertop was doing everything he could to save you. He wept over you."

Rip saw Goodman breathe heavily, but the man made no reply.

"I, too, was worried about you," continued Rip. "But Feathertop showed me a tiny shoot—a new branch with green leaves—coming out of that tree." He reached out tentatively and touched Goodman on his arm. "Feathertop told me there was hope for the Sleepy Hallow."

The Puritan bowed his head and nodded slowly. "Now it is high time to awake out of sleep," he murmured, "for now is our salvation nearer than when we believed."

Rip tilted his head. "What's that?"

Goodman exhaled deeply. "It's from the Bible, my wife's favorite chapter. She read it to me when I became the thirteenth Hallow." He paused before slowly rising to his feet. "Well, then, what do we do now?"

All eyes turned toward Rip, and he looked back at group in astonishment. "You're asking me?"

"You're a Hallow," said Goodman, cracking a smile. "You must have some idea as to how we might save Boston."

Nathaniel cleared his throat. "Pardon me for being a pessimist, but Mistress Hibbins and the Minister have Stormalong's flying ship. Even if we *did* have some sort of plan, we couldn't possibly catch up to them!"

"Uh, Nathaniel," said Goodman, "need I remind you that you are perched on the finest Lightning Horse in New England?"

Gunpowder let out a loud whinny, and Nathaniel sheepishly tucked his beak under a wing. Pearl helped Rip to stand in the meantime.

"Hang on," said Rip. "You're saying that horse can take all *four* of us to Boston?"

Goodman grinned and put his hands on his hips. "Just tell him where you want to go, and he'll take you there! Do you know what that witch is planning?"

Rip bit his lip. "She said something about Blaxton's Beacon."

"Blaxton's Beacon?" repeated Pearl, furrowing her brow. "The tower on Beacon Hill?"

Rip nodded slowly. "Yes, why?"

Pearl held up a hand. At length, she pointed at the raven. "Nathaniel! You know everything. Isn't there something special about the watchtower on Beacon Hill?"

Nathaniel blinked and cocked his head to one side. "Well, there's a legend . . . but it's never been confirmed."

"All right, what is it?"

"Well, according to the legend, the watchtower was commissioned by Governor Winthrop and designed by William Blaxton. The original idea behind it was that it would be less of a watchtower and more of a magical beacon, a torch, a lighthouse—"

"A light in the darkness," said Goodman.

"Exactly," said Nathaniel. "After all, it was Governor Winthrop who said that Boston would be a 'city upon a hill' and that all eyes would be upon it. The intent was for the beacon to fight the Terrible Slumber with light while simultaneously drawing other Luminaries to Boston."

"It's true," confirmed Goodman. "The watchtower *is* a magical beacon. It was enchanted by the original Hallows to magnify the magical light within the community. Of course, once the Terrible Slumber took full effect, the citizens forgot about the true intent of the beacon, and it became a simple watchtower. It's no longer used to invite people in, but to keep them out."

Rip was watching Pearl. She was rubbing her temples and thinking feverishly. "Pearl, what is it?"

"I think I know what Mistress Hibbins is planning."

"What?" asked Rip.

"Well, she said that the Midnight Minister drains the life out of others, right?"

"Right," said Rip.

"Well," began Pearl, "if that's true, then the Minister's primary power is death. We saw that when he killed all those dogs."

"And when he raised the dead," added Rip.

"Exactly," said Pearl. "When the lantern came into his hands, it no longer glowed with light; it . . . it 'glowed' with darkness."

"The lantern was magnifying his power," said Goodman.

"Yes," said Pearl. She knelt down and used her finger to draw an almond shape in the dirt. "All right, pretend this is Boston. Now, near the center of the city is the watchtower on Beacon Hill." She put a dot in the center of her makeshift map. "It's like a lighthouse on a hill—a light on a candlestick. The idea behind the beacon, as Nathaniel said, was to fight the Terrible Slumber with light. But what if, instead of lighting that candle with light, it was 'lit' with darkness? What would happen if the Midnight Minister lit the beacon using the pumpkin lantern?"

Goodman let out a low whistle. "His power over death would be magnified by both the lantern and the Beacon. He would drain the life out of everyone in Boston—possibly all of Columbia—in an instant."

Pearl nodded grimly.

"Well, what a wonderful predicament!" squawked Nathaniel sarcastically. "Mistress Hibbins is about to destroy Columbia, and we can't stop her. She can't be killed!"

"That's not *entirely* true," said Pearl slowly.

Nathaniel narrowed his black eyes. "Come again?"

"Mistress Hibbins *can* be killed."

"And how do you know that?" asked Goodman.

Pearl let out a deep sigh. "Long ago, I was cursed by Mistress Hibbins to remain a child, both in body and in mind. In the decades since then, I've watched nearly everyone I know grow old and die—and yet I remain. My mother spent years looking for a way to reverse the spell, only to learn that as long as Mistress Hibbins is alive, I'm trapped like this. But if she were to die—"

"Then the curse would be broken," finished Goodman.

Pearl nodded. "So ever since my mother went missing, I've been studying Mistress Hibbins, trying to learn her weakness."

"And you think you've found one?" asked Rip.

"The Midnight Minister," said Pearl. "He's her greatest strength, but also her secret weakness. Do you remember what happened to Chillingworth, the man, after his imp was killed?"

Rip frowned, trying to remember the details. "He got up and ran into the forest."

"That's right!" said Pearl excitedly. "Once Chillingworth was free of the imp, his health came back to him and he ran away."

"The same thing happened to Jonathan," said Rip, eyes wide with amazement. "He was weak when he was in the cage made by the imps, but as soon as he became free, his strength returned to him."

Goodman rubbed his chin. "So, if Ann's link to the Minister were broken, her death would be returned to her. Kill the Minister, kill the witch."

"Exactly," said Pearl, a look of triumph in her eyes.

"Well then," said Nathaniel. "We have a most excellent idea of how we can stop her in the, ah, long term, but how do we stop her in the short term? She's heading to Boston, and I'll wager she's almost there by now!"

"We don't need to stop *her*," said Pearl. "We just need to stop the ship. Because of Mary Dyer's blessing, Mistress Hibbins cannot set foot in the city. If she did, then 'all life would turn against her.' At least, that's what my mother said. If we stop the ship, we stop Mistress Hibbins."

"But she still has her broomstick," said Rip. "Even if we stopped the ship, she could still fly to Beacon Hill."

Pearl grinned. "No, she cannot. I destroyed her broomstick earlier tonight, remember?" She nodded in the direction of the trees near the cottage. "It's over there, burned to ashes. I'm telling you, all we have to do is stop the ship."

Goodman grunted. "And just how do you propose we do that? My horse can't magically appear onboard *The Courser*."

"Ah," said Nathaniel, raising a wing, "there *might* be a way to board the ship."

All heads turned toward the bird, waiting for him to go on. Nathaniel appeared nervous.

"Yes?" prompted Rip.

Nathaniel shrugged. "Well, it's just that . . . well, it is a little mad . . . and it calls for, ah, a great deal of bravery on the part of the only one of us who can *actually* fly . . ." The bird swallowed hard and fell silent.

"And?" snapped Goodman impatiently. "Good heavens, Nathaniel! The *one* time you're at a loss for words!"

Nathaniel's wings slumped. "Stormalong and his crew are tied up below deck, right? If you get me close enough, I can fly up to *The Courser*, find some rope, tie one end to the ship, and send the other end down to you. From there, any one of you can climb to the top, sneak down to the lower decks, and—I don't know—release Stormalong and his men? Take back the ship? Mutiny, and all that?"

"Nathaniel," said Goodman with genuine amazement in his voice, "*that* is the most useful thing you've *ever* said.

Nathaniel did not appear to know whether or not this was a compliment. "Thank you?"

The Puritan turned to Rip. "What do you think?"

Rip exhaled slowly. "Well, if Nathaniel's all right with going up there—"

"*All right?*" interrupted Nathaniel. "Don't be ridiculous! I've never been more terrified in my entire life! But if I'm to die, then what a magnificent way to go!"

Despite the gravity of the situation, Rip couldn't help but smile. The bird's declaration had reminded him of his first encounter with Nathaniel and Jonathan. Rip felt a pit form in his stomach when he thought about the preacher. "Wait, what about Jonathan? Is he still in Dogtown?"

Goodman shook his head. "We saw him being loaded aboard *The Courser* shortly after our arrival. No doubt Mistress Hibbins is using him like a mule—forcing him to use his power over wind to drive the ship toward Boston."

Rip tightened his jaw and clenched his fists. The thought of the witch hurting the preacher made Rip's blood boil. "We have to stop her!"

Goodman cracked a broad grin. "I think so, too. First things first—we'll have to find *The Courser*. Now, I imagine the witch will be cutting across land, approaching Boston from the north, near the mouth of the Massachusetts River."

"Where's that?" said Rip.

"*Charles* River," corrected Nathaniel. "Close to where the Puritans settled before meeting Blaxton."

"If we arrive there in time," continued Goodman, "Nathaniel can fly up to the ship. If he gets the rope just halfway down, I can use my magic to pull it the rest of the way. Then we can climb aboard and find Stormalong and his crew. Fortunately for us, both Gunpowder and *The Courser* produce heavy storms—so I imagine we won't have to worry about being especially quiet. With any luck, we'll be able to take control of the ship, and then we can deal with Mistress Hibbins."

Nathaniel let out a loud caw. "You realize that, given the witch's power, it is highly unlikely any of us will make it out alive? I hate to be the pessimist, but things do seem rather hopeless."

Goodman let out a laugh so deep and rich that it surprised Rip. He had never heard Goodman laugh so merrily. "You're starting to sound like a younger version of myself," said the Puritan while adjusting his hat. "Why are ye fearful, O ye of little faith?"

"I know that reference," said the raven testily. "And for your information, we are, quite literally, deciding whether or not to ride into a storm."

Goodman nodded grimly. "We may very well be riding into a storm— the darkest of our lives. Victory is uncertain. But how can that matter when this is the right thing to do? Our lives are meant to be a light in the wilderness, and so we must go into the darkness—forward in faith."

Nathaniel rolled his eyes. "A fine speech, Goodman. Bravo. Right, then. Forward it is!"

Goodman turned to his horse and gently stroked its sleek neck. "'The night is far spent, the day is at hand,'" he murmured. "Perhaps tonight old Goodman Brown finds his redemption."

With that, the Puritan grabbed the saddle horn and hoisted himself up onto Gunpowder. In the distance, dark clouds began to roll in. Holding the horse's reins in one hand, Goodman turned and held out his other hand to Rip and Pearl.

"You ready?" he asked.

Rip pocketed the pumpkin seed and glanced over at Pearl. She nodded back at him. The two climbed onto the horse and sat behind Goodman.

Nathaniel, who was now sandwiched between Goodman and the horse's mane, let out a snort and rolled his eyes. "The only time they listen to me is when I offer a plan that puts my life in mortal peril. Brilliant."

Rip looked down at the ground and tilted his head. "Wait, do you see that?"

"See what?" asked Pearl.

"Your map of Boston," said Rip, pointing to Pearl's almond-shaped sketch of the city. "What does it look like to you?"

Pearl squinted before taking in a sharp breath. "*An eye,*" she whispered.

Once seen, the symbol couldn't be unseen. The outline of the peninsula looked very much like an eye, with the center dot of Beacon Hill as the pupil.

"Good heavens," muttered Nathaniel. "I've flown over Boston hundreds of times and never before noticed that. It looks exactly like the symbol of Columbia. I suppose it just goes to show that everything we see in life is a symbol for what we cannot see."

"Indeed," said Goodman. "It would seem that tonight is destined to be the battle for Boston's Great Awakening." The Puritan leaned forward and whispered something into the horse's ear. Gunpowder whinnied and pawed the ground with his hoof.

"Hold on tight," Goodman shouted over his shoulder. "And don't mind the tingling sensation in your eyes. That's just the lightning!" He whipped the reins across Gunpowder's neck, and the horse took off at a gallop. Rumbles of thunder and flashes of light came from every direction.

Rip tightened his hold on the Puritan as he felt the hair on the back of his neck rise up, and his eyes begin to sting. Then, all at once, there was a brilliant flash of light, and everything went white.

23

THE CITY ON A HILL

IN WHICH THEY RIDE INTO THE STORM...

*R*ip felt the horse come to a stop, but he had to blink several times before he could see clearly again. Still sitting astride Gunpowder, the riders were now on a low hill near the mouth of the Charles River. Before them stretched Boston Harbor, dotted with numerous islands. Goodman tugged on the reins, and the horse moved closer to the harbor. Even at this late hour, the lights in Boston made the city glimmer in the darkness.

Nathaniel—who had wriggled out from between Goodman and the horse, and was now perched comfortably on Rip's shoulder—murmured, "City on a hill."

"Look!" exclaimed Pearl, pointing at the sky above the river.

But she did not need to point. A monstrous green and black storm was approaching from the northwest. The mere sight of it caused Rip's mouth to go dry.

"All right, Nathaniel," said Goodman, an undeniable note of humor in his voice, "let's see if this plan of yours will really work."

Rip felt the bird tremble slightly. "Are we sure it's the best plan?" asked Nathaniel. "I mean, we really never explored other options . . ."

"That's because we're running out of time," said the Puritan firmly. "Come on, now, Nathaniel. Boston needs you."

The bird puffed out his chest. "Boston needs me, eh? Well, I suppose I can't shirk my responsibility now. But I must say, those are the largest storm clouds I have ever seen—"

"Nathaniel . . . ," growled Goodman.

"No matter! The harder the conflict, the more glorious the triumph!" The raven spread his wings and turned his head to Rip. "Write that down," he said. "I'm sure it will inspire future generations. And if nothing else, you can put it on my tombstone."

With that, the raven took off in the direction of the clouds, flapping his wings wildly until he disappeared from sight. The storm, meanwhile, was passing over the river and moving quickly toward Boston.

"The witch is heading for Beacon Hill," shouted Goodman, "just as Pearl said!"

Rip thought about his family and clenched his fists. "We must hurry!"

Goodman slapped the reins, and the children tightened their hold as Gunpowder reared up and whinnied. Rip closed his eyes when he heard the familiar rumble of thunder. The next thing he heard was the sound of the horse's front hooves slapping down on wood. He opened his eyes to see that Gunpowder was now standing at the edge of Boston's Wharf, the long wooden dock that stretched out into the harbor. An icy wind whipped against their faces. Swirling in the sky before them was the foul green and black storm of Mistress Hibbins and *The Courser*.

As the three looked up at the monstrous storm clouds, Rip felt a shiver in his soul.

Goodman must have sensed Rip's uneasiness. He glanced over his shoulder at the boy. "This is when being a light in the darkness truly matters." Then he dug his heels into Gunpowder and roared: "Forward!"

The black horse snorted and thundered down the wharf at a ferocious speed. In no time at all, they were galloping down King Street, directly into the path of the storm.

Soon they were in the midst of a torrential downpour. All around him Rip could hear the shouting and screaming of the people of Boston as they awoke to large chunks of hail smashing down on their rooftops and shattering their windows. Goodman yanked on Gunpowder's reins, and the horse made a sharp left down Tremont Street, toward the center of the storm. As they passed King's Chapel, Rip couldn't help glancing at his house and praying that his family would be safe.

"There's Nathaniel!" roared Goodman, bringing his horse to a full stop.

Rip looked up and saw the bird struggling to fly against the wind. In his talons, he carried a thick rope. The Puritan extended his arm, clearly trying to draw upon his powers to guide Nathaniel down to safety.

"Come on, Nathaniel," he murmured. "Just a little farther."

The raven, still fighting the wind, spotted the trio below, folded his wings, and made a mad dive toward the Puritan.

"There!" exclaimed Goodman. With a twist of his hand, he magically pulled the bird toward them. Nathaniel came down at such great speed that he nearly collided with Gunpowder's neck, but Goodman caught him and pulled him close to his chest.

"I have to admit, Nathaniel," said the Puritan with a grin, "I didn't think you'd make it out alive."

"Oh, ye of little faith," said the bird, panting. "Although I am utterly exhausted."

Goodman chuckled and passed the end of the rope to Rip and Pearl.

"I should warn you," began Nathaniel. "I don't think there is a lot of slack left on that rope. And *The Courser* is still moving."

"What are you saying?" asked Rip.

Nathaniel shrugged. "Um, hold on?"

The words had no sooner left Nathaniel's beak than the rope jerked forward, yanking Goodman, Rip, and Pearl right off the horse's back.

Nathaniel, whom Goodman had inadvertently dropped, shook his wings and called out to them as they skidded down the cobblestone street: "Shall I just wait for you here, then?"

The trio continued down the street at a fast clip, but Goodman merely roared with laughter. "It's been a long time since I've felt this alive!" he shouted, and immediately started pulling himself up the rope with super-human speed.

Rip and Pearl followed after Goodman, although at a much slower pace. With the wind and the rain whipping past them, it was hard enough to hold on to the rope, let alone shimmy up. Rip began to worry about how long it would take them to reach the ship—if indeed they made it to the top at all.

But before he had much time to worry, Rip felt the rope being reeled upward at a rapid pace. For a moment he feared they had been discovered and were now being pulled in by the witch. But as they drew closer to the hull of *The Courser*, Rip was relieved to see Goodman's round hat leaning over the deck. The Puritan was using his magic to pull Rip and Pearl aboard.

As soon as they reached the top, Goodman quietly hoisted them over the rail, and they all ducked down behind a cluster of apple barrels. The Puritan had apparently been helping himself to Stormalong's shipment. He removed a half-eaten apple from his coat and took a large, crunchy bite.

"What are you doing?" hissed Pearl.

"What?" said Goodman innocently, his mouth full of apple. "I'm hungry." He gestured to the deck with his head. "Mistress Hibbins is at the front, and her undead army is scattered throughout the ship. She's got Jonathan tied to the main mast—poor fellow looks exhausted."

Rip peered out from behind a barrel. Sure enough, there was Jonathan, tied to the mast with thick, dark ropes. The preacher was unconscious, head lolling to one side.

"What about the Midnight Minister?" asked Rip. "Where's he?"

Goodman took another bite of his apple. "Up in the crow's nest—*with* the lantern. Now, first things first," he added, tossing the core of the apple overboard. "Stormalong and his crew are tied up below deck. Pearl, it's a long walk from here to the door that leads to the lower levels. Can you use your magic to sneak over there?"

Pearl smirked. "Oh, please. Give me something hard to do."

"That's the spirit!" said Goodman. "Now, while you free Stormalong and his crew, I'll use my magic to move the helm and send the ship toward Boston Neck—that will draw the witch's attention away from Jonathan and hopefully lure the Minister down the mast and to the helm. Then Rip can run out and get the preacher. With Stormalong, Jonathan, and the crew on our side, we'll have a fighting chance against Mistress Hibbins in case anything goes wrong."

Rip and Pearl nodded. The Puritan stuck out his tongue, reached up over his head, and pushed his hand into a barrel. He felt around for a moment before producing another large, red apple.

"Sorry," he said, savoring the smell of the apple. "It's just been so long since I've been able to really enjoy these." He took a bite. "Incredible! You have no idea how torturous it was, standing outside the Simmons Sisters' house the other day. I'm willing to bet that Heaven smells like home-baked apple pie!" He suppressed a burp. "Do they still bob for apples at the Harvest Festival? That's how I met my wife, you know."

Pearl waited a moment, and then strode out from behind the barrels and gently waved her hand through the air. Rip blinked in astonishment as he watched Pearl vanish before his very eyes! He fixed his gaze on the door that led below deck but saw only a momentary flicker of light as the door opened wide enough to let Pearl slip beneath it.

"Pearl's really quite powerful," Goodman whispered to Rip. "Most Luminaries only have one or two powers—Pearl has many. She's well on her way to becoming the most powerful Luminary in the Confederation. But . . ." he trailed off.

Rip furrowed his brow. "But what?"

The Puritan shook his head sadly. "Pearl is a wounded soul, Rip—most of us are, of course—but Pearl is wounded more than most. She has a long and difficult road ahead of her."

"She'll be all right," said Rip reassuringly. "She'll live with my family in Boston. She'll have a home."

Goodman opened his mouth to reply but was interrupted by a cry from Mistress Hibbins.

"We've nearly reached Beacon Hill!" she said excitedly.

Goodman smiled coyly and pointed at the helm. "Not quite," he whispered, wagging his finger. The wheel jerked from side to side, causing the ship to rock to and fro. Confused, Mistress Hibbins ran to the helm.

Goodman turned to Rip. "Brace yourself."

Rip wedged himself tightly between an apple barrel and the ship's rail. The Puritan jerked his hand to one side and the wheel followed suit. The ship made a sharp right turn, sending the witch's undead army sprawling across the deck.

"What's happening?" she shouted. The length of black chain magically appeared at her wrist, and she gave it a swift tug. "Get down here!"

The headless form of the Midnight Minister began climbing down the ladder of the crow's nest.

"We're heading toward Boston Neck!" roared the witch. She glared down at Jonathan. "Are you doing this?" But the preacher was clearly still unconscious.

The Minister placed the pumpkin lantern on the deck and calmly took the wheel. The ship moved back on course.

"Ah," whispered Goodman, nodding toward the lighted pumpkin. "He let go of the lantern. Marvelous turn of events."

The Puritan raised his hand again. "Just when she thinks everything is going according to plan . . ." He brought his hand down hard, causing the wheel to spin with so much force that the Minister was thrown to the deck and pinned under the wheel.

Goodman laughed so loudly that Mistress Hibbins spun around and looked in the direction of the apple barrels.

"*Goodman!*" she hissed.

The Puritan winced and shook his head in disappointment.

"I know it's you," barked the witch. "Show yourself!"

Gesturing for Rip to stay hidden, the Puritan rose and faced the witch. A look of mockery danced in his eyes. "Good evening, *Ann.*"

The witch descended the stairs slowly, a mass of corpses following close behind her. "What are *you* doing here?"

Goodman tapped his chin thoughtfully as the undead bodies staggered in around him, forming a tight circle. "Well, if I were a betting man, which I'm not—at least not anymore—I'd say I was about to put an end to the devil's favorite witch."

"You?" laughed Mistress Hibbins with a sneer. "The Judas of the Hallows? And what makes you think you can stop me?"

The undead warriors moved in closer, drawing weapons from their tattered clothing. In response, Goodman removed another apple from his pocket and took a bite. "We have a bigger army."

Just then, Captain Stormalong burst through the door and onto the deck. In his hands, the giant brandished a massive sledgehammer. He glared at Mistress Hibbins with savage eyes of steel. "GET OFF MY SHIP, WITCH!"

The Captain immediately set to work, smashing the living dead as if they were no more than bugs. The rest of Stormalong's crew poured out of the lower decks and began battling against the undead. Pearl emerged behind them, a red bolt of fire glowing in her hand.

Mistress Hibbins pointed at Pearl. "You! I should have killed you and your mother years ago when I had the chance! You're to blame for *all* of this!"

Pearl's eyes narrowed into tiny slits, the red fire casting dark shadows across her face. "What's stopping you, witch? Are you afraid of a little girl?"

Mistress Hibbins stamped her foot and ran forward, but Stormalong intercepted her. With one hand, the giant scooped up Mistress Hibbins and brought her close to his enormous chest. He grinned, baring his teeth. "How 'bout a dance, love?"

Without waiting for a reply, he flung the witch across the ship, and her body smashed against the mast with a loud crack.

From the helm came a burst of green light. The Midnight Minister wrenched himself free of the wheel and leapt into the fray. In his hand he brandished a black, curved sickle and seemed to move as swift as lighting. Sweeping his sickle from side to side, he was like the grim reaper, hewing down anyone who stood in his way.

Seeing this, Goodman let out a roar and flung his arm toward the Minister, but nothing happened. The Midnight Minister was immune to the Puritan's magic. Raising his sickle high, the headless figure ran toward Goodman Brown. Rip watched as the Puritan unsheathed a shining sword and met his attacker head-on, parrying the Minister's blows with expert ease.

Rip, meanwhile, rushed to Jonathan and set about untying the preacher's ropes. All around him, Rip could hear the sounds of battle. Out of the corner of his eye, he saw Pearl exchanging magical blows with Mistress Hibbins, while a group of undead warriors swarmed over Captain Stormalong. The Captain was putting up a good fight—throwing bodies across the ship—but it didn't look as if he could last much longer.

Rip turned his attention back to Jonathan's ropes. He had just about untied the last knot when he heard Goodman cry out in triumph. Rip turned his head in time to see the Puritan run his sword through the middle of the Midnight Minister.

The Minister dropped his sickle and fell to one knee, clutching the sword protruding from his body. Breathing heavily, Goodman started toward Rip, a look of grim satisfaction on his face. But the Minister was on the rise, his sickle raised, aimed at the Puritan.

Rip's eyes widened in alarm. "Goodman, look out!"

Rip ran forward, barreling into the headless man with full force. The two toppled to the deck in a heap. The Minister quickly rolled into a crouching position and regained his footing. Rip watched helplessly as the Midnight Minister grabbed the handle of the sword protruding from his stomach and effortlessly pulled it out. From somewhere on deck, Rip heard the voice of Mistress Hibbins.

"Fools!" she roared. "The Minister cannot be killed. *He is death!*"

The headless man raised the point of the sword over Rip and brought it downward. Goodman, without a weapon to defend himself, rushed forward, throwing himself between Rip and the Midnight Minister. The sword sank deep into the Puritan's chest; Goodman, in shock, grasped the handle, staggered backward, and fell to the deck.

"No!" cried Rip.

The Puritan rolled his head to one side as if to look at Rip, but too soon the light from his eyes faded into darkness.

"No!" repeated Rip. He was now kneeling over Goodman, shaking the man roughly. "Please! Don't die! You can't die!"

Rip heard the Minister speak in his two-tone voice. "It's too late, boy! He's never coming back. He's dead, and you killed him!"

Rip whirled around and looked up fearfully as the Midnight Minister, pumpkin lantern in hand, strode toward him. The lantern oozed a black mist. Rip scrambled backward awkwardly on his hands and feet.

"No!" he cried tearfully. "I didn't kill him. *You* killed him!"

"But it's all your fault," said the witch through the Minister, raising the lantern higher. "You killed him just as you killed your sister Charity."

A thick darkness spilled out of the pumpkin and enveloped Rip. The sounds of battle faded into nothingness. He could no longer see anything but the Minister and himself. The smell of death filled his nostrils. He was alone—alone with the Midnight Minister. He felt blanketed—suffocated—by a cold darkness.

"There is no hope!" hissed the Minister.

Hope.

Instantly, Rip's mind was flooded with memories. He saw his sister Charity at the Harvest Festival and his brother Duncan under the bed. He saw the Delaney sisters wandering the streets of Boston with their dying mother, and he saw his brother Joseph clutching a wooden contraption to his chest. He pictured the twins huddled in a corner of the State House and his brother Gabriel sitting alone by a fire. He saw Matthias and Zachariah reaching for the light they had seen within him.

Light, thought Rip. Then, he saw a scarecrow—a scarecrow with a giant, glowing pumpkin for a head—a pumpkin lantern with a smile as warm as the sun.

"*Have faith, Rip,*" the scarecrow had said, after placing a seed into his hand. "*Believe in yourself, and believe in me—for in me there is always hope. No matter how dark things may seem, remember that the sun will always rise. Light will always triumph over darkness.*"

On the deck of the ship, Rip reached into his pocket and, with a trembling hand, found the seed that Feathertop had given him. He pulled it out and stared at it with a renewed sense of wonder.

"What's this?" shouted the Midnight Minister. "The boy thinks he can fight me with a seed? Your power is nothing compared to mine! Death destroys all!"

"No, it doesn't!" exclaimed Rip. "Light is greater than darkness. And life is greater than death!"

The Midnight Minister merely cackled. "Nothing can stand against *my* death! Who do you think you are?"

Rip leaned forward and pushed the seed into a crack in the wood, and then glared up at the Minister with a look of utmost defiance. "I am Rip Van Winkle!" he shouted. He could feel the energy from the pumpkin seed course through his veins. "*And I am a Hallow!*"

Rip squeezed his fists together, and a beam of yellow light shone from his eyes. Instantly, the deck of the ship cracked and split as pumpkin vines the size of tree trunks sprang up between the planks. The pumpkin lantern, once filled with darkness, erupted into a ball of white flame—as bright as starlight. The Midnight Minister staggered backward as the witch's spell of darkness was shattered. Rip himself was surprised by the sudden burst of light; nevertheless, he focused on the plant, willing the pumpkin to grow faster. The vines swept toward the front of the ship, where they wrapped themselves around the remaining undead warriors and crushed them. Stormalong and his crew fell back in surprise, their eyes wide with wonder. Pearl, who stood near the helm of the ship, marveled at the pumpkin vines winding their way past her and around every surface.

Rip heard Mistress Hibbins let out a foul curse. He glanced up and saw the fiery pumpkin lantern hovering in midair as though suspended by some unseen force. Like a living creature, it shuddered violently before erupting into a brilliant flash of yellow light, brighter than the sun at noon. When the light disappeared, the pumpkin lantern was gone.

Brandishing his sickle once more, the Midnight Minister roared and sprang toward Rip. Just as the headless man was about to bring his blade down, a figure intervened, slicing the Minister's sickle in half with a bright silver sword. Rip's jaw dropped. Standing in front of the Minister, shielding Rip from harm, was Goodman Brown! The Puritan's eyes burned with strong yellow light.

The headless man fell back a pace, and Rip sensed the witch's fear emanating from her puppet.

"Impossible!" whispered the Minister. "You're dead!"

Goodman cast his yellow gaze on Rip and smiled warmly. "No, I am awake—redeemed by Feathertop. And he sent me back with a message." He turned to face the Midnight Minister, his sword erupting into yellow flames. "The harvest is over; it is time to burn the weeds."

The headless man raised his broken sickle to fight with Goodman Brown, but the Puritan knocked it away and drove his blazing sword into the Minister's chest. There was a flash of green light, and the Minister fell to his knees. Still gripping the handle of the sword with one hand, Goodman grabbed the Midnight Minister by his wrist, grunted, and hurled his body off the ship, into a line of trees.

Rip heard a high-pitched scream to his left. Mistress Hibbins had fallen onto her back, an unseen force tugging at her arm, pulling her toward the ship's rail.

"What's happening?" exclaimed the witch.

"Your curse has been broken," said Goodman, eyes aglow. "Your link to the Midnight Minister is no longer immortal and infinite; it is mortal and finite. Your time is up, Ann Hibbins."

The Puritan nodded toward her wrist, and Rip was amazed to see that the chain, once hardly visible, was now fully exposed; it went all the way across the deck and over the side of the ship. With the weight of the Minister's body pulling on the chain, the witch slid, on her back, toward the edge of the ship. Kicking wildly, she was able to swing her body sideways and stop herself against the rail balusters. For a breathless moment, she wriggled pitifully against the weight of the chain. She lifted her head and shot one terrified expression before the chain wrenched her overboard and into the darkness.

There was a moment's pause before Goodman turned to Rip and nodded. "The night is far spent and the day is at hand," he said, eyes glowing brighter than ever. "This next part belongs to you, young Hallow."

And with that, the Puritan vanished.

Rip breathed a sigh of relief and glanced around the ship. Most of the crew members, weary from battle, were still trying to catch their breath. Captain Stormalong sat with his back against the broken mast. A little blood trickled down the giant's forehead, but he winked at Rip none-theless.

Rip heard a moan from somewhere on deck. Pushing aside a giant pumpkin plant leaf, he discovered Jonathan Edwards, who was just managing to free himself from the loosened ropes. The preacher looked up at Rip and grinned.

"That was impressive," said the preacher. "I take it you found Feathertop?"

Rip nodded.

"What was it like?"

Rip was thoughtful for a moment. "Real," he said at last.

Jonathan leaned his head against the mast and glanced out at the horizon.

"Rip!" he gasped. "Look!"

Rip followed the preacher's gaze and saw, to his astonishment, that the top of Blaxton's Beacon was shining, glowing with a glorious white light.

"The Great Awakening," whispered Jonathan, tears streaming down his cheeks. "It has begun."

Rip was about to sit down next to the preacher when he heard Pearl scream, "Rip, watch out!"

Just then, he felt an icy hand grab his neck and yank him backward, bringing him face-to-face with Mistress Hibbins, eyes ablaze with murderous rage.

24

ALL HALLOWS' DAY

IN WHICH LIFE OVERPOWERS DEATH...

*Q*uick as thought, the witch wrapped her other hand around Rip's throat and began to squeeze. Desperate to break free, he tried to pry her fingers off but her skin was too wet—slick with blood. Rip's eyes widened in horror. Mistress Hibbins had liberated herself of the chain, but not without injuring herself.

Stormalong and his crew tried to rush to Rip's aid, but Mistress Hibbins was alive with an unparalleled fury. She screamed a word that Rip did not understand, and soon they were encircled by a wall of green fire. The crew shouted in dismay, unable to cross the tall flames.

"Rip Van Winkle," hissed the witch, tightening her icy hands. "I'll kill you, and then I'll kill your family. I'll snuff out all the Van Winkles forever!"

Rip felt a surge of anger but he could not break free! She was too strong! Then, from somewhere beyond the searing pain in his throat, Rip felt a familiar—comforting—sensation.

The pumpkin plant.

Gritting his teeth, he peered over the witch's shoulder and saw a large pumpkin ballooning out the top of the crow's nest, fed by a vine that had climbed the ship's mast. Like the pumpkin from his mother's garden, this one swelled rapidly, growing until its sheer weight caused the mast to creak and groan.

Mistress Hibbins apparently sensed that something was wrong. She relaxed her grip, looked up, and let out a yelp of terror. At that very moment, the pumpkin (which was now the size of a small cottage) broke free of the crow's nest and crashed onto the deck. The impact sent everyone sprawling, including the witch. She let go of Rip, and they both fell onto their backs.

The ship swayed, and Rip craned his neck to see the pumpkin teetering from side to side, as though it were inwardly debating to go starboard or port side. From somewhere on deck, the voice of Jonathan Edwards, stern and clear, rang out.

"RIP! Get out of the way!"

Instinctively, Rip rolled his body toward the bow of the ship and made eye contact with Jonathan. The preacher set his brow and sent a blast of wind across the sky and against the pumpkin, forcing it to roll toward the witch.

It all happened in a matter of seconds. The ship, under the pumpkin's immense weight, tilted to one side, sending everything and everyone skidding to the port side.

Rip, alongside the pumpkin, rolled toward the rail at an alarming speed. He reached out, desperate to catch something, anything, that could anchor him to the deck. But it was useless. Both he and the pumpkin hit the rail of the ship and pitched forward, falling into the night toward the ground below. The air whipped past him, causing his eyes to water. He looked down and saw that he was fast approaching the gate at Boston Neck, and braced himself for impact.

The giant pumpkin landed first. It smashed through the wall and split open, annihilating the gate. Rip tumbled after it, landing in a large, soft mound of pumpkin pulp. For a full minute, he lay there in breathless silence, blinking up at the underbelly of *The Courser*, hardly daring to believe that he was still alive. He stood up and shakily began wiping slimy pulp from his clothes and hair. Trembling though he was, he felt a strange desire to laugh. For the second time this week, he had fallen from a flying ship and miraculously survived.

He heard a growl from somewhere beyond the shattered pumpkin and turned. His heart leapt into his throat; in the darkness, he could see the outline of a hulking figure bounding toward him. It was tall, gray, and covered in fur.

It was Katy Cruel, the werewolf!

Rip brought his arms up to shield himself, but the monstrous animal leapt clean over him. He turned just in time to see it collide with Mistress Hibbins. It took Rip a moment to realize that Katy wasn't trying to kill him —she was trying to protect him! Mistress Hibbins hurled a bolt of green fire against the werewolf, but Katy ignored it and raked her claws across the witch's stomach. Mistress Hibbins cried out in pain and staggered backward, grabbing at her mid section. She glanced down at the blood on her hands, a look of shock spreading across her pale face.

"The Midnight Minister is no more!" said Rip. "Your spell is broken!"

The witch looked up at Rip, her face white with terror. Her lip trembled and curled before she let out a terrifying screech and struck Katy's face with a magical blow—one so powerful that it produced green sparks. The werewolf let out a groan and toppled over, unconscious.

Mistress Hibbins, covered in blood and pulp, straightened her back, swooned slightly, and staggered out of the broken pumpkin shell. Rip guessed that the witch was delirious with pain because, instead of going across Boston Neck toward the mainland, she headed straight for Boston.

Rip furrowed his brow. Wasn't Mary's blessing supposed to prevent Mistress Hibbins from entering the city? How was she still alive? Rip didn't know what was happening; he only knew that he couldn't let Mistress Hibbins hurt his family. Wading through a thick mound of pulp, he soon reached the grass and ran after the witch.

After a brief sprint, he had nearly caught up to her. They were both running across the Common, but Rip was much faster. As he drew near, he noticed something odd about the way the witch was moving; she kept stumbling and tripping—as though something was grabbing at her ankles, pulling her downward. When she finally fell to her hands and knees, Rip moved close enough to see what had slowed her down. Small roots were shooting out of the ground and coiling themselves around her wrists and ankles like thin brown snakes. Mistress Hibbins let out a cry, then forced herself to stand and struggled forward, attacking the roots with small bursts of green fire.

Rip, about to intercept her, stopped short when two large brown roots shot out of the ground and wrapped themselves around her arms. Mistress Hibbins was once again forced to her knees, where she struggled in vain to break free. She looked up and screamed in horror.

Standing in front of her, surrounded by an orange haze, was the ghostly figure of Mary Dyer. Directly behind the martyr was the Great Elm, shaking like a giant awakening from a deep sleep.

Mary Dyer addressed the witch in a stern and unyielding voice: "Ann Hibbins, in your long, unnatural lifetime, you have been the epitome of selfishness. You have made a mockery of nature and have favored your own life over the lives of all others—including the life of my own child. And so, Ann, as you have turned against life, life has turned against you!"

Rip glanced at Mistress Hibbins and saw, to his astonishment, that she was aging rapidly. Her dark hair turned gray and her smooth skin began to wither and wrinkle; the dried blood and strands of pumpkin pulp clinging to her face gave her the appearance of a rotting corpse. The Great

Elm gave a mighty twist and snapped to life. It glowered down at the witch, causing her to tremble with fear. Then, bending at the base of its trunk, the tree heaved itself toward her. Ann's scream was cut short by the weight of the Great Elm thundering down upon her.

Rip shielded his eyes against the twigs, dirt, and leaves that flew up and scattered in every direction. After a momentary silence, the tree slowly straightened itself up and resumed its normal position.

Rip took a cautious step forward to examine the place where Mistress Hibbins had knelt moments before. But both she and Mary Dyer were gone. The branches of the Great Elm fluttered peacefully in the morning breeze.

Feeling concern for his companions, Rip turned and hurried back to the obliterated gate at Boston Neck. As he entered the forest, he encountered Jonathan, Katy, and Pearl. Katy had transformed back into a woman, and the preacher looked as pale and tired as ever but he nevertheless grinned at the sight of Rip.

Pearl, on the other hand, sprinted out and threw her arms around Rip. "We've been searching all over for you! We feared the worst!"

"Well, if it wasn't for Katy," said Rip, glancing up at the tall woman, "I would surely be dead."

Katy ruffled Rip's hair. "I warned you not to trust Jonathan," she said warmly. "He's never been the strongest werewolf. How many times were you captured, Jonathan? Three times? Four times?"

The preacher shook his head. "Just twice," he muttered.

"Oh, just twice?" said Katy. "Just twice. And how many times was I captured? Oh, that's right, not once!"

Jonathan rolled his eyes. "What happened to the witch?"

Rip quickly explained everything that had happened since his fall from the ship, detailing the appearance of Mary Dyer and the death of Mistress Hibbins.

The preacher nodded grimly. "Such is the way of a selfish soul. In seeking everything, they eventually lose everything."

"So she really is dead, then?" asked Pearl. Rip nodded and she threw her arms around him. "Then that means my curse is finally broken!" she cried. "Rip! I'm free! Thank you."

Rip blushed and nervously patted Pearl on the back. "Um, you're welcome?" He quickly wriggled out of Pearl's embrace. "So, where's Captain Stormalong? Is he all right?"

Jonathan chuckled. "Stormalong? That giant's happier than ever—you've given him another story to tell. And *this* story is even more unbelievable than any of his others—if such a thing is possible. He'll probably want to see you. Come along."

They moved farther into the forest and found *The Courser* docked against a pair of tall trees near Boston Neck. Once they climbed aboard, Rip was amazed to discover that Stormalong and his crew had made remarkably quick repairs to the ship. Despite a few giant pumpkin leaves that had yet to be removed, it looked almost as good as new. Stormalong, meanwhile, was cheerfully loading what remained of the giant pumpkin into empty barrels and crates.

Upon taking notice of the companions, Stormalong grinned and wiped pumpkin pulp from his hands. Rip started apologizing for the damage he had caused, but the giant waved his hand dismissively. "Nonsense!" he bellowed. "My crew's been through worse storms than this. They've learned how to fix the ship quickly. Besides, this pumpkin is the best thing that's ever happened to me!"

Rip screwed up his face in surprise. "It is?"

"Of course it is! Do you realize how much this pumpkin is worth? Why, with the money I'll make from the pulp and seeds alone, I might actually be able to expand my business and buy a second ship. I might even buy . . . a ring."

"A ring?" said Jonathan with a smile. "Do you have something you want to tell us, Alfred?"

In response, the giant's face turned as red as a beet. "Well, when Mistress Hibbins had me chained below deck, I got to thinkin'," he said, scratching his head. "I thought to myself, 'You know, there's really only *one* witch I'd want to imprison me for life.'"

A familiar voice piped up from above them, startling them all. "Alfred, promise me that's not how you're going to propose to Amanda."

"Nathaniel," said Jonathan with a laugh. "Good to see you, old friend. I hear you played a critical role in the salvation of Boston."

The raven was positively beaming. "Why, yes, as a matter of fact, I did! Honestly, I wouldn't be surprised if someone from Boston wrote a poem about it."

Katy rolled her eyes. "A poem about a raven? Maybe. But never anything more."

"I heard that!"

"Wait, where's Gunpowder?" asked Pearl.

Nathaniel squawked. "I have no idea. And frankly, after how rude he was, I don't care. I was keeping him company and reciting—from memory, mind you—John Bunyan's remarkable novel, *The Pilgrim's Progress*, when that nag bucked me right off and galloped into the night!" The bird shook his head. "Really! After spending so much time with Goodman Brown, you'd think that horse would be starving for a bit of culture! Speaking of," added Nathaniel, glancing around, "where is Goodman?"

Rip's smiled faded. "Goodman . . . Goodman's gone."

"Oh dear," said the raven, his tone somber. "He died?"

Pressing his lips together, Rip looked out across the Common. He realized that Goodman, like Mary Dyer, had given his life to protect the city. Now, with all of Boston bathed in the morning light of All Hallows' Day, Rip felt an overwhelming sense of peace. Beyond the Common, he could just see the outline of the trees growing within the South Burying Ground. He thought of his sister Charity, picturing the day his family had laid her body to rest.

"Yes, Goodman died," said Rip at last, "but death isn't the end of life—it's merely the beginning of a new one. I think that's what Mistress Hibbins could never quite understand: to sacrifice yourself—to give your life in love to help another—is a power that somehow multiplies your own life. Mary Dyer and William Blaxton learned that. And I think my parents know learned that, too." He paused, realizing something he had never before considered. "They woke up one night, left their home, and went into the darkness, into the wilderness, to save me. They sacrificed their own lives, the lives they had known, to become parents—to give life to others. *That's* the great awakening—to have the faith to give up the life you know and go into the wilderness to give light and life to others. Goodman sacrificed his life to protect me—to save Boston. So, even though he died, I think . . . his light lives on . . . in the lives of those he saved."

Rip glanced up at his friends, who smiled back at him and nodded. Jonathan looked particularly proud, and his eyes sparkled with something that Rip had never before seen in him.

"Rip Van Winkle," said the preacher with a smile. "The boy who was ripped from the grave—raised from the dead—to give light and life to others. There's something divinely poetic about that. Perhaps we are not really sinners in the hands of an angry God, after all. Perhaps we are all more like seedlings in the hands of a wise gardener."

AFTER HELPING Stormalong load up the last of the barrels, Rip and his friends bade him and his crew a fond farewell, then headed toward the city. High above them, a puffy white cloud moved northward—no doubt heading for a gingerbread treehouse where they would joyously celebrate All Hallows' Day.

Jonathan and Katy came to a halt at the edge of the Common. "This is where we say goodbye," said Jonathan wistfully. "In order to cross over into Charlestown, Katy, Nathaniel, and I will need to travel back through the Boston Burrows. It's the fastest route."

Rip gave a sad nod, and Jonathan reached down and shook Pearl's hand. He then offered his hand to Rip, who ignored it, choosing instead to wrap his arms around his friend. When Rip pulled away, he noticed that the preacher's eyes were a little misty.

"Thank you," whispered Jonathan, squeezing Rip's shoulders. "Thank you for everything. I—well, you two take care. And have a happy All Hallows' Day."

The preacher stood, but before turning around, he paused and removed his hat. "You know," he began thoughtfully, "You two should come and visit me in Hartford. I could always use some help in the library at Yale College . . ."

Rip brightened. "Really?"

"Especially after I found this." The preacher reached into his coat and removed a rolled-up piece of parchment.

Rip recognized it immediately. "The map!"

Jonathan nodded. "I found it on Stormalong's ship earlier this morning. Do you realize that it's one of a kind?"

Rip shook his head.

Jonathan rubbed his chin. "Apparently, it shows the location of Norumbega—the lost Viking city. Rumor has it, the city contains a vast treasure, and," he added, mysteriously, "*a dark secret.*"

Katy raised an eyebrow, and Rip and Pearl exchanged glances of wonder and excitement.

Jonathan shrugged. "Perhaps the two of you can help me figure out what that is. Besides, I'm sure Nathaniel would *love* to have someone to talk to."

The raven ruffled his feathers indignantly. "You know, I resent the insinuation that I talk too much." Then, turning his attention to Rip and Pearl, he added, "But yes, I would love to have someone to talk to."

Rip and Pearl both stifled their laughter. The preacher tipped his hat, and he, Katy, and Nathaniel headed off in the direction of the Great Elm Tree.

Rip waited until his friends had disappeared from sight before he and Pearl headed down Tremont Street. In the distance, Rip could see his home. He squinted his eyes and felt a lump forming in his throat. There, standing by the front door, was his father.

Josiah spotted Rip almost immediately. He let out a gasp and his eyes grew wide. "Rip?" he breathed. "RIP! Abigail! Abigail! It's Rip! He's here! He's home!"

And though Rip was yet a great way off, Josiah ran up the street and soon had his arms wrapped around his son. Pearl, meanwhile, slipped behind Rip, out of sight.

"My boy, my boy," whispered Josiah, his voice heavy with emotion. "We were so worried about you!"

Rip's chin was trembling. "You were?"

Josiah stared back at Rip in amazement. "Of course. You're our son. You *belong* here." The judge put a hand on Rip's cheek. "Where have you been?"

Rip smiled. "It's a long story," he said. "But first, I want to introduce you to someone." He turned and tugged gently on Pearl's elbow, bringing her to his side.

"This is Pearl," he said. "She's my friend, and she doesn't have a home. Can she live with us?"

Josiah took the girl by the hand. "Pearl," he repeated. "We would love for you to live with us—our home is a belonging place."

Pearl looked up at the judge and smiled. They walked together back to the house, where Rip's brothers and sisters poured out the door and came running up the street. Behind them was his mother, her hands over her mouth and her eyes shining with tears of gratitude.

"Rip!" shouted Silence.

"It's Rip!" said Gabriel. "Rip's back!"

As the children ran toward their brother, Rip took Pearl by the hand. "Come on," he said reassuringly. "Let's go home."

25

THE PUMPKIN SEED

IN WHICH RIP SEES THE BOSTON SEED...

he Harvest Festival in Boston in the year 1730 was considerably more lively than previous celebrations. For one thing, most citizens, who had been terrified by the storm that had swept through the night before, were simply grateful to be alive. For another, a handful of people reported seeing strange things during the night—a flying ship, a giant pumpkin falling from the sky, and a massive gray wolf running down the street toward Boston Neck. Old Mrs. Gookin even swore that she saw a headless figure galloping away on a horse as fast as lightning!

But of all the things that had been seen and heard, none could dispute seeing the glorious flash of light that had seemed to turn the night into day. Those who had been awake rushed to their windows, and the few who had been asleep rose from their beds to marvel at the sight of such light. There were those who believed it was the beginning of something terrible, and those who believed it was the beginning of something great. Regardless of what they thought, the citizens of Boston could not deny how they felt. The air seemed sweeter, the sunlight seemed brighter, and despite a strong November chill, they each felt warmer. It was almost as if someone had lit a candle inside of each of them, filling their gray community with a warm and wonderful light.

High above them, for those who had the eyes to see, Blaxton's Beacon glowed with a wonderful, white light.

AFTER THE HARVEST FESTIVAL—LONG after everyone had returned to their homes—Rip lay awake in his bed, pondering everything that had happened. For some time, he simply lay there, fidgeting with his blanket. At length, he slipped out of his covers, dressed himself, and silently made his way to the South Burying Ground.

After crossing the threshold of the iron fence, he took a deep breath and reverentially approached a grave that stood near a maple tree. Rip felt a lump form in his throat as he knelt down and ran his hand across the name on the gravestone.

CHARITY VAN WINKLE
1716–1730

For a long time, Rip sat there in silence, struggling to find the right words. Then, from somewhere behind him, came a low, gruff voice.

"Rip Van Winkle."

He leapt to his feet, whirled around, and let out a gasp. There, sitting on a gravestone and smoking a long clay pipe, was Goodman Brown, surrounded by an orange haze.

"Goodman!"

The Puritan grinned before tilting his head and clicking his tongue. "Still sneaking into graveyards at night? Haven't you learned your lesson?"

Rip couldn't help but laugh. Goodman was right. All of his struggles— the burial of his sister and the beginning of his adventures—had begun in the South Burying Ground. Thinking back on it all, Rip thought it strangely ironic for a graveyard to be both a beginning and an end. Like the death of a seed as it begins its life as a sprout.

"What are you doing here?" asked Rip. "Aren't you helping Feathertop now?"

Goodman's grin widened, and he slid off the gravestone to stand on his feet. "Why, yes, as a matter of fact, I am." Walking toward Rip, the Puritan reached into the pocket of his coat and removed something. "Here," he said, holding out a clenched fist. "Feathertop asked me to give this to you."

Confused, Rip held out his hand, and Goodman released something small into his open palm. Rip brought the object close to his face.

"A necklace?"

"Not just any necklace," said Goodman. "A *Hallow's* necklace."

Rip peered down at it. The cordage, made out of soft brown leather, was braided all the way down to the center, where it wrapped around an exceptionally large seed, which seemed to glow ever so slightly.

"A pumpkin seed," whispered Rip.

"It seems Feathertop has a terrific sense of humor," said Goodman.

"Why do you say that?"

Goodman tapped his chin with the end of his pipe. "Well, remember when all of us were sitting astride Gunpowder and we noticed, for the first time, that the symbol for Columbia was shaped like Boston?"

"Yes."

"Does that shape remind you of anything else?"

Rip furrowed his brow before looking down at the necklace in his hand. His mouth dropped open. "A pumpkin seed."

Goodman nodded. "Each of us is like a seed, planted by the Good Gardener so we might grow into something majestic." He paused and took a long draft of his pipe. When he exhaled, his smoke ring was an outline of Boston—the shape of a pumpkin seed. "As it turns out, all of the colonies of Columbia are like seeds." A glowing ember rose out of Goodman's pipe and floated toward the center of the smoke ring.

"You lit the watchtower of Beacon Hill," continued the Puritan, pointing at the ember. "And then your pumpkin destroyed the gate at Boston Neck." He swiped the pointed edge of the smoke ring. "The seed, or the eye, has awoken." A web of light streamed from the ember and through the narrow opening. "The Great Awakening has truly begun."

Rip's eyes filled with wonder as he watched the web of light pour outward, stretching before him like an intricate network of plant roots. Then, in a flash of white light, the image vanished.

"As I said," continued Goodman, placing the end of his pipe back in his mouth, "Feathertop has a terrific sense of humor. I'd take good care of that pumpkin seed if I were you."

"Is it magic?" asked Rip.

"Indeed it is," said Goodman. "As magical as the pumpkin lantern itself. Feathertop thinks you'll be needing it in the future."

Rip cocked his head to one side. "Why? Mistress Hibbins is dead. The light on Beacon Hill is lit, and the Great Awakening has begun. The darkness has been defeated. Why does Feathertop think I need this?"

Goodman let out a wistful sigh. "Ah, Rip. You are very brave, and yet you have much to learn about life. Yes, a light has been lit, but light always casts a shadow, and that shadow always resents the light. As with a lantern in the cold night air, darkness will surround the light, desperate to smother it out of existence. You must always be on your guard, lest the forces of darkness overtake you."

Rip closed his fist around the necklace and bit his lip. His last struggle with the darkness had nearly killed him. Would he have the strength to fight against it again?

As if sensing his thoughts, Goodman smiled and placed a comforting hand on Rip's shoulder.

"Never fear, Rip. Don't give in to the darkness, for there is so much life ahead of you." Goodman paused and glanced around the graveyard thoughtfully. "So much life because you live."

Rip opened his hand and stared thoughtfully at the pumpkin seed. Goodman reached out, lifted the necklace, and reverentially placed it around Rip's neck. Instantly, Rip felt a familiar warmth ripple through his body. He tried to smile at the Puritan but instead cast his eyes downward.

"What is it, Rip?"

Rip paused, not knowing how to ask the question that was on his mind. "All this talk of pumpkin seeds and being planted in the ground makes me wonder . . . who planted me here? Who left me in this graveyard thirteen years ago? Who are my real parents?"

Once again, Goodman tapped his chin with the end of his pipe. "Who left you in the graveyard? That's a good question, Rip," he said slowly. "A *very* good question. Keep asking questions. For questions often lead to unexpected adventures."

Rip breathed heavily and nodded.

Appearing satisfied, Goodman turned as if to leave, but then he paused and looked over his shoulder. "Oh, and Rip? Will you do me a small favor?"

"Yes?"

Goodman's eyes twinkled with mirth. "Try not to lose that."

Rip smiled back at his friend. "I won't."

The Puritan winked. "I know."

And with that, Goodman Brown vanished into the night, leaving Rip, once again, alone in the graveyard. Touching the necklace at his chest, Rip turned to face Charity's grave. He knelt down and placed a hand on the cold gray stone. It was a long time before he was able to find the words he wanted to say.

"I will always carry your light with me," said Rip, blinking back tears.

He touched the ground gently and then ran his hand across the letters of the gravestone as a large green plant grew up beside it. Before long, small buds emerged from the foliage and blossomed into stunning red roses.

"Rest in peace," he whispered.

ACKNOWLEDGMENTS

This book would not have been possible without the encouragement and support of numerous people. First and foremost, I'm thankful for the love and friendship of my wife, Kim, who guided me through my numerous "dark nights of the soul" and helped me "look to the light and keep moving forward in faith."

I'm grateful for my family (Mom, Dad, Shannon, Stephanie, David, Sean, and Jaimie) who have supported me through all things and always, always, *always* encouraged me to write.

I'm extraordinarily grateful for the Gonzalez family (Gonzo, Kerry, Logan, Aly, Ben, and Kalee). You are the inspiration for the Van Winkle family. Thank you for being my family, and for giving me a belonging place in Florida. I am particularly indebted to Gonzo, who encouraged me to write my novel while we were driving through the Smoky Mountains, listening to Toad the Wet Sprocket.

I'm thankful for Howard and Shari Lyon, who—like Josiah and Abigail Van Winkle—saw and believed in Rip long before I had fully risen from the creative bed of my own "Terrible Slumber." In more ways than they realize, the Lyons brought life to the boy who had been "ripped from the grave."

I express my appreciation for everyone who went to Howard's studio to pose as characters for the book: Isaac Lyon (Rip Van Winkle); Shari Lyon (Mistress Hibbins); Paul Cardall (William Blaxton); Tina Cardall (Mary Dyer); Jonathan Johnson (Jonathan Edwards); Ganel-Lyn Condie (Katy

Cruel); Andy Proctor (Goodman Brown); Kim Stephenson Smith (Mother Rigby); Nate Bagley (Captain Stormalong); Candice Madsen (Amelia Simmons); Kirsten Smith (Amalia Simmons); Leavitt Wells (Amanda Simmons); Kelty-Lyn Dagley (Pearl Prynne and Mary Delaney); Teagan and Campbell Dagley (Martha and Molly Delaney); Nat Harward (Governor Chillingworth); Lindsay Hadley and her sons, Milo and Mason (Matthias and Zachariah); and the Craig and Dawn Armstrong Family (Josiah and Abigail Van Winkle).

I'm grateful for the unyielding help, support, and friendship of Jeff and Juliana Pooley—their initial feedback was crucial to the foundation of the book (and their continued friendship is crucial to my overall well-being). I am also grateful for the others who read early iterations of this manuscript and offered their feedback: Sharli Ruth Bronson, Charlotte Ashlock and Mark Rice.

I am particularly thankful for my friend and Berrett-Koehler editor, Neal Maillet. A native of Massachusetts, Neal enthusiastically listened to portions of my story and took time out of his vacation to give me a tour of some of the locations mentioned in the book—specifically, the ruins of Dogtown. Jonathan Edwards speaks a line in chapter 15 that was originally spoken by Neal—although Neal said it with a lot more humor. I'm sorry I forgot the map, Neal! The upside is that you inadvertently inspired the sequel!

I am unbelievably thankful to Joyce Winnett Horstmann, a former (and favorite) creative writing teacher of mine who agreed to review and edit the manuscript. Her feedback was timely and priceless, and I am ever so grateful that I signed up for her class thirteen years ago.

Speaking of editors, I am grateful for my final editor, Elissa Rabellino. Elissa is a wonderful editor who has edited two (now three!) of my books. She somehow manages to turn manuscripts into gold, and I thank her for her patience and persistence. Her work has truly been a blessing to me.

I want to acknowledge the tremendous contributions of Vanae Keiser. It is impossible for me to describe the extent of my gratitude for Vanae's work. For some inexplicable reason, she poured her heart and soul into this book at a time when I needed it most. It kept me going when all I wanted to do was give up. What she did for me is (at least in my mind) an echo of what William Blaxton did for the Puritans. Thank you, Vanae.

I am grateful for the ANASAZI Foundation (particularly the Ezekiel and Pauline Sanchez family) for inspiring the idea of a "belonging place." For years, the ANASAZI Foundation in Arizona has been a belonging place for me (and so many others), and I hope this book offers a sense of belonging to all those who wander.

It is my hope that after you close the covers of this book, you will search for ways to become like William Blaxton, Mary Dyer, and Rip Van Winkle. I invite you to become a light to the world and open your heart and home to those who are searching for a belonging place.

ABOUT THE AUTHOR

Seth Adam Smith is a best-selling, award-winning author and blogger whose writings have been translated into over thirty languages and featured on the *Huffington Post*, *Good Morning America*, Fox News, CNN, the *Today* show, *Forbes*, and many other news outlets around the world. In 2015, his book *Your Life Isn't for You* was awarded a gold medal for inspirational memoir.

A survivor of a suicide attempt in 2006, Seth is an advocate for resources and understanding concerning depression and suicide prevention, and he regularly writes about these topics in his books and on his blog. He and his wife, Kim, currently live in Arizona but have "belonging places" throughout the United States.

Rip Van Winkle and the Pumpkin Lantern is Seth's first novel.

Read more of Seth's writings at www.SethAdamSmith.com

ALSO BY SETH ADAM SMITH

Marriage Isn't For You

Your Life Isn't For You

You, Unstuck

Made in the USA
Coppell, TX
27 November 2020